Dalton

❧ Book Four ❧

Mistress & Master
of
Restraint

𝔇alton

Copyright ©2012 Erica Chilson

Wicked Reads
PO Box 29
Nelson, PA 16940

www.ericachilson.com/wicked-reads

Printed in the United States of America

First Printing, 2015

ISBN-13: **978-0692565674**
ISBN-10: **0692565671**

Dedication

To my very patient fans

Titles by Erica Chilson

Mistress and Master of Restraint
-series order-

Restraint
Unleashed
Dexter
Dalton
Queen Omnibus*
Jaded*
Queened*
Checkmate*
King
Faithless
The Hunter
Integrated

-Coming Soon-
Hero/Empowered (tentative title)

BLENDED
-Series order-

Good Girl
Wildly Wedded Wife (Blended #1.5)
Widow
Wanton (Blended #2.5)

-COMING SOON-
Warped

RUSTY KNOB
Rusty Knob
Tarnished
Stainless (coming soon)

For the past four years, Dalton Fontaine Marconi has been living incognito as Dalton Thompson. After his grandfather's murder, Dalton's self-preservation led him to Dominion, New York.

As Restraint's resident antagonist, Dalton has been doing his mother's bidding. Olivia Fontaine always wants something from someone, and she always uses her son to get it. In order to deal with the ramifications, Dalton finds comfort in the fact that he's doing it for altruistic reasons. But thinking it and feeling it are not the same beast, and the pressure is suffocating him. As a masochist, Dalton balances on a knife's edge between self-punishment and the point of no return.

Restraint was plagued with riots, leading the rest of Dalton's family to Dominion, and together they set out to protect the Masters of Restraint. But as Restraint crumbles down to its foundation, Dalton's life does as well.

While trying to hide his true nature, Dalton pushes the members of Restraint, oddly finds Pretty Boy Whittenhower taking a shine to him, joins Generation Next, and tries to locate the mole leaking the information published in the Mistress & Master of Restraint books.

Walking down a lonely path of alienation, Dalton discovers those he's trying to protect are actually protecting him from the very monster who set it all into motion.

Chapter One

Leaning against the dry-erase board, Dexter looks relaxed and replete after last week's scene with Katya, where she drew blood and caused harm– which demonstrates why we're training again in the first place. "Students, I know you're all worked up right now. Since everyone was so attentive this evening, you're all excused to play in the dungeon. Don't do anything I wouldn't do, boys and girls." In a rare good mood, Dexter winks playfully at us.

I gather my things and try to exit the room before anyone looks at me. I hate '*play in the dungeon*' time. I love all aspects of BDSM when I'm able to be myself. After growing up in a bordello fronting as a BDSM club, I enjoy my training because it feels like home. It's also my first taste of the classroom experience after being homeschooled by my masters: by my father and my bastard brother in *How to be a straight mafia kingpin 101*, by my mother in *How to be a subservient whore*, and by my grandfather and his partner in *How to be a whipped, molested pup*. I even enjoy the sound of Marc's and Dexter's voices as they drone on, explaining the dynamics of our lifestyle. I missed Marcus after the year he spent with us during my childhood, and have enjoyed his company in the past four years of adulthood.

What I hate is the pressure to perform that the dungeon demands. I'm not one to be on display, especially around those I've turned into enemies. After the attack a few weeks back, I'm riddled with anxiety just thinking of stepping foot into the dungeon. But now that outsiders aren't allowed in, it's more comforting. What isn't comforting is the fact that the dungeon is now filled with all those I've targeted with my assholeness.

Just a few years ago, I watched movies and read a lot of books featuring high school because I was obsessed with something I wanted to experience. Dungeon time reminds me of being picked last during gym class. No one in their right mind should want to play with the douchebag who purposely baits their classmates. So it confuses me that anyone would want to play with me.

After all, I act like the biggest asshole on the planet, yet I still attract ladies. With my brown hair, brown eyes, out-of-style clothing, and my short height, my blahness should be a deterrent. I'm starting to regret playing the asshole. Maybe I should have gone with the nice guy friend approach. Nah– nice guy is way out of my comfort-zone. At this point, I believe an asshole creates pheromones that are impossible for a woman to resist.

"Dalton," Kristal brazenly drawls my name, proving my thoughts correct.

Freezing mid-movement, my eyes dart to the floor, silently praying she's a figment of my imagination. I can't do this tonight. It's too much for me to take. Anxiety to perform as Dalton Thompson overpowers me. The shakes start in the tips of my fingers and my stomach roils. The need to release the pressure is overwhelming.

"Will you play with me tonight?" Kris cocks her head to the side, dark hair covering one eye. I recognize the move of looking at me through the lace of her lashes as one taught to me from a very young age. It's meant to be enticing, but all it does is freak my ass out. *I can't do it!* "I don't mean a scene. I just wanna fuck." Her mouth wraps around the words as if she's giving me a verbal blowjob.

I nod because I can do nothing else. The majority of the membership is here to fuck, turning deaf ears to Marcus and Dexter when they explain BDSM is *not* about sex. It would look odd if I suddenly turned celibate. Bile rises in my throat as the word fuck is repeated in my mind in Kristal's sultry voice– she'd do my master proud in the pay-for-play racket.

Unable to speak, the shakes move from my fingertips to my hands, and then run up my arms. I'm quivering like a leaf, unable to shut my brain down. The panic rises as I think of having another person's mouth wrapped around my limp cock. I swallow down the need to retch when I envision sliding into Kristal's body.

I won't be able to get through it this time, failing my master.

A firm grip clutches my shoulder and I relax into the touch. "Kristal, may I join you two this evening?" Whitt asks politely. He's always polite, especially now as he massages the shame from my shoulder.

Kristal's eyes widen and her lips form a large *O*. Whitt releases a throaty laugh filled with lust as my muscles clench in revulsion, both of us envisioning those pouty lips begging for oral sex.

"Yes, please…" Kris is practically panting. Doesn't she see I don't want her? Am I that good of an actor? "God, I loved last time. It was fucking fantastic." Her eyes have dilated, pupils blown until they eclipse her irises, like she's high on the prospect of sex. Her skin is flushed crimson with tiny beads of sweat forming above her upper lip.

I don't know why Kristal targeted me when she has Whitt as a master and my friend, Alex, as her boyfriend. Why me? Really, *why?*

My body quakes as I remember the last time I was with Kristal. Whitt joined us that time too. The remembered terror as Kristal begged to suck my cock intensifies this time around. Whitt saved me by allowing me to fuck her while she sucked him. Her cunt was less personal than her mouth. Stomach clenching, throat tightening, I'd vomit if it wasn't for the fact that I haven't eaten today as I remember what her pussy felt like as it clenched my dick as she came.

Oh, God. What if Whitt wants to fuck Kris this time? I can't allow her to take my dick in her mouth. Ever. I spent more than ten years of my life using my cock for my masters, but I can't do it anymore.

Panicking, my breathing becomes labored. I think of my master to try to calm myself. I repeat my mantra: *This is for Master. You are not a whore. You are an asset– a son. Do not disappoint Master.*

I stare at the floor and school my breathing. But my terror must be apparent because Whitt begins massaging both of my shoulders at the same time. His fingertips bite into the muscles in a soothing rhythm, spreading a delicious warming sensation throughout my body.

"Have you ever taken two men at once, Kristal?" Whitt asks with a smile. "I'm pretty sure you have," he teases in a mischievous tone. His fingertips venture south, rubbing at my back.

"Not since Queen put a stop to it," she replies excitedly. "You know, my addiction."

"Which is why I'm your master now." Leaning in, Whitt whispers conspiratorially. "I've never done a DP, but I've always wanted to try it. What do you say Kristal?"

I notice that Whitt doesn't ask me my opinion. I'd like to bitch about his highhandedness, but this means Kristal's eager, welcoming mouth is off the table.

"Fuck, YES!" Kris yells, alerting all those who are still in the classroom about our odd arrangement. Kristal is a tiny spitfire, attractive and exotic. I'm sure she's exactly what the pretty boy loves in a woman. She's his complete opposite in all ways. She's also the most difficult submissive at Restraint. Hell, I think she's more dominant than Dalton Thompson– not me. He's my alter ego.

Aesthetically, I can see Kristal's appeal with her caramel skin and dark features. I just can't see her as a sexual being. Bile rises again at the thought. I've heard stories that she used to be even wilder than she is now. Everyone says she was a sex addict. I witnessed her brutal punishment at the hands of Queen. Ever since that night, Kris has only been with Alex, Whitt, and, for some unknown reason, me.

Blue eyes glittering with naughty thoughts, "I want to pound that tight pussy of yours, if that's okay with Dalton." Whitt's voice is filled with taunting amusement.

My eyes lift when my name is spoken, until this moment I've been ignored. I don't know why I have to be involved at all. Maybe they get sick of screwing each other and need someone to make it more thrilling, or maybe Whitt's trying to humiliate me because he figured out why my father was ashamed to call me son.

"Are you okay with anal sex?" Whitt asks in the same way Kris had earlier, with every word infused with the sex act to come. My cock fills with blood for the first time on its own in almost three years. Whitt's voice paired with the word *anal* is devastating as my mind begins playing its greatest wants involving Whitt's well-sucked cock inside my ass.

I lick my suddenly dry lips a few times to moisten them. "Yes," I mumble, answering my unspoken thoughts, not wishing to fuck Kristal ever again.

Lips curving into a devastating smile reveal dimples, Whitt seems awfully pleased with himself. "Have you done it before? Anal?" I nod my head yes, eagerly so. "DP?"

"Yes." I lick my lips again.

"Good." Whitt's eyes twinkle with mirth. He's acting different than usual. He's always picking and joking around, but now he's more commanding as well. Like a moth to flame, Whitt's voice is lulling me to do whatever he wants.

The group files out the door, with Alex trying to have a silent conversation with Whitt, then me, and I don't know how to answer his loaded look. I drag my feet, trying to delay the inevitable.

The firm grip is back, but this time on the back of my neck, steering me– pushing me forward. Whitt will not allow me to avoid the dungeon. I fantasize about breaking free from the herd and running to the closed end of the hallway where the hidden entrance to the upper floors is located: the nexus to nirvana– my apartment. I want to be in my own space where I can hide away and finally breathe deeply. My apartment is the only place in this fucking town where I am me. Font.

I blink out of my reverie when I'm tugged to a stop. I cringe when I see that we're in the middle of the dungeon. I bristle at being on display after years of being used like a tiger in a cage at a zoo. No one here has seen an inch of my covered body, not even the cock I fuck them with.

My eyes seek Alex for help, but my only friend is sitting on the sofa talking to Queen. I silently beg him with my eyes to intervene. Alex knows all of my secrets, so he must realize why this is a very bad idea. His ruby-red lips smirk at me while shaking his head slightly, causing his hair to swing along his jawline. Alex's silence is loud. *No, you're on your own.*

Eyes flicking about wildly, I stop to watch as Whitt nuzzles Kristal's throat. When he begins undressing her, I take a few steps back, clenching my eyelids tightly. Whitt keeps dirty talking, and it confuses the hell out of me.

Isn't there a single person at Restraint who has a sexual orientation and sticks with it? Ezra is gay yet married to a woman. Cortez doesn't know what the hell he is, but no doubt Ezra knows because I sure as hell figured it out. Alex is straight, my gaydar not even pinging a tiny bit, but he gives out handy jays like party favors– sadly never to me. All of the women do each other because they think it gets the guys off, and only a few of them actually enjoy it. Whitt is straight, so what is he getting out of me joining him and

5

Kris? Maybe he's more malicious than I ever thought, more like his sister, Adelaide.

Swallowing down the panic and the disgust, I decide to concentrate on Whitt even if he's only doing this to harm me. I reach out to touch Kristal's naked back, just above the swell of her ass, but my hand freezes in mid-air when I lose my nerve.

I can't do it.

I can't do it ever again.

With an oily film of evil caused by years of defying my true nature, my skin tries to crawl off my body. The things men of my nature have to do to hide, the loss of our self-respect. It's not that women are inherently disgusting. They're beautiful in their own way; I just don't want to touch them.

Whitt smiles at me provocatively, lips still spewing naughty acts. Commanding blue eyes hold me in place as he removes the last piece of Kristal's clothing. My eyes follow the movement of his hands. With a sharp smack, Kristal's ass reverberates, then he's palming the reddened flesh while looking pointedly at me. Whitt mouths, "*Yours*," and laughs infectiously. Pretty Boy is so irritatingly beautiful, I smile before I can stop myself.

"Such an eager, little pussy you have." Releasing a moan that runs a shiver up my spine, Whitt rubs his fingers between Kristal's legs. "Always sopping wet, ready for a rough fuck. Aren't you, Kris? You can't wait for Dalton to take your ass, can you? With both of us in you, it'll be like our cocks are fighting for space. Imagine it… being able to feel Dalton's cock trying to touch mine."

Dalton Thompson is an asshole while the real me is shy. As Whitt goes off at the mouth about all the dirty things that make me envision him fucking me instead, I glance to the floor, skin flushing with embarrassment.

Whitt's firm grip surrounds my wrist, tugging me forward, and then he places my hand on Kristal's ass. I rest my palm on the swell of her behind as I tunnel deep into Whitt's eyes, connecting to him as if Kris doesn't exist. It's unfair to her, but right now I don't give a shit. I block out everything in the dungeon except for Whitt's eyes, the way he's panting for breath, and the feel of his thumb caressing the inside of my wrist– the touch so much more intimate than his fingers spreading Kristal's folds.

Breaking the odd connection Whitt and I have established, Kristal rears back into my hand, demanding my attention. I rub the compact swell of her ass and close my eyes, pretending it's Whitt's ass beneath my touch instead. Blocking Kristal's whimpers, I focus on the deep grunts Whitt keeps making. My face goes slack as I picture silky blonde hair and drowning pools of blue seas. My cock grows harder, beginning to tent my pants, as I play pretend that Whitt is groaning for me.

I moan softly when a hand rubs a circle on the center of my chest. Instinctively I know it's the hand I crave. I keep the image burned into my mind as my hands grip and then release Kristal's ass cheeks– tenderizing. I part the globes, my forefinger skimming until I find the tight ring of muscle barring my entrance. I know from personal experience how anal needs a lot of moisture or it'll hurt badly. The thought of touching Kristal's pussy juice has my semi-hard cock limp in half a second. I refuse to spit on her– that is just gross. Panicking, I fear harming Kris.

My eyes flash open at the sensation of something hot, wet, and silky drizzling down my fingers. Whitt's eyes catch mine, lips curving up in a mischievous smile. Movement draws my attention– Whitt's fingertips rub more of the liquid around Kristal's ass for me. His finger slides easily into her hungry anus. He pulls out, and then pushes my finger inside her. She moans loudly at the invasion, but all my focus is on the fact that I am doing as Whitt wants.

"Rub this on your cock." Startling me, one hand latches onto my wrist and the other smears more of the fluid onto my palm. I look at Whitt in confusion. Who the hell carries around a bottle of lubricant? He must have a lot of impromptu sex. One side of his lips lifts revealing a devastating dimple.

"If you're slippery under the condom it feels like you're riding bare," Whitt says in explanation. "Just make sure the condom doesn't slip off."

I don't want to rub my cock because it no longer hardens beneath my touch. Lately, I'm lucky to be firm enough to get it into the person I wish I wasn't fucking. But I'm large enough that they never notice. I ride them until they climax, and then I fake it. It's been at least a year since I came by my own hand, and never since I came with someone who wasn't my duty. That's just fucking pathetic and depressing.

My thoughts don't help the situation as I push my slippery hand down the front of my jeans and knead my dick. I sing sweet nothings to it hoping to coax some blood into my limp shaft.

"Look at me," Whitt commands, and my eyes instantly obey.

Kristal's wrapped around Whitt, mewing like a cat in heat. Whitt's head is resting on her shoulder while he patiently gazes at me, all the while his hand is rapidly moving between her legs. He's still fully dressed except for the mouthwatering flesh that hangs between his thighs and the hard length pressed between the lovers. I blink my gaze away from down *there*, worried I'll insult Whitt or blow my cover with my interest.

"Rub your cock along her ass," Whitt coaxes me in a raspy voice warping with lust. "It'll feel amazing."

"Maybe it'll feel amazing to you," I think to myself as I close my eyes and shore up my reserves. How the fuck does Whitt know I have a problem with this? He's far too observant for my comfort.

I get as close as possible to Kristal's behind, shielding my limp cock from view, and then I unzip my pants and tug to bare the eleven inch length of meat between my thighs. My masters have whored me out for profit and power since it grew obscenely large, and it disgusts me to even look at the flesh that makes me feel worthless.

"I have to put a condom on first," I reason with Whitt, voice warbling with fear and embarrassment.

Whore rule #1: always have an impenetrable barrier between you and your mark.

Whore rule #2: pretend your cock isn't attached to you while you work, and hope like hell you remember it does when it's time to use it for personal reasons.

Whore rule #3: soap– you can never have enough soap to wash it all away.

Whore rule #4: cleanse your soul any way you can.

Whore rule #5: lie by pretending this time is the last time.

As a seasoned dominant, Whitt yanks me from my thoughts, somehow sensing what's playing out in my mind. "Hey… You're safe to rub, as I said. When you're *ready*, you can put the condom on." Pinning me with his demanding stare, he commands, "Do it!"

Pretty Boy Whittenhower has got my number, knowing my true nature: a masochistic gay switch. Beautiful, commanding, dick-hardening, Whitt feeds all of my needs.

Obeying, I close my eyes as I rub against Kris. It does nothing for me, forcing a song of frustration from the back of my throat. I'm a blink of an eye from telling Whitt to step off and let me do this the way I always have.

Fake it.

"Isn't it slippery and silky smooth," Whitt murmurs about the lubricant I'm rubbing around in. Words a suggestion, It suddenly feels exactly as he said. My dickhead slides against soft skin, kissing the bud, dipping in a bit.

Shuddering, "Yes," I agree, voice dreamy since I'm pretending I'm touching Whitt instead of Kris. "It's perfect."

"I've been using it since my first hard-on." Lips twisting so evilly Whitt looks as seductive as the Devil, yet his sunshine-kissed skin, blond hair, and blue eyes glow with innocence. "It's my precum."

Lightning strikes me so hard I take a step back, giving Whitt a flash of my cock growing from flaccid to rock-hard in an instant. I haven't had a real erection in so fucking long, and it's debatable if I've ever been *this* hard. I stop swirling my cockhead in the stuff and stare open-mouthed at him.

Surely Whitt's lying.

Not saying, "*Just kidding*," as I thought the prankster would, Whitt demonstrates instead. I watch as his hand disappears between him and Kristal. His arm pumps a few times, and then he pulls his hand away and presents me with his palm. The cup of his hand is filled with glistening liquid.

Fuck! Whitt's spunk is on my dick.

I lick my lips and stare in awe at his palm, wanting it all. My dick begins to insistently throb and make its own contribution to the moisture slicking Kristal's ass. This is the closest I've ever been to consensual sex with another male.

"Now you're ready for the condom." Whitt raises a brow toward my engorged dick, getting more than an eyeful. "*Jesus.*" I'm so distracted by Whitt's whimper that I don't tune in until he's moving. "I thought you'd enjoy me more than Kris." Whitt pulls his hand from between Kristal's thighs. Eyes holding mine, he sucks the moisture off his fingers– one at a time, sucking down to his knuckles. I stare enraptured as his mouth works his digits, pretending he's not some straight boy-next-door, but a dirty gay guy like me, wanting a rough fuck. My knees ache to be bruised on this tile floor.

"Condom– now!" Whitt commands, snapping me out of the depraved vision in my head.

The switch in me luxuriates as someone takes dominion over me, someone who isn't using me right now but wanting to give me pleasure for the first time in my life. My masters are now down to only one survivor, and they've always used me as a pawn to hurt others. In a hurry, I oblige Whitt by easily rolling the latex down my cock for the first time in a long while, not having to struggle to get it to cover a flaccid dick.

"On the count of three, we'll enter Kris at the same time," Whitt coaxes me, voice so eager it warbles. Finding his enthusiasm infectious, I quickly nod my head in assent. "One...Two... Three..."

To the hilt, I force my way into Kristal's ass as Whitt thrusts into her cunt. I nearly come as Whitt and I fight for space inside of her, pressing against the shared membrane separating us as if we're gliding against one another instead.

Neither of us moves for a few moments as Kristal writhes between us, whimpering in pleasure. I ignore the fact that Kris loves what she's getting, concentrating instead on the beat of Whitt's cock as he struggles not to climax. I mirror him, trying to maintain control. It goes against my needs, but I want to prolong this experience for some strange reason.

Woman held upright between us, we stand in the center of the dungeon with all eyes on us. Whitt stares at me over Kristal's shoulder, like he's peering into my soul and sees what I've painstakingly hidden. I don't know how, but he knows many of the secrets I've managed to keep hidden here at Restraint for nearly four years.

One: I'm a switch. Whitt's demonstrated that knowledge by yanking my leash and reveling in my submission.

Two: I'm not straight, not even a little bit bisexual. I one-hundred-percent crave men. Whitt knew to give me this end of Kristal. And the trick with the semen was such a fucking tease– I want to bathe in that slippery shit.

I have no idea how Pretty Boy knows my secrets, or how he knows that I'm struggling daily with the difficulty of maintaining my straight image. The struggle gets worse every day, more so than the last. I just pray he doesn't know the rest of my secrets.

That last thought kills my erection. I deflate in less than a second and depression envelops me. Masculine hands grip my hips and pull, fingertips splaying toward my ass. My eyes snap back up to find Whitt giving me a calm and reassuring expression in return.

He tries to project that he understands and will help. But why the fuck would he help me? I'm the asshole of Restraint– the drab pariah. I'm our weakest link. Not me, my alter ego, I try to remind myself.

Font, you are not this Dalton Thompson asshole!

Giving up all pretenses, Whitt's hands slide farther back to squeeze my ass, slowly tugging my pants lower so he can get at my bare skin. My eyes drift shut at the intoxicating sensation of a touch I welcome. Whitt manipulates my flesh as he begins to thrust inside Kris, using my ass as leverage. I ignore Kristal's moans and focus on the sounds Whitt releases– sharp, primal grunts as he thrusts deep. Rubbing along my cock, I can feel him moving inside of her. That combined with his hands on my ass has me insanely erect, growing larger and larger.

I find the same rhythm Whitt is riding, and in seconds I'm hanging from the edge of release. I bark out a loud cry that echoes around the dungeon, stunning myself with the sound. Turning enthusiastic, Whitt pushes and pulls me in tandem with his thrusts until the shock fades and I join him in movement.

Kristal moans and whimpers between us as she starts to climax. I try to ignore the sound, worrying it will reduce my pleasure, but it leaves me feeling guilty because I'm using Kris to get closer to Whitt, a man who is just throwing me a bone.

"Just feel, Dalton," Whitt coaxes in a voice gone rough with lust. His fingertips sneak into the waistband of my pants, dipping in to caress my bare ass to ride along the top of my crack. "Ladies may not be your preference, but Kris is fucking tight and her ass will milk you dry. Just experience the pleasure."

The caress of my name on Whitt's lips pulls me closer to the edge, but combined with his heavy-lidded blue eyes and his parted lips releasing grunts of pleasure, I'm a goner.

Whitt's fingertips tighten on my hips and ass, digging in with bruising force. His thrusts become erratic, just as Kristal screams bloody murder in the throes of orgasm. Her body spasms around mine, gripping me tighter and drawing Whitt that much closer to my cock. His reaction to our contact baffles me– he comes violently. I stay my release just so I can absorb his. I want to imprint it into memory to hopefully use to masturbate with if my cock will allow.

Whitt's beautiful face contorts in agony, gasping raggedly. Simultaneously his deep blue eyes snap open to snag mine and his hands grip my ass tight in his fists. A sneaky fingertip grazes my pucker, yanking a thrilled gasp of shock from my throat.

Knowing exactly what he's doing to me, Pretty Boy's lips curl into a wicked smirk– the bastard.

Feeling the pressure of Whitt's release inside of Kristal is my undoing. A cry from deep within my chest is painfully expelled from my throat. It's never-ending, flowing and flowing in painful waves of pleasure.

Exhausted, I sag when it's finally over, my face less than an inch from Whitt's as we share Kristal's shoulder. Our breath mingling, my body jerks every few seconds as aftershocks shoot lightning throughout my body.

"Trust me," Whitt whispers.

My startling reply rushes to my lips, "*yes, Master*," but it's cut off by a loud clapping.

"That's my boy!" Devlin cheers from the seating area as he gives us a standing ovation. My cheeks flame in embarrassment, and I worry Devlin's actions will reveal our secret, disappointing my one true master.

Mortified, I dip my hips to disengage from Kristal's body, even in my need to flee I won't harm her by pulling out too quickly. Covering my junk the best I can with my small palms, I turn my back to everyone. I yank the soiled condom off my cock, and I'm stunned by the amount of fluid inside. A shiver of remembrance works its way up my spine because of the fact Whitt contributed his precum. I tie the condom off, having no idea what to do with it– Whitt turns helpful by taking it from me as I try to vanish by turning invisible. I quickly tuck myself back into my pants and turn back around.

Good, no one saw an inch of my body except for Whitt peeking every chance he got. My flesh is private– it belongs to me even when I'm whoring myself out. My right to privacy was torn from me too many times to count, and I refuse to allow it to happen ever again.

I try to leave, gaining a foot closer to the hallway, but Whitt's strong fingers bracelet my arm. "Kristal, clean Dalton up." Whitt's usually sweet voice is commanding. "We don't want his cum to stain his pants."

I freak the fuck out at the prospect of Kristal's mouth on my dick– arm yanking violently to disengage Whitt's hand. He said to trust him. *What?* Trust in the fact that Whitt plans on humiliating me in front of the entire dungeon. He knows damn well I don't want Kristal's eager mouth anywhere near my cock. Ever.

Why is Whitt doing this to me?

"No… no, that's okay. I'm good." Shaking my head frantically, I use my fingertips to try to pry Whitt's hand off my arm. He gives me a look that shouts, "*HEEL!*" and my struggle ceases, the fight bleeding right out of me.

"Clean me, Kristal," Whitt commands, eyes never leaving mine, nor does he let go of my arm. "Don't leave a drop behind."

Suffering, I stare at the floor, being subjected to listening to suction noises and slurping sounds, feeling it vibrate up through Whitt's arm to his hand clutching at my arm. Eyes knitted together, confused, I chance a glance when Kris doesn't stop sucking after a minute.

Whitt's hard again, with Kris sucking him towards his second release. I suddenly feel more depressed than before for a myriad of reasons. Whitt was asserting his dominance and screaming how he was heterosexual at the same time.

Yeah, I get it, Pretty Boy. I understand how you were dominating me, not coming on to me.

Lost in my destructive thoughts, Whitt's seductive groan draws my gaze. I watch as he climaxes again, body wracked with pleasure from Kristal deep-throating his cock. For some bizarre reason, he watches me watch him the entire time he comes. Enjoying my attention, his lips twist up into a smug smirk of satisfaction.

"Kiss Dalton in thanks," Whitt commands Kristal as soon as she sucks his cock dry.

"Oh, fuck no!" I shout, yanking so hard I finally break free. I make a run for it, not giving a shit since everyone already thinks I'm an asshole. I don't want to add freak to the list too, but hell no!

I make it ten feet toward the hallway, heart pounding out of my chest, before I make the mistake of looking over my shoulder. Whitt's gaze cuts to mine, and I'm captured. Freezing, my feet refuse to move.

Swinging her hips with evil intent, Kristal stalks toward me. Flinching back, I try to avoid the lips getting closer to mine, but my feet refuse to move me. I never kiss females, even if I fuck them. I'm already a whore, so I've adopted their practices.

Tentative, doing as her master bid, Kristal presses her pouty lips to mine anyway. I resist at first, because her smaller mouth feels weird when I long for strong, firm lips.

…And then I taste him– so salty-sweet I release a primal groan. Going mad, I grip the back of Kristal's head and roughly pry her mouth open with my lips and tongue. I feed from her mouth, the taste of him bursting on my tongue. I lick every crevice, down around her gums, and even the roof of her mouth, sucking every drop of Whitt I can taste. The pressure is instantaneous. No build up– it just explodes.

I quickly turn my back on the voyeurs, Kristal, and even Whitt. I stand still as I try to contain the release flowing through my veins and flooding out my cock to saturate the front of my pants. Trembling, against my will, small whimpers escape between my clenched lips.

Humiliation and shame slam into my body with a force that almost takes me to my knees. Pretty Boy was just toying with me, most likely seeking revenge for one of the many nasty slights I've performed on his friends. I deserve it, even if I've never directly attacked him. He was always sweet and kind, and it felt like kicking a dog when it's down.

The second and third Daniel Whittenhowers were my intended targets. My master felt they were the direct line to getting access to Adelaide Whittenhower. My duty was to cut off the flow of information being released about the BDSM Lifestyle Authority. But even if I was sent here with that purpose, I disobeyed my master, unable to harm Whitt. He's less than a year younger than me, but not in life experience. There's something almost childlike in his demeanor.

I was wrong, so very wrong, and I'm paying for it now. I underestimated Daniel Whittenhower II. Whitt is a master manipulator who is able to sense our darkest secrets. Even after being born and raised in the lifestyle, I couldn't sense his power. Whitt obviously has the ability to mask his will, just as I have been doing all along in Dominion.

Doesn't Whitt realize I already punish myself harder than anyone else could? The pain from my actions hurts my soul, but he's adding humiliation to it now.

Seeing the smug look of triumph on Whitt's face is a stab to my heart. My control fractures and I lash out. I push my palms into Whitt's chest as hard as I can and shove with force. The satisfaction of momentarily feeling vindicated weaves its way through me as Whitt is flung back several feet, where he stumbles to stay upright.

"Did I pass your test?" I hiss between clenched teeth. "Are you fucking happy now?" I glare at the pretty boy and show him every emotion that is raging through my system: betrayal, broken trust, and pain.

Turning on my heel, I run from the room, knowing no one will ever chase me for a positive reason. They never have and never will. If anyone ever follows me, it's to harm me, never to care for me. Unable to deal with the shameful dampness in my pants for a second longer, I choose my private room to hide out in instead of my apartment upstairs.

I fling the door open to my room so hard it reverberates against the wall and rebounds back, hitting me in the head. Seeing stars, it knocks some sense into me.

Pull it together, Font. You have a mission– complete it and get the fuck back home!

Chapter Two

My cellphone rings a Cabaret song, and I immediately fumble for the device in my back pocket. The song is like Pavlov's dog. I hear the sound and the invisible leash that is tethered to my master's hand is yanked tight in her fist.

Hands shaking, "Master," I breathlessly answer, almost dropping my phone.

"I call for your nightly report." Her French accent is thicker than usual, so I know she's worried. I can feel it in my soul.

"I'm sorry, Master. But tonight was fruitless. Restraint is still closed for business due to the problems with security, and we're still being retrained, as per your request." As I speak with her, my accent thickens and becomes more pronounced. I will forever be Font with her, never able to hide behind Dalton Thompson in her presence, which is why she avoids Restraint even though she is currently in Dominion.

"It's for the best that Restraint is closed." Her voice rises in pitch, seeming pleased with the outcome. "I think it should remain closed indefinitely. It would solve a lot of problems."

"Master, you don't mean that," I chastise, but I'm pretty sure she does.

"I do. Look what happened to you a few weeks ago." Voice thickening with hostility, I shouldn't allow it to warm my blood, allowing myself to feel as if she cares for my wellbeing. But I know deep down, she is merely speaking of their weaknesses, not about how they allowed her son to be harmed. "They can't even keep their masters safe."

"That wasn't their fault. Someone set all of this into motion, and I fear it might have been an outside hit. I'm working my ass off trying to figure out why this is happening and who is leaking the information about our masters. I'm trying," I whine. "What if who I am is drawing my enemies near?"

"Doubtful," Master disregards my words, as if it isn't a very real possibility that my enemies are targeting Restraint because it's where I live. The more dominant the master, the more narrow-minded they become, and mine is the most dominant of all. "Soon it will be too late anyway." Master sighs heavily, the sound warbling through the cellphone. Without it directed toward me, I still wince because I know she feels I'm failing her yet again. I've been conditioned to feel worthless unless she's directly praising me.

"I'm trying my best, Master," I plead. "Please don't be disappointed in me. I will get us the information–"

A sound jars me from my conversation. Turning to gaze over my shoulder, I notice Dexter is standing in the doorway with my death in his eyes, leaking menace.

"You should have shut your fucking door if you didn't want to be caught." Dexter snarls, baring his front teeth as he pushes into the room. With force, he kicks backward to close the door, locking us in together, where no one else will find us.

"Dexter, it's not what it sounds like." My voice is pleading as I hold out an arm in front of myself in a stay motion. "It's not what you think." I know it will do little good because I've done too much to Dexter for him to see reason. He's losing control and reveling over the fact, thinking he's finally found the reason his club is in shambles.

With instinct his driving force, Dexter moves so quickly I have no time to react. With a telltale snap, fire spreads through my left side and I collapse to the floor. Rolling into the fetal position, not putting up any fight, I wait for the agony to set in as I slip into shock. Tears form in my eyes because I'll finally receive the atonement for all the evil deeds I've committed in the name of my master.

Pain gurgling up, "It's not what you think, Dexter," I try to reason with him again. The glazed hate in his eyes screams my defeat, and I come to terms with my fate. This isn't my first beating, nor will it be my last. At least this time it's not by those who are supposed to love and protect me.

"I'd fight back if I were you." Dexter growls menacingly and lunges for attack.

Fingers outstretched, seeking anything to protect myself yet coming up empty, I use my last resort. "Master, help me!" I scream piteously into the cellphone lying on the floor beside me, knowing she'll think me weak and an utter failure.

Warbled with terror, "I love you," Master lends me false strength.

The blows rain down heavily all over my entire body, the blunt force of a punch and the sharp burn of a swift kick. Arms curled around my head, I protect myself, leaving my chest as the target.

Fist… Boot… Boot… Slap… Fists wrench silent screams from my throat, the death knell of a wounded animal. My flesh parts beneath Dexter's clenched fists. All the while, he shouts and hisses his hatred at me for daring to touch his wife and his club, and I don't blame him for the violence.

My breathing becomes shallow as each breath fires agony into my lungs. I concentrate on the sensation of my tears slipping down my cheeks. I imagine the cool wetness draining from my flesh as my body's way of weeping– blood, not tears.

My vision clouded with agony, my mind swirls with all the sins I've committed yet haven't paid for. Weak, eyes closing, I seek my final atonement, praying for absolution.

The pounding ceases at the same time I hear my salvation. I whimper in thanks to my master, knowing it wasn't out of love or loyalty but out of necessity.

Devlin's, "What would you have done if I hadn't come upon you?" kills me more than the act of violence– my master didn't call for help. My master, as I'm unable to call her mother, left me for dead.

Seething with fury, Dexter's sanity has not returned. He reels back to strike me again. I clench every muscle in my body, but the hit never comes.

"Don't move, or I will beat you," Devlin threatens, voice deep with rage– the animalistic rumble a comfort. "I promise you won't like it any more than the child did."

Gazing down at me with unveiled disgust, "Child?" Dexter mutters in confusion, eyes tracking the devastation he's wrought.

"You don't understand what's going on, Dexter." Tentatively moving my arm, I blink several times to clear my vision, finding Dexter held at arm's length by the huge man.

"You've allowed your emotions to cloud your judgment, no longer thinking clearly." Devlin releases Dexter, no longer finding him a threat. "Dalton is not the mole, and he's still a child. You're beating the hell out of someone who isn't fighting back and is fifteen years your junior. Wake up and get some fucking control."

Shaking his head left and right, Dexter tries to regain his restraint. "Dalton has to be close to my age. No fucking way is he a kid," Dexter says dismissively.

If I could work my mouth, I'd tell Dexter how he's wrong. What the members of Restraint see is Dalton Thompson, not Font. I had turned twenty a few days before Dexter met me the first time. To Devlin, I'll always be a kid even if I just turned twenty-four last month.

"We'll get you patched up," Devlin promises, voice a rolling purr along my agonized flesh. Strong arms slide beneath my body, cradling me gently, and then lift. Clutching my side, I scream out in pain as my ribs revolt. Devlin gently presses me to his chest, pulling a string of whimpers from my throat.

The pain makes me utter a word I've held in check since Devlin arrived in Dominion, even in private. "Dad," I cry, face pressed against his neck, dragging in a lungful of his familiar scent.

"It's okay, son. I've got you." Devlin's voice rumbles next to my ear as he speaks. "Dexter, follow me. I'd like a chance to explain."

Carrying me, Devlin glides to the hidden door at the end of the hallway. The walk up the flight of stairs is smooth, managing not to jostle me with every step, for which I'm thankful. I don't look back to see if Dexter follows. I can feel his confusion and shame wafting around us.

"Um– Dad? I don't know how to tell you this, Devlin, but you're a six and a half foot tall black man and Dalton's a tiny man with skin the color of wallpaper paste. It's a genetic impossibility," Dexter says from behind us as we enter my two-room efficiency apartment.

Devlin settles me gently on the bed that dominates the main room. I wince from the sharp stab of pain that radiates from my left side. I use all of my strength not to curl up into a ball and cry like a baby. Master's son does not cry, at least not with witnesses.

"Dalton's sperm donor is dead." I can tell Devlin is annoyed by the way his deep voice lowers into the depths of hell. "Blood doesn't make you a parent, Dexter."

"I'm sorry," Dexter placates, sounding ashamed of himself. If I had the strength, I'd let him know I don't blame him for beating me. "What happened to Dalton's dad? I didn't know you were married."

"I'm sure as fuck not sorry. But a son will always long for the love of his father, so I will not speak ill of the dead– at least not in Tony's case. As for married, Dalton's mother and I are close. I'm Master's right-hand man." Devlin's voice is as deadly as the knife we wielded to kill my master's master and his pet tormentor. "Clearly, I'm willing to kill for her."

Ill-at-ease, mind reeling over the fact that he just learned I'm Olivia Fontaine's spawn, Dexter starts shifting toward the open door. Devlin's large strides eat up the space in a second. He firmly closes the door and snaps the deadbolt into place.

"I promise I won't harm you, as I understand your motivations for beating Dalton. I've been waiting for this moment to happen, and I realize I have to tell you what's going on."

"That would be a refreshing change," Dexter mutters to himself. "But I realize I haven't exactly been receptive, fearing the answers."

"Understandable, under the circumstances." Devlin and Dexter share a cryptic look that I don't understand. "But I must care for my son first. Please have a seat." With the polite air of a man playing host, Devlin pulls a chair from the small dining table and places it near the head of the bed.

Dexter reluctantly sits and glances around my humble home– one room with an attached bath. His eyes drink in every detail, missing nothing.

Devlin leans over the bed, trying to get to me. His fingertips snag my brown wig, trying to work it free of my scalp. Panicking, I realize Dexter will see me. Trapped with Dexter on my left and Devlin on my right, I try to slide off the foot of the bed. Moving too roughly, a sharp stab pierces my side as my broken rib protests. Falling to the mattress, panting in agony, I'm unable to move, let alone think through the pain.

Pressing on my side, Devlin offers me some much-needed relief. "Shh… It's okay. We have to place our faith in Dexter. Trust in how he will put Restraint first above all other personal negativities."

Clutching my side, an ironic snort is torn from my throat. "In theory, you may be right," I gasp through the pain. "But fuck a guy's wife and see what happens."

Dexter looks ashamed of himself, but Devlin chuckles, knowing I have a warped sense of humor. "I know you can't trust Dexter, so trust in me instead."

There is no saying no to a man who is triple my weight and a foot and a half taller than me. I'm just shy of five and a half feet and one-hundred-and-ten pounds sopping wet. My dad is nearly seven feet of coiled power in the package of a bald midnight-black man.

I obey.

Once the wig is removed, strong fingers comb through my chin-length black hair. It's a relief to feel the strands brush my face after having it tied up all day long. Those same fingers slowly move toward my eyelids, and I freak by pulling away too quickly. The movement spears agony through my left side.

"I have to remove the contacts, or I can't see your pupils." Devlin's tone holds a wealth of patience. Inside my head, I can hear him telling me I'm only harming myself with my reluctance to allow him to help, just as he's said time and time again to our master. "I need to see how they dilate to determine if you have a concussion. Relax," he orders as a heavy palm pushes my chest until my back is pressed into the mattress. His hand is so large that it covers my entire chest, so I couldn't struggle if I wanted to.

The fingers are back, getting closer and closer, prying my eyelid open. Devlin moves the hand from my chest to reach over to pluck the brown contact from my eye. He repeats the process with the opposite eye. Then he's smiling down at me warmly when my green eyes are finally revealed.

"There's my boy," Devlin murmurs in obvious pleasure. "I've had a hard time looking at you since I arrived in Dominion. It's creepy how different you look." He places the contacts in their appropriate spots in the case, squeezes some solution into the wells, then twists the caps into place, finally stowing the case in the nightstand drawer.

Devlin's hands return for my shirt, and I freak the fuck out, hurting myself in the process. I grab his wrist, trying to stop him, but my fingers don't meet. "No!" I protest loudly, infusing what little strength I possess in the singular word. My eyes are huge, pleading, as I pointedly stare at Dexter.

I don't want Dexter to see me– I never want anyone's eyes to take in my flesh ever again.

"Dammit, Font! The shirt has to go!" Devlin loses his patience, no longer taking no for an answer. "I know you have broken a rib. Let me bind the damn thing before they get here."

In an instant, the urge to fight bleeds out of me. My master may not have sent out an SOS, but she'll eventually show up with my baby sister in tow like last time. Devlin's right– he always is. It would be worse if they witnessed the injury. I hate the look of disgust on my mother's face, not the shame and guilt, as it should be. She looks at me like I'm weak to have allowed my father and brother to mark me when I was a small child, mark me because of the power struggle between my parents and my grandfather.

None of which was my fault– more than half of which was my mother's fault. Olivia Fontaine is evil incarnate, and as a son it is my duty to obey and worship her.

"Hurry," I mutter, frantic, trying to help tear my shirts off. "I don't want Spy to see me like this. She'll cry."

"Spy?" Dexter's interest ratchets higher, no doubt knowing my baby sister is his blood too.

With giant hands, Devlin lifts my t-shirt over my head. I lean forward and suck in a pained breath to allow the shirt to leave my back. The thermal shirt is next to go, leaving me naked from the waist up.

The rib pain is nothing compared to the look of horror on Dexter's face as he sees the ruination of my skin. My entire torso is covered in burn scars. They aren't deep, but obvious next to the pale of my flesh. The scars cover my back and parts of my arms as well. I'm slowly covering myself in tattoos. Four prominent ones are displayed on my back. I simultaneously feel pride and shame over those particular tattoos.

"What happened to you?" Dexter's look of horror changes as he sees me clearly for the first time. I finally look my age and nothing of Dalton Thompson.

"A misunderstanding," I reply shallowly. "My father and brother abused me, not telling me it was a power struggle with my mother at my grandfather's bidding."

Huffing a surprised laugh that I'm being so candid, Devlin leaves the room in search of bindings. I debate talking to the man who beat me until my bones broke and my skin burst like over-ripened fruit.

"Some grandfather you have…" Dexter can't peel his eyes away from my emaciated torso.

"Pierre Fontaine is dead," I snarl with conviction. "I murdered him."

"So I've gathered." Dexter reaches out a tentative fingertip to trace one of the worse scars above my nipple, but he flinches back. "How old were you?"

"I was raised in a whore house– tiny and pretty. Feminine. French. My mother taught me how to be a whore. My Italian mafia Don of a father didn't appreciate that too much." My fingertips skim my burn scars, now fond of my father's mark of ownership instead of the pain it held when he was still alive. "He was burning the fag out of me because my grandfather and his henchman were trying to molest me."

"What?" Dexter's eyes bulge from his skull– Marc had the same reaction when I first met him during the act.

"Being pretty around a pedophile is not a wise thing… Pierre and his pet sociopath, Jon, they would play these sick games, pitting my parents against one another. My mother didn't like to lose, and my father didn't like to see me hurt. Either way, I always lost."

"How did Devlin get involved?" Why Dexter chooses that question to ask is beyond me.

"Jon was Devlin's father– I killed my own dad's father, then we took turns at my grandfather," I say with pride and not an ounce of remorse. "Other than to avenge my father, I'm a nonviolent person. I'm here to find your mole, not harm you."

"What exactly were you trying to accomplish by fucking my wife?" Dexter tries with all his might to keep the fury out of his voice.

"I'm acting like an asshole to get Adelaide Whittenhower's attention, or whoever she works for. I want them to think I'm on their side so they will invite me to join them in their plot of evil. I fuck with each one of you equally. You're all so strong that the only way to get to you is to grind you down, knowing eventually one of you will lose control." I smirk at Dexter, my morbid sense of humor showing. "Congrats! You're the winner."

Dexter looks at me with an expression I can't fathom. I hear the key in my door and freak. "Dad!" I yell.

Devlin comes striding in from the bathroom, staring at the bindings in hands. "What? Which size works best on your tiny rack of bones?"

"Master's here." My voice warbles in fear. "Cover me up. I don't like her seeing my weakness."

Ace bandages long forgotten, with hurried movements, Devlin finishes tucking a blanket around me when the door is flung open.

"Oh, my God! What have you done?" Furious, Master charges to the bed, leaving the door wide open. Upon seeing Dexter, her demeanor changes to false concern. Fist curled between her ample breasts, "I was so worried about you. Are you okay?"

"I'll be fine, Master." I lie, knowing even if I was bleeding to death I'd never tell the truth. This woman has sat by and watched me be beaten bloody and raped, and she hasn't shown any concern or empathy. Deep down I know my mother is a sociopath, so narcissistic she feels I should suffer in any way she has had to suffer.

The victim becomes the ultimate victimizer.

Master's hands flutter over me, looking for a safe place to touch. She finally settles for my hand, touching me for the first time in years. I smile up at her in absolute adoration and hate my fucking guts for it. If all you ever experience is pain in your quest to make someone proud, the instant they give you any comfort, you need it like it's your lifeblood.

Amber eyes bugging out, face flushed, I watch in mild amusement as Dexter sees Olivia Fontaine in the flesh without her cowl covering her from head to toe. I don't see my mother as a woman, but I know that she makes one hell of an impact on the opposite sex. Her tall, curvy figure combined with her flowing black hair and green eyes is a stunning combination. It seems conceited to admit that since I look exactly like her, only even more feminine than she is.

"Master, I'm fine." Dexter looks at me crosswise for calling my own mother master. Not many are given the honor of using her first name, and only Spyder is allowed to call her mother. "Quit fussing over me." I push my luck, grabbing her hands before she can pull the blanket down to see my chest.

Master derives sick pleasure from the sight– the only worthy act I've committed is ridding the world of Pierre Fontaine and Jon

25

Wilson. Every other breath I've taken has been an utter disappointment.

Dexter's eyes rove between my mother and me, noting our likenesses. Worry etches across his face as the impact of his actions comes into sharp focus. From his point of view, it's probably not wise to beat the son of Olivia Fontaine while she's on the phone with said son. Not wise at all.

"Hi, Dexter." I mutter in a chipper voice, hand reaching out to him for a cordial shake. "I'm Dalton Anthony Fontaine Marconi. Font for short. I just turned twenty-four, and I apologize for all I've done to you in the past and for what I may have to do in the future. It's for the sake of the BDSM Lifestyle Authority, so suck it up." I allow my true voice to shine through and smile when the tone hits Dexter's ears.

My mother and I share our accent as well. Even with living in the United States, the effect of my grandmother's inability to speak English has worn off on me. I'm fluent in French, Italian, and English. My true voice holds a strong accent and sometimes I mix the wording on accident.

To say that my nights at Restraint have been difficult would be an understatement. I have to watch my accent, the language I speak, act as an asshole, and act straight. I do all of this while making sure no one notices that I'm in disguise while I pump them for information. I should get an Academy Award.

I reach my hand out for Dexter to shake in acquaintance. Bewildered, he stares at my hand for a few seconds before his manners kick in and he gives a few pumps of a shake. His broken and bloodied knuckles are rough under my fingertips.

"Master, could you take Dexter into the bathroom and aid him with his hands, please?"

Master flashes me a look– *how dare I order her around!* But her need to play the doting mother supersedes her ego just this once.

"You and I need to have a talk in private, Dexter." He flinches at the implications, but I know my mother well. She wants to offer an explanation as to why she sent me here. She places a hand on the smaller man's wrist and directs him toward the only room in my apartment that offers privacy– my tight fit of a bathroom.

I breathe a sigh of relief when the bathroom door is closed. I need my ribs bound, but don't want my mother to see the scars. On a time crunch, Devlin tightly wraps a stretchy bandage around my torso. The pressure offers instant relief, allowing me to breathe easier. Expanding my chest, I take in several large breaths in ecstasy.

"There is a long-sleeved shirt in the middle drawer." I point while speaking. "Will you help me put it on? And I need some pajama bottoms."

Moving quickly, Devlin brings me the soft gray shirt, and I snuggle into it. My attitude changes as soon as my nightmare is covered. I struggle with my jeans because I refuse to be undressed like a baby. I wad the soiled jeans in my hands in shame. Passing them to Devlin with outstretched fingertips, I make sure he avoids the soiled part as I pass them over so he can toss them into the hamper.

"Dad, I need a damp cloth." Filled with shame, I cast my eyes downward. "There are dishcloths next to the sink."

"You've had an adventurous night, eh?" Devlin hands me the cloth, facing away from me so I can wash my earlier shame and excitement from my crotch. My hands tremble as I remember what I did with an audience. How Whitt embarrassed me in front of everyone I've ever tormented. I know I deserved it, but it doesn't take the sting away. I pull the soft pants over my boney hips and breathe a sigh of contentment.

Devlin approaches me with intent, a bottle of rubbing alcohol and a bag of cotton balls in his hands. Uh-huh. Not happening.

"I'll do that," I take them from Devlin. "I don't need to be coddled." I place the items in my lap. Thankfully my face was spared by my upraised arms and my cowardly fetal position during the beating. It was the mildest beating I've ever had. I'll live. My hands and forearms are covered in bruises and cuts where the skin ruptured from the force of Dexter's hits. For such a small man, he rages like a bull.

Dexter and Master return to their seats while I tend to my broken skin. Dexter looks at me with pity. I flinch, hating that look since I was eleven and the burns began. I'm saved from his pity when a spider crawls through my open front door. Well, not crawls– runs and lunges.

"Oomph!" wheezes out of me as my lungs empty of air. My sister crawls on the bed with me, and I'm thankful that it's my right side.

"Watch the rib, Itsy Bitsy," I warn with a wince as I draw my sister to my side.

Spyder and I are the same size, but she has a few pounds on me. She isn't a big girl, just curvy like our mother. On the other end of the spectrum, I'm emaciated to the extreme. I've had no control over myself since birth, which is a difficult notion for someone as dominant as me. I use my food intake as a form of control, which drew me to Dexter's wife in the first place. Hunger pains are also a proper form of self-punishment.

"Are you all right?" No hand fluttering for my sister. Spyder rubs whatever her hands can reach. Worrying her bottom lip, tears glisten in her brilliant eyes and it kills me to see her upset. We're six years apart in age, but we're more like twins.

I don't answer Spyder; I just hold her to my side, happy to be in the presence of someone who loves me unconditionally. I've only seen her a handful of times since she and my mother came to Dominion, but never in private. It was torture to ignore my sister, worse than it has been to ignore Devlin. It's been easy to ignore Master.

I snuggle Spy onto my chest, not caring when the pain radiates from my side. The past four years apart haven't been easy on either one of us. A girl without a real father needs her big brother— no mark against Devlin, but his guidance and comfort aren't the same as having the validation of the person who created you in their image.

Not learning any lessons from my upbringing, my mother uses Spyder's affection and wellbeing as currency. Married, but living apart while running competing empires, my parents bartered for time with me, down to the minute. My mother never saw me as a human being, using me as an agenda against my father while he struggled to deal with the father-in-law she sicced on him. There wasn't an act of violence that I didn't suffer at their hands as a way to punish the other.

Spyder was used as leverage against Marcus Zeitler. My mother's history was how she was given to my father in an arranged marriage to solidify two mafia families. She would cry false tears while sobbing how she was a virgin and my father raped her on their wedding night, with me as the result. I hated my father for most of my life, until I was able to see through my mother's manipulations. My mother was no virgin, nor was she raped. She played the victim while victimizing others, using those same very real tactics to create Spyder with another man while torturing my father in their marriage.

My mind cannot come to terms with the fact that I equally loathe and love my mother.

Every muscle in his body frozen, Dexter's gaze devours my sister as she snuggles with me. Face set in awe, it takes me a moment before I understand the implications of Dexter seeing my sister.

"Does she know who I am?" Dexter asks in wonder, eyes glued to the curls springing from my sister's head– curls identical to his.

"Yes," I reply, surprised at the emotions lacing my tone. My sister hides her face against my chest, suddenly shy, asking me to lend her strength. "Master wouldn't tell Spyder who her father was. I was forbidden to speak of it, but remained in contact with your cousin, trying to pass along your family traditions and religious practices. Generation Next didn't have such loyalties to Olivia Fontaine, and told Spyder the instant they were able to meet with her."

I stare between a distraught Dexter and my sister. Her eyes no longer hold the tears back, dampening my shirt. I decide I should formally introduce the pair.

"Dexter Hayes, this is Spyder Zeitler." I ignore the fact that Master is glaring at the side of my face, taking everything I just said as a slight. Devlin has a firm hand on my mother's shoulder, holding her in place. No doubt it's to protect me from her wrath. I will regret this later on, but I will never regret connecting my sister to her family.

"Call me Spy," her voice wavers as she crawls off me to give the man a hug. He pats her back and twines a curl around his finger. He stares at the coil and smiles. He gives her a tight squeeze and laughs a sound of pure joy.

I'd allow Dexter to beat me nearly to death over and over again as payment for this moment. As melodramatic as that sounds, my sister needs strong men in her life who can counteract the villainess we call mother.

"Cousin," Spyder's voice warbles as she clutches Dexter. "Generation Next has told me all I needed to know about you– not the publication but the people. They wanted me to know you before I met you."

Master looks stunned, as if her only daughter is betraying her– it's a look I know well. Every time I looked at my father with any form of affection, my mother acted like I was gutting her. However,

29

he just looked sad when I would return the same look to my mother, knowing a Black Widow can't feel real emotion. I watch with curiosity as my mother rebuilds her composure, ignoring the fact that the world doesn't revolve around her.

"Let's leave Dalton in peace," Devlin suggests, knowing how draining this is for me. "He needs to rest so he can heal."

With patience, Devlin pulls Spyder away from Dexter's arms. She was slowly mapping the man's features with a fingertip in awe. I understand the fascination, but it isn't polite to randomly touch virtual strangers, relatives or not.

Master stands, and it's a cue that the impromptu visit has met its conclusion. She kisses my cheek, lips never coming into contact with my skin, and then departs to the outer hallway.

Dexter pats my shoulder and gives me that damn look of pity again, this time it's accompanied by shame and guilt. Tomorrow, when I act heinous, he will rethink these emotions.

Spy leans down and brushes a kiss to my cheek, her lips firmly connecting with my flesh. "Mon frère, feel better."

"Bonne nuit, Itsy Bitsy." Sadness burrows into my soul, knowing how this was just a respite, because tomorrow I'll be Dalton Thompson again. If I see my sister, I have to act as if she doesn't exist in my world. Worse, I may have to be mean to her in my quest of ferreting out the mole. I feel queasy at the prospect.

"Do you need me to check on you in the morning, son?" Devlin's deep voice rumbles with concern.

"I'll be fine. As you know, I've had much worse," I say loudly, hoping my mother is haunting the hallway. "I'll see you tomorrow sometime. I think I'll wait a few days before I initiate *operation piss off the Devil*. I don't think I could withstand your punishment so soon after Dexter's." I chuckle at the look of horror that flashes across Devlin's face.

I keep teasing how I will push Devlin to punish me in front of the members in my quest to gain Adelaide Whittenhower's attention. I'm not teasing. Eventually it will come down to that.

I watch as the group converges in the small hallway outside my front door. Devlin locks my deadbolts in place and I'm safe and tucked in for the night. I drift off to visions of crystal blue pools of water feeling confused, ashamed, and in pain.

Chapter Three

"You little freak, I can't believe I sired you. You're an abomination." A rough voice growls in my ear. His rapid breath scalds the shell of my lobe. "Why won't you listen and learn? If you act like a little faggot, your grandfather will pass your ass around. I'm trying to protect you!"

His meaty fingers twist in the rope of my ponytail, wrenching my head to the side with one hand while the other strikes me with an open-fist across my cheek. The force of the hit almost pulls his fingers from my hair. A few strands yank out at the root, others snapping. The sting from the slap and the ache from my scalp are nothing compared to the burns that flame my skin.

"Bruno, show my nancy of a son what it means to be a real man." The man yanks my head farther back, bowing my spine, presenting a perfect canvas for Bruno's ruination.

The father commands his bastard son to burn the faggot out of his legal son. All because my ass is too round, my waist dips in from my hips, my face is too beautiful, my movements are too fluid, and my grandfather is finding them too enticing. The heart of the matter is that big manly Bruno can't give Tony Marconi an heir, but he'll condition the faggot son until he can. If my grandfather molests me, then he'll turn me into a fag, and Tony still has time to change my fate.

Nothing I can change, but I suffer anyway.

Fury washes over Bruno's strong features, blaming me for what he has to do simply because he couldn't do it otherwise. My brother sneers at me in anticipation as he relights his cigar. Eyes avidly focused, I watch as he cuts the end off the hand-rolled Cuban. He swirls his lighter in a circle, igniting the end. He puffs out white plumes of smoke, stoking the cigar to flame. Bruno's brown eyes never leave my face as he takes a few drags. He's building the moment, eyes glazing with his eagerness to cause pain to relieve his own frustrations.

"Dalton, I swear you think you're a girl. It's one thing to ruin your father's hopes of a future with your love of cock. But I'm starting to think you wish you had a cunt." My head is yanked farther back, pulling a whimper of defeat from my lips. Several more black strands break from the force of his fist. *"Maybe I'll make you wear a dress since you're so fond of kissing boys."*

"I'm not sorry," grits out between my clenched teeth. *"I won't say I can't help it. It's who I am."*

"I know," my father mutters with great regret. *"If you weren't born to your parents, I'd appreciate you as you are. But you were born to us– Bruno, burn the faggot out of my son."*

At fourteen years old, I'm more evolved than Bruno is at twenty. All he knows is what my father has taught him, never questioning anything. My bastard brother is great muscle for my father, which is apparent as he slowly moves in with the lit end of his cigar.

Neck bowing, tendons cording with strain, flames sear in white-hot agony on my chest. The sizzle of flesh and the scent of my burning skin has me retching in my father's hold. Nothing comes up my throat because I haven't eaten since the night before. I don't scream, knowing that it will feed into how they see me as a pussy, drawing this torture out even longer. I drag in large breaths of air that are tinged with the putrid scent of my burnt flesh and cigar smoke.

Bruno draws on the cigar, stoking its flame hotter and hotter. I watch as embers ignite the end to cherry-red. The torture stick is applied to my left nipple and I cannot control the death wail that frees from my throat. My body gives out at the knees, and the only thing keeping me upright is my father's hold on my hair.

Dangling from my father's fist, my body flashes with sweat as I try to accept the pain. I huff in more of the noxious odor, trying to calm myself before I hyperventilate. I hang like a rag-doll, enduring the pain. I learned a few sessions ago, how if applied long enough, the cigar deadens the nerves, searing the pain away. Bruno has improved his technique. He no longer leaves it longer than a few seconds in one spot. Every time, he stokes the end hotter by sucking a drag off the cigar before he applies it to my skin.

This time my punishment is harsher than the last. My last offense was an erection that came unbidden when they brought a couple in to touch while I watched. When my father noticed my fascination with the boy, I was punished with a whipping across my *back. I didn't ask to be gay, and I cannot control my baser urges. My father sets me up in impossible situations, waiting for me to fail, just so he can have my brother punish the gay out of me.*

When I'm on my mother's time, Master celebrates my homosexuality by using my cock to her advantage, destroying all of my father's conditioning. Since my father can't punish my mother, and my mother can't punish my father, and they absolutely hate each other's guts, they use me to harm the other. My father does love me, but I highly doubt my mother sees me as more than a possession that she doesn't wish to have broken. Then there is my grandfather... the man pulling both of their strings, getting off on our shared misery.

My parents are both strong dominants, yet they both want me to kneel at their feet, and then punish me for being subservient. It's worse when they punish me for flexing my dominance.

My current offense is my first kiss. I knew I was being watched, but my defiant nature forced me to do it anyway. With premeditation, I leaned over and kissed my crush. A few seconds into the kiss, before it could turn into something more, I was wrenched from his embrace and thrown into my father's office.

I wish I had the balls to tell them that no matter how much they punish me, I can't help what triggers me. I will avoid the contact in order not to be punished, or I will learn to be more discreet to ensure I don't get caught, but you cannot punish me for something that is the core of my personality.

I scream as searing pain radiates across my chest. The cigar burns hotter as it's applied to a previous burn– the burn from yesterday when my father said he needed to burn the pansy accent out of my voice. There isn't a cell in my body that doesn't need to be punished. I'm too effeminate. I'm too French. I'm too much like my mother, not enough like Anthony Marconi. Not anything like Anthony Marconi.

My small, pale body isn't golden or brawny enough. I show no resemblance to the man who bought my mother's virginity. I would hate him just for that, but not as much as I loathe my grandfather for it. The Italian father respects the French grandfather, but not the son. I'd love to burn the French out of that bastard. Maybe Bruno could help.

My body lulls in place, attached to the head that Tony grips in his fist. My mind disjoints until I no longer feel the pain of the burns.

Floating dreamily, I lost count at twenty. The door slamming into the wall brings reality into sharper focus.

My eyes roll up more than six feet and meet the white-blue gaze of my dad– not my douchebag sperm donor who doesn't think I'm good enough– Devlin Conrick, the one who not only loves me but takes care of me, playing interference between my parents.

"Enough," growls the deep timbre of his voice.

"Fine, Conrick, take Olivia's spawn back to KINK, where she'll sell his soul for a few bucks." Tony releases his grip on my hair, and I slump to the floor. Against his will, Tony actually tries to soothe me with a loving touch to the inside of my wrist. "I'll see you in two weeks, son. Remind your mother not to make you late, or I will earn extra minutes."

"No, Dalton will not be coming back to your abuse." Devlin's voice is vehement, just as it has been bi-weekly since my birth. I would love to believe him, but we both know I'll be back until the bastard finally punishes the life out of me.

"Do you say the same to my wife when she has our son brandishing his cock for her clientele? That's child abuse too," Tony reminds Devlin how they are both equal when it comes to evil, and Devlin is just as guilty for allowing it. "You will bring my son back to me in two weeks, or I will take action against everyone who resides at KINK. There is a lovely child who I can't wait to get my hands on, simply to hand her off to her actual father."

Devlin sputters, actually debating if Spyder is better off with the man my mother raped– she couldn't lie or manipulate her way out of that since I saw it with my own two eyes. It's hard to spin yourself into a victim when you keep a man against his will for over a year. Tony actually tried to save Marcus more than a dozen times, losing a month's worth of my time in the tug-of-war struggle for dominance over my life.

That was almost seven years ago, so my parents are currently back to fifty-fifty custody, each destroying me half the time.

"Fine. Two weeks." Strong arms scoop me off the dirty floor and press me to his broad chest. I inhale his familiar scent– the scent of safety. I sigh in relief as I replace the putrid scent of my burnt flesh combined with the cloying scent of tobacco with Devlin's comforting musk.

"Make sure my father-in-law and your father keep their disgusting hands off my son," Tony shouts after us. "If Jon so much

as lays a finger on my son, I'll murder anyone with Wilson blood running through their veins, especially you!"

"This will end one day– I promise. It can't last forever." Devlin sounds so sure of the future as he strides out the office. The din of illegal gambling drowns out what he says next.

"I have to die sometime," I whisper underneath my breath, knowing he can't hear me. I prophesize, "This will end with death."

Chapter Four

I wake with the lingering effects of the memory. As always, it sucks the will to live right out of me. My shame and regret, the worthless feeling of being lowered to a possession, flood back as if it's happening in the here and now. Hidden beneath the depression is my smug attitude that I was the one who survived.

I avenged my father while protecting my mother. But I'm not sure I'm strong enough to live with what I've done for the sake of her vengeance.

Scrubbing my face against my pillow, I brace myself for the agony to come. As a masochist, normally I'd feel a release from the pain– a type of soul cleansing. But as I lay on my stomach, my broken rib doesn't lessen my burden. For some reason, it seems to intensify it.

Gathering my courage, I place my palms on the mattress and push up to right myself. Sucking in a pained-filled breath, my rib protests my movements. I wish the memory would have stayed hidden, because I always thrash in my sleep when I remember. It's not a wise thing to do when your body is broken.

I silently count to three and roll to my back. "Mother Fucker!" Clenching my teeth, my hands immediately seek my side. If I hadn't deserved it, I would find Dexter and beat the living piss out of him. Who am I kidding? That would just result in a broken hand. I'm as weak as a baby. I'm pretty sure the Zeitler toddlers could kick my ass right now.

My fingertips snake down the edge of the bed, searching between the mattress and the box spring. The shakes never leave me for days after I see my mother. Hearing her voice is bad enough, but seeing her play pretend to my face is worse.

Tony fought to protect me, using unconventional methods, but I've had four years to come to terms with why my father abused me. To show me affection would have put me at risk with my grandfather. In the game of global domination between mafia kingpins and sociopaths, they use those you love against you.

I miss Tony. Just before he died, we had found a happy medium, both of us enjoying our relationship. Every few months, Bruno visits me. He looks and sounds so much like our father that I break down every single time.

Bruno doesn't call me a nancy boy, or a pussy, or a pansy, or a faggot– he cries with me. We love those who refuse to love us back the most, while taking those for granted who love us freely. My brother keeps me in check, making sure I'm objective when it comes to Olivia Fontaine. He also keeps my mother in check because I gave him the deed to KINK as my first act of independence, or as my mother called it– willful disobedience.

On autopilot, my fingertips pop the latch on a thin cigar box that used to belong to Tony. I'm sick in the head, but I miss my punishments– they bonded me to Tony and Bruno, because afterward, Tony would hold me and tell me how proud of me he was. Eyes held wide, with a sure stroke, I slice a perfect line across my thigh near my hip.

Red. Blood slowly wells to ooze from the cut, the flow symbolizing a physical manifestation of my mental anguish, or so Alex said when he saw the marks on my body. All I know is that I feel relief as I watch the blood trickle out of the wound.

"Dalton?" flows from my open door. I was so mesmerized by the red that I hadn't heard the door swing open. I quickly flip my blankets to cover myself. In a frenzy, I stow the razor blade in the cigar box, and then tuck it back between the mattress and box spring, hoping one of my dirty secrets stays hidden.

Wincing, I sit with my back to the headboard. "When I saw you after my attack in the dungeon, I thought you were a figment of my imagination. But then you kept showing up."

Leviticus walks into my apartment, shutting and bolting the door behind him. As Devlin's nephew, Levi was my savior while he lived in Las Vegas– he was my grandfather's and his grandfather's outlet, taking the molestations in my place, until he moved away and left me to fend for myself.

Being born into such evil bonds strangers into brothers, always making us question how and why Pierre Fontaine and Jon Wilson bonded together.

"Bub? Are you okay?" My eyes flash away guiltily as Levi stares at the blood blooming on my sheet. "I understand," he murmurs as he pads softly across my floor, making no sound. Settling on the bed like a ghost, the mattress doesn't dip under his weight. "You have to remember to call me Wil when you see me, okay? But you don't have to pretend I don't exist."

Levi is older than me, older than Bruno by a few years. He keeps his life a secret, to the point I don't even know if he has a wife and kids. But the instant he walks into the room, I know I'm safe.

"I'm an asshole, remember? I can't be buddy-buddy with our security. Too many questions will be asked."

"True," Levi mutters to himself while his hand fishes beneath my mattress. "I took this job to keep you safe. You know that, right?"

"I know," I breathe the truth. "Did Stanton send you?" I ask of Stanton Green, Dominion, New York's kingpin. "Are there more hits on my life?"

Levi chuckles a sardonic sound, the desolate tone resonating with me. "Well, bub… that kind of shit tends to happen when you rat out your competition to the FBI after committing three counts of patricide."

"I didn't kill Tony," is spitting out of my lips before I can stop it, never denying offing our grandfathers. "They all deserved what they got."

"I know." Levi pops the lid on my cigar box, gazing expressionlessly at my bloodletting kit. "Yes, Stanton thought it best *Gunner*–" he stresses, because I keep fucking that name up too, "– and I keep an eye on you. The dungeon incident was a hit on your life, having nothing to do with Restraint. Stanton's following a few leads, furious that anyone is stupid enough to set foot into his territory."

"Bruno said the hit didn't come from anyone in Las Vegas, and my brother isn't malicious enough to take me out by himself when I give him anything he desires."

"That's what worries us the most, not knowing who is trying to harm you… Look, bub–" Levi takes a fresh razor blade from my kit, and before I can blink, a cut is welling on his forearm. "No matter how lonely you feel, you have many people who love you, and not the type of love that hurts."

"Master–"

"Never call her master." Suddenly furious, Levi's eyes glow with bitter hatred. "Olivia is *not* your master. She's your mother. We shouldn't have been born as a way to draw our grandfathers' attentions away from Olivia, while she sat by and watched them harm us in the way they used to harm her– how she was fine with them molesting Gunner and others as long as they never touched her. We were born to be the playthings of our *masters*. Olivia Fontaine is as much to blame as Pierre and Jon, even if she never laid a finger on us. Never let her forget that fact, because she'll sure as hell make sure you do."

Quickly, before I can react, Levi slices a mark across my forearm. I don't even get to enjoy the sight of the red flow, because he's pressing our wounds together in an instant. "Blood brothers?" I snort, releasing an uncomfortable laugh because I'm basking in the warmth of Levi's attention.

Gazing at me with eyes so blue they're eerily white, "*Brothers*," Levi stresses. "Does it bother you to look at me? Do you see Jon instead?"

Remembering Levi as the boy who used to protect me, it's hard to see that kid in the man sitting on my bed today. In his thirties, Levi's brown curls are shorn off so close to his scalp, his hair is a shadow on his head. He's the light to his uncle's dark, with the Wilson line coming from a white sociopath with eerie eyes. The dark skin comes from a different branch in the family tree– one of my mother's whores gave Devlin the Conrick surname since he was born a bastard.

Levi's body is unassuming, small and nonthreatening, but I know in this case looks are deceiving. Leviticus Wilson is deadly but impartial. "I see *you*," I finally respond, voice as grave and serious as Levi's always is. "Awake or asleep, nothing will ever overwrite the memories. My entire life, you and Devlin have had my back. So what if the man who gave you those creepy eyes used to rape me? I put a stop to it permanently."

"Thank you," Levi whispers, face turning away to seek some privacy to hide the tears threatening to fall. "I don't want to see Pierre when I look at you, or Spy, or Olivia–"

"But you do."

"Yes," Levi breathes. "You're obviously stronger than me, because it bleeds into my life. Stanton was mourning the loss of Bianca's innocence when the call came. He charged into my bedroom to tell me my grandfather was dead, and I celebrated."

"When I got to Dominion three days later, Stanton vowed I'd have his unconditional protection for life– his version of a thank you card."

"We had a party– a huge celebration." Levi's cruel lips curl into a smirk. "With you mourning Tony's death, we figured it would be disgusting to invite you."

"Why did you stay away?" I ask the single most important question that has plagued me since I saw Leviticus a few weeks back after the dungeon attack. "Is it because I remind you of Pierre?"

"No." Levi grinds our wounded forearms together again to stress home his point. With quick efficiency, he stows my bloodletting kit beneath the mattress. "We both look like our grandfathers. I feared what you'd see when you looked at me."

"Never," I vow.

"Now that that is established." Levi rises to his feet, only to bend at the waist to kiss my forehead. "Stop harming yourself– let the shit go. Finish whatever bullshit Olivia has you doing, and then tell her to fuck off once and for all. She's pure toxicity. Trust me when I tell you how liberating it is to say it to her face."

I peer up to Levi like he holds the answers to the universe swirling in his pale blue stare. "How'd you do it?"

"My stepmother taught me about unconditional love. After she died, even when my grandfather yanked me back to hell, I kept that warmth inside me." Levi fists his chest. "I left the first chance I got, and then I found people who actually gave a fuck about me– that's how." With a quick jerk of his t-shirt, Levi bares the side of his muscular torso, showing off a series of scars. "Leave this addiction behind, okay? It seems to flow in our blood, but the relief only lasts a second. Deciding you're not worthless lasts forever." And with that, he leaves as quietly as he arrived.

For a few quiet moments, I lie in bed letting my mind wander, trying to read between the lines of Levi's cryptic words, and it frightens me about what may have been revealed. Everyone I care about is currently in Dominion with me, no longer halfway across the country where I have to worry about them. Except for Bruno, but I know that brute can take care of himself. Most of my enemies are dead, and I'm unsure if my mother is my enemy or not.

As if sensing my thoughts, my cellphone sings a cabaret song. Unable to help myself, I grit my teeth while I reach for my phone resting on the nightstand. "Master?"

"What did Leviticus want? What did he tell you?" Unveiled suspicion is thick in my mother's voice, proving she has eyes and ears everywhere. Which begs the question, why does she need me then?

"Levi was being nice by checking up on me," I answer without hesitation. "Why is that a bad thing? Don't you want people to care about me, Master?"

"Never forget how half of his blood runs Wilson," Master warns cryptically, answering my suspicions more so than if she came right out and told me the truth.

"As does Devlin's," I remind her just to be an asshole of a son. "As did Levi's father. He was your best friend."

"Never speak of Jonathan," Master snarls, taking my bait by proving my father correct.

Master said she was a virgin when she spun her woe-is-me victim tale, and Tony kept saying she was in love with our tormentor's son who spurned her affections and moved to Dominion to marry. Master called Tori Wilson a fat, black, old hag purely out of jealousy. Tori and Master were complete and total opposites and Jonathan loved her instead.

Tony assumed Master stole the allegiance of her lost love's baby brother– Devlin –on purpose, just so Jonathan would have to look her in the eye and bring his wife, daughter, and Levi to visit. If being gay wasn't in my DNA, Master's crazy female revenge bullshit would have done it. According to both Tony and Devlin, Master would flirt with Jonathan, burn Tori to her face, and call their daughter's darker skin ugly, which was courting death since Devlin was standing at her back while she insulted his niece.

Tori died of an aneurysm around the time I was born, and a few years later Jonathan died of a heart attack after refusing my mother's advances while he grieved for Tori. I doubt my mother has ever gotten over Jonathan– grief, jealousy, and hatred have destroyed all goodness in her.

"Just do your job." The click of the phone disconnecting leaves me in deafening silence.

Time to do my job by becoming Dalton Thompson.

After a struggle to stand, I cross my apartment in a few strides. I scan the contents of my refrigerator, and I decide on an energy drink for breakfast. I look to the clock on the microwave– I guess it's a mid-day snack. I can't eat this late in the day. I usually eat a healthy breakfast, and at the end of my night, I will try to hold something down. No way can I eat so close to becoming Dalton Thompson. I usually retch up whatever I ate during the day.

Can of Amp in my hand, I fetch Thompson's identity and head into the bathroom to start my nightly routine. I stare longingly at the shower stall, but I can't get my bindings wet. At times like these, I wished I had a bathtub and some creature comforts. I could call Devlin and have him rebind me, but I don't want to be coddled or be a bother. The man has his hands full with my mother and her people.

I give myself a poor excuse of a sponge bath out of the dinky sink. I try to avoid all the bruised and broken skin with each pass of the soapy washcloth, but wince and hiss when I miscalculate.

Unbidden, my first kiss pops into my thoughts. I hate it when the memories resurface. I try to forget, but when I can't, it's like getting hit by a semi. Sebastian was my friend turned submissive. My sweet and completely straight lifelong friend– my first kiss.

I know Sebastian is in Dominion, hiding out at the Edge building with my mother, sister, and Devlin. I miss him like crazy, but it's best if I'm not in his presence. He'll do anything for me, and I feed off it. He was safer in Las Vegas, away from me. My thoughts veer from innocent, dark brown eyes to ones that resemble water and twinkle with mischief.

My cock greets me for the first time in a long while because we're usually disgusted with one another– he wants me to screw men and I blame his grotesque length for making me a whore. I stare down in awe as he swells at the perverse thoughts rolling through my mind. As a test, I touch my cockhead lightly with a fingertip. I arch a brow when he doesn't deflate but grows to its full eleven inch length. It's been almost a year since I've masturbated and didn't find it a chore. I reach down and grip him tightly– painfully. I moan a sigh of relief at the pleasure that radiates from my groin. Eyes drifting shut, I recall two different men as my hand picks up a brutal pace– both men are off limits and straight, but my cock doesn't give a fuck. Within seconds, my head flops back and I howl a cry of release.

Insane laughter bubbles up my throat when I see the mess I've created on my sink, and even the vanity mirror. Spunk everywhere. "Holy fuck! Thanks for staying hard for me. I guess you're telling me what you want. Sorry, but it has to be girls for you. If you get hard for me again, we can pretend Sebby is with us."

I stare at myself through the spooge-spattered mirror. I'm fucking insane. I run a hand through my chin-length hair, wishing I didn't have to wear that nasty wig. I've always preferred my hair long, even if it made me look more feminine. But I cut it to this length after years of having it used against me. My grandfather's pet sociopath, Jon, would yank my hair while he–

I'm safe now, but I still won't grow it longer. Sliding my fingertips through the silky strands while saying goodbye for the day, I pull it back to fasten it at the nape of my neck. I glare at the offending mass of bland brown hair resting on the edge of the sink, and stifle a resigned sigh. I adjust the wig until Font's hair is completely covered. I place the left contact in my eye covering the brilliant green with a muted brown and repeat the process with the right. I gaze into the mirror and a stranger looks impassively back.

I smooth concealer underneath my eyes to cover the bruise-like shadows. No matter how much sleep I get, the haunting bruises remain. They're a part of me, but I don't cover them out of vanity, rather one more part of Font that is concealed. Lastly, I cover my lips with tan cream. Just as the dark circles, my lips are an unnatural shade of red– the unnatural mark of a Fontaine.

Over my boxers, I pull on a pair of baggy jeans to add extra bulk to my body. If I were Font, I'd wear skinny jeans, but Thompson doesn't wear those. He's a thirty-four-year-old drab asshole who gets in your face and challenges you at every turn, not a twenty-four-year-old who wants to wear black to fade into the shadows and observe. I gingerly pull on a brown thermal shirt, trying not to disturb my rib, effectively covering all the markings on my body. I pull a boring t-shirt over it, when I'd usually wear something a bit edgier. To add more weight to my body, I add a jacket, even if it's late spring. Since it would be strange if Dalton Thompson appeared emaciated, I layer to cover my slight build and the telltale curve of my ass and hips that my grandfather was so fascinatingly absorbed with.

I huff in several breaths, storing Font to the back of my mind and bringing Dalton Thompson to the forefront.

You are Dalton Thompson– antagonistic and belligerent. You don't speak Italian with a French accent because you're from the Midwest and English is your only language. You crave pussy, not cock. You don't want to make friends, or be nice to anyone, or take comfort from those you're harming. You don't recognize half the people who are lurking in the shadows, even if you don't know what game they're playing. You're here to do your business, gain Adelaide Whittenhower's attention while protecting your ass, and do as your master bids, your happiness be damned.

I repeat the mantra several times over, allowing the persona to settle over my mind like an ill-fitted costume. Dalton Fontaine is gone. I was given the identity of Dalton Thompson after I ratted out my competition. I was hidden where Stanton could keep me safe.

I want my life back. I want my family back, especially my father. I don't want to walk past Levi and not give him a hug. I don't want to pretend my mother loves me. I never want to snub my baby sister. I want to deserve hopes and dreams and fantasies. I'm sick to death of looking over my shoulder, waiting for a knife to be shoved deep into my back.

I miss me, not my mother's tool, my father's son, my brother's greatest shame, my grandfather's toy, Jon Wilson's victim, or Devlin Conrick's burden. I don't want to be a victim any longer, or a murderer, or the head of the Marconi and Fontaine crime families partnered with the Green crime family.

Dalton Anthony Fontaine Marconi wants his life back for the first time ever.

I hate my mother. The acts I've committed in her name are heinous. I love her with every cell in my body, and I thank her for giving me life. She's a strong and formidable woman, but she allowed one monstrous act to change her life and to shape mine by allowing the same men who molested her to do worse to me. She lied to me my entire life, creating a web of fallacy and betrayal to force my hand. She endured a childhood of distress, losing the only person she ever loved, while I've endured a lifetime of cleaning up her messes. She is a victim, but an even better victimizer.

The sins of the father shall be visited upon the son– except I sin for my mother because of her father. I love her, I hate her, but mostly, I resent her.

I glare at my reflection and allow all the pent-up hate, pain, and shame to infuse my soul. Font hides in the depths of my mind as Thompson erupts in a wave of unadulterated hatred and disgust.

Chapter Five

Stepping from the hidden doorway leading from the staircase to the upper floors, I unleash my anger on the first target I find. Daniel Whittenhower III is stalking down the hallway to our classroom. Burly. Rosy-cheeked. Innocent. Happy. Dalton Thompson must hate him for having the life I never got to lead. He's not much younger than I am, but I guarantee he hasn't experienced even a tenth of the torture I have.

Sidestepping from the shadows, I startle the young man. "Niel, how's it feel to be a pedophile?" I taunt him because that's what Thompson does. My stomach roils, protesting my behavior but finding no food to eject since I haven't eaten in nearly two whole days.

"What?" Niel gasps in shock, looking at me like Font is attacking him, not my nasty alter ego. Visibly hurt, it makes this all the more difficult for me to go through with. I've never targeted Niel or his pretty boy uncle with my hate, even though they were my intended targets. I've left them alone because I know they aren't the guilty parties. Well, Niel is guilty, but not of feeding information to his aunt.

"Ava," is my answer. Ezra and Katya's oldest is guilty as well, but too young to be playing with Niel. I'm fond of the pair of idiots. They're ingenious and have taken my sister in with open arms. The three of them are such a bad idea, but I wait with amusement to see what they will accomplish. I actually respect the brats, and relish the idea that they will live their own lives without anyone pressing an agenda upon them.

Operating on a hair-trigger, "Don't talk about my girlfriend like that, asshole." Niel rushes toward me, and my hand flares out to grip the front of his neck. I flash him my eyes, holding the baby dom in check with my will. I may be gay and small and beaten, but I'm a strong dominant– switch or not. I was raised in this lifestyle from birth. A fledgling master is nothing for me. Niel could beat me with his stocky body, but my eyes freeze him in his place.

"What?" Niel's eyes glaze over, and I smile at the information it provides.

"Keeping secrets, are we, Daniel?" His green eyes widen impossibly large, bottom lip quivering. "I guess I understand why you let Ava lead you around on a leash."

"I-I-I—"

"Get to class, Niel. I won't tell anyone." I drop my hand from the front of his throat to pat his chest. My asshole persona is not worth harming the boy. I pat his chest, trying to comfort and reassure him. "Your secrets are safe with me. If you have any other secrets, especially those pertaining to your bitch of an aunt, I'd tell me if I were you. I don't think you'd like your secrets made public. I hear your grandfather is a real old-school motherfucker. He wouldn't take kindly to your temperament."

Niel watches me in confusion as I display my force of will, turning agreeable. "I will, sir. I promise to let you know about Aunt Adelaide– she just published the sequel. But I'll see what else I can find out for you."

I shove Niel towards the classroom and follow after him. He stops abruptly in the doorway. I plow into his back– a grunt is forced from my throat as my rib protests the movement.

"Niel, do I have to put taillights on that big ass of yours? Move it, mini-shit-Whitt." I give him another shove into the room. We're late and I hate being the last one in the door. All eyes latch onto me with a wide variety of expressions– disdain wins out.

I glance around the room, trying to figure out what stopped the kid in his tracks. My eyes immediately find my mother as if she holds a gravitational pull on me. She's at the head of the class, chatting with Dexter and Marcus. But that isn't what captured the kid's attention– Ava is in attendance. The fourteen-year-old is sitting next to her mother with a pissed off scowl on her face, with Syn sitting on her other side. I guess the child is in trouble again.

A smirk pulls at my lips, wondering if their little secret was revealed.

It's too bad they don't know who I am. I could be a valuable source of information on how living in the lifestyle fucks with a child. I was born into it, schooled in it, excelled and failed in it. Ava had almost twelve years of innocence, way more than I received.

The past three years have warped the already too mature child into a miniature version of her adoptive grandfather.

I want to bitch at my mother for forcing Katya to drag her daughter here, knowing Kat must be unsettled by the decision. She's the type of mother I'd wished I had, while I'm surprised my mother didn't demand the Zeitler toddlers to attend. The only consolation is that Ava's entire family, minus her tiny minions, is in attendance. It's like a goddamn diabolical family reunion.

In fact, every single member of Restraint is packed into Dexter's personal room. There are so many, I can't pick out individuals, but Gunner and Levi are bracketing the only exit, keeping us in the room.

The side of my face warms as eyes avidly stare at me. Curious, I turn towards the sensation. Hand clutching the nearest desk to remain upright, I gasp audibly and my knees go weak. My heart beats a rapid tattoo beneath my chest. I clutch my side as my rib throbs like a toothache. Tears form in my eyes as the gravity of his presence hits me. Hard. I'm going to kill whoever brought him here—

My mother is evil incarnate.

I stare into guileless deep brown eyes, and they stare back. His soft brown hair curls above his chiseled jaw. His firm lips lift slightly at the corners in a silent hello, while his hand gives a slight wave in recognition.

I'm not sure how Sebastian recognizes me as Dalton Thompson, but I guess I would recognize my master in disguise— when isn't my mother in disguise? I watch as he stands and approaches me. Then I unfreeze by my feet moving without thought toward Sebastian. We meet in the center of the room in front of the desks. I yank his taller, lithe body to my broken one and wince when he squeezes me too hard.

"Master," Sebastian whispers against the side of my neck, his breath ruffling at my hair. "I've missed you."

I start to bawl. I try to hold it in and fail, but there is nothing that could stop the torrent. It's been one thing after the other my entire life, with all of these people who truly love me showing up on the same day. Gripping him as tightly as possible, I sob against Sebastian's shoulder, feeling centered and at home for the first time in four years. It was my twentieth birthday the last time I saw him— my wedding day. The day my father was executed. The day I killed for the first time to protect him, and the same day I killed for the second time to avenge all of their victims.

Sebastian has been in my life since his birth. He was my playmate and best friend, my study buddy in all things. He was my solace against the pain I lived through on a daily basis. Later, when I grew strong and he didn't, I bent his will with mine. From a very early age, the sensation of unconditional love, respect, and adoration became an addiction, a vice I had to kick.

I hate Sebastian for being here, because it brings up the feelings– the memories. Because it makes me miss him all the more. Absence doesn't make the heart grow fonder, it gives you the ability to play pretend and forget. With Sebastian standing here, it's proof I'm a murderer and will never have a normal life. Not that I'd have any idea how to live without the constant shadow of death hovering over my head.

I rub my tears against Sebastian's shoulder to clear my vision. Then I roll my eyes to look to my master. The genuine expression on her face informs me that she brought Sebby here as a reward, trying to appease how unsettled I've become. It wasn't an act out of love, but another form of control on her part. Balling up all of my bitter resentment, I show my mother all the loathing I feel for her with one single glance.

My mother turned me into a murderous whore, but that was forgivable because I was strong enough to take it. What is unforgivable is how bringing Sebastian here put him into danger, not only from everyone at Restraint and those who keep trying to harm us, but from me.

"Sebby, I've missed you, too." I draw away from him, but he's reluctant to let me go– physically stronger than me, he refuses to uncurl his hands from the back of my shirt. "You know why it's best if I'm not around you," I murmur near his ear. "You know how easy it would be to take advantage, to abuse your trust, and I can't allow that. But that doesn't mean I don't love you. It means I want you to have freewill and be happy."

Brushing a platonic kiss against my neck, Sebastian is able to communicate with me without words– if anyone understands my reasoning, it's Sebastian Vance.

I was a focal point when I entered the room, but now I'm the center of attention. All eyes are on me as they look on with curiosity. The asshole is bawling like a child as he holds a submissive male in his arms. The straight asshole Dalton Thompson wouldn't create such a spectacle.

Sebastian looks at me with acceptance. I turn and walk away as if I didn't just embrace him. I leave him standing in the center of the room as I take my seat in the back corner, guilt and shame burning through my system. I glare at anyone who dares to look in my line of sight. I feel nauseous over what I must do to defuse the situation. I look around the room until I find my next victim– the one with the biggest payoff.

After class I will hit my target.

We all sit quietly as Master, Marcus, and Dexter furiously discuss something in the front of the room. My eyes drift to Sebastian and drink him in, starved after so many years of separation. I close my eyes to cut off my sight, knowing better but doing so anyway. I try to stop the memories from flooding my mind, but there is nothing that will stop the torrent once the dam has broken.

"Is he hard?" The gruff voice of my father demands as I receive my very first blowjob. The female at my feet shakes her head no since she's unable to talk with my flaccid cock rammed into her mouth.

"Well, suck him harder," he hisses in frustration. "Dalton, you have to learn to take a woman. Not only for the Marconi legacy, but you know your grandfather is using this as a test."

I grit my teeth as she pulls harder, both of us doing our damnedest to get me hard. I'm not a moron. After years of this shit, I know the more desperate my father becomes it's because Pierre has him by the balls, and I'm the one who will be punished. My father loves me too much, and his tough love is actually for my benefit.

"Figlio di puttana," Tony snarls. "It's just a blowjob. Close your fucking eyes and relax. There isn't a man on the planet who doesn't love a wet mouth wrapped around their cock."

My dick shrinks more, trying to get away from the bruising force she's drawing on us. The harder she pulls, the limper I become. Alone in my bedroom with this woman would be humiliating, but slumped against my father's desk with my father and brother looking on like I'm a bitter disappointment... with my sociopathic grandfather sitting on the sofa watching with avid fascination.

Bruno is beefy and suave, but he's known for being gentle and kind with the ladies. He walks onto the main floor and drags any woman he wants to his office, and the girl is thrilled to be chosen. Me? The future head of the Marconi and Fontaine organizations? I'm limp. Being born in the unholy state of matrimony shouldn't be a deciding factor on who is your successor, judging by my brother and me.

"Get the kid," Tony commands Bruno. Then Italian flows in rapid succession over how his faggot son acts like a blowjob is a punishment, not a reward.

Tears fill my eyes as the young woman at my feet sucks without results. This is my first blowjob and it's my punishment, no matter what Tony says. I didn't want it from her, but he forced me to put my dick in her mouth. I'd feel worse if she were here against her will as I am. It's something Anthony Marconi is known for, using sex as a form of interrogation or punishment. But I've seen this woman working the floor. She's one of his prostitutes, and no doubt she's getting paid overtime for trying to suck the gay out of Tony's son. She probably takes it as a great honor, a duty she is providing.

"We will flip that switch in your head that seems to think sex is evil. You will finish with Sandy," Tony demands. "I have a treat that will no doubt swell your worthless cock. But, as always, there are consequences set by your grandfather."

"No!" I shout when Bruno escorts my treat into Tony's office— Sebby. I've tried to protect him, and I've finally failed. I wrench away from Sandy, nearly a foot of my damp, worthless cock flopping out of her mouth. I pull my submissive behind my back in protection.

Tony and Bruno are sadistic bastards when it comes to our enemies, but never to me. My lessons are to avoid Pierre's machinations. The pressure to get hard with Sandy sucking me off was partly because I knew that if I didn't get hard, there was something far worse in my fate.

Pierre sits on the sofa and watches with a supreme expression on his face. We're all his toys to do with as he wishes. "Relax, Dalton. I wish your friend no harm. I just need him to give you some encouragement. We'll save our fun with him for when the stakes are higher."

Eyeing Pierre like he's a rattlesnake readying to strike, Tony pushes me into the center of the room, then he points at Sandy to get back to business. Seeming protective, my father takes Sebastian over near his desk to watch me.

I cast my eyes to the floor as the female continues to pull on me without results. Wet, it's just a meaningless tugging sensation and little else. Shame and embarrassment flood me. In the years since my punishments began, I've abstained from touching for pleasure. This is my final test. The douche-bag is testing me. He has a female at my feet and my submissive at his side. I groan deep in my throat in frustration. Sandy will not get a result, but Sebby will. Tears flood my eyes and stream down my face.

"You do me proud," my grandfather's accent thickens. "Both of your parents fail me, and you fail them. You're an endless source of entertainment." The proof in his words is obvious as the attractive, young woman continues to pull on me with her mouth and I stay limp.

Ignoring Pierre's attempts to bully me, "What are you to my son?" Tony asks Sebby. "Are you gay, too?" He doesn't say the word with disgust as he does when it's directed at me. He sounds curious. I don't like the look of his thick sausage-like fingers gripping the arm of the only person who belongs to me. Possession flares thick in my veins.

"Dalton is my master, sir. I'm straight." Sebby being the most honest person I know, answers just the questions that are asked and nothing more. It is a trait I taught him at KINK. He's too naïve and easily led. I had to train him for the past few years to get him to only heel to my command. Even at eighteen, he's still too innocent with all we've seen. I've tried to filter the violence of my life so that it didn't impact him. Today is his first meeting with my sire. He has met Pierre previously on countless occasions. Pierre always watches Sebastian with unadulterated lust, and I fear I can't protect him today.

"Well, I will admit it's admirable that my son is so strong-willed even at his age. I take credit for that. I blame his mother for his weak body and how the frou-frou French bullshit turned him into a pansy. Has he commanded you to service him?"

I see the panic hit Sebby as he tries to figure out how he should answer– truthfully, or in defense of me? I close my eyes in defeat because I know the truth will always win out with Sebby. I'm not proud of my actions.

"Yes?" Tony mutters, eyeing me with revulsion. "You forced yourself on an innocent boy?" His voice is tinged with equal

amounts of pride and disgust. Pride that I'd be brutal enough to take what I want, but disgust because anyone can see Sebastian is incapable of telling me no. It's not okay to be gay because you won't propagate the lineage, but you can rape men as a form of torture. I've seen Jon do so several times as he punishes my grandfather's associates.

"No, not force... you cannot force those who are willing," I begin to ramble, forcing the words out between clenched teeth as Sandy sucks the flesh from my dick, leaving me raw. "It isn't what you think and it was a long time ago."

My first kiss.

"Did you enjoy it?" Tony asks Sebastian, voice pitching higher with incredulity.

"Yes, if it's my master's pleasure, it is mine." I sigh heavily as I hear the reverent tone in Sebastian's voice. He's a normal kid except when it comes to me– if you can call growing up in a brothel normal. He wants to obey me and it's addictive, especially with how young we are. Most of our time is spent protecting him from me.

"Fine, take yourself in hand and allow your master to gain pleasure from it." He twists the word master as if it's a dirty thing, not the gift those in my lifestyle see it as.

Tony doesn't need the lifestyle to feed his needs. He lives his life as a criminal. There are no safewords with Anthony Marconi or Pierre Fontaine.

I try not to watch as Sebby takes his length into his hand and strokes himself from root to tip. He isn't obeying my father. He's obeying the need to please me. He was told to do this for me and he will. Thick and ruddy, he hardens under his own touch because he must.

I've never touched Sebastian in this manner because I'd never know if it was because he wanted me, or because it was his need to please me. I see how he looks at the girls at KINK, so I allow him to enjoy their company. I know he doesn't see me as a lover, only as a master, while I see him as a companion and the object of my misplaced desires. I avoid this part of our relationship like the plague because I'm insanely attracted to Sebastian. The consequences of that attraction could become a disaster. I know I could command him to be my lover and he would willingly obey, and most likely even enjoy it. But I don't want that. I need someone who wants me for me.

I try not to notice how perfect and smooth he is as his hand glides over the silk covered steel of his cock. Enjoying the sight, my dick starts to harden. I try to think of anything other than what it would feel like to have his lips at my mouth— pretend his lips are wrapped around my cock, sucking me with force, eager to taste my release. The more I push the thoughts away, the faster they stream in my mind, playing out in a montage of memories of our innocent touches over the years.

Neck arching, I shout to the ceiling as my release flows into Sandy's willing mouth. She makes hungry noises as she devours me down her throat, and that lessens the pleasure and pulls me out of my thoughts.

Disgusted with myself, I look to Sebastian in shame. He found no true pleasure in the act. He's still hard in his hand, and he won't finish unless commanded. I refuse to give him the right, but not out of punishment. Respect. I don't want Tony, Bruno, or Pierre to know the pleasure of Sebastian's release.

The look of pity on Sebastian's face turns my stomach. I drop to the floor and crawl to the corner to vomit. I heave and heave until my stomach protests and my muscles seize. A sharp kick to my side accompanies a simultaneous telltale snap. It isn't the first rib I've broken and doubtful it will be the last.

"Sebastian, get the fuck out of here and never come back to this God forsaken hellhole!" I scream hoarsely from my acid-burned throat. Even while reliving the memory, I know Sebastian will come back here one last time.

I'm beaten nearly to death, not for the proof that I'm gay, not for vomiting on my father's carpet, but because I failed my father and now he has to suffer by watching Pierre's glee as I'm trapped in the snare.

My face is smeared in the mess while Tony and Bruno taunt me, both blaming me because they have to watch. Pierre's hand is the one tangled in the hair at the nape of my neck— hair just like his. He sets up these impassable tests for my parents, knowing I will fail. It's always an either/or stipulation, and I'm never privy to any of it, making the game more sporting for Pierre and Jon.

I'm not a human being. I'm not an animal. I'm a possession to be toyed with. We're all Pierre's playthings. Using me against Tony, me against Olivia, and Sebastian and Spyder against me.

If I do A, my mother suffers B. If I do C, my father experiences D. But A through Z involve my torture, so it's a lose-lose for me and anyone who loves me. Simply because my grandfather gets off not on my pain, but on a father's pain of watching his son be brutalized by a monster.

Pierre brings in his partner, Jon, to enjoy my torments. The four of them kick, beat, and abuse me. They humiliate me while Jon uses me for his own sick pleasures. The torment doesn't stop until my visitation ends and Devlin comes to fetch me, where Pierre will come with me to play this game with my mother. It's been an endless cycle of abuse for twenty years.

Even in the memory, I loathe my mother for allowing her father to do this to us. Tony's hands were tied. He had his son to lose, as I learned while I tortured Pierre unto his death. Pierre admitted that if my father hadn't played his sick games, he would have killed me. My father chose torture to death, knowing someday the torture would have to end.

I love and miss my father, and I will every day until the day that I die.

Pierre admitted one more thing about my mother. How the only thing my mother feared losing was KINK. I would have suffered through anything to keep my family safe, but not for a building of brick and mortar and no flesh and blood.

My mother doesn't realize, but KINK no longer belongs to a Fontaine. In retaliation, I gifted it to Bruno for the loss of our father.

"I'm sorry to announce that the *Mistress & Master of Restraint: the Collapse* was released today." The French accent snaps me out of my memory. My mother is standing at the head of the room with a large book in her hands. A tome– the hardcover book is at least five inches thick.

"The reason all of you were called here today was because I needed to give you each a copy." Master points to several boxes filled with the large books. "I'm sorry to inform you that each and every one of you is included in the text. However, I don't believe that absolves you from being Adelaide Whittenhower's informant. It's quite the opposite actually. It's a great cover to reveal a few of your own secrets for the greater good. I'm appalled to say that five minors were included in the book, my daughter being one of them. The three Zeitler children and young Master Whittenhower were also reported in the text."

Being overly dramatic, theatrical, Master drops the offending book on the floor with a large thud. She glares at it as if she wishes her eyes could ignite the piece of trash.

My snort is loud, echoing around the room like a gunshot, as I replay her, "*I'm appalled to say that five minors were included.*" Said the woman who would parade me around KINK in nothing but a collar, allowing her customers to bid on who got to suck my cock. I was fourteen. Then she'd do the bait and switch, taking an exorbitant amount of money from them to suck some decoy off through a glory hole.

"There will be no training today or tomorrow. Masters Devlin, Marcus, and Dexter will be unavailable for the duration of the evening. I fear for your club. The fact that it's closed is just the first step. I wonder if it will ever reopen," she muses with a wicked glint in her eye– one I recognize and fear.

The expression of supreme arrogance on my mother's beautiful face turns my stomach. Since I look so much like that vile creature, I now hate myself for looking as I do. The hair, the skin, the eyes, the color of my lips, right down to the worthless meat dangling between my thighs.

In this moment, my blood boils with my hatred for my mother. Her eyes seek mine, and I see confirmation that she reads me clearly. Following on the heels of that is shame, deep-seeded shame. Good, I shouldn't be the only one who suffers with the fucking shit.

I stand, still glaring at her, channeling all of my fury into the actions that I have to provide in service of my master. Knowing she's no different than Pierre, she expects me to fail. For that reason alone, I will succeed for the good of Restraint.

Chapter Six

"Cassie?" I growl to gain the young brunette's attention as she sashays down the hallway to the dungeon. "How's the sobriety?"

Alex brought the submissive to us a few months ago. She's an addict that he counsels at Transcend. I don't want to be mean to her right now, especially since my friend brought her here, but I'm furious and she's an outlet.

Cassie can't strike back, and maybe this will gain the real mole's attention.

Beaming brightly, "Ninety days sober," Cassie announces with great pride.

"That's awesome!" Voice saccharine and false with praise, I smile predatorily at her. "I love how we have to give fuck-ups a medal when they behave. I would think it should go to those who never fuck up. What's the incentive to behave if all you have to do is get shit-faced and steal shit for years, but after ninety days on the straight-and-narrow, we have to pat you on the back for being a good girl?"

Cassie gazes at me with huge, glassy brown eyes forming tears of shame. She worries her full bottom lip between her teeth and tries not to blink. In this, I don't actually feel bad. These are my real thoughts. Kids like me got left behind because money buys off Child Protective Services. I needed help, and there was none to be had. Yet this chick got high, stole a car, robbed a convenience store, and we wasted tax dollars on her instead of making sure kids weren't being abused. Her excuse? Her boyfriend asked her to do it.

"Squeaky wheel syndrome. But hey, what do I know?" I shrug one shoulder, face set into fake amusement. "It just seems like the system is flawed. The good little boys and girls don't get the recognition and positive attention that a crack-whore thief gets."

Cassie blinks, and the surface of her tears breaks. Blinking several times, her shame streaks down her cheeks.

"Go you!" I shout sarcastically. I give Cassie a thumbs up, and then turn to walk down the hallway.

Holding the hallway wall up, Alex chuckles at me when I pass. "Cold... that was just cold, dude."

That was so bad that I have to laugh or I'd puke. I shake my head as my belly contracts from laughter. "Score on my newest asshattery?" I ask my partner in crime.

If I didn't have Alex, I'd scream. I'll owe Marcus forever. He stripped me bare until Font was naked in the impact room at the Brownstone. Then Alex walked in from his side of the house and shook my hand in welcome– instant best friend.

"Ah..." Alex taps his chin in thought, and then the bastard tucks his black hair behind his ear. I growl at him because he did it on purpose. He knows how much I miss the feel of my hair swinging at my jawline because of this nasty wig.

Alex arches a perfect brow above his turquoise eye and smirks. He runs his hands through his hair and groans in pleasure. "8.5. It was a decent attempt, but you pulled your hit. You're too soft. I bet you were scared you'd make Cassie relapse."

"Yeah," I mutter bashfully, guilt already weaving its way through my system.

"Not happening, bud." Alex crosses his arms over his chest, perfecting the look of a slacker. "I'm just that fucking good at my job. But I better go do some damage control." He stands upright, ready to go after Cassie. "Don't hurt any more subs. Pick on the big bastards. They may bite back, but their egos are delicate."

"Hey?" I pull Alex back. "I was serious. Why do we cheer for the damned and ignore the innocent?"

"Native American atheist, here," Alex points at his chest. "As your spiritual guru, or whatever you call a Jewish dude, I'd suggest you talk to Marcus about that... or maybe you better hit up Toby. The kid loves God. You guys share the same god, right?"

"I don't mean about God," I sputter in exasperation. "Why do *you* praise women like Cassie, while the good kids at Transcend get ignored?"

"I'd say it's because they're attention whores." Alex chuckles underneath his breath. "But... it's because they wouldn't have fallen down the rabbit hole if they didn't need the extra attention. Those who are secure don't need a pat on the back. I sold the bad shit for years, but it never passed my lips."

"Dude, I've smoked with you," I remind Alex. "I've seen you passing out goodies to Kat and Dexter."

"Pot," Alex grumbles, rolling his eyes. "I sold the hard shit to the weak, and I don't work at Transcend for people like Cassie. I work there for those who come there and work their asses off, not being a victim to extenuating circumstances. Someday you should ask Cassie what pushed her over the brink. Because, Dalton, I bet you've been close many a time."

"Thanks," I grunt, feeling sucker-punched.

Alex shrugs at me, smiles, and then walks off to help the girl I just tore apart. That's teamwork.

I wander to the dungeon, feeling lonely and sad. I miss the sounds of a full dungeon. I miss the craziness of the club. The lights, music, and the flow of alcohol reminded me of home. Vegas gets into your bloodstream and can never be removed. I fear I'll be lost when I no longer have all this pressure hanging over my head. I wouldn't know how to live a normal life should one present itself.

I hear my mother's voice trail down the hallway and my stomach twists in knots. I used to lie to myself by pretending she was the perfect mother. It was the only thing that kept me from self-punishment. Then the memories sharpen into clarity and the animosity screams inside my mind until all I am is hatred.

Self-hatred.

Furious that the dungeon is suddenly filled with children, I target Tobias Kline with good intentions. The preacher's son is staring down the hallway, longing to hang out with Dexter, who's too busy with my mother. Just like me, Toby needs some friends his own age. He's a few years older than Niel and Spyder, and way older than Ava, but he's a good boy with an even cleaner soul.

"Toby?" I pull his attention from behaving like a pup awaiting its master. "I need your help with something."

"Yes, sir." Toby comes to attention, standing a few inches over me. I have to admit, the kid is adorable, sexy in a corruptible sort of way. But he doesn't swing my way– more's the pity. I think any and all attraction I feel is that Tobias Kline reminds me of who Sebastian Vance would have been if he had been born into a real family, not in a brothel run by the mafia.

"Any chance I could convince you to get the kids out of here? As the youngest actual member, I think you'd be a good influence on them."

"Me?" Tobias gestures at his chest, surprise coloring his voice and cheeks. He seems pleased I think so highly of him. But his baby blues are looking through me, like he can see Font resting beneath Dalton Thompson's drab exterior. As my eyes dart around, I notice no one is looking at me with animosity anymore, and I have no idea why.

"I-I-I– I grew up in the lifestyle, and I don't think it's a place for kids to be. Ya know?" I turn bashful while speaking to the quietest, nicest guy we have at Restraint. "Why don't you take the kids for pizza, or go hang out with them somewhere? Watch a movie? Just something not here."

"Of course, sir. That would be fun." Toby's cheeks pink and his eyes brighten. "Katya was trying to figure out how to get Ava home, but got pulled into the office by Ez over some Restraint business."

Leaning against the wall, laughter bubbles up as I watch Toby practically skip down the hallway with my baby sister as his destination. Awkward, I can tell he's stumbling over his words, drawing Niel and Ava's attention. Not that my sister seems to care. I can see the blush staining her pale cheeks from twenty feet away.

Cellphones pulled out, they're no doubt texting parental units who actually give two shits. I bet Spyder would call Devlin, Marcus, or even Dexter before my mother was notified. Not that Master doesn't know where Spyder is located every second of every day. She just doesn't care as long as her property isn't being broken beyond repair. I wonder what it would have been like to have Katya looking after me, or even Uncle Pretty Boy. The kids await replies before departing out the backdoor where Albert, the Whittenhower's driver, is always parked if Niel or Pretty Boy are on the premises.

Gunner becomes visible, ghosting down the hallway to exit to the parking lot. No doubt he was hired to shadow the Whittenhower prince, or maybe Marcus Zeitler's princesses. Instead of feeling jealousy over someone caring enough to protect them, I feel relief that they are safe and secure. Gunner is a solid family man, who found succor with the Marine Corps instead of wallowing in what Pierre, Jon, and Gunner's grandfather did to him as a child.

There are a lot of Pierre's and Jon's survivors wandering around Dominion, exponentially so if you add in their nasty friends who victimized others as well.

With the kids gone, I'm not sure what to do next. They were a happy diversion in an otherwise sucky existence. In a different world, Toby and I might have been friends, going to a concert or studying for exams. I'm twenty-four, and I have no idea what people my age do outside of reading about it.

"Won't you introduce me?" Whitt whispers in my ear, startling me. My emotions are stuck on hatred, so even his smooth voice doesn't flip my switch.

"To whom?" I give Whitt impassive eyes. The corner of his mouth lifts into a dimple and his pale blue eyes sparkle with humor.

Great– Whitt's going to play with my emotions again, and I don't think I can handle it two nights in a row.

Blunt yet sounding annoyed, "Is he your boyfriend?" An expression flashes over his face so quickly I can't interpret it.

Well, Whitt's question answers one of mine– he knows I'm gay. Asking a guy if they have a boyfriend is a huge **NO**, even when you're standing in a BDSM dungeon.

"No, he's not my boyfriend. I haven't seen Sebastian since I moved here four years ago." I don't offer any more information. Whitt pissed me off last night, even though that was one of the best orgasms of my life. I blush bright red when I remember how I stroked one out this morning using Pretty Boy as a fantasy.

Whitt really is too goddamn good looking for my own good.

"Mmm… what's the blush for?" His lips skim the shell of my ear as he murmurs to me, eliciting sparks of electricity that shoot throughout my body.

"I don't know what you're talking about." I lie as if my pasty skin isn't flooded with rosy health and my baggy pants aren't tented.

"Hmm…" Whitt purrs into my ear. "Who is he?" His demand is stronger this time, while catching my gaze. Like a switch being flicked, my body falls lax as he bends my will.

"My submissive," I reply immediately, using Sebastian's tactic. I only answer the question, never offering any other information on the subject, even though it's what he wants. Whitt practically growls at my refusal to play along with his game.

"More," Whitt demands as he glares in Sebastian's direction. Eyebrows knitting in the center of my forehead, I look at him in confusion. Sebby's making quick friends with anyone who will speak to him, so easy-going and laidback that he's addictive.

"What's your problem?" I defiantly hiss at Whitt.

In a move that shocks me, he pushes me up against the wall, caging me with his larger body. My eyes go into a frenzy, making sure no one else saw. My cock fills diamond hard from the dominance he forces on my will and the feel of his body grinding into mine.

Whitt makes a strangled sound in the back of his throat and moves our hips apart– distancing contact with my erection.

My blush returns with a vengeance as I struggle to get away from the commanding man. He's making my head spin. His personality is jovial and innocent, and then he pulls this domineering bullshit with me two days in a row. I thought I was fucking insane for having both Dalton and Font taking up residence in my mind, but they are self-created. Pretty Boy may actually have two personalities.

"What is your problem?" I repeat slowly, hoping he will answer this time without turning me on any further than I already am.

"Who is he?" Whitt repeats just as slowly, signaling that we're at an impasse and he's not going first.

"Sebastian Vance– I grew up with him since birth." I force air out my nostrils in annoyance. It's none of Whitt's damn business, but when he looks at me I want to spill my deepest, darkest secrets. "I've always been like this. When we were twelve, I took him as my submissive because he was in desperate need of a keeper."

"You were a Master at twelve?" Whitt mutters in disbelief, face open and honest.

Whitt was trained to become a master at eighteen, with mini-shit-Whitt at sixteen. Twelve is a little young, but that is why I can sympathize with how confused Ava must feel with all these emotions swirling in her head.

"I was trained from birth," I admit. "I grew up in the lifestyle."

"Is Sebastian just yours?" Whitt presses his chest against mine. It should hurt from my broken rib, but all it does is spread delicious warmth throughout my chest.

"I left Sebastian under Devlin's care, but he listens to Master."
I curse my fucking mother for bringing him here.

"So, is that the only reason he's here?" Whitt coaxes out of
me, with his forehead a hairsbreadth away from mine. His sweet
breath is fluttering at my lips. I wonder if he'd knee me in the nuts
if I kissed him. Serve the pampered bastard right.

"Master brought Sebastian back for me– I think." I scrunch
my eyes in confusion. I don't know why he's here, or why Whitt
gives a shit.

"Is he your lover?" He stares at me intensely, gaze boring a
hole through me. He rotates his hip so that the outer curve of his
thigh is cradled along my pelvis. My breathing deepens as I harden
for him all over again. He presses harder into me, grinding his leg
on my worthless dick. Shocked, my neck relaxes until the back of
my head lolls against the wall.

"Why do you care?" I growl at Whitt. My anger is returning
because he's manipulating me, toying with me, and teasing me
with his hip. Just because it feels good doesn't mean he's being
nice.

I notice Whitt turns his pelvis from me so I have no idea if he
is enjoying the contact. I bet he isn't. I've seen him in the dungeon
with his cock shoved into countless females' mouths. Daniel
Whittenhower II loves a good blowjob as much as I hate them.

My breathing deepens and becomes ragged, and it's not only
from arousal. I push against his chest, trying to untangle myself
from where he's pressing me to the wall. I look around again, and
I'm shocked that no one has noticed us. Whitt chose the perfect
spot for his interrogation– a dark corner.

Whitt grips my chin with his soft fingertips. It doesn't hurt,
but it draws my attention to his eyes. He holds my will, forcing me
to answer.

"No, Sebastian's not my lover. Dammit!" My head jackknifes
into the wall, the hit so hard I see stars. Self-inflicted pain.
"Sebby's not like me."

Whitt releases his hold on my will and his fingertips glide
down my neck, shooting pleasure straight to my cock. But his look
of supreme satisfaction boils my blood and deadens my arousal.

"What? I'm such a loser asshole that I don't deserve a lover?"
I hiss out between my clenched teeth. "You don't think I deserve

to have friends? Or to be touched in a nice way? Or have someone care about me?"

Whitt, momentarily stunned by my outburst, gazes quizzically at my face, trying to gauge my emotions. Sometimes I hate dominants, especially when they use your own tactics against you. Why was I born a switch? Why do I respond to his call? Why do I give a fuck what this entitled, rich pretty boy thinks about me?

"Does it please you that you know my secrets? That you can jerk my leash?" I grind my erection into Whitt's hip and I hiss at the horrible pleasure that tries to pour out my throat. "Does knowing you turn me on get you off? I've never done anything to you, yet you try to humiliate me." I try to keep the betrayal from my tone, but a tinge seeps into my voice.

Whitt's hand slides back up my throat and tightens into a noose. I hold his gaze as I still my breathing. His eyes cloud and a pained expression engulfs his face. He makes a loud, frustrated sound in the back of his throat. Hand leaving my neck, he swipes a thumb across my lower lip.

Shocked, I watch Whitt's back as he angrily storms down the hallway. I hear surprised voices as he passes by, and then the slam of a door.

Chapter Seven

I charge out of my private room like a man on a mission. I had to take a few minutes to relieve the horrible pressure Whitt put me under. I go three years without having a sustainable erection and that prick toys with me for two days in a row, and I harden with a stray thought. I've whacked off twice today– I think that may be a record. I have to do my duty, not play with myself all night. I will channel my energy into catching the mole instead of figuring out Whitt's angle. I know the pretty boy isn't the mole, just the bane of my existence.

Since I never went to school, all of my playmates were whores and mobsters and all of my energy was placed on Sebastian's safety, I never experienced a crush. I hate it– it's a bit like being insane. Heart spiking when you think of the person, they affect you even when they're not near. I need to get the pretty asshole out of my head since I'm not the type who will ever have a normal life, with a partner and a house and kids. It's just not in my stars.

I chastise myself because the second I enter the dungeon my eyes seek Whitt out instead of my quarry. Heart thudding in my throat, depression rolls over me when I see what he's up to. Whitt's entangled with Kristal, sucking on her breasts while one hand is hidden between her thighs. Kristal pants in ecstasy because Whitt is totally into her. On her knees, Heidi is bobbing her strawberry-blonde head up and down on his cock. Aaron and Kayla watch with smirks on their faces as their lover services another master.

I've always hated sex, especially oral, and Pretty Boy always has his cock shoved into a willing mouth. I have nothing to offer him, even if he wanted it from me. I might sound like a chick, but I've been used my entire life, so the thought of a quickie in the dungeon makes me puke a little bit in my mouth. Too bad I have to fuck someone tonight– and not at all a kneejerk reaction to Whitt. No, not at all… never.

I freeze in place as I watch the scene unfold before me. The sounds of pleasure emanating from Whitt's throat leave me aching. It was only two minutes ago that I found my release and my cock is already twitching for attention. I should feel proud of my prowess, but it just leaves me feeling empty. I need to use my reaction to Whitt to help when I whore myself out for my mother.

My eyes hunt for prey. I skip the usual suspects, especially my target for the night. I notice Queen is hiding out by the impact toys again. She longingly flutters her fingers along a flogger. I know how she feels– empty. Queen has been acting strange for the past few months. She hasn't engaged with anyone. She doesn't do scenes. She just lurks around the periphery– just as I do.

Sensing a kindred spirit, I decide Queen will do for my vindictive make Whitt jealous sex– I mean, for my sexual conquest of the night. I'm nothing like my mother or father.

I get into Queen's personal space, rising on my toes to bring us face-to-face. I hated it when Whitt did it to me, so I try it with her. It's annoyingly effective. Her green eyes widen in surprise. Yes, Queen, I'm not weak.

"Regina, why do you stand all by yourself?" I bat my long eyelashes at her.

Yeah, you'd think a gay man wouldn't know how to turn on the charm for a lady. At KINK, I was a whore for both men and women. At Restraint, I play an asshole, but that doesn't mean I can't be pretty. I wish I wasn't in disguise, because all this brown and concealer negates my appeal. My androgynous appearance has been helpful over the years for my master when she'd parade me through KINK. After Tony came to understand I'd never be like Bruno, he used my *French* wiles to extract information.

Queen's large eyes see right through me. "Dalton?" She smirks, playing with me as I play with her. The first day I arrived in Dominion, I was delivered to the Brownstone unto Marcus Zeitler's care. Queen was one of the first people I met, looking through my disguise that day as she is now.

"Regina Regal– The Queenly Queen," I murmur smugly.

"Dalton Anthony Fontaine Marconi," she whispers in reply, lips curving up at the corners.

Speechless, I wanted to read her and she read me instead.

Biting her lip, Queen is trying not to full-out smile. I stare at the woman who's more than half a foot taller than me and a decade older. Her blonde hair is pulled tight and twisted around her head. It reminds me of what I first did so Pierre couldn't get a handle on my hair before I finally gave up and cut it. But no one is pulling Queen's hair.

A thought flashes in my mind. I lean forward to kiss Queen's neck tenderly as a diversion. I don't do the mouth with the exception of when Whitt demanded it– prick. I nibble on her skin gently, and she gasps in shock.

"Regina, why do you pretend to be gay when you're not?" I nibble her neck some more when she doesn't yank away from me. "We all know you're straight, but the lesbian rumor never dies."

"Dalton, why do you pretend to be straight, when we all know you're gay?" she fires right back. "How did it feel to finally get off?"

"Confusing," I answer honestly before I can stop myself. "Do you miss the touch of a man?" I taunt her, trying to figure out why she isn't fucking her way through the dungeon like everyone else.

"Who says I'm not getting any elsewhere?" she murmurs like she has a secret yet knows all of mine at the same time.

"Tell me why you hide and I will tell you why I do," I negotiate.

"I can't tell you why I hide," Queen mutters in a panic. "Will you answer me if I tell you *a* truth?"

"Yes," I say intrigued.

"You know I'm straight, but I had to pretend I was gay when I first came to Restraint." She sounds ashamed– shame in pretending, or shame of everyone thinking she was gay? "Then I just gave up and never had sex with anyone– it seemed easier."

"I know how that is." I laugh without humor. I look at Queen for a few seconds, realizing her inherent masculinity would come in handy with keeping me aroused. She's blunt, honest while skirting the truth, and I decide I like her as a person.

Queen will do because I can't use my usual outlet. The thought of touching Kristal makes my stomach twist in knots. Goddamn you, Pretty Boy! But I do have to fuck someone since I need to show the members I'm not the pansy they saw bawling and hanging onto Sebastian in the middle of the classroom. An asshole doesn't behave that way.

"Would you like to have sex?" Bashful, fearing rejection, my pale skin flames in embarrassment. I wait for her to say no, then I realize my mistake. Babbling, "Shit. I mean with me. Ya know, not in general."

"Do you want to have sex with *me*?" Queen murmurs wryly, green eyes sparking with humor. She nods her head yes while smirking at me. She's laughing on the inside, but not *at* me. I'm amusing the ever-loving fuck out of her.

Queen's up to something.

"I think you and I could be good friends," Queen declares. "Welcome to the game, Font. The bench was getting mighty crowded," she says ambiguously.

"What?" I breathe, and she nods her head at me. "Font? You called me Font."

"How about we get another guy to join us? Hmm… that would help, wouldn't it?" Queen has my number. "It might help your jealousy mission if you use that Sebastian beauty of yours."

Eyes narrowed, I gasp, "What?"

"My Pretty Boy," Queen hitches her thumb over her shoulder, pointing in the general vicinity where Whitt is still getting his cock sucked, probably for the fourth or fifth time. The motherfucker always has his cock in a mouth– his libido is on crack. "Choosing me was a good idea. It's guaranteed to piss him off. But I saw him questioning you about Sebastian earlier, so if you *really* want to get him to lose his shit, a combo of me and Sebastian will do it."

"Seriously, what the hell? I can't be *that* transparent."

"Introverts, we lurk in the shadows watching," Queen murmurs, fighting back a grin. "So while you were watching everyone else, you failed to notice I was watching you."

"Lovely," I mutter begrudgingly. "Do you know who the mole is, then?"

Queen looks at me dead to rights. "I believe you need to sit down with Marcus, Devlin, and Dexter, and just have a conversation… but that's for another day. I'm bored, so let's entertain ourselves by watching Pretty Boy lose his shit."

"You're twisted, lady." I have a new appreciation for Queen.

I bite my lip, thinking over how to proceed. Eyes darting around the dungeon, I find Sebastian getting to know a handful of submissives. I catch his eye, silently communicating my needs. He nods in my direction, asking for a moment to finish his conversation.

I don't feel badly over asking Sebastian to join us. It's not like I'm demanding he service me. Sebby's favorite partners are more experienced mature women. He eyes Queen in a way I never could, with lust, seeing her as a sexual being.

"Take off your clothes," I order Queen, while I look around the room to find a yoga mat. What I have in mind requires lying down. I'm not Whitt with his penchant for having sex while standing up so he can be the center of attention.

I drag the cushioned mat over near the back wall, hidden by the corner, and position it. I only want to draw one person's undivided attention, while showing the others I'm not a pansy-ass crybaby.

"Lay down on your back." I continue to order Queen once she's naked– we both know she's only humoring me for her own entertainment.

My eyes take in the landscape of Queen's body. She's a beautiful woman– ripe and supple, with huge tits and wide hips. She looks more feminine with her clothing off. Her female parts soften the firm edge to her jaw. She's exactly what most men would love to nibble on, but she doesn't do a thing for me. I will have to borrow Sebastian's enthusiasm as I did Whitt's last night.

I don't look at this as whoring for my mother. But the idea doesn't bring bile to my throat, so that's a plus. I'm intrigued by Queen, wanting to bore into her mind and discover all of her secrets. First thing tomorrow morning, I will call my contacts and know every second of importance that has ever occurred in her life. We need to be on equal footing, Queen and I, because she seems to know all about me.

Walking with a rolling gait, Sebastian sees Queen laying out for his enjoyment and lust fills his features. I've watched him have more sex than I've had myself. Most of my experience was with my hand as he found pleasure in the warmth of a woman or three. Usually he would turn me on so I could do my duty for Master.

Sebastian was my fluffer by visually stimulating me. Tonight will be no different.

"Strip." Tone salacious, I can't keep the heat from my voice. The word came out as a mixture of English, Italian, and French, like my brain was overloaded on having Sebastian so near. I'm just thankful that Queen is as enamored with Sebby as I am, so she didn't notice.

I groan loudly when Sebastian exposes his body to our sight. He's even better looking now than he was at twenty. Miles of tan skin, with mussed up hair and eyes glinting with lust and amusement, Sebby's presence hits me hard– right in the cock.

Finally filling out in the shoulders and chest like a grown man, his body is still lanky but corded with taut muscles. Tonight won't be a hardship. I just have to make sure I don't touch him, because if I do, I'll order him to do very bad things to me.

"Queen, stand," I demand in a tone that brooks no room for argument– I may be dressed like Dalton Thompson, but Queen knows I'm Font, and I can't be anyone else but me around Sebastian. "Lay down on the mat, Seb. Then I want Queen to lie down on top of you– mouths to genitals." I arrange our scene, not realizing until it's too late that I murmur, "*S'il vous plait,*" and "*Merci,*" a few times when they do as I say.

With grace, Queen mounts my submissive and takes his perfect cock in her mouth. My mouth waters at the sight, wishing I was Queen. I've never had the pleasure– envy takes my breath away. I close my eyes against the sound of Sebastian groaning when he makes contact with her warmth.

Skin between my shoulder blades burning with interest, eyes are boring into my back. I turn to find the culprit, finding Whitt studying us as he thrusts into Kristal. I turn my back to him. I don't need Whitt– I lie. I don't want him to think I do. I will not play whatever game he's trying to start. Instead, I enter a new game with Queen.

Fully clothed, kneeling on the edge of the yoga mat, I watch Sebastian and Queen devour each other. In theory, I can understand why oral sex is so addictive. But after being forced to eat pussy, to have my cock crammed in strangers' mouths, to never have chosen a partner, the thought turns my stomach.

For some bizarre reason, I want to suck Whitt's cock– it'd be a first for me, and I know I'd enjoy every nasty second of it. He's also so impartial with who he sticks his dick into, he probably wouldn't reject me. But that's not what I want. I long to have a real lover, someone who wants me for me, whoever the hell I may be.

Snapping out of my thoughts, I find Queen mewing in pleasure. The sound doesn't annoy me as usual since she's driving Sebastian insane with need– Mon Dieu, I'm addicted to the animalistic sounds pouring out of Sebby's throat.

I ignore the pink flesh before me, concentrating on the way Sebastian's tongue curls around Queen's clit, leaving a glistening shine behind. Leaning to the side a bit, I try for a better vantage point to view Sebby's perfect cock. Sliding past Queen's lips, he's wet and ruddy with arousal– the perfect length and girth to top. A sound of pure frustration rumbles up from my chest, knowing that's a pleasure I'll never have, as well.

I stare in rapt fascination as Queen sucks Sebastian's cock like she hasn't had the taste in an eternity. *I'm right there with ya, Queen.* I lick my lips, fearing drool will pool out. I swallow audibly.

Deep down, I know I could have Sebastian and he'd revel in it. He wouldn't blame me, and he'd find pleasure in the act. But I want Sebastian to find the girl of his dreams, just like I should find the guy of mine. I'd rather have Sebastian the friend than the reluctant lover.

Resting my knees between Queen's spread thighs, I draw her calves up. I watch as Sebastian's tongue delves into her, lapping up all her juices. He rolls his eyes up to me and they shine with pleasure. I had missed this intense look Sebastian gets when he's riding high.

I turn my back so that no one but Sebby can see my cock. Ordinarily I would just pull my dick through the fly of my jeans and slap a condom on it. But for some sick reason, I pull my pants to my knees, wanting my balls to be in touching range of Sebby's face. It's not like he hasn't seen me at my worst. I want this first touch in years to be more intimate than a nasty fuck in a BDSM dungeon.

I struggle hiding my cock because it's engorged at over eleven inches– there will be no putting him away until I get off and go soft. We're on display, and I make sure they can only see my bubble butt and skinny thighs, hoping they don't find it too girly and guess things they shouldn't about me. Thick excitement is riding the air as the members watch a newcomer submissive, a fake-lesbian domme who never scenes in public, and the asshole engage in a three-way.

What an odd pairing we make.

After sheathing my cock in latex, I rub against Queen's slick slit. Since I don't puke in the first two seconds, I push in a little to test my resolve. It's not that Queen is gross, judging by how enthusiastically Sebastian is going to town eating her out, the opposite is true. It has nothing to do with being gay, and everything to do with being forced to fuck girls. If a guy bent me over right now, I'd probably pass the fuck out from PTSD.

Now, Whitt… that might have a different outcome. My lust for the pretty boy outweighs my past. Sebastian? He could have unlimited access to every square inch of my body without permission, simply because I trust him that much. With anyone else, I'd probably turn into a rabid animal lashing out to protect itself.

Other than Kris and a few stolen touches from Whitt, I haven't engaged with anyone else in this dungeon. Kris somehow senses that I have to be in control and doesn't give me any shit, most likely because Alex asked her nicely.

When nausea doesn't wash over me, I plunge in to the hilt. Queen rears up and screams, the sharp sound echoing around the dungeon. I didn't hurt her– I hope. I think she liked it. Hell, if I know. I know nothing of the female body. I'm fully erect this time, instead of just hard enough to enter a woman, so maybe that's the difference.

Hand resting on the small of Queen's back, "Did I hurt you?" I whisper in concern when she stills.

Looking over her shoulder, Queen's eyes are watering. "Yes and no. You're motherfucking huge. It hurt, but it was a good kind of hurt… My lover is big, but dang, Dalton." Turning her head, she simultaneously sucks Sebastian back into her mouth while rearing backward onto me.

With an inward shrug, hell if I know what she meant. I close my eyes and find a rhythm that is pleasing to both of us. The background noise of cries, moans, and the pound of impact toys wash away with the wet sounds and moans of my companions. I gasp when a warm, wet mouth sucks at my balls. I nearly combust from the pleasure of the sensation.

"Sebastian, don't tease me," I chastise weakly, voice bordering on begging. "I won't be able to control myself." I pull out of Queen so I can gaze down at Sebastian from between Queen's goodies and my groin.

"I've missed you. Let me please you. I know how hard this is for you to do." Sebastian pleads with his huge brown eyes. "I don't want sex, but let me help you stay happy." He smirks when he says happy– the cock-tease.

"Forever my fluffer," I mutter wryly.

My poor attempt at seduction with Queen is apparent in comparison to what a true submissive can do. The cunning look that brightens Sebastian's face almost has me coming from the sight of it. His need to please has me shoving deeply into Queen.

My companions groan loudly in unison. Sebastian's mouth beneath me goes into a frenzy on Queen's pussy, tongue sneaking to lick my shaft to keep my interests high, with Queen's mouth sucking Sebastian until she's deep-throating his perfect cock. I don't move as they writhe beneath me.

Everyone firmly back in control, I begin to thrust in smooth rolls of my hips. I try to ignore the fact that my ass is jiggling, but fail. Blushing red from the attention, I can feel eyes staring at my ass. Breath sawing in and out in time with my movements, I know Queen is close when her body starts to jerk and her muscles tighten and she moans in a way that sounds like weeping. Sebby is beneath me, grunting as his climax floods Queen's mouth.

I watch as they both orgasm, neither of them pushing me off the precipice. Skin flushing, I look over my shoulder at the person who's burning a hole into my jiggling ass with his avid gaze.

Whitt's no longer engaged with Kristal and Heidi, cock drained by both women. Closer than anyone else, he'd crept to stand a few feet off to the side of us, where he's watching with obvious interest. I notice too late that he's in the perfect position to see my cock. I'm uncomfortable with that knowledge, and the feeling pushes the pleasure down to a level that removes all need for release.

Whitt raises his hand and rubs the back of his neck in a nervous gesture. My eyes eat the sight of his body. My breath becomes labored as I watch his biceps bulge from his movements. Rare, he's wearing a t-shirt, which rides up his torso, showing off the deep V of his waist. Eyes flicking downward, I take in the obvious bulge in his pants, even though he came several times in the past hour.

Slowly, my eyes work their way back up to Whitt's face. I meet his hungry gaze, so filled with need that I moan from the sight of it. I don't know who he's craving, but I go into denial and pretend it's me. My release rushes from my balls, but doesn't find the force to exit my body. I'm stuck at the precipice with the pressure building to painful levels. My mind, body, and soul know that I'm mating with the wrong person and it refuses to release.

I scream in frustration, fingers clenching against Queen's hips. She tries to rock against me, but to no avail. Sebastian knows my body better than I do, giving me desperate relief. Teeth bite into the pathway of flesh behind my sack and sink in. Deep. My taint is on fire. Screaming for a new reason, the intense pressure releases in a torrent out my cock as I fill the latex with my shame.

I collapse from the force of my orgasm, with my head resting on the swell of Queen's ass, and I couldn't care less. I watch Whitt as he watches Sebastian soothe my tender skin with his tongue. An indescribable look crosses Whitt's face just before he flees the dungeon.

Chapter Eight

Done for the night, totally drained, I'm walking through the dungeon with my apartment as my destination, only I cross paths with my mother instead. I want to ignore her, but there is no ignoring Olivia Fontaine. "Joli garçon?"

Eyes narrowed with fury, "Maître? Pourquoi tu t'en préoccupes?" I whisper in a hurry, asking my mother why she gives a shit about whether or not I'm getting off on Pretty Boy. I hate how she pushes all of my buttons, making me feel awful about myself.

"Maîtresse Reine? Vous jouez avec le feu," she warns me that Queen is going to burn me, only I no longer trust my own mother's motivations.

I repeat, "Pourquoi tu t'en préoccupes?" knowing my mother doesn't really care about me, only that I'm not doing as she orders.

Words clipped with rage, "Se rendre au travail," she proves me right by telling me to get back to work before striding away, leaving a cloud of bitter resentment in her wake.

Mood plummeting to hell, I do as my mother bids simply because I'm so keyed-up I'll be able to do my job well. No doubt that was exactly what the cunt had in mind, to twist my emotions while I was still riding the endorphin crash of post-coital tristesse.

I catch my quarry in the hallway before she can make it to the safety of Dexter's room. I lean against the wall, waiting for her to come to me. I'm a patient hunter, or so I tell myself. In reality, I was using the wait to try to talk myself out of targeting an innocent woman with my assholeness.

"Well, well, well… If it isn't the incompetent baby sadist," I murmur, a sneer thick in my voice. Are you going to Dexter's room to abuse him some more?" I raise an eyebrow at the shame that crosses Katya's face.

Yes, it's wrong to exploit her shame. I know how Kat feels more than anyone possibly could. But I'm not Font right now, and the asshole demands his payment for the night– we mustn't disappoint our cunt of a master.

"Did you leave many scars?" I taunt, evil leaking into my voice. I'm a bit angry with Kat for not standing up to my mother and demanding her fourteen-year-old daughter didn't step foot into Restraint. But Kat gave in, and we need women strong enough to protect their young against the predators looking to exploit them. "You already scarred the wife, why not the husband?"

Visibly shaking with either fear, anger, or shame, Katya doesn't answer me. She tries to step away from me to defuse the situation. I'm thankful that she's a small woman, or she could beat me or outrun me. But Kat can't do either of those things. She steps to the side, preparing to go around me, but I angle myself to cut her off. We do this dance several times before she bares her fanged-caps at me. I laugh at her– Font, not Thompson. It was rather cute in a pissed off kitten sort of way.

I feel awful that I have to bully her, but Kat is Adelaide's biggest nemesis, and this will surely get the woman's attention. I know Katya isn't Restraint's mole, but if the mole is watching who else would love Katya being fucked with more so than Adelaide Whittenhower. Kat was my ultimate target, but I hadn't had the stomach to use her until now. I have the feeling I'll have to do it a few times.

"What do you want?" Kat hisses at me, irate. "Just leave me be."

"Don't you think it's inappropriate to allow your child to watch the fun and games in the dungeon? I had to send Ava and the rest of the minors from the area. What kind of mother are you?" I accuse. "What's wrong with you people?"

Actually, this is Font's question. My mother allowed me to see so much debauchery that I don't know what's normal anymore. I don't want that type of confusion to plague the angelic beauty.

Katya flinches at the accusation, then she takes a step back to flee me. So I rotate and herd her until her back hits the wall. Now she can go nowhere.

"Tell me, do your children understand why their father is sucking off their grandfather?" Flinching backward, she looks as if I've physically struck her. The nausea starts to build, but I can't stop now. I've attracted an audience, so I have to finish this. Now.

"Does your daughter know how you married your rapist?" I shudder at the thought, imagining a lifetime of looking Jon in the eye across the breakfast table, sharing a bed and children with him, and I want to vomit on the spot. "I bet you get off on force. I bet you loved every second that Ray Hunter pounded into you. Did you come for–"

"You bastard!" Kat's small fist swings out and deflects off my shoulder, the punch not landing. I hope after this they teach Katya some self-defense moves for her own safety.

I finally step from Katya's path for two reasons. One: I hit a nerve. She must have climaxed for one of them, and it makes me feel dirty to have said it. I wouldn't have pressed that trigger had I known. Kat's tiny face is set in lines of betrayal, with angry tears of frustration sliding down her cheeks. Reason number two on why I must retreat: I'm so nauseous that I can barely contain my dry-heaves.

I walk down the hallway at my regular pace, chuckling Dalton Thompson's evil laugh.

I don't change my pace until I reach the end of the hallway to enter the hidden staircase to my apartment. I run flat out up the stairs and make it inside my apartment just in time for the heaving to start. I huddle over my toilet as my throat constricts, and the only thing it draws up is bile. The fluid burns my throat and mouth and I welcome the pain. I deserve it. It isn't a just punishment for the wounds I opened for the young mother and wife. Not to mention what I did to Cassie earlier in the night, or for trying to spark jealousy in Whitt.

Self-loathing settles over me like a comforting coat I wear on the coldest of nights.

I reach for a towel to smother the scream that's forming inside my chest. The excruciating pressure is building and building, suffocating me with bitterness and regret. I need to have the pain exorcised. I cannot survive collecting the sum of my actions, taking it in and holding onto it. I'm not big enough of a masochist to contain the misery.

Standing in my bathroom, I glare at my reflection in the mirror– Dalton Thompson. He's an evil bastard created by my mother, by her father, by her father's partner, and by the United States government as a form of protection– all of them used me for my body, my mind, and my secrets. I yank the ugly brown wig from my head. With hurried movements, I pull the tie for my hair and watch as the black strands swing around my head. Looking at the wig, I'm tempted to burn the goddamn thing in the sink basin.

The freedom to walk out of this apartment completely naked, makeup-free, without the trappings of Dalton Thompson. It would be a high like no other.

I don't want to do this any longer. At first, my mother said she sent me to Dominion because she was worried about my longevity after murdering Pierre Fontaine and Jon Wilson, following up my revenge plot by turning state's evidence on all of my mafia competition. It was the largest mafia bust in recorded history, leaving the organizations I entrusted to Bruno and Stanton Green's organization in Dominion as the most powerful. I know without a shadow of a doubt, if I walk outside as Font, I'll have a target on my back, no matter how hard Stanton tries to keep me alive.

Then my mother convinced me I needed to keep an eye on Spyder's father, stating she was worried about Marcus. She had me keep an eye on Marc and tell her anything that was worrisome, not that I told her everything because I truly enjoyed Marc's company.

I had a few months of nothing major in my life. All I did was help Bruno run the Fontaine and Marconi crime families from a distance, while secretly meeting with Stanton Green on a biweekly schedule. I was able to build a friendship with Alex, while learning who I was no matter what I was wearing. I kept to myself, only being an asshole to keep people at bay.

Then when Adelaide Whittenhower resurfaced, my mother commanded me to locate who was feeding her information. I would do anything for family— even family that isn't directly related to me, because I love my sister that much.

Restraint? KINK? The BDSM Lifestyle Authority? It's not worth it. All my mother ever cared about was her precious club. Her lineage— the same lineage that bore Pierre. Her children are pawns. I was born out of a lie. She fed me a story and I suffered the consequences. She tricked Spyder's father. According to the lying bitch, Marc never even had sex with her. She's a spineless, coldhearted bitch.

The more I whore myself out for my mother, the more I want to add matricide to my list of sins. It isn't anything worse than I've already committed. The only reason I don't retaliate is because of my sister. The only reason I keep up this charade is because even though I've bullied everyone, I've come to care for their wellbeing.

I pinch the contacts out of my eyes— my mirrored reflection finally revealing who truly am. But this time, the resentment, bitterness, and hatred do not subside— it's turned inward. Tears flee my eyes as my frustrations beg for an outlet. If I don't take care of my needs, I will implode.

Snaring a razorblade from the medicine cabinet, I rest my forearm against the sink basin. Eyes held wide, I slice parallel to the mark Leviticus laid into my flesh. Red. Lifeblood. The color of fear, betrayal, fury, and shame. Beading crimson dots of misery, the red tide flows across my pale skin. The drips splatter to the porcelain, and then weave their way down the drain.

Breathing shallowly through the burning pain, the suffocating pressure doesn't subside, doesn't even lessen marginally.

Again.

My hand arcs the blade again… and again… and again.

Again.

The pressure worsens.

Again.

Heart stilling, breath stalling, panic overpowers my vital functions.

With numb, shaking fingertips, I pull my cellphone from my back pocket and text a message that I send when I can't contain the misery any longer.

PAIN!

Completely naked, stumbling, dripping blood in a ribbon across the floor, I move my small dinette set to the side near my bed. I need a big enough space for the large male to work in. I unlock the deadbolt and crack the door so he can enter without delay.

Prone, kneeling with my forehead on the floor, the top of my head brushes against the wall. The cold tile is soothing beneath my shins, as is the steady flood of blood cooling beneath my arm. I wait for what feels like hours as I school my breathing for the release that is to come. I register his arrival when the deadbolt is clicked into place.

"We can't do this, son," Devlin tries to reason with me. "Not with your injuries from last night. You have a broken rib. I don't see why that wasn't enough to relieve you for a while."

Devlin's deep voice is rough with remorse, but I'm thankful there isn't a trace of pity. He understands better than anyone on this planet what she has put me through– he's had to stand by and watch it with his hands tied, after suffering at the hands of the same men who were torturing me.

"I just broke a wife and mother because my mother demanded it of me," I admit, stomach twisting with revulsion. "I made Kat relive her rape, and I know better than most the torture that that is."

"Son?" Devlin's shoes come into view in my periphery, but he knows better than to touch me with anything other than pain when I get like this.

"Master brought me Sebastian, knowing I can't be around him because he isn't safe with me. The temptation is too great, especially since I have no outlet for my needs. I'm not sure if she meant for Sebby to soothe me with his company, or if she didn't care for his wellbeing as I take his will away to suit my own needs. Knowing her brutal nature, I would say she doesn't give a fuck about Sebastian. She just wanted to placate me so I would continue to whore for her. She's willing to make Sebby my whore in payment."

"I know." His deep voice is filled with a wealth of sadness and resentment. "I tried to dissuade Olivia. I don't know why she does the things she does."

"Because she can," I say in spite.

"Pierre and Jon, they were monsters, molesting and raping anyone they could get their hands on, and not just our bodies but our minds. But there is something even more evil about Olivia, because we knew who Pierre and Jon were. Olivia does have kindness and love rooted deep inside her, but it's tainted. We see that spark, and it gives us hope, not realizing she's infecting us as we fall deeper and deeper into reverence with her."

"Only you understand– maybe Levi. Spyder will never understand and it breaks my heart that someday she will learn who her mother truly is."

"I'm so sorry." The pity finally appears in Devlin's voice, but it's projected inward because he's in love with my mother. Devlin feels for Olivia what his brother, Jonathan, never could. Only now it's too late for my mother to recognize it. "I should have done something more to protect you."

"You did when no one else would," I murmur, eyes darting to watch the blood well from the twenty perfectly parallel lines I carved into my forearm.

"It wasn't soon enough." Devlin shifts, and I can sense his intense need to soothe me right now. I know he's witnessed the blood all over my apartment– he's seen worse from me too many times to count. "The damage was done before I intervened."

"Fate pushed me to that defining moment in my life." I reach out to wrap my fingers around his ankle, needing to center myself through him. "Devlin, do it!" I plead, voice warping with desperation. "I'm suffocating– I need it. I feel dead inside."

"So be it," Devlin faintly whispers, ankle pulling from my grip.

The snap of the cane on my back draws enough pain that I enter my mind instantly. I float from the present and enter the past. It hurts as much to experience it again as it does to go through the loss and grief once I return to reality. It wasn't until after their deaths that I needed the punishment, because before I'd received it on a weekly basis, drawing my sins from my soul.

I had self-punished until Devlin's arrival at Restraint. I withheld food until I was faint, used bloodletting, and caned myself across the tops of my thighs. Sometimes it took all three to remove the agonizing pressure.

I smile as the sting radiates across my back. The next vicious hit against my thigh is brutally satisfying.

"Olivia, I give you a choice: come to my bed one more time and give me another child, or add more time to my visitation with Dalton." Tony's voice is sweet and thick like honey. His face is glazed with lust and a small amount of love as he gazes at my mother. She's resting on the loveseat– posing seductively at an angle to showcase her hips and breasts, purposely amping up his desires.

My grandfather is sitting next to my mother, barely containing the smug satisfaction pulling at his lips as he watches a game he set into motion. Why they don't just kill the sociopathic bastard is beyond me– it seems cleaner, simpler, less painful for me.

They speak of me as if I'm not in the room. I'm an inanimate object in their never-ending game of tug-of-war. They're discussing parental visitation for an adult. I'm still a possession for the both of them even though I just turned eighteen. Both hold my currency and use it to their advantage.

But in the end, I know it won't matter who wins, because Pierre has placed his own price on either choice. If my mother chooses to give Tony another child, Pierre will harm me in a way to harm Tony as the ultimate sacrifice. Pitting them against one another, if my mother chooses either to give into Tony's demands or to refuse him, there will be another set of painful results.

83

My parents battle on my behalf, both knowing the price they pay, never knowing the price their spouse pays until Pierre collects it from my hide. Desperate to save me from a predestined fate of Pierre's machinations, they fight it out.

"You already have half the month. What's in it for me?" My mother negotiates, sounding flippant and dispassionate.

"I could kill everyone in your establishment and raze it to the ground," Tony's threat is without heat. "I could take sweet Itsy Bitsy and use her to birth my children when she comes of age. Or I could whore her out like you do our son– children catch a fair price. Or I could hand Spyder off to her father who you're toying with worse than me. Or I could just kill you and take complete ownership of Dalton, handing off your youngest to the wolves in Dominion. Your choice: him or me?" His eyes narrow in a combination of lust and hatred.

Tony's hand reaches over to stroke my hair, but not out of affection. Possession. My devoted father disappears the instant Pierre or my mother enters his office. Another pass of his heavy palm against my scalp– it's the same gesture Tony uses before his fingers tighten and he restrains me with his fist.

I try not to flinch– flinching is for pansies. It's a punishable offense because Pierre deemed it so.

"No more kids from me." My mother scoffs, acting put out by the suggestion. The gleam in my grandfather's eye and the way Tony's hand stills on my hair utterly petrifies me. "Fine, one extra day per month, or an added fifteen minutes per visit– your choice."

It takes everything in me not to lunge at the woman who created me and kill her for betraying me. I envision wrapping my hands around her throat and choking until the evil light dies out in her eyes. Fantasy so real, I can even feel her fingernails biting into my forearms carving furrows of violence. The satisfying way the capillaries in her eyes would burst– her crimson lips turning blue as bubbles of apologetic words tried to reach my ears.

Instead of sacrificing herself, my own mother fed me to the wolves. Pierre laughs tauntingly when he sees me lean forward with unadulterated violence in my eyes.

"I think I will take Tony's fifteen minutes now," Pierre purrs in a husky tone laced with lust and madness. "Olivia, I insist that you stay while we visit." He gets up from his seat on the sofa, practically prancing theatrically, and then opens the door a crack.

"We're ready to play," Pierre murmurs to someone on the other side. He stalks across the room to Tony's desk, and produces a kitchen timer from a drawer. Grinning menacingly, he spins the dial until the fifteen minute line.

Tick.

I know this game well. I start to hyperventilate knowing what's coming next. Because of my grandfather's insanity, my mother's selfishness, and my father's cowardice for not murdering his wife and father-in-law, I will be subjected to fifteen minutes of whatever trips Pierre's trigger. My body beads with sweat, and the nausea that I feel more often than not makes its presence known. The tick of the timer is a sound I hear in my nightmares.

Tick.

Tick.

Tick.

Seconds of my life warp into a never-ending nightmare for all eternity.

Tick.

Tick.

Tick. The sound of my dignity being torn away.

Bruno and Jon glide into the room. My brother's darker skin is tinged green with disgust and fear, while Jon's pale skin is glowing with anticipation. Bruno waits for instruction, eyes finding me as his ears register the timer. He winces. No brother has the stomach for what's to come. He may like punishing the cheaters and thieves, but he lost his taste for punishing my flesh years ago.

"May I offer my services?" Jon's face is alight with pleasure, his eerie blue eyes nearly glowing white as he envisions my punishment beneath him. "I would enjoy this immensely."

Slumping forward out of my chair at Tony's and my shared desk, I'm a hairsbreadth from passing out, something I pray to God will actually happen. My mind won't even conjure what's to come, knowing I won't be able to handle it.

"You may, but no permanent damage," Pierre allows, appearing benevolent, like he's doing so for my benefit. "Don't be rough. This is Dalton's first time, and I wouldn't want to break my favorite toy."

My mind tries to come up with an escape plan as Jon leers salaciously down at me. I barely weigh a hundred pounds, and I'll *never hit five and a half feet tall. There's no way I'm getting out of here before I receive my mother's punishment.*

Feeling on the edge of unconsciousness from terror, I glare at my mother as she sits impassively on the sofa next to her sadistic father.

Like father, like daughter.

The betrayal is so deep, I feel it resonate in my soul. I come to terms with my fate and swallow my pride. Pierre said no pain or damage, but that is only physiological– psychological? A cerebral fuck is mandatory.

So what if the last of my virginity is torn from me by force? It's not like I haven't already endured rape by mouth and by cunt. Both were in a quest to prove I could bed a woman, training for my future wife so I could propagate our bloodline, which is exactly why I'm being punished because my mother refuses to birth more playthings for Pierre to toy with before she hits menopause.

This last piece of my virginity... I was saving it for when I found a real lover. Instead it will be thrust away by Jon– my grandfather's partner in crime. Devlin's father will steal the last piece of what makes me Font.

Tick.

Fifteen minutes at a time.

Tick.

I don't believe my mother's lies, but I do trust the facts. Our lives were destroyed long before I was born with a barter between Pierre and Tony's father, Anthony Sr. The Marconi and Fontaine's alliance was wrought through the exchange of my mother's body to Tony, with the signing of a marriage license, resulting in my birth as the legal heir to both the Marconi and Fontaine crime syndicates.

I was forged to be nothing but a pawn in a game played for over twenty years. A game of dominance, one not of masters but mobsters.

It's a game with no rules or safewords.

"Ne vous inquiétez pas, petit-fils." Pierre has the arrogant audacity to tell me not to fret, knowing it will spike fear in my veins. "You're gay, more woman than man. It's what you were made to endure. I'm sure you'll love it." He gloats and taunts with a single laugh. "Carry on, Jon, time is ticking."

Crawling on my hands and knees, trying to hide underneath our desk, curled around my father's legs, I'm yanked harshly by my hair.

Tony cries out but is frozen in fear, knowing if he intervenes, my grandfather will slice my throat in front of him without hesitation.

Scrambling, I scuttle out from beneath the desk, losing a fist-full of hair in the process. Bruno's at the door, pounding, fingers tearing at the doorknob, trying to open it but Pierre controls the security system, ensuring the locks stay engaged.

Tick.

We're held hostage, feral animals turning rabid, locked in Pierre's sadistic cage until we consume each other.

Tick.

Pierre watches with great amusement as my brother tries to protect me, laughing loudly when my father has to take my brother to the ground to protect me when my current fate is worse than death.

"He'll kill him," Tony predicts as he pants roughly. With force, he presses Bruno to the floor, riding my brother's back. "You know the drill: don't look, go inward, and pretend you're not here."

Tick.

Logically, I know this is worse for Tony and Bruno than it will ever be for me. Logically, I know this same thing has happened to countless others. My mother. Devlin. Levi. But terror is not logical.

Tick.

Knowing running will make no difference. Tick. Knowing fighting back will make no difference. Tick. Knowing there is no escape. Tick. I run the timer down, even though one second will last my lifetime.

Tick.

Lashing out like a wild animal, I shriek like a banshee, loud enough that even Pierre flinches. My pants are ripped from my rear and a large hand presses my forehead to the ground.

White-hot searing pain radiates across my backside. Neck arching, I scream my shame at the ceiling, exorcising my demons in a mournful song filled with violence and worthlessness. I'm thrust back into the present with that last strike of the cane. I blink the tears away until my vision returns to clarity.

"How about a shower?" Devlin's voice floats down from high above, jarring me into reality. "I'll wait for you, then rewrap your rib and put ointment on your back when you get out. Okay, son?" His large hands engulf my shoulders and lift until I find my footing.

Mortified but feeling better, I shuffle into the bathroom in a daze. I try to ignore the viscous moisture running down my thigh that's dripping from my dick. It's shameful that Devlin knows the end result of my punishment.

I take no pleasure from the release, nor do I ever remember it. I'm always too far into the past, reliving my nightmares in an alternate reality that is more real than my present.

Standing underneath the cascading water, I'm in a fog of my own creation. I no longer feel the need to scream or murder. I start to weep as the emptiness returns. It isn't a void that can be filled by the love of a parent, or a sibling, or even a friend. It's the void of losing yourself, of never knowing who you truly are.

When the void is at its darkest and seemingly infinite, I long to be held and comforted– not out of pity, but love. When Master dotes on me, it's out of pity, or obligation, or reward. Devlin and Spyder do it out of love and acceptance. But it's not what I need. I need a connection, intimacy, affection, but I doubt I'll ever find it.

I lean my head on the tile wall and weep until my eyes are as empty as my soul. I'm a shell of a human being, fashioned in my mother's image, not knowing my true purpose without being told by my master.

Chapter Nine

Sitting cross-legged in the center of my bed, I wait for Nurse Devlin to take care of me. I'm nude– a very rare occurrence. Usually I'm naked just for the amount of time it takes to shower and redress. The rest of the time, it's too terrifying to be out of my Dalton Thompson disguise.

Right now I feel exposed, not just in the flesh, but to the depths of my soul.

Devlin is a formidable master, able to read me like an open book. I haven't been able to stay the flow of tears leaking from my eyes. They fall in a strange pattern– sometimes in a torrent, and then a moment later a trickle, only to pick back up again.

Strong hands wrap a sports bandage tightly around my midsection. It hurts sharply for a moment, but then the relief sets in as I breathe easier. It dulls to a mild ache, easily forgotten unless I make a jarring movement. The cool touch of ointment smeared into my inflamed skin is soothing and comforting. Venturing from his caretaking, Devlin's fingertip traces the four tattoos embedded into the skin on my back. Two large tattoos are over the bulk of my shoulders with two smaller ones directly beneath.

Devlin follows up the nursing with basic comfort by helping me dress in pajama pants and a soft long-sleeved shirt. The feel of the jersey cotton is a blissful luxury for my skin. The paddle of a brush pulling through my hair is eliciting vocalizations from my throat.

"You don't have to do that, Dev," I mutter in protest, hoping he ignores me because I secretly love it. Every pass of the brush has my scalp tingling, crackles of pleasure zinging around my body. "I can take care of my own hair."

"I want to," Dev murmurs gruffly, intense emotions thick in his voice. "Besides, it would hurt you to raise your arm to do it. So let me take care of you as you take care of all of us. Let me show you how much I love you. Please, son," he pleads.

I don't answer. I sit contently as Devlin runs the brush through my hair. It's a gesture that one's mother should do, but not one my mother ever used. Devlin picks up on all of her failings when she allows it.

"Devlin, I don't think Spy and I could have prayed for a better father. You and Master were never together, but you took responsibility for us. And for that, I thank you from the both of us." I wipe a stray tear from the corner of my eye.

"Ah, no matter what anyone says about you, Font, you are a joy to have as a son." In a rare gesture of affection, Devlin wraps his arm around me in a half hug.

Punishment always brought us together. When it was Tony, he and Bruno would take care of me. When it was Pierre, Master would take care of me. When it was Jon, Devlin would take care of me. A thread of sickness lies buried deep in my psyche, needing punishment in order to accept affection.

"Don't allow your broken mother to ruin you. You're stronger than her in so many ways. She's one of the strongest of us, but in a way, the biggest coward. I haven't respected her in a long time. She's a hard woman to deny in the moment. But when I have time to think, I can't stand by her decisions."

"Me too. I loathe her as much as I love her," I whisper the words that have plagued me my entire life.

"Me too, son." His deep voice rumbles with sadness. "Me too."

"I don't trust Master anymore. I don't trust why she sent us here. Even with all the bad things I've said and done to the members of Restraint, they still treat me with respect. I want to stay here and I want her to go home."

"I agree. It makes no sense for Olivia to come here, bringing all of our people with her. She handed me the reins at the helm of the BDSM Lifestyle Authority. Then she left KINK, completely walked away, and that has never happened before."

"Never," I breathe ominously, shuddering in fear.

"I don't trust Olivia's motives. I'm rethinking everything she's said and done. But don't stress yourself, son." Devlin gives me a squeeze of reassurance. "You could go downstairs as you are and be yourself, Font. You don't have to keep up this charade."

"You mean denounce her as my master?" I ask in surprise.

"Olivia will always be your mother, for better or worse. But she is a bad master for you, and you don't need anyone to pull your strings. You're more than capable of being your own man. Just think about it. I know you fear the repercussions of being Font. But those loyal men and women would keep your secret."

"All of them except for the leak," I muse.

"Maybe they would, too." Now it's Devlin's turn to go introspective. "You never know. People do things for different reasons. You have treated your fellow masters with disrespect at your master's command, never questioning her motivations to her face. Perhaps the mole is in a similar situation, but doesn't want to be."

"Perhaps," I agree, looking at this from a new perspective.

"What do we even know of the leak, or Ms. Whittenhower? While you've been obtaining information for your mother, I've been looking for the source. I have nothing concrete yet, so don't ask."

I relax with the rhythm of the brush. I close my eyes and try to clear my mind of everything. I concentrate on my breathing, in and out... in and out... in and out.

"Font, I don't want you to be angry with me, but I need you to do something for me." Devlin's hesitant voice breaks into my meditation.

"I don't like the sound of that." I'm surprised to hear a teasing lilt to my voice. "It's always a bad idea when a sentence starts with *don't be angry with me.*"

"Not necessarily," Devlin murmurs sheepishly. "Tomorrow night at midnight, I have someone who wants to spend some time with you. So I need you to trust me and do as I say."

"What do you mean?" Voice warping with suspicion, I freeze in fear. "And yet again, the *trust me* makes me think I shouldn't."

"You need to make friends your own age, gather some hobbies and interests. So I found you an outlet that's a helluva lot safer than starving yourself, cutting yourself, or forcing me to beat you. You need to have your basic human needs met."

"I've gone twenty-four years without that happening," I mutter underneath my breath. "I don't think it's a pressing issue right now, Devlin."

"Just be here at midnight. Be yourself. He wants Font, not Dalton Thompson. Dress as yourself, but wear the mask I put on your bedside table until he tells you otherwise. I know you can't trust anyone, but you can trust me. Just do this. You need it badly."

"Did you hire someone, or force them to spend time with me?" Heart breaking, I'm extremely offended. "I don't need you to find me lovers."

"No, dammit," Devlin sputters. "Font, trust me. I'm keeping his secret. He came to me and requested that I set this up for the both of you. Just enjoy something for the first time in your life. Don't act, just be yourself around him. It isn't even about sex. I have no illusions that it's not on his mind, but I think he wants to be around someone who is um–" He hesitates as he thinks up a word. "Like-minded."

"Do you mean gay, Dev?" I tease him. He's one of the straightest men I know, which is saying something since our BDSM community is teeming with men in comparison to women.

"Yes, I mean gay. But you're in a similar circumstance, hiding in the closet. As I said, it's not just about sex. But I do think like-minded was an appropriate word," he defends his word choice.

"Fine… but if I don't like it, I'll tell him to leave." I fall back on the bed and snuggle into the blankets. I'm overcome with lethargy. "It's the best I can do right now."

"Get some rest." Devlin actually tucks my blankets around me. "I set the alarm on your cellphone and there are fresh bagels on the counter for breakfast. You don't need to worry about your stomach tomorrow. Class is dismissed and you aren't scheduled for duty in the dungeon."

"Thank God for small blessings," I murmur into my pillow.

"Eh?" Devlin hesitates. "Your sister outed you to her new friends. I'm sorry, but it's unavoidable." I struggle to sit up, but his heavy palm pushes me right back down. "Under the circumstances, we can agree that they are exceptional at secret-keeping. So tomorrow afternoon, I need you to take them to a movie or something. Ava needs to talk to you."

"I agree about Ava needing a mentor who's been in a similar situation. But I don't like that they know. First, Dexter. Now, Ava and Niel know my real identity. Who else will find out? Hell, Queen called me by my real name tonight. If the mole knows, I lose my in with Adelaide. But worse is if the cartels find out. I don't want Dalton Thompson's name on a hit-list too."

"You're safe. The ones who know who you are will protect you. No fear. Get some rest. I will call for an update on your meeting." He winks as he says meeting– Devlin the matchmaker.

"Speaking of updates, Master didn't call." I avoided bringing up the sore subject earlier, but it's unavoidable now.

"I called Olivia while you were in the shower. She won't call you tomorrow, either. She's busy, and I told her to leave you the fuck alone or there would be consequences." His voice drops an octave as he speaks.

"Did you really threaten her?" I ask in awe.

"Yes, and I meant every word I said."

"Yeah, you can mean it, but it doesn't mean she does."

"Olivia knew I was being serious. I don't give a shit if she tries to bend my will. I'm three hundred pounds of pissed off. She got the hint… besides, technically I'm her master now." Devlin releases a sardonic chuckle. "Olivia shouldn't have given me the reins."

"Dev, did she come with Sebastian?" I pray I am wrong. "I saw her during your initial meeting with the membership, then a glimpse during Dexter and Monica's wedding."

Devlin just nods his head sadly.

"Thanks, bonne nuit." I roll into a ball underneath the covers and sigh in pleasure. "Good night to you too, son." He bids me adieu as he locks up behind himself.

Chapter Ten

Wrapped up in intense warmth, I've never felt as safe and secure as I do now. My body aches, but my heart is slowly knitting back together. Groggy, rousing from sleep, I try to shift but a heavy weight is holding me down.

A bolt of terror spikes, but then I just instinctively sense who is curled around my back in a protective stance. "Are you my brother?" flows from my lips before my brain has time to catch up and stop me.

"Yes," Levi whispers near my ear, voice breaking. He pauses, unsure if I'm going to reject him or not. "I was ordered never to speak of it."

All of my life, Levi's been there, protecting me the best he could. My early childhood was filled with Levi and his little sister. As a team, Jonathan and Devlin kept Pierre and Jon at bay, but I could sense Levi changing. He would leave for months on end, most likely here in Dominion. When Marcus was with us for a year, I had Levi to myself the entire time. When Marc left, so did Levi… and neither of them ever came back.

"I don't understand," I murmur, confusion thickly lacing my voice. I'm angry, more furious than I've ever been, but I dampen it down because it doesn't belong to Leviticus. Master is always at the heart of all of my rage. "I could sense you around this whole time, but you never approached me."

"I-I-I–" Levi curls around me tighter, resting his cheek against the top of my head. "Dad died and I had important obligations that kept me here in Dominion, leaving you open to what you've lived through."

"It's not your fault, if that's what you're getting at."

"I know– I had to raise my sister as a parent, plus work and run a home. I trusted Uncle Dev to keep you safe the best he could, knowing what would happen whether I was there or not." He squeezes me tighter, and I instinctively know I won't like what he says next. "I couldn't stick around and watch. But then Jon forced me to choose. I felt you were stronger than my sister. If I hadn't raised her, Jon would have."

Shuddering, I imagine Jon raising a little girl– she's a grown woman now, but still. The implications are terrifying. "You made the right choice."

"When you get up this morning, you need to eat, and then you need to walk out of here as yourself, Font. Fuck Olivia and all of this master horseshit. She is not your master; she is the world's worst goddamned mother to have ever walked this planet, and I know some atrocious cunts."

"Tell me how you really feel," I mutter sarcastically, trying to defuse the violent energy radiating through Levi.

"Olivia seduced my father, you know? Taking one look at her, who would deny themselves a few stolen moments of pleasure? Dad was honest with her, how he didn't love her more than a childhood friend. But she thought sex would change it, and he thought all they were doing was being teenagers who were fooling around, and then he was sent here for– work."

"Is this the story of how we learn why our mother is evil incarnate? Because she blames that on Pierre, then Jonathan, then Tony, sometimes she even blames me. Hell, I've heard her blame Marcus for Spyder's conception, and we both remember that man locked in a room for a year."

"Olivia is the common denominator. You and I are proof that you can be victimized without becoming a victim."

"From your mouth to God's ears."

"She got knocked up by my dad, only she didn't tell him. She ranted and raved about how impossible it was that Dad didn't want her when she was Olivia Fucking Fontaine," Levi bites out, enunciating each word. "Away from her toxicity, Dad met Tori in Dominion."

"Tony came after this, but he was well versed in the tantrums our mother threw, and he'd tell me stories to counteract her propaganda."

"Dad didn't know I existed," Levi whispers against the side of my cheek. "I was handed to Jon as soon as I was born, and I was lucky that he brought me to Dad instead of keeping me– not that it mattered anyway, since he still got his goddamned hands on me."

Hesitantly, I ask something important. "You're better now, though, right?"

"Sure," Levi replies, not sounding very sure at all. "I lived the first seventeen years of my life looking my goddamned mother in the eye and having her look at me like I was a stranger." Levi pulls away from me, unable to touch me while he's filled with rage.

"I was relieved when you showed up in Dominion, Dalton." Levi shifts on the bed. It's pitch-black, so I can't see him, but I can tell he's sitting cross-legged. "So I kept watch from a distance, with Stanton keeping tabs on whether or not anyone learned your identity. But when our mother came to town, I did all I could to get into this fucking building to keep you safe."

"Your Trojan horse was a comfort," I mutter wryly, causing Levi to chuckle. "Dexter didn't buy Gretchen's story for a second... Why not just tell me who you were to me, and let me into your life? I know nothing of who you are as a grown man, Levi, and I'm just now learning you're my brother."

In the dark of my shitty efficiency apartment, when I could afford to live anywhere else but it's not safe, my brother rests his forehead against mine. "As long as you call Olivia Fontaine Master, the only part of me that I can give you is protection. If you want to know me as a human being, as a brother, you must cut the cord," he warns, absolute fury vibrating in his voice.

"I can't just reclaim my identity," I grumble, completely taken aback by Levi's passion.

"You can," Levi promises, leaning away from me. "Bruno is the figurehead of Fontaine and Marconi, with Stanton watching out for you here. When you removed those men from power, those who usurped them owe you a big fucking thank you. They haven't put a target on your back, and they never will. Just as I wanted to shake your hand for murdering Pierre and Jon, they wanted to shake your hand for the same thing. I said we had a party– it was all the heads of organized crime celebrating their demise and your courage."

"Then where are the hits coming from?" I struggle to sit up in bed, my rib protesting. "Where? I know of nine separate attempts on my life, with one only a few weeks ago."

"It's not mafia related, I can tell you that." Levi's voice is hoarse, and he swallows so thickly I can hear him gulp. "Cut the cord with Mommy Dearest, and you can have unlimited access to every facet of my life. But for now, I've removed anything sharp from your apartment."

"Hey!" I protest, struggling to reach underneath my mattress for my bloodletting kit.

Slapping my hand away, Levi ignores my protests. "You're unnaturally hairless, so if I see you buying a razor blade, I'm going to break your fucking fingers," he threatens, meaning business. "Gunner is guarding the Whittenhowers and Zeitlers, and my job is the rest of you fools– including you. So when you go for a walk, I'll be going with you a few paces behind. Don't think of buying anything sharp and pointy, I mean it."

"I didn't forget how bossy you could be," I murmur like it annoys me, but I secretly love it. Levi was always pushy in a way where he made sure I didn't step out in traffic or stick my finger in a light socket. Where Master was bossy in a way that harmed me inside and out. As a switch, I find it a comfort.

"Devlin said he brought you bagels, but I went ahead and stocked your fridge. You will eat three meals and two snacks a day, and I don't mean energy drinks. You'll find your cane is no longer in this apartment, but down in your private room– mounted to the wall, completely unusable."

"I-I-I–"

"You're probably going to wish I never found my way into this half of the building. It took me a few months, but I weaseled my way in. My wife is the biggest bitch you've ever met– a complete control freak. So you're being forewarned that I'm going to micromanage your life since she won't let me live my own."

"You have a wife?" I don't mean to sound super excited.

Levi releases the oddest laugh I've ever heard, and it trails on for several long minutes. Awkward, I find myself laughing with him like I know what's going on. "Gunner's real big on exercise. After we get Olivia out of Dominion, you'll be expected to join our survivors' workout group. We run from our demons until we're too tired to have nightmares– masochist or not, the only beating you'll be doing is your soles on the pavement and your fist on your cock. Got it?"

Suspicions rising, "Are you trying to replace our mother as my master?"

"No," Levi stresses firmly. "I'm helping you see that you don't need her. There are healthy alternatives to all the coping skills you've learned. I want you to find yourself and enjoy whatever you make out of life. I don't want to control you, but I will if I find you being stupid. So once the cord has been cut, I expect to see my brother reemerge."

"What if I can't let Master go?" I mutter sadly, animosity and devotion warring inside my mind.

"If you want to survive to see twenty-five, you'll do it," Levi predicts.

Chapter Eleven

The world is brighter by the light of day seen out of green eyes instead of drab brown. My face luxuriates in the feel of my hair sweeping across it in the light breeze. I lay on my back in the grass at the park with a smile stretched across my face.

This morning I ate breakfast with my brother, chatting about nonsense, but it felt freeing. Then I called Bruno because seeing Levi made me miss him. Then I left Restraint in a pair of skinny jeans, a thermal with a printed t-shirt over top, and a pair of Chucks. No wig. No concealer. No contacts. I stepped out of Restraint as Font, walked across town to the Brownstone, where I chatted with Alex while playing dirty word Scrabble with Jamie. As I was leaving, Marcus was coming, and he gave me a hug.

Sweet freedom. But my reprieve is short-lived, because I won't be able to quiet the call of my master and I can feel the target on my back buzzing, even if Stanton and Bruno promise everything is right in the underworld. I allow those who know I'm Dalton Anthony Fontaine Marconi to see Font today, but I will be Dalton Thompson the next time they see me.

"Ruff… ruff… ruff… grrr…" startles me upright. I almost butt heads with the young idiot. "Bark… bark… Font." Niel laughs at me, bringing his face so close that he looks like a Cyclops.

"Back off, mini-shit-Whitt." I mock-punch the kid in the chest so he'll get out of my personal space.

"You have a nice smile," is his reply. I throw him a confused look and he smiles at me again. "I've never seen it before."

Rising up on my elbow, "What's up with the look, Daniel? I know I look different, but you're gazing at me like I'm fascinating."

"Because you *are* fascinating," a girl murmurs from behind Niel, and I'm hit with a sense of déjà vu.

"Who's she?" I ask of the teenage girl who looks so much like Whitt it's surreal. She's tall and curvy with sandy-blonde hair and bright blue eyes. She smiles at me shyly and blushes, with Ava Zeitler and Spyder flanking her.

"My little sister, Ella." Niel points at the ground where he wants his harem of ladies to sit, like he's used to ordering them around.

Big brother syndrome, everyone becomes your little sister or brother and they are to automatically obey you. Niel is definitely a Whittenhower, even if he didn't inherit the blond hair and blue eyes.

Ava rolls her eyes while folding her willowy frame to the ground. Next to her, my sister smiles at me like she has a secret. Bubbling with excitement, Ella gazes at me, refusing to blink as if afraid I'll disappear.

"Kid, I thought you were an only child, an orphan? I'd ask if you meant an adopted sister… but dang, Ella looks exactly like Whitt." I shake my head in mystification. If the girl wasn't so close in age, I'd swear Whitt was her father. She looks old for her age, but I'd guess her to be around fifteen, give or take, and Whitt's only twenty-three.

After the morning I've spent, I believe I know who sired these kids. Seeing Niel and Ella side-by-side, their features reveal their lineage. I suspect that's why they never travel in a pair.

While eating breakfast, I stared at Leviticus the whole entire time, finally seeing beneath the Wilson trapping to the Fontaine beneath. It would've probably been noticeable to others if Levi stood next to Spy or me, but not when apart. It's the same phenomenon with Niel and Ella.

"Shh… no telling, or our mom will kick your ass," Niel warns. The girl nods her head up and down in agreement, and I do believe their overprotective mommy would murder me. I add another mother to my list of mothers I wish Olivia Fontaine would've been, alongside Tori Wilson and Katya Waters.

"I feel ya." I smirk at Spyder. "I have a bratty little sister, too." She scoffs, slapping at my chest, while her new friends giggle at her.

It was kids' choice of activities today, a picnic and sunbathing in the park. Yeah, what a lovely idea for the pasty white guy, his sister of the same skin tone, an ethereal being, the freckle-faced boy-next-door and his sister, the girl-next-door.

"Whose idiot idea was it for us to get a sunburn?" I ask when Niel doesn't explain why he keeps gazing at me fondly.

"I thought since this was our first official meeting, it would be nice not to be in the dark." Ava, the youngest of our group, gives the best insight. "I grew up in the country. But now our lives are spent in a dungeon, castle-like homes, and learning institutions. We need a little sun to brighten up our lives."

"I wouldn't call the five of us a meeting." I shift, already feeling the heat of the sun bearing down on me. "I do like the location, but I hope someone remembered sunblock."

I help spread out the quilt that Ava brought, and smile when I see a huge hamper full of food and drinks.

"We aren't the only members–" Ava cuts her words short when Niel gives her a '*shut the fuck up*' look. "One member couldn't make it today."

"I assume that the member is a secret– good to know." I turn sarcastic as I feel eyes focused on me. "Dammit, Daniel, why do you keep staring at me?"

"You're very pretty." I look at Niel like he's lost his mind. I know damn well the boy only has eyes for Ava. He isn't crushing on me so what's his issue?

"You look just like your mom, almost identical– except on you it's better." Examining me, he gives me a slow perusal. "You'd be beautiful if you weren't a guy."

Blushing, feeling oddly exposed, I shove Niel out of my personal space. "You're creeping me out, kid."

"That's a perfect combination– beautiful and pretty." My sister snickers like I'm the brunt of an inside joke. I roll my eyes at Spyder, pretending I'm not curious. But my suspicions are confirmed when Ava looks at me from her peripheral vision and blushes.

"You wouldn't happen to be matchmaking, would you?" I tease and sigh dramatically. "Have you been talking to Devlin? Spyder, is nothing sacred?"

I receive four pairs of innocent eyes: two green, one gray, and one blue. All four blink their lashes at me. Well, this afternoon is like the preschool I never attended, but it's entertaining.

"So how many members are there, really?" I ask Ava– clearly, she's their leader.

"Six members," Ava stammers. "Us and one other person."

Impressed with the kids, my question rolls off my tongue without thought. "Whose idea was it for your organization?"

"Niel and I came up with it, and then we got some help from our silent partner." She smiles at Daniel, all proud of herself for not mentioning the missing member. "We found your sister, and now you."

"What are the rules?"

"It's like Fight Club. You don't talk about Fight Club. One extra rule– you don't state the name of the club or the members. Lastly, we come first. I know that sounds strange, but your loyalties lie with us first and foremost." I crack a grin as the angelic child-woman gives me the rules of Fight Club with a straight face.

"Kids, I'm from Vegas, as my sister probably told you. I know those rules very well."

They all nod their heads like happy puppies.

"All right, I'm in charge now." I will not have a fourteen-year-old child boss me around. No freaking way is my sister going to, and a hell no on mini-shit-Whitt and mini-pretty-Whitt.

They all shake their heads no. I stare them down. Ava's too strong-willed, my sister is immune, and Ella refuses to meet my eyes… Daniel caves.

"The silent partner's in charge," is his answer.

"Who's older?" I arch a brow, setting my trap.

"You may be by a few months– I think." Niel scrunches up his face and rubs the back of his neck in a gesture that is so similar to his uncle's that I have to blink the vision of Whitt from my mind.

"Well, I'm the oldest, so I'm in charge now." I really don't care. I'm baiting them so they'll slip up and tell me who their silent partner is.

"Stop answering him, you fool!" Spyder snaps at Niel. I glare at my sister for messing up my plans.

"No, he's still the one in charge." I laugh when the kid keeps it up. I fall back to lay in the grass, silently laughing so hard I have to hold on my chest to still my aching rib.

"Ah– you guys are fabulous." More laughter bubbles up, painful or not. "Thanks for making my day– hell, my year. I don't know how you've gone undetected for so long. It's a fucking miracle." I sit up and wipe my eyes. "I bet your silent partner, Marcus, your mother, and Devlin are all running interference to keep you out of trouble."

The four of them look at me in confusion, not understanding why I find them so amusing.

"Ava, from now on, you're the spokesperson." I chuckle underneath my breath, marveling over how gullible Niel is for someone who's almost eighteen. "I hope and pray chatty-Daniel is only so free with his speech around those he trusts."

"I'm good at keeping secrets," Niel reminds me, looking offended. "No one knows who my parents really are. The Whittenhowers have more skeletons in one closet in Misery Castle than most families will accumulate in a century... and we have one hundred and seventeen closets in our castle."

"Jesus, kid." My heart clenches. I wanted to meet with Ava today, needing to give her some advice on how to deal with her family being in the lifestyle and with all the publicity. I hadn't realized they all needed someone who wasn't their parents' age but old enough to have made mistakes yet young enough to be their brother.

"You guys know too much about me, and frankly, it could get me killed." I hate admitting it, feeling weak and defenseless. "So you better mean what is said at '*do not say the name of the club*', stays with us."

"Lips are sealed." Niel demonstrates how he's still a kid by zipping his lips and locking it with a key, then he tosses the pretend key over his shoulder. The girls giggle as they pretend to catch the key out of the air and fight over it.

So innocent. Jealousy momentarily slams into me. But then warmth filters in because they are experiencing something I never got a chance to experience. Childhood. The angst-filled teenage years.

Freedom.

Adelaide Whittenhower, may she rot in hell. She'd be good company for Olivia Fontaine. Pierre Fontaine and Jon Wilson already reside in its fiery depths.

Leaning back on my elbows on the grass, I try to look nonchalant, hiding my thoughts. "Go ahead and call Whitt to our meeting. I'm sure he's sad that he's missing all the fun." I raise an eyebrow at their shocked expressions. "That is, unless you've been able to keep your mouths shut for five seconds, and by some miracle he doesn't know who I am."

Varying expressions of disbelief, all jaws hanging open to catch flies, they look at me like I figured out the launch code to a nuclear missile.

"One: the silent partner has to be someone who is close to you and fits in the club's stringent rules." I chuckle as I tick off the numbers with my fingers. "Two: you told me that the silent partner is a few months younger than me. Kids, that doesn't leave anyone but Whitt. Third: you said he was male. Hence, the mystery silent partner is Whitt. Don't make me break out Scooby and Shaggy references."

Niel's fingers type with lightning speed on his cellphone. I lay back and relax– I'd be willing to bet my two mafia syndicates that Whitt is within sight distance. I'm sure the whitest kids on the planet didn't want to get a suntan any more than I do. We're here so we could be observed from a distance.

"Ya didn't fool me with the park, kids. It was clever, Ava, but we might as well be vampires when it comes to the sun. I'm sure Whitt knew his cover was blown before he received the text message."

I smile up at the man who makes my blood boil in so many different ways. I'm thankful that I received my punishment last night, or my mood would be drastically different. Relaxed and satisfied, I feel more like myself than ever. They accept me, even with knowing most of my secrets.

Smile so goddamn huge, his dimples are on display, blond hair glowing in the sunlight, Whitt stands over me, looking happier to be here than I feel. "I wondered how they'd make it without me. I'm in serious doubt of their intelligence at this point."

"I give them props for trying." I shift in the grass, uncomfortable with how Whitt makes me feel. A buzzing energy runs in my veins. It's the feeling that is described in countless books when the protagonist finally meets the person who will change the direction of their lives. I don't believe in fairytales, but I always read them. "You can thank your nephew for ratting you out. He doesn't know when to keep his trap shut."

Always playful, wearing a similar grin to the one I saw this morning on someone else, Whitt cuffs the kid in the back of the head. After messing up Niel's atrocious hair, Whitt drags his fingers through the curly mess, trying to put it to rights.

"I would think, with all the money the Whittenhowers have, someone would take the child to a hairdresser." I tease the pair of Whitts.

"We have– it's no use." Niel shrugs shamelessly. "Why bother at this point."

"I hear you're the one in charge, even though I'm older by a few months." I catch myself flirting with the older Daniel Whittenhower, and I don't know why.

"Ah, that's how you figured it out." Folding himself to the ground, Whitt sits so close he's almost in my lap. "No, I'm in charge because I hold your leash," he replies smugly.

Eyes darting in his direction, I scowl at Whitt because I didn't want the young ones to know that about me.

"Let's get the meeting started, and lunch will follow." We all sit upright when Whitt addresses us.

Pulling the device out of her mammoth designer handbag, Ava hands Whitt a tablet with what I presume is the minutes to the last meeting.

"I hereby call our eighth weekly meeting." Whitt says the following from memory. "We are the children who grew up within the lifestyle. We are the first generation of masters who aren't bound by the restraints of normal society. Our parents made the choice to live without boundaries, now we embrace our own choices and admonish the cowards who hide behind their money, influence, and power. The hypocrites who tell their children to live one way while they secretly live another. We own who we are– Generation Next."

Whitt smiles at us each in turn, his eyes sparking with mischief and pride.

"I have news." Whitt teases us by pausing until the kids turn antsy. "Four more chapters of GN have opened up. Our network is growing rapidly. The BDSM Lifestyle Authority thought they held all the power, but for every member there are a few children they created. Someday we will be more powerful than the organization we joined together to rise up against."

"Oh, my God," Niel whispers, green eyes glowing with pride. "So fucking bizarre. Grandfather would go mind-fuck on our asses if he knew."

"Knowing Grandfather–" Pink cheeks turning red, Ella chokes on her own laughter. "The old bastard would be proud of us."

"If your grandfather ever joined forces with my mother–" Spyder mimics her mind exploding.

"And my grandmother," Ava adds in, maintaining a straight face. "Diane Holden doesn't bake cookies and give hugs– she's utterly terrifying."

"Grandfather and Diane are already BFFs." Niel shudders.

"Care to share with the class?" I lean forward, eager to hear their secrets instead of dwelling with my own. "You do know Olivia Fontaine lived in Dominion and graduated from Hillbrook. I heard so many stories while I was growing up, I was sad that I didn't get to attend to continue the Fontaine tradition."

"Legacy!" Whitt, Niel, Ava, and Ella point at their chests, leaving Spyder and me out of the loop. Ava continues, "Yeah, Pop told me Grandmother and Olivia were the best of friends."

"What a nightmare," Niel mutters, knowing these people I've never met. "Which means my namesake knows Master Fontaine."

"We could spend the rest of our lives dissecting the interconnecting alliances of the rich, twisted, and influential, but back to the task at hand." Whitt stops Niel and the girls as they begin volleying back and forth. "The other chapters of Generation Next will supply us with fresh news, and we will print it. I've changed the membership requirements. We now charge a fee because the publication costs and websites are milking us dry. I know our subscribers pay a fee for their subscription, but it's ridiculous how much it's costing to reroute IP addresses to avoid detection. We seriously have to think about going public. While I love the Robin Hood feel of GN, it isn't cost effective. I would help with the expenses, but my trust fund doesn't mature until I turn twenty-four. Yours doesn't either, Niel, Ella, and Ava, and that's a long wait. My day job barely covers my living expenses since Father takes half for savings. He's insane since Adelaide's breakdown."

"May she rot in hell," is chanted around the group. My eyes roam from one to the next, trying to figure out what that was about, considering three of the chanters are the woman's closest relatives.

"Whenever the cunt's name leaves our lips, we say *may she rot in hell*." Whitt laughs ruthlessly about chanting his sister's horrific demise– scary.

"I have sources I can tap into for funding," I offer helpfully. "That is if you don't mind the money being dirty."

"Illegal money is dirty," Niel murmurs so quietly I almost can't hear him. "But our money stains our hands red with blood."

Narrowing his eyes at Niel, Whitt looks at him askew. "Thanks, Dalton. As long as it doesn't put you into any danger, we would appreciate the funding."

"Dad?" Ella says out of the blue, and it has me looking around for her father, who I know isn't in this park with us.

Huh?

"Whatcha need, sweet pea?" Whitt asks Ella, answering her *dad*, which confuses me more.

"If we tell Mom, she'll help us with the IP addresses." She shrugs, pretty skin flushing pink.

"Oh, she already knows, but she has so much going on right now that I don't want to bother her." Whitt pulls Ella into a half hug while saying, "That's all the new information we have. I open the floor for grievances."

"I'm good." Niel answers quickly, passing the question in Spyder's direction.

"I want to spend time with my father, but my mother won't allow it. She says since Marcus didn't want her, why would he ever want me? I'm almost eighteen, and I have to sneak around to see my father, and when my mother finds out, she cries and tells me how badly I've hurt her. But it hurts me, too, especially when I have to watch Ava and the twins have unlimited access to the man who is *my* father."

The quiver in Spyder's voice and the tears dotting her cheeks have me reaching over to pull my sister into my lap. I bury my face into her hair while rubbing her arms up and down, trying to comfort her.

"Our mother is a heinous, remorseless bitch. Don't take advice from her when it pertains to matters of the heart, and never trust her motivations. Always trust that she is putting herself first, and we're dead last unless it somehow helps her with an agenda."

"Mother told me how when Marcus looks at me, all he sees is her. She said she wanted to smear me in his face, but at the same time she never wanted him to lay eyes upon me, knowing either way would hurt him. She said he knew about me since before I was born, and didn't care– never tried to see me, never asked about me. Nothing."

"Bullshit," I snarl. "I was old enough to remember how our mother destroyed Marcus, and then kicked him out, never allowing him to return. I spent four years telling Marc every single detail I could about you. Then when I was with you, I made sure to tell you his ideals and religion, trying to negate our mother's influence."

"Then why don't you tell your mother to fuck off?" Whitt's words are said in a tone without heat, but their meaning is passionate. It's like Whitt and Levi are of a like mind when it comes to Olivia Fontaine. I know I need to get with the program, but I'm not ready to take my own advice yet.

"Itsy Bitsy, if you're worried about running a club, our mother will help you. But other than that, don't believe anything she says. Marcus is a tough man, but he's fair. He has an endless amount of love for his family, and he's a better man than to allow petty jealousy to rule his life. If we all looked at our loved ones with hatred because of who contributed to their blood, we'd hate everyone."

"I missed you, mon frère." Spyder smiles at me, wrapping her arms tightly around my shoulders, making my rib protest. I kiss her on the tip of the nose, and then set her back in the circle because my chest is aching sharply for dual reasons.

"Home isn't a very good place to be right now." Ava starts, impatient to take her turn. "My parents are oblivious. I hear and see things I shouldn't. It's not like it's out in the open. I'll admit I'm the one who goes looking for it." She trails a humorless laugh.

"Curiosity killed the cat," Niel taunts. "And you're Kat's kitten."

"Ah-ha-ha," Ava mock-laughs. "My apologies for what you're about to hear, Spy." She pats my sister's arm. "Cort attacked Marcus at dinner last night, and I don't mean their usual bantering. He flew across the table and tackled Pop, the chair breaking underneath their weight." Filled with rage, Ava's features have never looked more like her father's.

"Cort punched Marcus and blackened his eye. It wasn't funny, but it was incredible to watch them lose their shit." Fury etched across her pale features, Ava turns animated as she sets the scene. "Marcus stood up and walked right out the terrace doors. I wanted to stop Cort when he went to follow, but Dad laughed it off as if it were nothing." Resting her head in her hands, pure frustration bleeds from her voice. "I waited for two hours for them to come back into the house. I was scared they'd kill each other."

I look across the circle to Whitt. We share a knowing smile. I have no doubt why Ezra allowed them to work out their frustrations, just as I have a good idea on what Cortez's malfunction is.

"Ava, it's called foreplay." My sister schools Ava on the finer points of the male ego. It takes everything in me not to laugh hysterically at the absurdity of a daughter and granddaughter discussing their patriarch's sex life.

"Is she right?" Ava asks with all seriousness. "Is that all it is?"

"It's because Cort is having a hard time admitting he likes guys more than girls." Whitt makes a snapping sound out the side of his mouth. "Someone needs to tell Cort and Marcus that they're in a relationship with each other. The constant foreplay is obvious at Restraint. A few weeks back, Marcus all but admitted it."

"It was fucking wild to witness." Niel releases a strangled laugh. "I was there when they tackled each other. I was waiting for one of them to kill the other. It was a fight to the death or–" he cuts himself off when he sees Ava and Spyder, and his baby sister who doesn't need to know this shit. "Sorry. I apologize," he mutters bashfully.

"Be mindful of impressionable ears," I remind Niel, wishing I hadn't grown up in this type of environment. "Ava shouldn't be seeing it, but your sister shouldn't be hearing about it, either."

Niel gives me a quick jerk of his chin, understanding completely and showing a healthy dose of regret for bringing it up.

"So, it's normal?" Ava asks, refusing to let the subject drop.

"Pretty much," Whitt gives in when he catches me biting back a reprimand. "Cort says he's straight, but that ship sailed when he was twelve." Whitt laughs hysterically for some reason. "I assume there's a learning curve, but not one almost as long as I am old."

"Why won't they grow up?" Ava's angelic face fills with frustrated anger, and it pleases me that she sees the injustice of their actions at her young age.

"Ava, don't kill the messenger," I bluntly interject. "Cort and Marcus enjoy the game they play, or else they wouldn't play it. They're so blinded by whatever is plaguing them that they don't see how it's affecting your family. Most of the members only play in the dungeon. But they've expanded their playing field to include everywhere, especially your yard, it seems."

"You mean they were having–" Ava cuts off, turning green around the gills like she has a sour stomach.

"Sorry, but parents aren't asexual, especially those in the lifestyle." Whitt flashes a weak smile, empathizing with the girl while trying not to find it hilarious.

"Thanks, I guess that's my grievance for the week." Ava politely ends her turn.

"My grievance is the same as usual. I want my family to be whole," Ella directs at Whitt like he's the one who can change it.

"Tick-tock... Tick-tock... Tick-tock..." Whitt clucks his tongue. The mini-Whitts nod their heads like they understand it. Ava, Spy, and I look at them in confusion.

"You gonna elaborate on that, *Dad*?" I stress the dad because... *What?*

"I'm having an epic birthday celebration." Whitt grins while his minis laugh and clap excitedly. "The big two-four is coming right up."

"What are your grievances, Whitt?" Ava asks, a challenge in her voice.

Whitt waves his turn away with his hand, refusing to play her game.

"Oh, so your charmed life has no complaints?" I tease, trying to squash the flirty quality to my voice. "Sorry, kids, mine is NC17 and not appropriate for siblings. Guess that leaves me without a group to hear my grievances."

"Meeting adjourned," Whitt announces abruptly, an unspoken order in his voice. Scattering, the kids dive into the picnic basket, looking for snacks.

I lay back on the grass, unable to contain the smile on my face, and gaze at the clouds floating overhead. "In Las Vegas, there was never any time to just be outside. The underworld is run at night. This is a nice change of pace."

"Maybe we should ditch the kids next time. I'll show you around to all the places here in Dominion that are open during the day." Whitt lies next to me on the grass, crowding into my personal space.

"And where would that be?" I play along, finding my body curving more toward him for some odd reason.

"What do you do for fun?" Whitt asks, not going with the flow of our conversation.

"There isn't much downtime in my life– there isn't much time to *live* my life." I gulp, realizing how true that statement is, and it makes me sick to my stomach. "I read to experience other's lives."

"I don't have much time, either." Whitt's body seems to be plagued with the same condition that has mine curving toward his. Our bodies are seeking each other, meeting in the middle. "Between working, being Daniel Whittenhower's yes-man, taking care of the next generation of Whittenhowers– Niel and Ella, and Whitney and Prissy Preston. They all live at Misery Castle, and I want them to have the life I didn't get to have."

"God," I groan, hating how I'm warming to the entitled pretty boy.

Ignoring my protest, Whitt rambles on. "I draw. I've drawn since I could hold a pencil. Then I became obsessed with creating living canvases with flesh, but I personally don't have any tattoos."

"I love ink," flows out of nowhere, deep and not in a voice that sounds like my own. "I have them all over my body."

"Thank God," it's Whitt's turn to sound like an idiot. "So you read and I draw, and we both deal with our fucked up families. I'm a creature of the day, and you're one of the night. I think we should each show the other how our half lives."

"You've been to Restraint." I turn my head, staring at the side of Whitt's face. Fine blond stubble lines his jaw, like he missed a patch when he shaved this morning, and I want to lick it. "So you know how creatures of the night live. I don't mean just the dungeon, but the club. Add gambling, enforcing, and keeping everyone in line."

"Hmm..." Whitt purrs from deep within his throat. Then his head turns, eyes locking on mine. Heat burns through my veins, an uncontrollable fire rages. My breath seizes in my lungs– never before has this happened.

"I'm a suit and tie guy who doesn't know who he truly is. I think I'd like to give you a tour of Dominion– the place I learned to tattoo, Hillbrook, Misery Castle, the bookstore where I buy my books– I'd show you Restraint, but you live there. I'd take you to the Brownstone, but Alex won't let me in there without stopping me at the front door first."

"Ah!" My eyes widen, and Whitt gives me a queer little smile. "I'm up for a tour."

"What book are you currently reading?" Whitt goes from one subject to the next with dizzying speed. "I begged a book off of Katya that's about a twisted family– a lot of incest, and secrets and lies."

"So your reality, then?" I banter, unable to stop myself from flirting, and Whitt's answering chuckle was totally worth it. "My favorite genre is Young Adult," I admit, and Whitt bites back a laugh. "I like to live vicariously. I've moved onto New Adult. But someone gave me a book to read this morning."

It's Whitt's turn to go, "Ah! A James Atwater original, isn't it?"

"Ha-ha, yeah…" I blush, suddenly feeling shy. "I'm not much into reading BDSM because they always get it wrong. But the Roman Numeral titles always get me with their authenticity. So much better than ninety percent of the books where the author completely bastardizes our culture, making it about romance."

"And sex," Whitt adds. "Can't forget how all those books devolve into a sex-fest, showing dominants as sociopaths who can't control their baser urges and submissives as being unable to say no, even though they really want to."

"Making us all out to be rapists and degenerates," I continue on for him, turning sarcastic. "Exactly. I mean, I'm totally down to fuck 24/7, until I perish of sleep deprivation and starvation. Not even time to piss, shit, and shower off the body fluids."

"Yeah." Whitt grunts. "Okay, so that is mostly true in my case. I love to get off. But I do work fourteen hours a day, so it's a rare treat just to find time to do a sketch. I don't even have time to play with my ropes in my private room. I just go in for a quick BJ and get back to the castle to be Daniel Whittenhower's pawn."

"I live above the dungeon, and even I can't find time to go down there because I'm working… In books, we're just mindless fuck-machines," I mutter wryly. "And the masochists will have horrific arthritis from being beaten ten times a day– their life-expectancy will be remarkably short. Imagine the calluses on the hands of the whip-wielding sadists."

"I'm a fuck-machine in real life, babe," Whitt volleys back, causing me to blush harder. "Since I know a few authors personally, I've had this conversation dozens of times. But never with James Atwater. Have you?"

Heart aching, empathizing with his situation, I feel awful for Whitt. Neither one of us are able to voice the pain he must feel, knowing it's better left unsaid. "Yeah, I have. When I spot an inconsistency, I don't let him live it down."

Blue eyes glittering with mischievousness, "Cort!" Whitt shouts, then bubbles of laughter are spilling between his goddamn perfect lips. "My favorite thing in life is to hand that man his ass when it comes to his writing. So, what was his answer– with the book discussion?"

"It's fiction, is what he said." I'm reluctant to answer for some reason. "It would be boring to show all the in-between bits, so BDSM fiction makes us out to look like sociopathic fuck-machines hell-bent on forcing unsuspecting innocents. If a reader who's never been in the lifestyle comes upon a realistic book, they will call the author out for not being *romantic* and *erotic* enough, when the book was meant to be neither. Lose-lose, James Atwater said."

"Yeah, I can totally see that," Whitt muses. "It would be like if someone wrote a book about a billionaire, but was realistic in showing how he worked twenty-four hours a day, and didn't have time for anything besides basic hygiene. Gives a whole new meaning to filthy rich– so hot."

"Talking about yourself now, are you?" My voice dips an octave with seductive intent, and it's too late to take it back.

"Oh, babe–" there Whitt goes again, calling me that goddamned overused endearment, but it seems to be wiggling inside my mind and pulsing straight to my cock. "I make sitting at a desk, completely bored and exhausted out of my mind, the most erotic vision you'll ever see."

I croak out in a voice gone husky with lust, "I don't doubt that." Shifting nervously on the ground, I wipe my sweaty palms on the front of my jeans.

"So," Whitt's eyes flick to Niel and the girls feeding at the picnic basket like piggies at a trough. "While they're busy with Martha's yum-yums– Misery Castles' housekeeper/baker is Kristal's mom… anyway, while they're occupied, I'll listen to your grievances. I have strong and eager ears, awaiting the pleasure of your French-accented voice."

"I'm sure you would love for me to spill all of my secrets." I arch an eyebrow in Whitt's direction. "I didn't peg you as one of the gossip-mongers. You sure had me fooled."

"It's been a pleasure to watch them all squirm." Whitt's fair face glows, already picking up a bit of a tint from the sun. "I think Dexter figured out we were Generation Next when the '*hate Marcus*' edition was published the day after Marc lectured Niel and Ava about teenage sex etiquette. However, I did come clean to your mother and Devlin. I think we're avoiding Katya, Ezra, and Cort just for the fun of it, and I can't wait to see the shit-storm that brings." Whitt's laugh is intoxicating.

Suddenly acting nervous, Whitt finger-combs his hair. When he lowers his hand to the grass, it touches mine– he doesn't move it.

Tensing my muscles against the shudder that is building, I redirect my mind to more important matters. "Their entire life is a shit-storm brewing. I grew up like that– I'm still living like that. Look at how my mother is playing tug-of-war with Spyder against Marcus. This can't be good for the kids."

"Ezra and Katya always put the kids first– Cort is like the super stay-at-home-daddy right now, and that is where some of his bullshit with Marc is coming from. He's found his rebellious stage at age thirty-three. Truth be told, Ava snoops and finds things she shouldn't. That's her fault, not theirs," Whitt defends his friends.

"I know what it's like." My guts twist up painfully. "Ava has a big support system, though. She's a smart girl– she'll be okay."

"Are you okay?" As Whitt turns his face to the side, his nose brushes my cheek. The shudder breaks free, waving throughout my entire body. "I really want to help if you aren't. I know how lonely this life is that we lead. To be around all these people who say they love you, but deep down you don't believe it's true." He asks again, "Are you okay?"

"I don't know," I answer in all honesty, shocked senseless at what flows from my lips. "I fucking hate this shit. I just want to be me, completely me, and I want my mother to go home– or just leave me alone. I'm starting to see how toxic she is for me."

"Well, now you can use me and Niel as fodder in whatever game you're playing for her. We'll go along with you." He offers, but I don't like the thought of being mean to either one of them, drawing them into my troubles. "You could always get into a fight with Devlin. That would rile everyone up."

"It's a good idea for you and Niel, but I don't know... I want the mole to tell your sister that I'm on her team. If I were to target you both, it may bring that faster. But there's no fucking way I'm testing Devlin."

"What's your plan anyway? What does your mother really want?"

Trepidation boils in my blood, but for some reason I trust Whitt's motives over my mother's. "Master wants the mole, which is why she has me riling up everyone and spilling their secrets to her. She wants an in with Adelaide– don't do that creepy chant," I warn before Whitt's lips move. He chuckles, sweet breath wafting out to tickle the side of my face.

"I feel empathetic toward the mole, since I'm sure they're only doing it because of blackmail. I don't blame them– I've done horrible things for the sake of my family. What we really need to know is who's pulling your sister's strings."

"I agree." Whitt sighs deeply— the ultimate sound of frustration. "It's all I think about. I don't really want anything bad to happen to Ade— I still love and care about her. Miss her. It's just a way for the kids to blow off some steam while we fight the unknown. I don't like knowing that Ade's name is on those books when I know she didn't write them. She loves a few of the people it slandered," he says softly. "Including our family members."

Whitt's fingers brush my arm, a tentative touch, and I jerk in surprise. My eyes drift shut as he plays with the fine hairs running along my forearm. "You can confide in me if talking about it will help." He murmurs softly, still staring at the side of my face.

"I'm Jewish— we don't have confession, where a few Hail Marys will cleanse our souls," I mutter wryly. "So do you have several priests on hand? Because talking about it may lift some tarnish off my soul… but in the end, I'm still going to Hell."

Whitt rolls on his side, settling his hand on the center of my chest. Eyes widening, I look at him in surprise. God, he's so warm— his hand is burning a hole through my shirt. My lashes flutter from the deliciously comforting sensation.

"I'm sure you had to do whatever you did. If it was to save another life, it will be forgiven," he promises. "No matter the religion."

I turn my face to the side to look Whitt dead-on. This isn't one of the most intimate moments of my life— it's the only one. I'm lying on the grass in the park, cuddled up with someone I'm actually attracted to, someone I feel a deeper connection to, someone I could talk to for hours upon hours or just listen to their silence. I'm sure when reality sets in, it's just a figment of my imagination. But for now, I cherish it.

"Your looks suit you." Whitt whispers like it's a secret, or like he fears he'll offend me for calling attention to the very thing that my mother exploited. I have no doubt Whitt knows most of my dirty secrets. He's gazing at me fondly, just as his nephew did earlier, but it has a different weight to it.

"I kept imagining what you'd really look like." He sighs deeply— wistfully. "My imagination wasn't good enough."

"Why do the Daniel Whittenhowers of the world keep looking at me like that?" I smirk at Whitt, and then turn my face away from his. I watch the clouds even though every nerve in my body is in tune with the man cradled against my side.

"Not all– you haven't met the original Daniel yet," he mutters with wry amusement. Conversation changing abruptly, "Why did you have sex with Queen last night?"

"Why did Ella call you dad?" I volley back, refusing to play this game.

"My question first," he commands, voice calling to me. His fingers tighten into a fist against my chest.

"Why do you care? You didn't answer my question, so why should I answer yours?" I try for defiant, annoyed at Whitt's highhandedness, but it comes out more as teasing.

"Fine," Whitt concedes. "I was the throwaway heir, while Niel was made specifically to be honed into the image the original Daniel wanted for his legacy. So Niel and I were raised as brothers, but I've always been more like his father– older than my years, grieving for the loss of Niel's father– my brother, Grant. I stepped up because Niel had neither of his parents. As for Ella, I'm her father in all the ways that matter– the only one she's ever known. They're the two most important people in my life, and that's saying something since I have some incredible people in my life."

"Lucky you," I mumble begrudgingly, but it's thickly laced with jealousy and longing.

"Dalton, you do, too. You have more people who care for you than you realize," he says softly. His eyes heat the side of my face as he watches every thought I have flash across my expression. He's using our dominance training against me again.

"Why are you looking at me like that?" I blush underneath his appreciative gaze.

"Because you're gorgeous and I can't stop looking at you," he answers bluntly. "Niel is my closest confidant. I'm sure he was channeling my thoughts, and that's why he kept looking at you like that. Your turn, why Queen?"

"Are you trying to seduce me?" I ask incredulously.

"I wasn't aware I was merely trying… here I thought I was succeeding." Whitt rises up on his elbow, leaning over me a bit to look down at me. Casting a welcoming shadow, he eclipses my sight of the clouds and sun. No matter where I turn my head, he will fill my vision– Whitt surrounds me.

"Dalton, I beg of you to talk to me. Your accent is driving me mad." He leans forward and presses his chest to mine. My eyes bugout of my head at the incredible sensation of his firm body hugging mine. My mind reels with the possibilities he's offering. Fingers fisting grass against the need to pull him atop me...

I ache.

"Harrumph," a male throat clears. "Public," Niel warns.

My seducer throws his nephew a loaded look promising revenge.

"Why?" Whitt asks again. He backs off slightly, but he's still in my space, still sending that delicious, addictive warmth through my veins.

"I don't know," I answer in all honesty. "It made sense at the time– I thought it was a good idea but I have no idea what compelled me to do it. Now I wish I hadn't."

"Why?" comes from between gritted teeth.

"It was nice not to have to whore for my mother for once." A pleading tone is infusing my voice, and I hate it. "Queen knew as much of me as I knew of her– more even. It started out as me trying to get information from her, to her saying she was taking me off the bench and throwing me into the game. I have no idea what the fuck she was talking about, but it intrigued the hell out of me. I couldn't finish without extra help, but it was enough to arouse me. She just felt like a kindred spirit."

"So–"

I cut Whitt off. "I don't want to talk about this right now." I cast a look at the kids. They're finishing up their snack and pulling out a deck of cards. They might be out of hearing distance, but that doesn't mean they aren't straining their little ears to eavesdrop on things that aren't their business. Like Ava peeking at Cort and Marc behind closed doors.

"Okay, later." He gives me a significant look.

"You're confusing me badly, Whitt."

"Answer me this," he whispers so closely that his lips flutter against the shell of my ear. "Have you ever been with a woman and had it be just about the two of you?"

I squeeze my eyes shut tightly and pray. I don't want to say it out loud, but I don't want to lie to him for some reason, either.

"Yes," I say with hesitation.

Tan face etched in fury, his blue eyes are practically sparking as he glares down at me. I start to panic over the look of rage crossing his face. I don't know why that upset him so much, but it did.

"Who?" He demands.

"Calm down, Whitt. You're scaring me." He relaxes in the face of my fear. Looking guilty for losing control, he loosens the grip on my shirt, and then pats the fabric back down from where he twisted it.

"It better not have been Queen," he warns, giving me a clue as to what made him possessive and protective, and angry and jealous.

It was Queen all along.

I had hoped it was me. I recognize Whitt is trying to seduce me, and I thought it was because he truly wanted me, wanted to get to know me. I've been experiencing the most intimate conversation of my life, and the whole time he was just playing with me. He's still the straight Pretty Boy getting his cock sucked by countless girls in the dungeon.

Breathless, suffocating on hurt and rejection I have no right to feel, "Why?" I whisper, fearing the answer but somehow knowing he'll never give it.

"Who?" Whitt repeats his demand, voice tight.

The truth flows painfully. "My wife," I croak out.

Scrambling to my feet, I decide that was as much Font as I want to be for today. Lunging forward, I run away as fast as I can.

Chapter Twelve

Burying my face into my pillow, I lie on my bed in shame. I fled the park as soon as I dropped my revelation. The children heard what I said– all were shocked but Spyder. My sister tried to catch up with me as I ran back to Restraint. Only a handful of people know about my wife. I couldn't stop it from happening and I don't want to remember. But as I lie on my bed, mortified beyond words, the memories assault me.

"My son arrives," Tony announces proudly. The tone in his voice alerts me that I'm in trouble somehow– he never praises me with words, only actions.

With trepidation filling my veins, I enter our shared office and take my usual seat at our desk. I've been very good lately, not even registering men at all as I maintain a straight image. Pierre and Jon have left me alone for the most part, and I haven't seen or heard from my mother in months. Tony has been praising me, training me to be his second-in-command and his successor in the Marconi crime family, even though we both know Bruno is the man for the job. Bruno? He seems good with it, enforcing for the family, with his own office and staff, with thugs and whores at his disposal. Tony, Bruno, and I have been getting along famously, and I've been waiting for the bomb to drop.

Today is the day. I listen to my intuition, and it's screaming loudly. My life will change– for the good or bad, I have no idea.

I made Tony proud the day I was able to take a woman without complaint. It was nearly twenty years in the making, but his behavioral therapies finally paid off. I'm still gay; I just know better than to act on it with my grandfather and his henchman lurking in the shadows. Tony promises that after they find a new target, I can date men as long as I keep my future wife and children happy. But right now, Pierre would see me openly dating men as an invitation to abuse me and make Tony suffer.

I know there is a worse fate than fucking a woman. Tony does use my feminine features to his advantage. He whores me out to seduce clients. He doesn't truly whore me out, not like my mother. I merely entice and tease for him. I'm the bait for Tony's fish. While my mother used to only use me as bait, she placed me firmly on the hook for whatever she would catch. Which is why Tony won't allow me to see the woman anymore.

Tony is fine with Sandy being my only companion because I'm comfortable enough to touch and be touched by her after a friendship of sorts was established.

We've had a good year. Since I've proven my ability to maintain a heterosexual relationship, Tony has allowed me to run several of his businesses. I'm thankful for the work since my mother signed away more of my time. I'm not sure what she's going to do when Tony finally has complete and total control of my being, which means I'm no longer under her influence. As it stands now, I only have one day a month at KINK, where I spend time with Spyder and avoid my mother... or my mother avoids me.

The happier and more content I became around Tony, the more my mother would try to manipulate me, cry and act the victim. But when I didn't fall under her spell, she wrote me off entirely, saying Tony brainwashed me.

I'm sure Tony has brainwashed me to an extent. Tony offers me freedom as long as I toe the line. The only thing he wants out of me is a legacy, which every father wants of his family. A wife and children are a must, no matter my sexual persuasion, and I understand that. Other than that, he lets me roam free. I can feel that Tony genuinely loves me, whereas my mother only wants to control me, and that is not brainwashing but fact.

Entering our office, I gaze around the room as I walk to my side of the large desk. I settle into my seat with my father next to me. Pierre and a dark-haired man in his late thirties or early forties sit *together on the loveseat– Stanton Green, head of the Green family from Dominion, New York. Through ruthless efficiency, he took out his own father to reach the position he is in today, becoming one of the youngest heads of organized crime. At the time, he was barely eighteen. Stanton Green's reputation as a fair yet firm man precedes him. He's a good criminal.*

Caleb Green Sr. was of the ilk of Pierre Fontaine and Jon Wilson– friends through amoral practices. Stanton had the balls my father lacks, executing his own father because he dared to touch his little brother. I've met the junior Caleb Green on a few occasions when I was very young. Levi and Caleb were joined at the hip– where one was, the other was surely to follow.

The hair on the back of my neck stands on end when I see the foldaway bed against the rear wall. My suspicions are founded when I spy the young woman sitting in the guest chair. I quickly look away, not wishing to remember her if something horrible is about to happen.

Tony slides a single sheet of official looking paper across the desk. He demands, "Sign this," knowing I'll do it without complaint.

I would worry, except I've signed contracts daily for months. I'm now the majority owner of all of Tony's businesses as well as Pierre's. Their combined criminal empire hinges on their sole male heir– me. I sign the paper Dalton Anthony Fontaine. The last piece my mother holds is my surname. When Anthony wins me fulltime, I will add Marconi on my name.

"Are you positive Dalton's proclivity won't get in the way?" Stanton asks my father, but not in a way to pass judgment. I have no idea what they're talking about, but pity is lacing Stanton's voice, along with a lot of fear and shame.

I don't dare gaze at anyone in the room, as I fear whatever expressions are on their faces. I should be annoyed how they're talking of me as if I'm not in the room. But I've been an inanimate object for two decades– it's nothing new. I am but a pawn in their life-sized game.

"I assure you it is a nonissue." Tony places a heavy palm on my shoulder to calm me. "While my son may be gay, he understands the loyalty needed to be a husband and father. I have trained him to take to a woman."

"Trained to take a woman?" Stanton's voice is filled with disgust. "Just let the boy go find another boy and be happy."

"Stan?" Tony sighs, leaning into me heavily. "I understand my son. But I'm in a difficult place, as you know," he says cryptically while his brown eyes glare daggers at Pierre. "The Marconi and Fontaine families only have Dalton to continue our bloodlines. Family loyalty supersedes happiness."

"That is no way to treat the boy." Stanton tries to defend me, and I decide the rumors are truth– there truly are good criminals in this world. "I can tell he won't turn violent. But they're young and should have the ability to fall in love."

"Amour?" Pierre snorts, like it's a foreign concept.

"Dalton's extracurricular activities are none of your concern." Tony directs at Stanton. "If he has difficulty with the consummation, I have someone who will guarantee results. I know the first time will be difficult for him because of who is in audience. But he will be fine every time thereafter."

"Fine," Stanton allows, sounding as if he's going to be sick. "I guess neither of us have a choice in this matter, and neither do our children."

"Aucun." Pierre gloats, a vile sickness warping his tone.

"Bianca, sign the paper," Stanton says to the young woman, and I get the gravity of the situation.

I follow Bianca with my gaze as she pads to the desk to sign her name with a flourish. She smiles bashfully at me, half of her smile *quirking up at the side. She's a tiny girl, which is oddly perfect for me since I'm just as small. She can't weigh more than a hundred pounds and she barely reaches five feet. Her warm chestnut hair and vibrant blue eyes are a contradiction, soothing yet exciting. I begin to worry as Bianca continues to look at me expectantly and doesn't leave my side of the desk.*

I look a question at my father. Tony sorts through his desk drawer, purposefully ignoring me. He smiles faintly when he finds our official stamp– albeit illegal– and presses it to the document the girl and I have signed.

"Bruno," Tony mutters into his Bluetooth. "I need this to be filed immediately."

I look around in confusion while Bruno hurries into the room and takes the paper. He cracks a rare smile my way, usually never showing any emotions when Pierre is in the room. "Less than five minutes and it will be official with the government." He rushes from our office.

Voice breaking slightly, Tony turns in my direction to gauge my reaction while speaking to the room. "Congratulations, Mr. and Mrs. Fontaine Marconi, may your marriage be fruitful."

Swallowing down the bile flowing into my throat, I stare at the side of my father's face, burning betrayal filling my eyes, along with the prickling of unshed tears.

"Oh, don't look at me that way, Dalton," Tony mutters, flabbergasted. "I would have told you, knowing you'd do it if I asked, but I wasn't allowed. So blame your bitch of a mother and her sociopath of a father. It was their idea, and don't think they didn't blackmail Stanton and me into playing their little game."

"Maître du Jeu est amusant? Non?" Pierre is glowing with evil intent. "Oui... pour moi."

"Masters of the game is fun for you but not for us?" I press my luck by talking back to Pierre. "What the hell, old man?"

"Ignore him– Pierre is baiting you." Tony reminds me. "Your grandfather tried one last time to get your mother to have another child with me, hoping for a boy. No doubt he wants another male heir, but also another plaything since you're now a grown man and difficult to control. But your mother said no. So they got together with their cronies, finding a compromise, drawing Stanton, me, and you and Bianca into it. So, instead of having children with her husband, your mother decided her grandchildren would work just as well as playthings."

I stare at my lap and wrench my fingers into knots, trying to contain my fury. I gasp as I come to terms with the direction my life has taken. My soul shatters from the very people who were supposed to protect me. I don't know how it could get any worse.

My own mother sells me time and time again. My grandfather allows his sycophant to rape me so he can get his jollies off while forcing my father to suffer. Now Stanton, who I know is a good guy, and his daughter are brought into our mess of a life.

"We just have one more issue to settle, and then we can get on with our lives. You must consummate your marriage with witnesses." Tony looks pointedly at the foldaway bed, refusing to meet my gaze.

"NO!" I stand up for myself for the first time in my life– another incidence twenty years in the making. On instinct, I pull my new wife behind me as I walk backward toward the door. I have lived through this shit, but it's doubtful Bianca has lived in depravity her entire life.

"Dalton, would you like to know what is next on my list?" Tony's calm voice stops me in my tracks, meaning his nuts are being held over the fire by Pierre, and I'm the one who will get burned. Tony's nuts can't make legal heirs with a woman who refuses. My nuts are his now.

"Your mother refuses to act as my wife. I have never hurt, nor harmed her. After your conception, she stayed at KINK and I stayed at Marconi, and we lived separate lives. I would have done just as you will do with your wife– take her on occasion and live my life the way I please. I would have had lovers and she could have had her own too. I just required children. Instead, I get a gay son who doesn't have my last name, and your mother births a bastard by supposedly stealing her student's sperm." Tony rolls his eyes and puts air quotes around the word 'supposedly' as he speaks. Yeah, I don't fucking believe her, either.

Olivia Fontaine locked Marcus Zeitler in a room for an entire year, torturing him, raping him, doing so until she conceived Spyder. I have no idea why, but I'm positive it was of Pierre's making. I was only five years old when it started, and even I understood what Marc's captivity meant. As the gatekeeper, Levi would sneak me into Marc's room to keep him company, where Marc made me promise to keep his child safe after it was born.

Spyder has gone unscathed, except for our mother's guilt tactics to make herself look like a perpetual victim.

"I'm not the bad guy here," Tony's voice interrupts my inner turmoil. *"Well, I am, but you know what I mean. You're under some fantasy that I forced your mother into my bed. She was the instigator– no more a virgin than I. Pierre came to my father, and our marriage was performed the same as yours just was. Our fathers wanted to solidify their familial ties. I did it for family loyalty, but would you like to know why your mother married me? What she got out of it?"*

I stare at Tony in shock. It's a rhetorical question so I don't answer.

"Olivia wanted the deed to KINK. She sold herself so Pierre would sign it over to her. She willingly participated in your conception– many times. When she found my currency was you and any other children we would create together, she exploited it. I

wanted children and she refused. And do you know who still has the deed to KINK?"

Yet another rhetorical question, because Pierre unwittingly signed it over to me last week. For a controlling man, he's so intent on causing pain, he doesn't believe we'd ever betray him in business. For the past month, he's been legally signing all of his business holdings and properties over into my name.

"Olivia never got her precious KINK, but she did get two more children that she should have put first. Now, Dalton, I didn't want to force women on you, but I needed you to be able to fuck your wife. Our bloodline dies out with you. Everything generations of Marconi's have worked for will be for naught if you don't create the next generation. Blame your fucking mother!" Tony screams as his fists pound our desk.

"I don't like hurting you, but Pierre will make me. So don't make me enact what is to come next if you don't do this." Head bowed, Tony sobs into his hands. "Please, just consummate your marriage. It won't hurt– I promise. Bianca is an innocent girl who has always known her place in the hierarchy. She will submit for you– give you a semblance of control. Most important is how she is willing."

"I don't know if I can do it," I say of the small woman cowering behind me. She's pressed to my back with her tiny fist holding my shirt.

"You have no choice, son. Your mother always has a choice, but she will choose wrong. Every. Fucking. Time." Tony's hand pounds the desk in time with his words. "I promise to make it easy on you. If you can't perform, I have a solution. But you will perform for your sister's sake."

Freezing in terror, I know Tony won't harm Spyder, even with her paternity, but Pierre has no reservations on harming his own flesh and blood. "What does Spyder have to do with this?"

"Choices: choose A, receive B. Choose C, receive D." Tony reminds me how every choice as an obscure yet completely unknown consequence brought down by Pierre. *"Your mother no longer has any control over you. Marconi is your surname at last,"* he whispers in relief. *"Plus, now that you're a married man and business owner, it's ridiculous that we keep fighting over you. Olivia offered me your sister for KINK. Spyder's fourteen. I'm a sick bastard, but not that fucking sick. If I take her, I'm shipping her to Dominion to her father."*

"Then take her!" I shout, wanting just that.

"Look at your sadistic grandfather— he's practically salivating at the thought because that's a choice with a horrific consequence. Do you know why that bastard is always here? It's not my doing— it's hers."

"I know that," I mutter in defeat.

"Please, Dalton." Tony closes his eyes, as if in pain. *"Just fuck your wife. Knock her up. It's either that, or your mother is giving me your baby sister. While it sounds like a good idea, it's not."*

"You don't have to do what Pierre tells you to do!" My defiant nature is coming online at last. *"Kick him the fuck out of our property!"* Turning to my lifelong antagonizer, *"GO!"*

"Oh, but I do." Tony slumps forward at his desk, completely and utterly defeated. *"There are worse fates than death, my son. Sometimes I long for the sweet relief."*

"You know what she's trying to do to us, right?" I ask my father. *"Master is trying to force me to save Spyder from Pierre."*

"Yes, it's only a matter of time. Olivia believes herself to be a better puppet master than he is."

My grandfather smirks at us, knowing full and well that we're speaking of his demise. Pierre pushes our buttons, Master pushes our buttons, both of them just begging for us to murder Pierre. It's too bad he's too physically fit to keel over from a heart attack.

"Fine," I bite out, furious. "Don't watch– that's disgusting!"

"I don't plan on it," Tony assures me. "Nor does Stanton. It was a requirement of the contract, making sure you didn't just say you did. Best of luck getting Pierre to look away after I had to negotiate for two days straight to keep Jon out of the room... and you don't want to know what I had to do to ensure that."

Tony looks at some papers on his desk, and Stanton joins him in my seat. I recognize the paperwork. It's the contracts for businesses in the New York area. My marriage just became a business merger. I stare down Pierre and he smirks at me. Nothing will make him look away.

I walk the green mile with my bride holding the back of my shirt. I pull the foldaway from the wall and sit with my back to the room and my knees at the wall. Bianca sits next to me.

"You okay with this?" I hold Bianca's blue gaze and try to get her to submit. It will be easier on her if she bends to my will. I wish I had someone to bend mine.

I decide on the fast approach. Even after countless encounters with Sandy over the years, I can't do foreplay with a woman. I kiss Bianca softly as I run my fingertips up her thigh. I'm thankful that she wore a dress. It will cover what we need to do.

Bianca's legs part as my fingertips skim higher up her thigh. Mind completely blanking, I pretend my body parts are no longer attached to me. I should chat Bianca up, maybe get to know her– that's what my conscience demands, but I don't have the luxury of time, and I never want Pierre to witness something as intimate as a conversation.

Sex is just fucking– a biological need no different than eating or taking a shit. But our words and the connections they create are personal.

I work my fingers under the edge of Bianca's panties and try to make her comfortable with my touch. She moans softly against my mouth. We're no longer kissing, just resting our lips against each other.

Bianca's hand rubs at my groin through my pants as I swirl my fingertips around her clit. She's silky smooth and highly responsive to my touch. I slip a fingertip inside her and groan– not in pleasure– frustration.

"You're legal, right?" My father managed to find me a damn virgin. It wouldn't surprise me if the lord of the underworld wed me to a child-bride, thinking it would be a treat to give me a virgin.

"I'm eighteen," Bianca murmurs shyly.

I resume kissing her and fondling her gently. I try to get into the mood as her hand rubs me just the way I prefer. It isn't having the desired effect since I can feel the pervert glaring intensely at our backs. I think if Pierre wasn't in the room, I would enjoy my wife's tentative touch. She's mine now, and I accept that as fact. I like the idea of giving her pleasure by meeting her needs. I can tell Bianca actually desires me. The feeling mentally turns me on, but Pierre's presence is keeping my dick soft.

Extremely responsive, Bianca climaxes quietly as I touch her. I thought I would be serviceable before she found her release. It makes me feel even more frustrated, which makes it next to impossible to get a hard-on.

"Son?" Tony calls out, but I can tell by the tone of his voice he's not looking at me.

"It's Pierre," I mutter my excuse over my shoulder. "I'd have no issue if I didn't feel him staring at us."

"Je vais appeler Jon," Pierre announces with a wicked gleam in his eye.

"No!" I yell in fright, not wanting Jon anywhere near my wife.

"I'm sorry, Dalton." Tony looks haggard, even more defeated than moments ago. "It was part of the bargain. Jon has what will help you. If you hadn't needed the help, Jon would have stayed in Bruno's office."

"I swear, by everything I hold dear," Stanton directs at Pierre. "If Jon so much as gets within touching distance of my daughter, I will have Bianca's sister execute you and anyone who has ever aided you. Don't doubt Faith's capacity to dole out justice."

"Vous ne disposez pas de l'autorité." Pierre murmurs in rapid French, sounding petrified for the first time in his life.

"I don't need anyone's permission," Stanton reminds Pierre of who he is. "Levi will hold you down while Faith cuts off your dick and shoves it down your throat– you'll choke to death on the very piece of meat you used against my brother."

"Mon Dieu!" breathlessly rushes out past my lips. I look to my wife, finding her a grinning, bloodthirsty little creature who apparently hates my grandfather more than I do.

"My father is dead– only you and Jon are left of the original old boys club of molesters and rapists. I killed one of three, it won't be difficult for me to finish what I started."

"Maître du Jeu vous exécuter." Pierre warns Stanton he would be executed too.

"Do I look like I care?" Stanton glares at Pierre. "The only reason I agreed to this farce of a marriage is because Levi promised me Dalton would be kind to Bianca. I didn't want her to go through what her mother has had to endure when one of you assholes decided you wanted a Meyers child in your bloodline."

"Peu importe," Pierre grumbles like a spoiled teenager. A moment later, he's chirping into his cellphone.

Jon walks in, and my world falls from beneath my feet. I stifle my cry of alarm, clutching my wife to my side.

"Jon, don't torture us anymore than we already have been." Tony's robust face is drawn gaunt and he looks exhausted. "Just sit next to your cohort. Sebastian, please service your master."

Sebastian walks over to me and slides down the wall to kneel at my feet. His hands reach for the fly of my pants and I grab his wrist.

"No," I shake my head in denial. "You will never touch me like this."

Sebastian shows a rare burst of dominance. He pulls the collar of my shirt until we are face-to-face, and growls at me. "You have to do this. I can't tell you what comes next if you don't. Just let me help you to finish this." He hisses furiously into my stunned face.

I resign myself to my fate, mind reeling and heart breaking. I pull Bianca back to me and kiss her softly. I pull her panties off her and work two fingers inside her in preparation. I don't want to hurt her because I'm large and not what a virgin needs. I know Sandy loves what I can offer, but she's a seasoned whore.

I've been whored out just for my cock. I show them the goods, promising they will have the pleasure after they sign whatever contract Tony sent me with. After the papers are signed, I don't allow them to touch me thanks to Bruno as my backup. It works as punishment, too. Tony has me enter the room aroused and the accused male offers all their information. Tony offers more protection than my mother. She whores me out at KINK. Men and women alike pay top dollar to suck me off.

I've never had a true consensual sexual experience– and that's not about to change tonight, either.

"Your wife is beautiful," Sebby murmurs, distracting me from his fingers unzipping my fly. "What's her name?"

"Bianca," I mutter fondly. I already feel attached to Bianca as I do Sebastian. Not as a wife– as someone who needs to be taken care of. I'm just wondering when someone will take care of me instead of using me as a playtoy.

Stomach muscles bunching, I hiss at the first sexual contact I've ever had with Sebastian. Hot mouth wrapped around my cock, I can't enjoy it because he doesn't want to do it. We have kissed that first time, and I've touched him, but never direct contact.

Ignoring the sensation of my body betraying me, I pull my wife closer, fitting our mouths together. Unbidden, I moan as Sebastian's mouth smooths over the head of my cock. I nearly come when he rolls his eyes up and looks at me through the lace of his lashes. He looks at me with desire, and it simultaneously confuses me and turns me on. His gaze holds a wild, almost hysterical edge. He's desperate for this to work, and I don't understand why.

Eyes riveted to the sight of Sebby's pink lips pulling taut over my cock, my innocent wife surprises me. She demands my attention, already showing a jealous, possessive edge. Body empty and hungry to be filled, she takes three of my fingers as she watches Sebastian service me.

"Thank you– we're both ready." Voice slurred from shock, I order Sebastian to stop. Surprisingly he ignores me, refusing to release my cock as he stares at my wife. With a rough yank, I pull his curls until he releases his mouth from my cock.

I draw Bianca to the floor between the wall and the bed. I use the bed for cover, ensuring no one in the room except for Sebastian can see us. Sebastian sits on the bed, his body blocking us further.

I try to be as gentle as possible as I consummate my marriage to my wife. I slowly enter her and wait for her to accept my girth before pushing further in. She releases a raspy gasp and whimpers, and I can tell it isn't from pain. I twine our fingers above her head and do my duty.

"I need you to scrunch up in this corner and stay safe." I whisper in her ear after we're finished. "Can you do that for me?" Bianca nods her head yes in agreement, flashing me the trust in her big blue eyes.

Righting myself, I tuck my spent cock back into my pants. I notice Stanton Green did not stay for the entire show, and it makes me respect the man that much more. But it terrifies me for another reason, because life as I knew it is about to end.

Moving onto plan B. "In a few minutes, Sebastian is going to take you to a man who will keep you safe. I need you to trust him as you would trust your own father. His name is Devlin Conrick, and he looks scary big, but I promise you he will protect you. He's six and a half feet tall, black as midnight, and completely bald. If that isn't a good enough description, then look for his eyes. They are so pale blue they look white. You will listen to everything he says and obey him until I come back for you."

"What are you going to do?" Bianca's fingers tighten in my shirt, trying to keep me with her.

"I refuse to live this way any longer, and I will never allow anyone to treat you like a pawn in a game. What I'm about to do is for our future, so we may coexist in peace."

I cup the side of Bianca's face and take a long, last look at my wife. I may not live to see her innocent face again, but I'll always make sure she stays innocent. Then I flick my gaze to Sebastian, whose jaw is clenching tighter and tighter, teeth grinding.

"I'll always protect you," I vow. "I always have, and I always will."

The chiming of my cellphone draws me from reliving the memory. I'm so thankful that it broke me from my reverie before I got to the bloody finale.

Reaching over to my small nightstand, I pluck my cellphone up on autopilot. "Dalton," I mutter into the phone.

"Hi…" Bianca's voice is weary, hesitant.

"How come you didn't tell me? We talked several times a day, and not once did you tell me you were coming. Then after I saw you in the meeting room when Devlin arrived at Restraint, you haven't talked to me since, ignoring my phone calls, texts, and emails. Then I had to run after you at Dexter and Monica's wedding, but you avoided me. Where the hell are you, and why are you dodging me?"

"What do you think, Dalton?" Bianca sounds exasperated. "Olivia forbade it. I'm calling you against her wishes."

"As if you've ever obeyed anyone in any way. So why now?" I accuse. "I find your timing suspect."

"Oh, you mean because you were seen cuddled up with the middle Daniel Whittenhower in the park this afternoon?"

"Yeah, exactly," I mutter, suddenly furious. "I'm sick the fuck of all of you playing tug-of-war with me like I'm just an object. Be jealous all you want, and don't deny that's why you called an hour after I saw Whitt."

"No need for me to deny it," Bianca admits freely.

"I've never denied you a lover, Bianca." I struggle to sit upright, my rib protesting. But I'm so furious I don't give a shit. "Don't act like my mother."

"Jesus!" Bianca hisses, pained. "You sure do know how to stab a girl where it hurts, you motherfucker!"

"I don't want to fight with you, but I also don't want you dictating to me like Master does."

"Stop calling Olivia master," Bianca offers up a solution. "Problem solved. Never– I mean *never* –accuse me of acting like Olivia Fontaine. My issue isn't just with you seeing Daniel, okay? There's more to it."

"Like what?"

"Not my secrets to tell. But I am jealous because I can tell this time is different. Your attitude has changed. I'm happy about it, but at the same time I'm sad. I know I'm going to lose you– I can feel it."

"Bianca," I sigh my wife's name. "I love you, but I've never lied about being gay. We haven't had sex since the first few months of our marriage, when I decided I didn't want to bring a kid into this demonic circus we call a life."

"I know– it's just." Bianca pauses so long I have to look at my cellphone to make sure she didn't hang up. Then she whispers so lightly, "You've never been with a guy, Dalton, that's why it's different."

"Whitt doesn't like me like that," I mutter, heart beating out of control. "I'm not saying I wish it was or wasn't the case," I tack on to save face.

Bianca's strangled laughter flows through the phone, reverberating in my ear. "You know it's Whitt who's showing up to your apartment tonight, right? I overheard Devlin setting up the meeting with him."

"Thanks for being a jealous cunt and ruining that for me," I snarl, always having fought with Bianca like she was my little sister. She and I usually get along, having a lot of mafia business to discuss. But when it comes to our personal shit, we go for the throat. Tone filled with sarcasm, "You act nothing like your mother-in-law."

"You cocksucker!" she shouts, hurting my ear. "I'm your wife, and Pretty Boy Whittenhower is arranging midnight dates with my husband, and I'm the cunt?"

"How many lovers have you had since we were together, Bianca? I've never asked, and I never will. Nor will I tell you not to see anyone."

"That's the problem! Maybe I want you to give two shits about what I'm doing. Maybe I want you to be jealous!"

"What?" I gasp, confused and shocked. "I respect you, that's why I don't ask. We might not have sex, but I've always put your needs before my own. I've flown to Vegas to watch you perform, risking the chance of being exposed for who I am. I even flew up to New York City to watch you three months ago. I've left you to pursue your dancing career."

"Maybe that's not what I want." Even over the phone, I can hear Bianca pout.

"Don't make me out to be the bad guy because I didn't want to knock you up and play the doting husband. Stanton knew I was gay. Tony knew I was gay. You knew I was gay. So don't get possessive, jealous, and butt hurt because I can't fall in love with you."

"Have a good time tonight, Dalton!" Bianca hangs up on me, solidifying why I'm a gay man. I pity straight men for having to put up with the mind games, manipulations, and irrational behavior of the fairer sex.

Chapter Thirteen

It was Master's idea for me to be an asshole to the members of Restraint. I was to collect their secrets and deliver them to her... after my mind's walk down memory lane, I decide I can't trust the woman who gave me life.

Don't trust Olivia Fontaine– cut the cord. I've heard this from countless sources: Marcus, Devlin, Levi, Bianca, even Whitt this afternoon. They've all said there were people I could count on, and it's time I trust that as fact. It's also time for me to make a real difference, to put myself first, and to count on some people.

It never mattered how badly I treated the members of Restraint, they would always treat me with respect. After I was strung up on the rack and beaten, each and every member came to see me.

It's time I count on them in my quest for answers, and not the answers my master seeks.

The third piece of advice I received was given by Devlin. Whoever the leak is, they're most likely doing it to save their own ass. Maybe if we can prove we can protect them, they will help us instead.

I hope I didn't make a mistake, but I'm going with my gut.

"Dexter, welcome!" I show my guest in and offer him a seat at the table. I even pulled out a package of cookies Levi stocked in my small cupboard. I don't have any coffee, so I hope he doesn't mind energy drinks.

Dexter sits at my dinette set while shaking his head in utter disbelief. "It's like night and day. You're creeping my ass out. I like this you– it's just that I'm so used to..." Dexter moves his hands around and pulls an indescribable face at me.

"In almost four years, I've only seen this me when I shower." I go for broke, being totally honest, no matter how uncomfortable it may be. "Looking into the mirror isn't exactly fun for me."

"I'll bet. Are you going to stay like this? I saw you come up here without your disguise." Dexter takes a tentative sip of the yellow liquid, smiles, and then gulps down the rest when he realizes it's tasty.

Yeah, what dominant doesn't like caffeine running in their veins?

"The people who know can know. Since I've had hits placed on my life, I have to be Thompson. If I knew for sure no one was after me anymore, I'd just be me. Stanton Green is making sure that the criminal element stays away, but he's not infallible. I really don't want to be gunned down in the middle of the dungeon. When those guys strung me up that's all I could think. I thought my time was up."

Dexter looks down into his empty mug and I can tell by the expression on his face that he knows all there is to know about me–everything.

No doubt Devlin and Marcus have finally decided to let Dexter in.

"I have a few apologies to make, and a few thanks to give." My face burns bright in mortification. "I want to thank you for rescuing me in the dungeon. I know you didn't want to, but I trusted that your nature would make you stop them from hurting me. I also want to apologize for what I did to Monica. I would like to apologize to her face, if that wouldn't upset you."

"I've forgiven you for Monica," Dexter mutters in a gruff voice. "I'll never be able to forget, but that's not because of you. I failed Monica when she needed me the most by turning a blind eye to her problems, which allowed you to prey on her."

"It doesn't work that way, Dexter." My eyes dart away, unable to look at him while I speak. "Those nearest and dearest, we don't want to hurt them with tough love." My mind instantly goes to my mother and Bianca. "I read a lot, and most of the characters never tell their friends the truth, even when asked, because they don't want to hurt them. I'm guessing you didn't want to deal with Monica's anorexia because that would make the problem real."

"You read a lot?" Dexter chuckles deep and long. "That's precious... It's no wonder, then. When Marcus and I were having a chat with Devlin about you, we had to do so at the Brownstone. Your buddies, Alex and Jamie, are your biggest fans."

Blushing like a sonofabitch, "Jamie's cool."

"I think so, too." It's Dexter's turn to blush, eyes seeking the book on my nightstand. "You're right about why I turned a blind eye to the issue. I thought I could fix Monica with love and attention without actually healing her. So it left her wounded and vulnerable."

"I still feel sick about it." Shame burns brightly in me, even after all the punishments I've received lately. "I don't blame you for kicking my ass. I'd let you do it again if it'd make you feel better." I offer, causing Dexter to laugh while I rub my side.

"Don't you mean make *you* feel better?" Dexter murmurs knowingly. "I'm a sadist, kid. When you were in disguise, it was hard for me to see, but I still recognized it. Your masochism is shining so brightly right now, I'm being blinded by it."

"Shit." I rub at the nape of my neck with my palm, mopping up the sweat that's beading there.

"Who's been working you?" Dexter hitches an eyebrow in my direction. "A masochist as hungry for pain as you are can't go long without."

"I self-punish." Pouting, I remember my newfound brother taking issue with that. "I did self-punish, but I was told to behave myself."

"*Did*? Explain," Dexter orders.

"I was told to knock my shit off because I cut myself pretty badly, then asked to be caned even with a broken rib. It was my bottom, I guess. I was told I'm going to be exercised to death."

"Ah, Gunner?" Dexter grins across the table at me, looking so unguarded and like Marcus it's uncanny. "Gunner was tailing Toby and me this morning as our security detail during our daily jog. He decided to run with us instead, and the bastard never shut up about fitness. God–" Dexter rubs his thigh. "He murdered my ass on the pavement. So how did you do it before?"

"Cutting. Caning my thighs. Starvation. Devlin would take care of it when he'd visit. But last night was the first time since he arrived for good in Dominion. I feel sick that I made him do it, that I made him feel sick because he had to do it. Before… before I didn't need to do anything because I was punished on a daily basis."

Dexter stares at me for a long time, and I'm now positive he knows everything Devlin does– everything Marcus knows. It helps me relax. Unlike my mother, Devlin has never made a poor choice. If he trusts Dexter, I have to, too.

"I called you over for three reasons. I wanted to apologize, I want to talk about Spyder, and I need your help. So… Spyder. I will make nice with you for her sake and because I think you're a really good person, and those are a rare find. I want Spyder to have a whole family, but I'll need a strong ally to help me against my mother. I love her, but I hate her. But one thing I know for sure, Olivia Fontaine is the worst mother in all of creation."

"Marc, Devlin, and I have had our heads together on this. Spyder's almost eighteen. So, we either have to wait, or get your mom to agree to visitation."

The word visitation has bile rising in my throat. "Olivia Fontaine does not share," I utter in a cold voice. "There will be no allotment for visitation made if it doesn't suit an agenda."

"We sat down with Olivia while you were at the park. It was three against one, and she still wouldn't give in. Going as far as to say she'd hide Spyder."

"She'd kill Spyder if she knew it would hurt Marc," I warn. "But unlike me, Spyder's wilder, less able to be manipulated, and doesn't have a Pierre and Jon playing games with her as the token."

"Jesus." Dexter shudders, no doubt remembering my confession of murder during show-and-tell. "Marcus wants Spyder living at Shadow Haven and graduating from Hillbrook. He wants his daughter to be raised in the house with the rest of his family."

"I think it would be best for Spyder to live with them. She's already bonding with Ava, and Katya seems like a grounding force. Vegas isn't where she needs to be. She lived above Kink. It's not like Dominion and Restraint at all. Kink is a brothel, and I don't want my sister to ever go back there."

"I know a lot about you, Dalton." Dexter flashes me a look filled with sympathy that is blessedly devoid of pity. "But I have a feeling that I don't know all that's important. You need to talk with Marc and tell him what put that wounded look into your eyes. You really are still a kid, but more so in some ways. You need a support system, and you can trust Marcus. He will take care of you and Spyder, as if you were both his children. I promise you this," he vows.

"Divided loyalties at the moment," I murmur in explanation. "That might not always be the case. But right now, I have to pack my baggage with one parent before I take on another one."

Dexter smiles sadly at me, understanding everything I left unsaid.

"I need your help," I say the unthinkable, and instead of betrayal I feel relief. "Master sent me here to keep an eye on Marcus, wanting to know all I could find out, but I kept most to myself. Then when you started having problems at Restraint, she wanted me to figure out who and who. Then after the *Mistress & Master of Restraint* book was released, she wanted me to figure out who was leaking information to Adelaide Whittenhower. She made me act like the asshole, saying that would draw the attention of Adelaide to be welcomed into the fold."

"I know, Dalton," Dexter murmurs, face etched with sadness.

"But I can't do it anymore," I practically whine, slumping down to the tabletop. "I want to be me. I want to walk in the sunshine without a disguise. I don't want to be an asshole, baiting those I want to befriend. I don't want to have to fuck people in the dungeon so they won't look at me like I'm a weirdo. I don't want to feel the need to cut my arm thirty plus times and feel no relief. But I will find out who is the leak, just not on Olivia Fontaine's terms. I want to help because the mole is probably in a situation that is painful. Whatever I find, I'll tell you or Marcus, and I'll let you tell Devlin. Because I don't trust my mother anymore, and I don't know if Devlin can be trusted because he's in love with her."

"Good!" Dexter's voice holds a wealth of relief. Lips curved, he smiles at me and I can't figure out why. "I'll agree, but on one condition."

"Name it," I agree before I hear it. "Restraint has shown me more respect than I've ever gotten in my life. No matter how heinous I was, you all still welcomed me. I'll do anything to get our doors open again."

"Trust no one else. It's not that they are the enemy. It's just that someone may overhear, or they may say something unwittingly. Understood?"

"Yeah, um… what about Queen? Is she helping you? Because Queen said she was taking me off the bench and welcome to the game." My eyebrows knit together in confusion. I have no idea what's going on with her.

Dexter huffs a laugh and grips his belly. I watch in amusement as he laughs his ass off. "Is that why you fucked her?" He laughs some more. "Because I'm pretty sure she was sending a message to a few people with that little stunt." He keeps laughing. "Had to get them off their asses, she did."

"What?"

"Nothing… it's nothing." Dexter wipes his eyes with the back of his hand. "Queen's fantastic. Yeah, tell her anything you want. Marc's been going nuts since last night. He's finally met his match."

"I don't know what the fuck you're talking about," I mumble.

"I know, that's what makes it so hilarious." Dexter snorts like a pig, choking on his laughter. I'd be angry because I'm the brunt of some inside joke, but seeing Dexter so amused is amusing in and of itself. "Tell Queen anything, and she'll tell Marc after you do."

"So I can't trust her?" I ask in confusion.

"That's not what I meant. Queen's pissed that her dungeon isn't open for business. She's been running Restraint and the dungeon for us for years. She's been helping you more than you realize." He smirks at me.

"Fuck you, Dexter!" I growl a sound of pure frustration. "Quit talking in riddles."

"Jesus, make sure you growl for your secret admirer tonight. It sounds hotter than hell in a French accent," he teases.

"Asshole," I grumble, but I smirk anyway. "Does everyone know about Whitt showing up tonight?"

"Pretty much." Dexter's grin gets bigger.

"Never mind that– did you learn anything about those assholes who strung me up in the dungeon? Why were they trying to harm Restraint?"

Dexter's amusement dries up in an instant, then the pity pops out. "I can't tell you much because you're not ready to hear it. Hell, Marc didn't tell Devlin until after the custody meeting with your mother earlier today. Devlin went on a rampage after he heard... and Marcus thinks he's everyone's dad, so you have two of them on the warpath."

"What made them so mad?"

"Devlin was upset after punishing you, so he went to Marc to try to figure out a way to stop Olivia from yanking your leash. Marcus thought it was time to spill the beans. So he finally told me what's been going on at the same time. Shocked is an understatement."

Suddenly nervous, my body quivers with panic. "What? How can I help if I don't have a fucking clue?"

"You're not ready to hear it yet– that came from Ezra, by the way, and Dr. Lunatic knows his shit. I guess the assholes were more than happy to tell Wil and Gunner anything they wanted to know." Dexter shudders, and I realize he knows more than he's letting on.

"Gunner and Wil are great guys– more honorable than anyone you'll ever meet. And Stanton Green? I think if you'd meet him, you and he would have a lot in common. So don't get upset when a mob enforcer uses unconventional means to extract information."

"I just don't want to know." Looking spooked, Dexter mumbles something about a van. "They didn't randomly choose a master after they incited the riot. They were specifically told to target and harm you. In fact, they were told to create a distraction in the club to clear out the dungeon. They were supposed to kill you and make it look like an accident. The fallout would have made Restraint no more and you would have been dead– a two-for-one special."

Dexter calmly delivers the news how I was supposed to die weeks ago. I sit in stunned silence and think about how I've lived my life. I was given a few extra weeks of life, and all I did in that time was be miserable and make those around me even more miserable.

Hands clenched into fists against the tabletop, "The cartels?" I murmur in acceptance.

"No, Dalton. You're safe from them. Your father-in-law really is protecting you. Your guy, Bruno? He's your big brother, right? He's protecting you, too. Devlin swears up and down that the mafia families across this country see you as a goddamn hero. They're all pitching in to figure out who the hell is putting hits on your life. No one dares to collect on the hit, fearing they'll never survive to spend their reward."

"That's so–" the warmth blooming in my chest feels so foreign I almost choke on it.

"You're not ready to know who wants you to die, or why," Dexter says ominously with pity so thick his words nearly slur.

"Does Devlin know?"

"Yeah, when we told Dev, he called all of your contacts until he figured out the why. I'm sorry," Dexter says out of a need to comfort, but it seems to hurt more than it helps.

"I need to be alone," I mumble, but it's laced with demand.

"I understand," Dexter says quietly, rising to his feet. "I think you know who– I can tell. You need to talk to Marcus soon. It can wait for tonight, because you need to enjoy your date."

"Why is everyone making such a big deal out of this?" I ask myself more so than Dexter.

"We've known Pretty Boy since he was born, Dalton. All of us cherish that kid like we're his dad. Just hang out with him, where there's no BDSM politics or a dungeon– be young for five minutes and pretend the world isn't going to burn if you take some time for yourself."

"I'm so confused." Slumping forward with my cheek pressed to the tabletop, I sigh heavily.

"You'll be pleasantly surprised. Get your rocks off tonight. For *real* this time. You fucking need it," Dexter stresses. "Later– you know where to find me," he says in parting, leaving me to my depressive musings and unexplainable excitement.

Chapter Fourteen

I feel exposed sitting on the edge of my bed with a sleep mask covering my eyes and my front door cracked to allow my secret admirer entrance. I know it's Daniel Whittenhower II, so I don't understand the need to cover my sight. Devlin made it a point to say it wasn't about sex. Whitt is a conundrum– he acts one way, and then another. It's making my head spin in confusion and need.

I'm in a dark mood after reliving my past and speaking with Bianca and Dexter. To the point I actually want to be alone and just stew in misery.

A warm hand on my cheek makes me flinch. I was so caught up in my inner miseries that I didn't hear my visitor arrive. Thank God my enemies didn't sneak in the door– I'd be a dead man right now.

Touch fleeting, the handprint is still burning me with its warmth. I look up and silently swear because the mask impedes my vision. I receive a playful pinch to the tip of my nose, and then movement in the air flutters along my cheeks.

The click of my deadbolt sliding into place is slightly unnerving. Either we're locking people out, or me in– neither is a comforting thought.

"Why the mask?" I ask my visitor.

The hand is back– resting lightly on my shoulder this time.

"You won't speak with me?" I mumble, laughter infusing my voice.

I receive two squeezes on my shoulder.

"Let me guess– two for yes, one for no," I mutter sarcastically.

Two more squeezes and I laugh from the ridiculousness of the situation.

"This isn't your first time playing the guessing game. I can tell. I know exactly who you are. It's like someone got on a hotline after seeing us in the park together today. Everyone I've spoken with has told me to enjoy our date. So you don't have to hide from me." I pause, waiting for Whitt to speak to me. "Why are you hiding?" I coax him.

Breath caresses my ear as if he's tempted to speak. My body goes bowstring tight. The darkness creates an intimacy I've never encountered. My hands flex on my thighs with the need to touch him. I instinctively know that I'm not allowed until he offers. It makes the need that much stronger. I lean closer and I barely resist the urge to kiss him.

"I want you," I reluctantly admit, and I hear a hitch in his breathing.

Whitt continues to draw in heavy breaths next to my ear as if he's as affected by me as I am of him. It ramps up my need to touch him. I twist my fingers in the covers on my bed, using it to anchor me as I wait for permission to touch him in return.

The hot breath abruptly stops– Whitt holds his breath for a moment and lets it out in a great gust as he steps away from me. He tugs my hand for me to stand before him. His fingers grip the edge of my shirt and I protest.

"No, not even my wife has seen my bare skin. If you want to see me, then I have to see you." He makes a deep sound of frustration from his chest, one I'm familiar with, and I chuckle at the absurdity.

Whitt's demanding fingertips return– one hand pulls down my thermal shirt, promising it will stay, and the other tugs up on my t-shirt, signaling it has to go.

"I bet you're fabulous at charades," I tease Whitt, and his breathing picks up like he's trying hard not to laugh out loud.

I allow Whitt to remove my t-shirt. I always wear two shirts– the bottom one always has long sleeves to hide my marks. But never out of shame, simply because I don't feel the need to be gawked at, or have to explain them to everyone.

Next Whitt tugs on my pants. "Bizarre," flows from my lips, as I allow him to remove my jeans. I have nothing to hide on the lower part of my body that Whitt hasn't already snuck a peek or ten at while we were playing with Kristal. I hold the waistband of my boxers. He can see the show, but not the *whole* show. Yet.

I stand before Whitt, half dressed in the bright of my apartment. I can't see him, but he can see all of me with perfect clarity. Warmth spreads throughout my body. So far everything with this man has been a new experience. I've never had a lover. It was always force, then acceptance, and finally, it was duty. This feels different. A buzz radiates inside my veins, a new sense of life.

This is the first time I've truly wanted someone, and a small part of me that has never stopped hoping, no matter what I've been through, believes the feeling is mutual with Whitt.

"I want to see you, too," I flirt with Whitt, placing just enough pleading into my voice to catch his breath. The other half of my switch personality comes to the fore. A dominant can be commanding and comforting. A submissive has the need to please and will use anything in their vast repertoire to do so. A true submissive has an arsenal of seductions to make their master proud. I may not have the demeanor or charm of Sebastian, but I can seduce like a pro. Tony made sure I was proficient and I learned a lot from Sandy, but it was my mother who made sure I was schooled in the art.

"Do you like what you see?" I bow my head allowing my hair to cascade across my face, and then I tip my chin back up. It would have more of an impact if my eyes weren't covered. I would have looked at him beneath the lace of my lashes.

Whitt growls near my face, and a resulting smirk pulls at my lips. I know he knows I'm seducing him on purpose. Eventually he'll fuck up and speak. I could easily call him by name, but it'll mean more if he does it on his own. I want him to be so taken with me that he'll speak out by accident. I want to be the one who makes him lose control.

I hear the rustle of fabric, and my body ignites. My head snaps back up and I rapidly move it from side to side to pinpoint the sound. Nostrils flaring, I begin to inhale air at a fast rate. What will happen next? The suspense is killing me. We're seducing each other. We're both trying to get the other to say his name. I want to growl and make his frustrated noise, too.

With a heavy palm against my chest, Whitt pushes me toward the bed, and I take a clue and lie down. I hear his bare feet tap on my hardwood floor, first away and then back. He settles on the bed with me, mattress dipping beneath his heavier weight. Eager, I scoot over to give him some room. Deft fingertips pluck the mask from my face, leaving me to blink several times as I try to clear my vision.

"You turned the light off." My voice dips into a whine. "No fair."

The warmth and solid weight of his body drive me to a fevered pitch. I roll onto my side and face him. Just like earlier today in the park, I'm afflicted with the condition that has me curving into his body.

It's light enough in the room that I can make out his lanky shape, but no features. It doesn't matter anyway, since I know exactly what he looks like. His bare chest and arms glow bright white in the darkness– as do his thighs.

Whitt's only wearing a pair of boxers.

"What next?" I demand, voice gone husky with lust. "I want to talk to you. Are you trying to drive me mad?"

Whitt's hand slides up the side of my neck to cup my cheek. He holds me like that for several long minutes. I lay frozen beneath his touch, waiting in anticipation. My breathing accelerates and our chests touch with every inhalation.

Hesitantly, ever so slowly, Whitt leans into me. His breath caresses my flesh to fill my mouth. Hovering above my lips, it's my turn to make that notorious sound of frustration at the back of my throat. His fingers tighten on my face, completely immobilizing me. I so badly need to move that last inch to touch his lips with mine.

"Only my first kiss was with a boy," I admit, my whispered words more intimate in the darkness of my apartment. "It was a fleeting touch. I've never had the pleasure of it again. Are you worried?"

Whitt stays frozen– heart ceasing to beat, lungs not rising and falling. I can see the whites of his eyes glow in the darkness, reminding me of those paintings of spooked horses at the Rockwell Museum in nearby Corning, New York. Frightened eyes almost as large as the horse's face– instinctively knowing their doomed fate to fall off a cliff as their rider drives them forward to push the buffalo to their deaths.

Understanding dawns on me. "You've never kissed a guy before, have you?"

One of the fingers gripping my face breaks from formation to slide across my bottom lip, and that's answer enough.

"I'd like to tell you it's no different than kissing a girl… but, God, I hope it is." The need to connect with someone I'm attracted to is infused in my voice, sounding on the brink of starvation.

I can tell by the whites of his eyes that Whitt is staring at my lips. I can't take it anymore. I unearth a trick that Sandy taught me. I slowly lick my bottom lip, making sure to give a glimpse of tongue and to leave my lip saturated. I follow it up by biting my lip, leaving teeth indents behind. A rough gasp is torn from his throat, signaling I'm finally going to get what I want– a man to kiss me of his own volition. One I want badly.

Whitt leans forward, pressing his lips softly to mine. I don't nudge closer, allowing him to take what he wants. I soften my mouth and part my lips, becoming pliant for him. If all he wants is to brush his lips with mine, I'm fine with that. I will not take the lead.

I gasp loudly, the sound echoing around the room, when Whitt's tongue parts my lips with urgency, tip seeking mine. I throw away the notion of following his lead when his tongue twines with mine, rolling along my flesh. I moan, desperate to feel more of him, my fingers pull him closer. Wrapping my arms around his back, I knead his bare flesh, fingers sinking into firm muscles.

Man.

Whitt is all man. For the first time in my life, I'm lying in bed with a man not of my imagination. Not with a woman I was told to bed. Not with a wife I didn't want, but I did so out of duty.

I finally understand what it means to be innocent. Rough stubble scouring at my chin, with firm, demanding lips sucking at mine, and thick, strong fingertips taking what they want, and an insistent hard-on being pressed against my hip, I've never been happier to be a gay man in my entire life.

Sneaking, questing hands reach beneath the back of my shirt to touch me tenderly where previously all I've known was pain. The pleasure is agonizing in its exquisiteness. I allow Whitt to draw my shirt over my head, never once being naked with another human being. It's less than a second our lips are parted before we fuse them back together. As far as a real first kiss goes, I'd rank this as spectacular. It compares to nothing before it.

"Holy shit, you can kiss," I gasp out when Whitt finally lets me up for air. I take a huge gulp of air and move back in for more. I meld myself to his lips, pressing my bare chest to his, and run my hands down the back of his boxers all the while moaning in pleasure.

A heavy palm on my chest pushes me backward onto the mattress. Whitt rolls onto his back, gasping for air. I feel rejected for a split-second until I realize this is the most he's ever done with a guy. Maybe he was just curious and found it not to his liking. I try not to let it hurt me, but it does.

We stay like this for a long while– Whitt on his back, slowing his breathing back to normal, with me lying on my side, staring down at him with utter confusion.

Moving slowly, as if not to spook me, Whitt's warm hand returns to my cheek, slides down my throat, and finds the burn marks on my chest. I freeze as his smooth fingertip explores the ruination of my skin.

I gasp when Whitt takes my ruined left nipple into his mouth and sucks. Squirming on the bed, the sensation of a hot tongue lapping at my nearly numb nipple is inexplicable– it's almost like the nerve-endings are coming back online.

My fingertips curl, fisting the sheets, so I can't touch Whitt in a way that will make him push me away again. I recognize it was my hands groping his ass that had him pushing me away earlier. I will respect Whitt for wanting to explore this at a pace he's comfortable with.

Expert mouth working my chest, I cry out when the ache in my groin becomes unbearable. I thrust into the air and find no relief. He works his way across my chest, nibbling, licking, and sucking the scars. The need is so bad that my hand unlatches from the sheet to rub the heel of my palm on my aching cock.

Whitt moans his approval against my skin, and it leaves me gasping under his touch. Hand plunging into my boxers, I painfully fist myself, choking off all need for release. It hurts so fucking good.

Lost in pleasure, "Whitt," rolls out of my mouth before I can stop it. He nips my hip with his teeth in reply, tensing when he hears his name. I tense back, worrying that I just ruined the moment by pushing him with his identity. I don't breathe, or move, fearing he will stop and run out the door.

I need Whitt so badly I ache.

"Dalton," Whitt breathes just before he reclaims my mouth with his. The sound of his pleasant voice roughened with lust while saying my name has me moaning against his lips.

Whitt's fingertips pry mine away from my cock. The blood flows back in a torrent, pulling a cry of pain from my throat. I try to get my hand away from his so I can rub the pain away, but he tightens his fingers around mine, not allowing it. With fast movements, Whitt tugs my boxers down, yanking them off my legs. Then his hand is back, wrapping around my cock to soothe the pain away.

"Daniel," spills from my throat this time, and he doesn't hesitate.

Whitt wants to be called Daniel in bed. No different than my need to hear Dalton instead of Font. Nicknames are given to us by friends and family, and they have no place in something so intimate.

"Dalton," Whitt answers me, somehow reading my thoughts. Impatient, his hand starts to stroke and twist along my shaft– awkward and inexperienced.

Perfect.

I behave brazenly under Whitt's touch. My hips thrust into his hand, pulling my length through his fingertips in a slow slide, as I feed from his mouth. I want to touch him back so badly, but I'm not sure I'm welcome. It doesn't matter anyway, since one hand is trapped beneath his side and the other is in the tight grip of his fist.

My climax is barreling down on me, but then Whitt shoves my hand down his boxers, and my mind blanks to everything that isn't him. Fingertips curled around his length, I cry out in shock at the feel of him sliding against my palm– Hot. Hard. Silky smooth.

"Yours is the first I've ever touched," I whisper to Whitt, voice thick with lust and awe. Needing to be closer to him, to do something, I latch onto the side of his neck and suck. Hard. I'm rewarded with his favorite lubricant filling my hand. Unbidden, laughter bubbles up, as I remember our time in the dungeon.

"That's some good shit." Whitt laughs with me. "Let me have some of it." I rub my Whitt-moistened hand on my cock until it's slippery, and then I clutch him again.

"I love the sound of your laugh, Dalton. You're always so sad and miserable. I'd do anything to hear you laugh." He reclaims my lips before I can reply.

I could go hours with a woman– but with Whitt, in less than a minute I'm groaning my release. It's so powerful that I have to bite my lip and clench my jaw, or I'd scream to the heavens. But it's impossible to contain the erratic jerking of my hips and the writhing as my muscles quiver.

Whitt's more polite, just as I knew he would be. He moans softly into my ear as he floods my hand. I don't equate how loud he is to the amount of pleasure he feels. His body spasms every few seconds for at least a minute– quiet and deadly.

Whitt gives me a lingering kiss and pulls me tight against his chest. "You'll be my first everything," he whispers against my cheek.

"Are you gay?" spills out of my mouth before I can stop it. "I mean, I've seen you in the dungeon with the ladies– you enjoy it."

"I'm horny," Whitt mutters wryly, and it has me trying to pull away. The pain of rejection is injected into my veins, heart cracking when I thought it was incapable of breaking. "Whoa… Dalton, that's not what I meant. Take a breather, and then listen to me."

"You're either gay, or you aren't." I try to wrench out of his arms, but Whitt is stronger than me and refusing to let go. "It's black or white."

"I'm gay– my first memory is of me coming out." Arms squeezing me tighter, he forces me to settle against his chest. "I know very little of Kink, but I know it was your home. So imagine Restraint is my home, okay? I know you're imaginative."

"Okay." I allow Whitt's soothing voice to coax me. Losing the fight with myself, I seep into the heat of his skin and actually relax.

"I only had you wear the mask until I could turn out the lights, simply because this is so new to me that I wasn't sure I could do it, or say what I had to say, while looking in your eyes."

"That makes sense." Feeling stupid for lashing out, I snuggle closer, not realizing how badly I needed it. Getting off with someone I wanted was nice, but connecting with them is even better.

"I'm a Whittenhower– we're allowed to be gay but not act out on it. My whole world is working and Restraint. But Restraint isn't exactly teeming with gay guys."

"It's not?" My voice is light, teasing. "Could have fooled me. There's me, then Ezra, and Cort who seems to be in denial."

"Cort and Ez see me as family," Whitt mutters wryly. "While they might be into real incest, they aren't into pseudo-incest." I snort at the ridiculousness, but it's actually true. "So I know everyone– I love them. I care for them. They're my friends, and I enjoy their company. That was my horny comment. I'm not allowed to go out and date a dude, because what if he turns out to be after my money? God forbid he puts me into a book."

Getting a clue, "So you get off with your friends, because it's comfortable and they love you?"

"Exactly." Whitt seems happy that I understand his insanity. "I've only had penetrative sex with two women, both of which you've screwed too. The rest of the time I get my cock sucked. I love a good blowjob, and they know how to work it."

"I grew up in a brothel." Shudders wrack my body. "They really know how to give good head, and I still hated it."

"You're saying I'm not gay enough for you?" Whitt's voice drips with anger. "I was five when I came out to my family. How gay is that?"

"Very… wow," I murmur in awe. "Five? Really? It was just always understood with me. At one point, my father was fearful I was transgender. I put his fears to rest by saying I loved cock, including my own, but I wished everyone else would leave it alone."

"Shit, Dalton." Whitt squeezes me tighter. "The affluent are no different than the mafia. We have our patriarch, similar to the head of your family, but we're all actually blood-related instead of a family wrought through loyalty."

"Blood is not thicker than water, except in viscosity. Loyalty and a common enemy create a stronger bond."

"True– so true… The Whittenhowers consisted of Wilhelm, who had Jackson and Daniel. Wilhelm was jealous of Jackson, so he bypassed his heir for Daniel."

"So, you're saying your branch of the family shouldn't have inherited your kingdom? Kind of like how Bruno was passed over by Tony simply because he was a bastard? Only Jackson wasn't a bastard?"

"Exactly. Jackson was actually betrothed to Priscilla Atwater, but Wilhelm punished him by wedding his intended to his younger brother instead… and this is the story of how Grant, Katherine, and Adelaide were born."

"Blue bloods are just as ruthless as the underworld, I take it?"

"More so– we're the original mafia, creating laws to hide behind. Daniel wanted strong grandchildren, hating how weak his children turned out to be. He treated Grant horrifically because he was soft and soothing– the best person you'd ever meet. Daniel married Grant off to an heiress of his choosing. Then he made a good match with Katie to a man she actually fell in love with– Daddy Daniel is pleased his little girl will be the wife of the next Vice President of the United States."

"Kent and Katherine Preston belong to you?" Leery, I almost pull away, worried over the life I've led and still lead.

155

"They're the parents to two of my girls– Whitney and Prissy, growing up beside Niel and Ella. But Katherine will always be Katie to me," Whitt murmurs with affection. "So, I was five, hiding behind the draperies in Daniel's study." I notice he only calls Daniel Whittenhower Daniel, no modifier of familial connection. "I was a bit like Ava, lurking in the shadows. Sometimes I still hide against the walls, knowing Daniel will look right straight through me."

"Why does he treat you like shit? You're amazing." I blush the instant the words are out of my mouth.

Chuckling, "I'm glad you think so... I'm the forgotten heir. It's my rightful place to be the next in succession, but Daniel bypassed me for Niel. When I was five, Katie and Grant were already married, and Ade was a teenager. Daniel was discussing who to betroth Ade to, deciding on Ezra, who was my first crush. Being a little kid, I didn't think anything of it. I stepped from the shadows to announce I wanted Daniel to arrange a marriage for me with a boy. Ezra."

"Shit," hisses out from between my clenched teeth– the pain in Whitt's voice is a tangible thing.

"Daddy snapped," Whitt murmurs in an odd voice, like he's being transported back to being a five-year-old little boy. "He backhanded me so hard I flew across the study to hit the opposing wall, all the while shouting about how his family was plagued with the weak and the homosexual. Grant picked me up, placed me in his chair, checked me over... and for the first and only time in his life, he punched another human being. Grant was a pacifist, which Daniel hated."

"What happened?"

"Daniel never looked at me twice after that, no matter how hard I tried. No matter how hard I proved I was an apt pupil who would take to the helm of commanding the Whittenhowers, just like I was born to do. When Daniel found out Grant's wife couldn't have kids, he procured a strong woman– a genius, picking and choosing what traits he wanted in his grandchild. Then he forced her to bear Grant's child, bioengineering the next generation of Whittenhowers."

"Niel?"

"Yes," Whitt whispers gravely. "I was born to lead the family, named after Daniel. Even though I'm stronger than him, because I'm gay, he says that makes me Grant's temperament. As if being gay is synonymous with submissive and passive. Grant was *not* weak. Priscilla Whittenhower is a benevolent woman, and that is where our traits come from, which is a good thing."

"I think I'd like her."

"You would– she's an excellent mother and grandmother. She teamed up with Marc and Dexter's grandmother to form Transcend, as well as to offer scholarships to deserving children to attend Hillbrook. It's not phony bullshit to use as a tax write-off, or to feel above everyone else. Her charities are funded with her love and compassion first and foremost, and her money second. She'd like you," Whitt predicts.

"I have the feeling the only reason you'd want me to meet Daniel is to rub me in his face, right?" As much as it hurts to be used, I'd like to harm him for hurting Whitt.

"I've never hidden my sexuality– strangers at Restraint just assume I'm straight because I play with girls. But there were no guys to experiment with, and I couldn't chance finding the wrong guy who would exploit me. Kristal's known me since birth, so that's why I picked her. She's also amoral enough not to give two shits that she's a decade older than me and looks at me like a little brother. My sex life would be nonexistent if that were the case. I wasn't trying to be straight– I just hadn't met anyone to be gay with."

"I've never trusted anyone to be close to. Sex? I've had a lot of sex with people I wish I hadn't. So sex for me is not about a connection. It's a biological need, and that's it."

"What we just did didn't feel too biological to me," Whitt taunts me, voice suddenly flirty. "But... my belly is covered in your spunk."

"Dumbass." Unable to help myself, I laugh, and it sounds carefree. "If you could do anything, be anyone..."

"Independent," Whitt answers in a heartbeat. "Independent of Daniel. I'd want a home to call my own, working with my art, with someone who loves me for me. That's all Grant ever wanted. He wanted to be his own man. I miss the way he would ruffle up my hair, hit me upside the head when I was being a little shithead, and then let me sleep with him at night so he could read to me for hours– he'll never read to me aloud again," Whitt croaks out, with tears tingeing his voice. "When Daniel says I'm too much like Grant, I feel proud, never ashamed."

"Dammit!" I snarl to cover up the insanity leaking from my eyes onto Whitt's bare chest. "I–"

"I know," Whitt stops me. "I know, so don't. It's not your burden to carry. So… what would you do?"

"Tony accepted me for me, but he wanted me to get married and have children to continue our legacy. I understood it, which is why I was amiable when he finally explained. I can't have what I want, though. Even if the target was off my back, it wouldn't matter. I can't have a family with another guy– I can't see the resemblance to Tony at the same time as witnessing the traits of my partner etched across my children's faces. It's an impossibility I long for more than I can ever put a voice to."

"I know," Whitt rasps roughly. "I was obsessed with watching Niel's mother breastfeed him. Not because of the boob, which was a nice boob in a comforting sort of way." I laugh at how embarrassed Whitt sounds. "I was jealous because Niel was born to take my place, being able to call Grant daddy. I was jealous because I never got to nurse at my mother's breast. Plus, I was jealous that she loved Grant, taking Grant away from me, but also because I wanted her to love me, too."

"Oh, yeah!" I laugh, and this time it's without humor. "Every time I saw a good mom, I hated her kid because I wasn't him."

"While watching Niel nurse, filling his little tummy, strengthening him with his mommy's milk, I said I couldn't wait to watch my own kids nurse… that's when I found out it had to be a girl, and I cried for three days straight. I was almost seven, and Grant was beside himself, a mix between laughing and mystification. But I just didn't understand."

"You were an odd little kid," I murmur, smiling against his chest. "I want kids, but I don't want them with Bianca. I refuse to bring them into this environment. Because I love the idea of them enough not to hurt them the way my parents hurt me."

"I've seen that brunette chick wandering around, not knowing she was your wife." Whitt's voice drips with possessive jealousy, and I don't want to bask in it but I do. "Bianca's her name, right? Bianca is always staring at me, trying to talk to me. But after she found out about tonight, she kept glaring at me. We were about to have words, but Sebastian stepped in."

Voice awed, I drawl, "Sebastian did that?"

"Yeah. He pulled Bianca away from me, whispering shit into her ear. I have no idea what, but I decided not to hate him anymore."

"Instead, you found a better target?" Smothering a laugh against his chest, no doubt he feels it.

"Bianca is in love with you," Whitt snarls. "I can tell."

"I won't lie– she is. But I've also never lied to Bianca, either. She knew I was gay before I married her. We've only lain together a handful of times, back when I was grieving for Tony and I wanted to give him his legacy. But then I saw Bruno's bastard son, and I was happy for the first time in my life– relieved to see my father reflected in the baby's face. So I allowed Bianca her own life, while communicating with her daily about business but not much personal."

"French Uncle Dalton to a bastard Italian baby." Whitt's head jackknifes backward into the mattress, peals of laughter spilling from his throat. "Do you have pictures?"

"I have three nephews and a niece now– all by different mothers, none of which Bruno has wanted to marry. The kids were all given the Marconi surname, with the oldest being Little Tony. Bruno's a good dad, but piss-poor husband material."

"I still hate your wife's guts, but your brother sounds like an interesting character."

"Yes, I have pictures," I finally answer, cheeks burning furiously with a blush. I reach over to my nightstand to grab my cellphone. After opening up the gallery app, I hand it over to Whitt.

"The trust!" Whitt bellows while choking on laughter. "The trust it involves to hand someone your cellphone… I'm not going to find dick pics in here, am I? Please tell me I am."

"You're an idiot, Pretty Boy," I grumble as he scrolls through the images Bruno sends me daily.

"I'll do you one better," Whitt promises as he stares at Little Tony, Baby Bruno, Big Dalton, and Antonia– my brother named his children. "I'll take you to Misery Castle to meet the kids who fill my cellphone."

"Terrifying," I mutter, feeling inexplicably giddy. "Just don't expect me to fly your ass to Las Vegas. I wouldn't want you to get the impression I'm a badass when I'm actually a wimp."

"No impressions needed, because I can see you clearly." Whitt thumbs through, snickering at the pictures Bruno sent of Kink with a big banner scrolled across the front of the building.

Finders keepers! Dominion can keep Olivia Fontaine. Las Vegas doesn't want her back.

"Oh, I like your brother." Each picture makes Whitt snicker more.

"Bruno despises my mother." Hesitant, but still feeling giddy to share this with someone, "Would you like to formally meet my other brother?"

"What?" My cellphone drops from Whitt's hand to land on the mattress. "Heck yes!" Alligator rolling me, I find myself beneath him instead of resting on his chest. "Let's get some rest– we have a big day tomorrow."

After another hand job session, with a lot of heavy petting and kissing, I fall asleep for the first time in a lover's arms.

Chapter Fifteen

A knock at my door jars me awake. I find myself Whitt-free and disappointment simmers in my veins. I wanted to know what it would feel like to wake up next to him in the light of day. I wanted to see him with my own two eyes to know it wasn't a fantasy, or a figment of my imagination. The deadbolt is unlocked with a key, so I don't freak out. Only one person has a key. I lie back on the bed and cover my nakedness with a sheet.

"I guess you enjoyed your date." Devlin teases me as he enters my apartment with Bianca following after him.

My eyes latch on to Bianca, noting her pinched, pissed off expression. Her soft hair flows to her shoulders and it glows in the morning sunlight with bronze and gold. My wife is a beautiful woman, but she's not for me.

The three of us are at an impasse, looking around unsure of what to say. Devlin sets a bakery bag on the small dining table, and then looks everywhere but at Bianca.

"Well, I brought you some breakfast." Devlin points nervously to the bag. "And your wife." He huffs a laugh at the ridiculousness. "I guess I'll leave you two alone for a bit." Acting peculiar, he starts to head to the door, then he abruptly turns and whispers something to my wife.

I narrow my eyes at them, not understanding what's going on. After I left Las Vegas, Bianca went back to her father. She's been using Dominion and Las Vegas as home base, depending on where her dancing career was taking her. Bianca has spent more time with my mother, Devlin, and Sebastian than she has me. Whereas I've spent more time with her father these past four years than she has.

"Um… yeah. Later." Devlin runs out of my apartment like the hounds of Hell are nipping at his heels.

"What was that about?" I ask Bianca, my voice holding suspicion.

She just shrugs at me, eyes taking in everything in my apartment. "Devlin didn't want to bring me, but I asked nicely."

"You mean you demanded it by throwing a fit?" I sit up with my back to the headboard. "Stanton would kick your ass if he saw you manipulating a man."

"I'm not the enemy, Dalton." Bianca stares at my bed like it's going to bite her. "I'm not getting anywhere near the bed you screwed another man on." She drags a chair away from my dinette set, much stronger than she looks after two decades of dedication to her craft. Lithe, graceful, she takes a seat. "I'm not like your mother, no matter how much you push it into my face."

Bianca." I sigh, wishing Levi hadn't removed my bloodletting kit. I'm tempted to cut myself in front of my wife to show her how badly she affects me.

"You have to see it from my point of view… I saw your *lover* on our way up the stairs." She twists the words like they leave a bad taste in her mouth. "Whitt tried to bite my head off last night, but he succeeded moments ago."

I roll onto my stomach and groan– no wonder Devlin was uncomfortable. This is the weirdest, most uncomfortable conversation ever. I know Bianca has lovers. She knows I whore for my mother. But seeing my lover on the stairs is beyond disrespectful.

"I apologize," I say with all sincerity. "That was not how I wanted you to meet."

"I finally spoke with Daniel, and it wasn't exactly how I had dreamed it would go down." With an odd tone in her voice, she opens the bakery bag to distract me. "He hates me– and I don't say that lightly."

"Whitt doesn't hate you." I struggle to sit back up. "You sound nuts right now."

"Nuts?" Bianca leans forward, bringing her face level with mine. "Daniel Whittenhower II said to me, '*Are you Dalton's wife?*' When I said yes, he told me to leave you alone, or I'd regret it. He does not like me, and that's not the type of relationship I want with him."

"What? Why?" I sit up and notice Bianca's eyes drink in my chest. Eyes glued to my ruined flesh, her throat moves as she swallows.

Bianca's never seen me naked. I get up quickly, covering myself with the sheet, and grab some clothing from my dresser. I put the shirt on first to cover the marks. I worry less about my cock since she's felt it before– never seen it, though.

"You worry too much about what you look like." Bianca's cheeks turn an appealing pink. "You're very arousing."

"I know," I say without arrogance. "That's the reason I cover myself." I walk over to the kitchenette and pull two glasses from the shelf and a carton of apple juice from the refrigerator.

"Did you finally–"

"No." I cut Bianca off. "Not yet anyway. But you should know I do plan on having sex with Whitt."

"Of course you do," Bianca mutters to herself, the words ironic. "You can't love me, but him… you have a love note on your nightstand."

"You never explained what's going on between you and Whitt," I say as I grab the note. I quickly unfold it, feeling like a teenage girl– giddy with excitement. I roll my eyes up when I feel my wife watching me. This is too weird. I turn my back on her so I can read my note without her reading my facial expression.

When we married, Tony said Bianca would submit. What he failed to inform me was that Bianca was only doing so because she wanted to. Willful, stubborn, demanding, my wife is stronger than me in all things. She also has the uncanny ability to read my mind, and right now she wouldn't enjoy my thoughts.

Dalton,
I was reluctant to leave your bed this morning, but I had to make plans for our day. I promised you a day-in-the-life of Daniel Whittenhower II, and I always keep my word. While I'm gone, make good on a night-in-the-life of Dalton Anthony Fontaine Marconi, and set something up for us to do this evening.

Devlin swears you are safe to be who you truly are. No disguises. I want you to accompany me today, not Dalton Thompson. No fear, no one from the underworld frequents my side of town.

Thank you for last night– it was the first time I'd ever done something for myself without fear of the consequences. I'll see you

in a few hours.
DW II

With effort, I try to wipe the smirk off my face as I fold the note back up and place it into the drawer of the nightstand. It's my first note, and I'm going to save it after I read it a few dozen times. I feel guilty as I turn back to my wife, but nothing can dampen the way Whitt makes me feel.

Ignoring the elephant in the room, I sit across from Bianca and dig around in the bag for a glazed donut. I bite into it, waiting for her to answer my question.

"Whitt asked me if I was your wife, and then he looked me over for a few minutes with a grimace on his face."

"I'm sure you were a perfect angel," I murmur around another bite of donut. "You can be honest with me, Bianca. I love you just as you are, and I don't think you a manipulative bitch. But I do see you for who you are. Stanton Green's only child would never be passive, not even for a heartbeat."

"Okay, fine." Bianca rolls her vibrant blue eyes, muttering a string of Italian swear words she picked up from her father. "I may have reminded Pretty Boy how I'm your wife and he's trespassing, so he should stop glaring at me like it was the other way around."

"Of course you did," I placate Bianca, understanding how difficult this must be for her. "And I'm sure he said some not-so nice things to you in reaction, right?"

"Damn straight, skippy," Bianca mutters, sounding just like her uncle, Caleb.

"You're living with Caleb, aren't you?" I laugh when Bianca's perfect eyebrows knit in the center of her forehead. "You talk like him when he's around."

"Yeah, Caleb and I are sharing an apartment next to Dad. Not that he's ever home, always protecting the assholes of this town or jogging for hours on end. So, anyway... I was trying to be nice to Whitt," she gets back to her story.

"Of course you were." I grab another donut, and eat it in three bites. I'm never hungry, but after last night I wish Devlin would have brought me bacon and eggs instead.

"Whitt growled something about you being his. Devlin laughed, and it spurred him on, going as far as to say you're gay, and I need to stop pining for you. It was an uncomfortable exchange, to say the least."

"Wow. Whitt not being a gentleman is a first. He even comes politely." Bianca looks at me like she's envisioning strangling me, and I smile in reply. "I'm not kidding. He's super polite. I swear he walks around with an etiquette rulebook in his back pocket. And he has no issue with a pretty lady," I drawl.

"I don't ever want to hear the details of your sex life with *him*. Ever." Bianca shudders in revulsion. "Don't look at me that way, Dalton. It's not because you're gay– it's because I'm your wife, and Whitt is… Whitt."

"I want a divorce," I blurt out of nowhere.

Looking as if I physically struck her, Bianca recoils in her seat. After my words sink in, her beautiful skin turns green.

"I love you," rolls rapidly from between my lips. "You'll always be my family, but as a sister, never a wife. I can't do this anymore– I can't live my parents' lives. They chose this for me, not the other way around. Tony is dead, and his first born has given him four beautiful grandchildren. I gave Bruno both Marconi and Fontaine– completely. I gave my father's legacy away."

"But–" Bianca's eyes go huge with wonder and confusion. "But Bruno wasn't a Fontaine."

"I don't care," I mutter with conviction. "Mafia is about family, not bloodlines. After nearly slitting my wrists, begging Devlin to beat me, and then having Levi tell me he's my brother, it put my life into perspective. I was doing what heinous human beings chose for me. So yesterday, before I went to the park, I cut all the chains binding me to my old life."

"What do you mean?" Bianca's control snaps, finally allowing her tumultuous emotions to playout on her face. "What did you do, Dalton? My God!"

"I made a call to your father and my brother, and it was completed in minutes. I may be a masochist, but I'm not insane. Why would I want to live the life they chose for me? Why would I want a cent from Pierre Fontaine? Why, Bianca? It would make me the ultimate whore, like my grandfather was compensating me from the grave for raping me repeatedly for nearly ten years of my life."

Bianca refuses to meet my eyes, knowing Stanton and Caleb were in a similar situation. Only Stanton took over to protect his

165

people. I don't need to protect my people because I have Bruno in my life, and he was born to run my families. It comes naturally to him, whereas it doesn't for me.

"Okay," Bianca says in a calm voice, but she refuses to look at me. "I can understand wanting that portion of your life to be over. But we don't need to get a divorce."

"Yes, we do." I make my way over to my closet. With the flick of my wrist, I'm opening my safe.

"Dalton, no." Bianca's voice quivers, as if she already knows what I'm doing and knows she can't stop me. Desperate, voice panicked, "I'm in love with you. Please, don't do this to me."

"Bianca." Brushing the tears off my cheeks with the back of my hand, I hold a single sheet of paper. "Stop being your daddy's and my mafia princess. Dance. Live your life. Find your counterpart. You deserve to fall in love with a man who is capable of loving you back, get married, and give Stanton beautiful grandchildren. But that man has never been me."

"Goddammit!" Bianca hops out of her chair, running toward the door. But I step in front of her path, pressing the paper against her small breasts. "NO!" she shouts, tearing the paperwork in half, and then a thousand little pieces. Paper flutters in the air, landing in her hair, on our clothing, and all over the floor.

"Your father knows how you operate, Bianca." I produce three more of the same official document, all just as illegal as our marriage license was. "I'm not giving you away– I'm setting you free."

"Don't do this to me." Bianca slides down the door, ass hitting the floor. Tears springing from her eyes to cascade down her cheeks, agonizing sobs are pulled from her chest. "Don't do this to me… don't do this to me."

"I love you." Pressing a pen into her hand, I flutter a kiss to her damp lips. I hold the paper steady, while positioning her hand over the signature line. "You deserve so much– so very much. Your future children deserve even more."

Completely despondent yet desperate, "Don't do this to me," Bianca mutters over and over again, but her fingers move the pen in an illegible signature.

I drag Bianca away from the door, knowing Devlin would anticipate my moves and call for backup. Reaching up, I flick the doorknob, knowing Gunner and Levi will be waiting on the landing.

Levi looks proud of me, and I'm surprised to see the same reflected on Gunner's face. I thought for sure he'd want to beat me half to death because of what I'm doing. Levi opens the door wide, allowing his partner to swoop in next to Bianca.

"I'm not doing this to you, Bianca." I give her one last kiss as her uncle lifts her from the floor. "I'm doing this for you."

Chapter Sixteen

Dueling emotions assault my senses as I reluctantly shower Whitt's scent from my flesh. No doubt Bianca thinks I'm leaving her because of Whitt, but that couldn't be further from the truth. It was a decision Stanton and I had been discussing for more than a year.

Bianca was sent back to her father after the hell we lived through on our wedding night. After I was safe in Dominion, he sent Bianca to me, hoping I'd find her a comfort. After a few months, Bianca's attention wandered back to her dance troupe. I didn't fault her, knowing ballet was her life.

No matter how many ways I replay the past, it doesn't take the guilt away after seeing Bianca break down into hysterical sobs. The thought thrusts me into the past– into a memory best left forgotten.

After tucking my spent cock back into my pants, I make sure every private inch of Bianca is covered by her dress. Then I help her rise to sit on the foldaway bed next to Sebastian, who immediately takes up a protective stance next to her.

"Where's Stanton?" I ask Tony as I move around the foldaway bed, not knowing what will come next, but my primal instinct has me mentally preparing for battle.

"Stan left once he knew the deed was done– no father should be forced to play witness to that." Tony glares at Pierre, but then an odd smile twists his lips. "Do you like your wife?" He looks at me as if seeing me for the first time. "How many times did you get off? Twice? Three times?"

I surprised myself, too. My mind accepted Bianca as mine and my body wanted to fulfill its biological need. I took my wife three times in rapid succession without stopping in between. I'd love to say it was because of Bianca, or the fact that after ten years of lusting after Sebastian I finally had a taste of him, but it's neither of those things that spurred me on.

It was because of the anticipation and excitement over what I'm about to do. Bedding my wife was my first act as a free man.

"Yes, I'm very pleased with my wife. Thank you, Father." Tony looks pleased that he finally did something right by me, and it wrenches my heart.

"Get the fuck out of my office and never step foot in this building again!" I command Pierre, pointing at the door while glaring at my grandfather. "Take your pet psychopath with you."

"Vos boules finalement tomber?" Pierre taunts me, asking if my balls finally dropped. "I will not leave my own property." My grandfather issues me an anticipatory grin– one of a feral predator. "Besides, Jon still needs to collect on a debt."

I sense Sebastian move behind me on the bed, even though I can't look away from my grandfather to gaze over my shoulder to find out. But it's the way Tony suddenly appears ill that has me on red-alert. But then the look of triumph on Jon's face registers, and my stomach twists up on itself.

Leaving the sofa, Jon paces across my office like he owns the world. The sound of metal grinding on metal has my head jerking so I can look over my shoulder.

"What are you doing?" I demand when I notice Sebastian unzipping his fly.

Moving faster than I ever imagined I could, I grab his wrist. "Don't expose yourself in front of my wife, and never in front of Pierre or Jon. They will take it as an invitation."

"I need no invitation," Jon purrs from a few feet away, watching every move I make.

Voice shaking, Sebastian pulls out of my grasp. "I have to do this, Dalton."

I grab Sebastian's wrist again, just as he reaches for his zipper. "No, I'm your master." His hand freezes and his eyes widen in fright. "You're to listen to me and no one else. Obviously you're not able to make decisions on your own if you're willing to ever listen to Jon."

"It was a tough negotiation." Voice smug, Jon tries to rub it in. "I won Sebastian for fifteen minutes if you were unable to perform without his help."

"What?" I look at Tony in disbelief, understanding dawning on why he looks physically ill. "Sebastian is not allowed to be brought into this shit. Never. You promised!"

"The alternative was worse– much worse." Tony covers his mouth, like he just puked and is trying to keep it down. "Pierre wanted Jon to take your wife if you couldn't. Stanton was completely *against this, and I don't blame him– I didn't tell you because the pressure to perform would have made it impossible for you."*

"I don't accept this– any of this" I look around the room, completely flabbergasted. "You're terrorists, is what you are. I'm a grown man, a human being, and I will not be used as a pawn." Control breaking, mouth unhinging, I scream, "Get the fuck off my property! Now!"

Jon and Pierre ignore me as I bellow into their faces. Tony pushes away from his desk, giving himself room to maneuver, as if he instinctively knows where this is headed.

I look in question at my father, and he gives a slight nod with his chin.

Pierre walks across the room to fish in Tony's and my desk. His hand comes into view, holding a kitchen timer. With the twist of his wrist, the ticking begins.

Tick.

My body reacts as one does during a PTSD episode. Knees wobbling, I almost lose my footing to fall to the floor. Sweat pours off my forehead, clouding my vision. My hands shake so badly I can barely bend my knuckles. The longer the timer ticks, the worse it gets.

Resigned to his fate, Sebastian leans over the bed as Jon stalks toward him. Jon's eyes find my wife, and he grins down at her with evil intent.

"Close your eyes, Bianca," Sebastian orders my wife, and she immediately clenches her eyelids shut and puts her hands over her ears, with tears sliding down her cheeks.

Frozen, I stand in place. Shock. I'm entering shock. I can do nothing but watch as Jon removes the offending piece of flesh that has violated me countless times. Grinning, eyes perusing Sebastian, he strokes himself to full arousal.

Sebastian has always been mine to protect, and now Bianca is as well. I will not stand idly by like my parents have my entire life. When Jon's hand touches the small of Sebastian's back and presses, my body explodes in fury.

Jon will not take this from Sebastian as he has me, as he has countless others.

"The only one who has this right is me," I utter in a deadly voice. I look at my hands in surprise. One hand clenches the silken

171

strands at the top of Jon's head, drawing it back at an angle. The other hand holds a knife to his throat.

"Where did this change come from, Dalton?" My grandfather asks me as if I'm a toddler who is misbehaving.

"You never touch a master's pets," my father reminds Pierre. Tony's eyes hold mine, giving me all the strength he has left. I see the knowledge reflected back that he knew I'd react this way. Not once did Tony allow Sebastian to be touched by anyone, always protecting him for me.

I now understand why Tony moved his chair; he knew this was the event that has culminated since before I was even born.

"That's just fantasy bullshit!" Pierre scoffs, the sound arrogant, but beneath the surface is fear. "Just a way to work out the kinks while you have sex."

"Your dead wife founded a BDSM community, one your daughter runs. You don't leave your dominance in the dungeon, Pierre. You should know that."

Wrenching him backward, I pull hard enough on Jon's hair to force a pain-filled grunt from his throat. Pierre laughs at me like I'm just playing around, but Jon's eerie eyes tell a different story.

"You're so dominant, Dalton" My grandfather taunts me, but there is an edge of panic creeping into his voice. "Look at what you've allowed yourself to endure."

"Dalton did it for his masters," Jon strains to be heard. I crank his neck farther back, just because I can. "I think he's finally let go and is his own man now that he has too much to lose. I'd take him seriously, Pierre."

Jon tries to warn his partner, but it falls on deaf ears. I can feel the vibrations run down the hilt of the knife as he speaks. I firmly press in until I feel Jon's throat indent from the force– just this side of cutting.

"And just who are his masters?" Pierre asks haughtily, always assuming he's in control, even when he's not.

"His parents, you fucking idiot," Jon hisses through his clenched teeth.

"I'm done stalling." My hand is starting to cramp from the need to lash out and slice. "Jon, will you obey from now on?"

"No– I can't." Jon's reply zings up my fingers, drawing the hair on my arm to stand on end.

"I own you now. I am your boss." I try one last time. "Will you obey me?"

"You aren't his boss." I can hear a hint of confusion ring in Pierre's voice.

"This past year, even though you've never left our sides," Tony admits the truth. "Dalton has taken complete ownership of all your property. You own nothing, Pierre. The young man you have terrorized is your boss now."

"Bullshit!" Pierre stalks forward, tearing open a drawer in our desk. The ticking timer falls onto its side on the desktop, somehow amplifying the sound.

My hand shakes, drawing blood from Jon's throat to trickle down my fingertips.

"Here!" Tony thrusts a stack of papers at Pierre. "The last of the paperwork was signed this morning, with me signing my property away to him as a wedding gift. That is with the stipulation that I continue to be in charge until I officially retire." I expected Tony to sound arrogant. But he looks sad and sounds worried, like he doesn't expect his longevity.

"One last time, will you obey me?" I ask Jon for the third time.

"No, I never will." Before the word no completely leaves Jon's lips, I slice the blade against his throat. With patience and a steady hand, as if in slow motion, I slice from left to right, nearly from one ear, across his neck, to the other ear.

Blood spurting out in an arc to cover several feet around us, Jon doesn't release a scream; he just goes lax in my grip. I'm not strong enough to hold his dead weight. With great effort, I command my fingers to release my hold on his hair, and he crumples to the ground.

Staring down, I watch the light die out in Jon's eerie eyes. An odd, baleful sound erupts from his throat, as the final spurts of blood trickle from the cut that nearly decapitated him. I imagine Jon thanking me for putting him out of his own misery.

I feel nothing but relief.

Does that make me as evil as Jon if I don't feel guilt for ending his life? I just treated another human being as if he were an animal at the slaughter.

No, I did the world a favor.

Slow motion fast-forwarding, the words I uttered as I sliced Jon's neck finally filter into my ears to sink into my mind.

"Sebastian, take Bianca and get to Devlin as fast as you can. Tell Dev I said that he is to guard you both. Do it now."

From start to finish, it took no more than ten seconds.

Ten seconds to end a life, and to change many others.

Standing in the middle of a scene straight out of the movie Carrie, I'm covered in Jon's lifeblood from head to toe, with it dripping off my fingertips. It was a hot wash over my flesh, but it immediately began to cool as it coagulated when it hit the air. Sticky, its drops turn thready with the aid of gravity.

Pierre is frozen in shock– staring at his dead partner as Sebastian and Bianca flee the room. It's like he can't believe it happened. Not that I actually did it, but that he finally lost, failing to anticipate how someone would react to his unwanted stimuli.

Blinking out of his haze, Pierre finally comes back to life. "You will regret that," Pierre predicts as he gestures towards Jon with the barrel of his handgun. My eyes go wide when I recognize the weapon. My chest rises and falls in rapid succession at the sight.

"I know what's coming next." Pierre's voice wavers with terror, sounding like a cornered animal. "I will not allow you to kill me."

My grandfather moves so quickly I can barely track his movements. He fires the weapon with a crack of sound. Dazed, I watch the fire at the end of the barrel erupt as the powder ignites. I blink several times, waiting for the pain to radiate. But then my ears register the thump of a body hitting the floor.

"There, now you're truly free of your maître," is the last thing I hear as Pierre rushes from the office, nearly colliding with Bruno, who's running in with his weapon drawn. Seeing Bruno unfreezes me.

Running, shoes sticking to the floor with every step, blood snapping as if it's elastic anchoring me to the floor. "Oh, my God! Tony! NO!" I shout in a panic as I fall to my knees near his torso.

I pull my father's head into my lap, then my hands wave through the air in a panic. I don't know where to touch him. I don't know how to make the blood stop. Knowing it's wrong, but I have to do something, I remember a heroine pressing down on a wound in a book I read last month. With all of my weight on my palms, I try to stop the blood flow.

"I'm proud of you, son– no matter how I made it look." Voice thready, Tony wheezes a death-filled song.

Something vital breaks inside me when Bruno drops to his knees next to me, brown eyes already filled with loss, knowing the end is not only near, but now. My brother's arms surround me, supporting me so I won't collapse over our father.

"NO!" I shout again, cutting off my father's goodbye. "No, you're going to be fine. I'll get you help. I can't do this without you. I'm not strong enough to deal with all this shit."

"I didn't want to do the things I've done, but I had no other choice. Don't hate your mother because of this. He held your death over us. If we didn't do as he said, he threatened to kill you and Itsy Bitsy. The bastard got off on watching us hurt you." Tony continues to talk– to tell me his last thoughts.

His last words. His final goodbye.

I kneel in denial– everything is fine. Tony isn't going to die. He's too strong to die. I watch as Tony moistens his lips with his tongue so he can keep talking. He keeps swallowing back the blood that fills his mouth– that slides in a steady stream from the corner of his mouth to pool into the collar of his shirt.

"Bruno," Tony's eyes roll to gaze at his first born. My brother takes our father's hand and waits while he tries to form words. "I've always been proud to be your father. I love you, son– I want you to take my name, then take care of your brother. You'll always have each other."

"I love you, too, Dad." I watch as Bruno gets choked up and tries not to cry. "No one will ever harm Dalton again. I promise."

Near lifeless hand trying to reach for me, Bruno holds Tony's wrist so I'm able to slip my hands alongside my father's. He doesn't even have the strength to clasp his fingers over mine.

"If you ever want to lead a normal life, you have to end this with Pierre. Do you understand?" Tony's words rush out in a torrent in fright, as if he's worried he won't have enough time to finish what he needs to say.

"Yes, I'll do what needs to be done before this night ends." I solemnly vow to execute my own grandfather.

"Don't let your mother control you any longer. Make your own decisions– hers are never right. Save your sister from her as well. Olivia may be better once Pierre is out of your lives." Tony's hand slips free of mine, and I begin to cry in earnest.

"No," I beg, gripping his hand again. Tony's leaving us. "Don't go, Daddy. Please don't!"

"I love you, son. I never doubted your ability to do the right thing. Take care of our people." Tony gives one last squeeze to my hand, and then his fingers go lax.

Leaning forward, alarm spreads through me. Tony sputters up a large amount of blood– he's drowning in it. He tries to speak several times and can't get the words to form. I push his head up to clear his mouth of blood.

"Tell your mother I love her and forgive her," Tony rasps as he lets go of my hand. He uses the last of his life to profess his undying love to a wife who had turned her back on him.

I allow Bruno and myself a few minutes to grieve. We hold one another, curled over our father's body, releasing sounds no one should ever hear, let alone make.

Sobering before Bruno, I have to do as my father bid. Take care of our people.

"Devlin," I whisper into my phone, somehow feeling it's wrong to speak loudly around the dead. I fall back onto my ass in a pool of cooling blood– Jon Wilson's and Anthony Marconi's. I stare in shock at my dead father, never fathoming how my twentieth birthday would play out.

"I need you," I utter the words I've never said to anyone. "Sebastian is on his way to Kink. He has a girl with him– my wife. I need you to send Bianca Green back to Stanton Green in Dominion, New York. Be on the alert for Pierre. If he shows up, retain him. But watch out– he has a gun."

I listen to the silence on the other end of the phone. Bruno's sobs are overpowering any and all sound. I begin to wonder if I didn't hear whatever reply Devlin said, or maybe I'm losing it and he never answered the phone. I sit for a minute, and as I'm about to hang up, he finally speaks.

"What happened?" Devlin's deep voice is calm, but I can hear the underlying terror.

"I slit Jon's throat when he tried to rape Sebastian, nearly decapitating him. In retaliation, Pierre shot Tony." Devlin's gasp through the phone hurts my eardrum and makes this nightmare reality. "Tell my mother her husband is dead. His last words were that he loves and forgives her."

I hang up.

"I'm sorry, Bruno, but we have things we must do. I'll call the cleanup crew, because we need to get rid of Jon before I call in the Feds. I will not dispose of our father like garbage. Even if I get Pierre, I want it to be known that Pierre Fontaine was Tony's murderer."

Chapter Seventeen

Pacing in the back alleyway, having no idea when Whitt plans to arrive, I try to get the past out of my head. "Am I going nuts?" I grumble underneath my breath. I've always blocked the memories, only entering the alternate universe known as my past during subspace. Now the past is assaulting my present.

"Hey?" A calm voice reaches my ears a split-second before a body is enveloping mine. "You look like you've had a rough morning." Whitt wraps his arms around me, pressing my cheek to his chest. His clean scent wafts up into my nostrils. "What happened?"

Instead of hearing it as a command, I listen to the underlying concern. I'm trying my hardest to grow as a person, and not lash out because I'm hurting. Seeking comfort, I all but collapse into Whitt's embrace.

"Busy morning?" I snort without humor. "I forced Bianca to sign our divorce papers, and listening to her sobs nearly broke me." Whitt's hands freeze, and I instantly miss their warmth as they passed over my shoulders and down my back in a continual circuit of comfort. "Then I was taking a shower and the past caught up with me, so much so that I didn't realize until I was in the alleyway that I was dressed as myself, and not Dalton Thompson."

"You're never dressing like Thompson again." This time Whitt's voice has a commanding edge to it that I long to obey. "Your mother has you doing all of these things for her, and I'm going to help you today. No more Thompson. No more asshole. No more punishing yourself to cleanse away what you did or said while you were an asshole."

Pulling away, I stare up at Whitt. "Everyone sounds like a broken record."

"Well…" Whitt displays why we all call him Pretty Boy– the goddamn dimples. "Because you need to hear it. Olivia Fontaine is toxic. So instead of pestering a bunch of people who either don't know anything, or aren't going to tell you anything because of loyalty, I'm taking you to the source."

"What?" My eyebrows knit in the center of my forehead, and Whitt reaches up to smooth them back out.

"One visit will negate all the bullshit your mother is forcing you to do." Whitt tugs at my hand, twining our fingers together. We both look down in awe. "I've never held a guy's hand before."

"Me, either," I murmur, voice thick with emotions. I tighten my grip, wrapping my fingers around his. "I rather like it."

"Same here." Whitt flashes me a devious smile. "C'mon, babe. We've got an asylum to visit."

"What?" I practically shriek, voice echoing off the buildings in the alleyway. "I-I-I– what?"

Whitt tugs me out the mouth of the alley to a Roadster idling at the curb. "You're riding shotgun while I give you a tour. First stop on the tour is Adelaide Charlotte Whittenhower."

"You'd do this for me?" I settle into the passenger seat, firmly shutting the door beside me– not that it matters any, since there is no top to the car. I look overhead, making sure there are no rain clouds.

"Put this on, my creature of the night." Whitt tosses a tube of sunscreen at me. "I would have done this earlier had I known." He navigates through Dominion's downtown traffic while I slather cream on my face and the tip of my nose. "No one believed Ade actually wrote the book– not that she's not intelligent enough to do it, but because she's physically incapable right now. Nor would she harm us. Her best friends– the women she sees as sisters –and her actual family are smeared in the books."

"I didn't know that," comes out as a whine. "I was just doing as I was told. What I was conditioned to do after a lifetime."

"In Las Vegas, you knew Tony, Bruno, Devlin, and Sebastian had your back. In Dominion, you felt you were alone. So I get it." Whitt takes an entrance ramp, accelerating to seventy-miles-per-hour in two seconds. I quickly strap my seatbelt on, not that it would help any since there is barely any car surrounding us. "But you aren't alone here. All you have to do is ask. If your mother asks something of you, ask someone else if it's legit."

"Easier said than done." I grip the door, fingertips turning into talons. Eyes darting to the speedometer, we're doing ninety on the interstate. "Are Whittenhowers immune from State Troopers?"

Ignoring my concerns, Whitt actually presses on the accelerator until we're nearly doing one-hundred-miles-per-hour. "It's what I have to do with Daniel. If he wants something from me, I start with

Marcus first. Then I trickle down to a few select others, until I find a reason to actually believe him."

"I will admit, I've been stupid for trusting my mother." My voice comes out shaky, but not only from emotion– terror. Whitt is a good driver, but he has a wicked lead foot and a car that is capable of going way too fast. "But she's my mother– you're supposed to be able to trust your own mother."

"That will be another stop on my tour." Whitt flashes me a devious grin. Then his foot lets up off the gas, and he downshifts to take an exit ramp. In silence, he navigates a series of roads from memory, until the sign for Wintercrest Asylum comes into view.

"I live in Crestview gated community," Whitt informs me as we wait for the gatekeeper to let us pass. "Crestview… Wintercrest… same shit, different day."

I'm asking, "What?" when an older security guard pops up near my door with a clipboard.

"I'll need your driver's license and a signature, sir." He thrusts the board into my lap as I fish around in my wallet for my real license. "We already have Master Daniel on file."

Whitt continues speaking as if we're alone. "Wintercrest was founded by the same people who originally made Dominion a town, then a city. They packed themselves into a fifteen mile circle of land with a giant fence around it, and named their tiny affluent residential area Crestview."

"Thank you, sir." The security guard hands me my license back, and then removes the clipboard from my grip. "Dominion's founding fathers were Meyers, Whittenhower, Holden, Zeitler, Spencer, Fontaine, and Green," he rattles off from memory. "One other has come into power since. I believe Simpson was added to our board of trustees during my lifetime."

"Thank you, George." Whitt is ever polite. Pulling away from the guard shack, he shrugs one shoulder. "Wintercrest is where the rich dump their fuck-ups. We don't go to prison, or rehab– we go to the asylum. If you accidently come out at the tender age of five, you'll have Wintercrest as your constant boogieman."

"You mean…" my voice is filled with horror. "Instead of being told you have to behave or you'll get grounded, you were threatened with this–" I gesture to the large, formidable building coming into view.

"Yes," Whitt whispers. "Wilhelm Whittenhower built this place as an exact replica of Misery Castle."

"It's huge!" My neck hitches backward into the headrest just so I can take it all in. A three-story stone building with buttresses and gargoyles, covering several acres and surrounded by green lawns and densely wooded forest. "Impressive."

"I said my grandfather built the asylum as a replica–" Whitt sounds disgusted. "Wintercrest is smaller than my home."

"Jesus Christ," I hiss, heart beating out of my chest. "I take it Adelaide's threats of imprisonment became a reality."

Whitt slides from the car, quickly making his way to my side like a gentlemen. Refusing to be relegated as the girl in this relationship, I get out on my own. But I do take his hand in mine because it feels good and I'm suddenly nervous.

"Remember how I said Daniel was betrothing Ade to Ezra? Daniel and Ezra's mother, Diane, are the best of friends. Ade snapped because Ezra was marrying Katya, and that meant she had an express pass to Wintercrest, which Daniel made good on."

"It's no wonder– if Adelaide truly wrote the *Mistress & Master of Restraint* books, I don't blame her."

"Ezra's mother is a real piece of work, and she's bookended by the assholes who created us," Whitt says cryptically. When I don't respond, he explains. "Daniel is older than Diane, but they made an unholy alliance. Did you know Olivia and Diane were classmates from kindergarten on?" Whitt scrunches up his face like he's sucking on a lemon. "No doubt Daniel and Olivia are in acquaintance."

"Yeah, I caught onto that board of trustees bullshit your man George just spewed." Hand-in-hand, Whitt and I ascend the front limestone steps to enter a two-story curved entranceway. "I inherited everything of Pierre's, and I don't remember anything about Dominion listed in the paperwork."

"I'm sure your mother has control over whatever that entails," Whitt murmurs out the side of his mouth as we approach the front desk. While he signs us in, I look around in awe. Marble as far as the eye can see, with cascading chandeliers hanging from the ceiling.

I'm used to new money– gaudy and tacky Las Vegas. This isn't even old money. Old-world money is more like it. Pre-Industrial-Revolution era money.

"Come," Whitt grips my elbow to direct me. "You'll see this show when I take you home to meet my kids, only on a grander scale." We ascend another set of stairs, but not an entire flight to the second story, leading to a sunroom. "I don't enjoy being here after having it held over my head for all of my natural born life. I'm still at risk."

"What do you mean?" I stop walking, sneakers stilling on the slate tile.

"I've caught wind of how your life has been." Whitt rubs the back of his neck, looking decidedly uncomfortable. "Our practices are less in-your-face and more cerebral-fuckage. The age of majority means nothing. It's until the maturation of our trust funds. Which occurs on my twenty-fourth birthday, only two weeks from now. Until then, Daniel has my balls in a vice. With Adelaide, the stipulation was until she married, no matter how old she was– he had her power of attorney, deeming her unfit to rule her own life."

"I want to move to Alaska," the perfect solution rumbles up my throat.

"I have better plans." Whitt's dimples flash. "I'm going to beat Daniel at his own sadistic game, and he'll never see it coming… until then." Whitt gestures to the opposite end of the sunroom.

A frail blonde stares out the high-arched windows of the gothic Wintercrest Asylum. Her brittle hair is pulled atop her head in a loose bun. She's so emaciated I can see the bluish veins protrude beneath the paper-thin flesh of her hands.

Adelaide Whittenhower looks like an elderly woman, not a vibrant thirty-five-year-old. She rocks in a chair and gazes blankly at the street below. Time seems to have stopped for her, as Whitt and I have stood by watching her for the past half hour and she hasn't looked our way. It's taken Whitt that long to stop silently crying as he stares at his relative.

This is what many have meant. If you saw Adelaide Whittenhower, you'd know she was incapable of authoring the Mistress & Master of Restraint books. I'm not sure she can formulate a sentence from her tongue, let alone write a word with her feeble fingertips.

"I'm so sorry," I whisper to Whitt. I haven't stopped crying since I saw the pathetic waste of a woman, either. I've never met her, but I've met Whitt, Niel, and Ella. All the Whittenhowers look alike. I don't doubt that Adelaide used to look just like them, too.

Gripping my hand tightly, "I can't do this," Whitt's voice is filled with sorrow and frustration.

"Grant?" Adelaide calls out when she hears Whitt's voice. "Is that you, Grant." Her voice infuses with strength at the prospect of seeing her dead brother.

Almost looking like cataracts, Adelaide's blue eyes are clouded by whatever drug they use to control her. A heavy scar bisects her forehead, reminding me of Jamie's scar on his lip. It was from her fight with Katya. Katya has scars, too.

"It's me, Ade." Whitt steps forward and touches her hand. "Whitt... little Daniel."

"Silly, Grant. You're always such a tease." Adelaide's voice is light and airy, but there is panic hidden beneath. "Whitt is a child."

"Ade, I know I look identical to Grant." Whitt steps forward, standing between Adelaide's rocker and the wall of windows. "We lost him when he was twenty-six. Don't you remember?" He coaxes, sounding desperate. "I'm sorry that I look just like him. It's difficult for a lot of us."

"Yes, Grant was supposedly poisoned by Father," she growls. Her eyes immediately clear of their cloudiness. "But that wasn't true."

"No, Ade." Whitt tries to get her to remember. "Grant was poisoned by Cora– his wife. In a murder/suicide. She took the poison next."

"No, that's not right." Adelaide shakes her head left and right, trying to clear it. "They keep me so hopped up on drugs, but I was there– that's not what happened."

Whitt crouches down to Adelaide's level, trying to gain eye-contact. They stare at each other for a very long time, silently communicating. She turns her head abruptly as if she can't look at him any longer. I finally understand what Whitt meant by his family having a hard time looking at him.

"You're wrong," Adelaide accuses. "Father loves poison– especially poison of the mind. He poisoned your mother, too– drove her away. Grant was devastated. Father poisoned Cora in all ways because she was barren, so Grant left for good."

"Ade, our mother is still alive and well," he says softly. "And Grant didn't leave– he died. There is no Grant Whittenhower any longer."

"Good, you keep telling yourself that, Whitt. I know you know," Adelaide accuses, voice dripping with anger. "You were a curious child, always lurking around Misery Castle, sticking your nose where it didn't belong. Your favorite place to hide was behind the study curtains while Father plotted. It's safer if you pretend your ignorance."

"Ade, I pretend nothing," Whitt says calmly, but I've learned to read him and he's lying.

"Is this your lover?" Adelaide swings her blurry eyes toward me. It's unnerving when she looks at me. Beneath the drug haze is a stare full of life and knowledge, and it's at complete odds with her failing body.

"Dalton Fontaine Marconi, this is Adelaide Whittenhower." Whitt introduces us formally.

"It's nice to meet you." I mutter quietly as I shake her boney hand. Pulling away, I try not to cringe because touching Ade was like touching a skeleton.

"You're a poor liar," Adelaide accuses. "It's definitely not nice to meet me, but I appreciate the sentiment." She turns back to Whitt, with me long forgotten. "Very nice, little Daniel. I'm sure he's very pleasing to your sensibilities. You won't have to pretend with our chica any longer. I know how difficult that can be," she trails off.

"It's nice to finally be free." Whitt sounds happy yet sad.

"I wouldn't know," Adelaide grumbles.

"I'm sorry I failed you. I'm sorry Queen failed you. We're still trying." Whitt drops to his knees and buries his face into Adelaide's lap. She gently strokes his hair, trying to give what little comfort she has to offer. "I promise to get you out on my birthday."

"It's not the first time that bastard won, and it won't be his last. *She* can't even get me out of here. How were you and Regina supposed to circumvent it?"

"If we get you out, you'll go right back to her, won't you?" Whitt mutters hopelessly.

"I don't know… I haven't thought that far ahead because I doubt I'll ever get out. It's closing in on four years." Adelaide turns her head away from us, so we can't see the expressions crossing her face. "I was doing everything Father asked of me, and it never dawned on me that he'd put me here anyway. I do believe if I had married Ezra, I would have been untouchable. I'm in here because I

185

know too much and I'm a liability. If I ever get out of here, who would believe the traitor Adelaide Whittenhower after her stay in an insane asylum and the books she didn't publish? No one, that's who," she murmurs.

"I'd believe you," Whitt tries to comfort Adelaide. "Queen would believe you."

"You already know Grant's secrets even if you lie about them to my face," she says angrily. "I know you have something planned. Father thinks me a vegetable, and he purposefully talks about what you have planned when Diane and Regina visit. Then he tries to interrogate Regina. So I know I won't be released on your birthday, because my father hasn't gotten to where he is today by being anything but cautious."

"I'm not worried– my plans are set in stone, and Daniel can't hurdle them... Ade, what does your girlfriend want?" Whitt tries to lure the answer from her. "Why does she visit you?"

Girlfriend?

"Is that why you're here?" Adelaide uses the last reserves of her strength to push Whitt away from her. "Leave!" she demands, pointing at the exit.

"That's not why we came," Whitt whispers, sounding genuinely hurt. "I was curious. After everything that happened, I can't wrap my mind around Regina being forced to sit with Diane and Daniel. Why do you do that to her?"

"There are two sides to every story." Adelaide looks far off out the windows to somewhere we can't see, voice distant and ominous. "Both sides are right *and* wrong. It's not black or white, Whitt– it's all about perception."

"So you're saying it's okay that you allowed your father and girlfriend to use your name on those goddamned books, and then force Regina to sit next to them during your visits, after they smeared her all over the fucking place in the media?" Whitt's bellows echo around the cavernous room, shocking me senseless.

Standing to his full height of over six feet, Whitt curls his hands into fists, like he wants to battle an invisible enemy.

"Jesus Christ," I mutter in shock. "Why are all of these bastards terrorists? Ezra's own mother and your father were the assholes who are doing this to us? What the fuck for?"

"You're on one side and I'm on the other, but at the same time we're both right and wrong." Adelaide pulls out the crazies. "But it doesn't change the fact that I love you and that we're family. And at the end of the day, you and I want the same thing. We may go about it differently, but the outcome is the same. I went to Diane for help and you went to Marcus. But we both want our family whole and me out of this endless torture of a prison."

"How can you say Diane is right?" Whitt asks, sounding utterly flabbergasted.

"And how can you say Marcus is right?" she counters. "He's a monster for what he's done."

"And so is Diane," Whitt replies. "She's using us to hurt her own family because they like her husband better. Don't you see how insane that truly is?"

"Oh, now I see why Diane and my mother are the best of friends," I mutter underneath my breath. "They are the same woman in a different package."

"That was my point." Adelaide ignores me outright. "It's about perception. In order for there to be a war, there must be at least two sides. Take America and the Middle East. In America, we cheer when we gain an inch in our war, and they hate us for it. When they take that inch back, we hate them even more. Which side is right? Does it make it right simply because it's the side you're on? Because they're on their side, so wouldn't that make them right in their eyes and you wrong, and vice versa? Diane's not right, but neither is Marcus. Diane's not wrong, but neither is Marcus. It's wherever your loyalties lie."

Eyes held wide, I mouth to Whitt, *Ade is Coo-coo for Cocoa Puffs.*"

"We *are* in an asylum," he murmurs back. "When it comes to you personally, I guess we're all on the same side. We all want you out. But, Ade, never forget who put your name on those books. Don't forget who made you the martyr for their cause. Diane chose your side for you by taking you away from us."

"Father took me away from you all in the first place. Never forget that, Daniel. That is where your vengeance should lie. Diane gave me a choice, and I chose her, even if it was allying with the same person who stuck me here."

"I wish I would have thought to record you, so I could play it back and force you to hear yourself. You just said Daniel was at fault, how he locked you in here, yet you're okay because Diane said so. Do you hear yourself?"

"Your lover is with us today. Don't forget that you can't choose who you love. Don't make me choose between Diane and Father versus the rest of our family, because to me they are mutually exclusive."

"You're mentally stronger than I remember," Whitt mutters in shock. "Queen warned me of this."

"My body may be frail, but when the drugs clear from my mind, all I have is time to think. My mind and will get stronger the longer I sit here. It's been well over three years of sitting in this chair, watching the world revolve while evolving and devolving. That is the point, whether it's an asylum or a prison, both are prisons of the mind. You get sharper as your body rots before your very eyes."

"I'm sorry–" Whitt's breath hitches, then he chokes on a sob.

"You didn't ask to be born male, as I didn't ask to be born female. Neither of us asked to be born gay. Father never treated you properly, and he's tried to hide what is rightfully yours. You're an incredible, giving person. I don't doubt your sincerity or your ability to help. However, I do doubt that all your bases are covered. Never forget what happened to Grant when he tried to get out," she warns.

"My birthday is in less than two weeks." He can't hide the quiver in his voice. "You will be out of here on that day. That will be my gift to you, Ade. I promise."

"Don't make promises you can't keep," Adelaide mutters pessimistically. "While I'm a neutral party, not everyone is. Don't tell anyone who isn't already privy. While your guy is pretty to look at, I wouldn't tell him anything while his mother is playing on the same team with your enemies. I'm not saying he will betray you. I'm saying watch what you say and where, because you never know who's listening. A lot can happen in two weeks."

"I won't breathe a word of it. I won't even speak of it with Queen," he promises.

"Good– if I get out of here, I will tell you why I'm really in here. The second coming will happen on your birthday, Whitt. I promise you that."

"Until my birthday, Ade." Leaning down, he presses a soft kiss to her cheek, but she doesn't react to the affectionate touch.

"In case I don't see you on your birthday because father caught wind of your coup, happy birthday and I love you. I hope you're still breathing on your twenty-fourth!"

"You can count on it. I love you, too."

Holding hands, both of our minds spinning, we walk out of Adelaide's cold, stone room and down the hall. While passing so much opulence, I can't help but shudder, feeling as if the woman is trapped inside the most impenetrable gilded cage I've ever seen.

"I never thought I'd say this, but I'm glad I grew up in Vegas. Trash with money was easier to live through than old world money." I shake my head, bile I've staved off for the past twenty-four hours makes itself known.

"Why do you say this?" Whitt asks in confusion.

"Because where I come from, we just put a bullet into the brain of someone that holds our secrets. Here, you put them into an insane asylum and watch them rot, watch the sane turn insane. My way was humane– your way is cruel."

"I won't argue with you on that point. But my way at least gives you time to plan and execute a rescue, and I will get Adelaide out of here," he vows.

"That creepy shit she was spouting. She's not totally batshit, is she?"

"No, she's not."

"And you actually understand what she was talking about?"

"Yes," he admits reluctantly.

"You're Catholic. Isn't the second coming about Christ? I'm pretty sure Adelaide is batshit on that. I just don't see Jesus coming to your birthday party." I try to lighten the mood. When Whitt sighs, I know it's not happening.

"Ade wasn't talking about Jesus, Dalton."

"And you know who she's talking about?"

"Yes, I do. Not only will I tell you. I'll do you one better by driving past Jesus' house. You can see for yourself that Ade isn't crazy." After waving to the lady at the front desk, Whitt leads me to his deathtrap of a car. "If we're lucky, maybe he'll even wave to us on our way by."

Chapter Eighteen

"Welcome to the driving portion of our daylight Dominion tour." Whitt sounds remarkably lighthearted after our painful visit with Adelaide. "That large cathedral to our right was my educational institution for twelve years. The nuns were vicious creatures, whose wooden rulers snapped the knuckles of the innocent and guilty alike."

"I was homeschooled by Tony and Olivia…" I part my hands like, '*there ya go*.' Turning in my seat, I stare avidly at the large stone structure near the center of downtown Dominion. Kids of all ages are strolling down the sidewalk in their plaid uniforms, wearing blazers and leather shoes. "Do you guys have a hard-on for stone?"

"Stone lasts forever," Whitt replies absentmindedly as he waits at the crosswalk. A gaggle of teenagers push and shove at each other– poor or rich, all kids have the ability to act like assholes to get attention. "During college, everyone was impressed with my pedigree. But going to Hillbrook was very lonely for me. I was the lone gay kid at a Catholic school. I didn't have any friends who were my age."

"At least I had Sebastian," I murmur wistfully.

Now that the crossing-guard signaled we could pass, Whitt accelerates to the next stoplight, then he makes a left-hand turn. "I used to seek out the little kids, so I could hang out with Niel. I was made fun of for that… all the time."

"Oh, Whitt." My heart clenches, knowing exactly how suffocating loneliness can be.

Driving down a very familiar street, Whitt stops directly in front of the Brownstone. The crimson door with the cheery gargoyle knocker greets us, but we make no move to get out of the Roadster.

"Niel and Ella's father owns this house– *my* father." Whitt sounds lost, voice breaking. "Marcus trained me here from my eighteenth birthday, for nearly two years. Every. Single. Day. I didn't know."

"I figured it out after I spent some time with you... it just so happened to be the same day I spent time with him. It was beyond obvious once I wasn't blind to it."

"I didn't know– I thought I was Daniel's youngest unneeded heir, knowing deep in my heart it felt wrong. I didn't know until recently." Whitt pulls from the curb to reenter the flow of traffic.

We sit in silence while Whitt navigates through traffic, taking us out of Dominion proper toward the impenetrable Crestview gated community. We go through the same procedure as before with this gatekeeper, going as far as giving me a permanent pass to show the next time I visit. The security around the community is ten times denser than at the asylum.

Driving through the thick iron gates, Whitt begins pointing out homes. "Fate grew up in that house– Fate Simpson."

Staring at a stone mansion hidden behind another set of iron gates, "As in the new addition to the founding members of Dominion?"

"Exactly. Fate's father was an industrious man who died in prison for a Ponzi scheme. It was only natural for Fate to walk in her father's footsteps by going into finance." Voice dry, Whitt is being hella sarcastic.

"That's why I decided to get out of my family business." Pensive, I look to the identical houses, hiding behind their identical gates, wondering if the residents are dwelling in just another form of an inescapable gilded cage.

"Dominion's forefathers are connected in other ways– I'm just not sure how yet. We're all related, either by blood or business. We're a mix of enemies and friends... and we're all locked in here together. Trapped by a twelve foot fence and multiple gates."

"Shit– keep your friends close and your enemies closer."

Whitt points to a house two doors down and across the street, identical to the house Fate grew up in. "My mother lives there," he says without emotion. "Gwendolyn Meyers. I have many siblings in this community, I just don't know who."

"What?" My neck cranks my head to the side so I can take a good look at Whitt. "You're kidding, right?"

"No." Whitt pulls up to the curb in front of his mother's home. "I spend so much time looking at everyone's eyes and hair. Blue eyes. Blonde hair. Mark of a Whittenhower– of a Meyers. But it's hard to tell because people wear contacts or dye their hair dark." Slumping against his seat in defeat. "I gave up. For all I know, we're all inbred. It wouldn't shock me– just another way to keep the money and power in the family."

"Have you spoken to your mother?" I reach over to squeeze his hand where it's clenching the stick shift. "How the hell did this come to be?"

"Gwen knows who I am. I've waited for her to come to me, like a mother should. But she never has… I mean, I live here– with *her*."

"You're a man now," I remind Whitt. "And if your grandfather is anything like my mother… since you said they are probably friends, I bet Daniel acts like Olivia. Maybe this Gwen woman was terrified or blackmailed to stay away."

"Do you think so?" Whitt turns to me, hope blazing from his blue eyes. He squeezes my hand tightly. "I was Daniel's first failed bioengineered grandchild. But he raised me as his, telling me I was the last in line to the Whittenhower throne, when I was the first in line."

"That's what your birthday is about, isn't it? You're taking your birthright from him?"

"Yes," Whitt answers immediately. "My grandfather had it written up that he would retire upon the twenty-fourth birthday of his heir. Everyone assumes that's Niel– Grandfather doesn't realize I know my true paternity. I'm the heir, as Niel is my younger brother."

"Why did Daniel try to pass you off as his kid in the first place?"

"Grant was going to marry Gwen– awestruck and in love with her. Daniel got wind of it, so he took my mother away, telling Grant she left him. Nine months later, I came to be, and my grandparents raised me as theirs… Grant suspected, but I don't know if he knew I was his or not."

"He knew– there's no way he didn't. It's probably why he'd rather die and lose all of you than live in that house with the enemy."

"Grant was an introvert, hating all the politics, and just wanted to be left alone. Daniel saw this as a weakness, and after I came out as being gay, he… it's my fault Niel and Ella were born the way they were. If I'd been straight, Daniel wouldn't have trapped their mother… so maybe? So maybe Gwen was treated the same way? Do you think?"

Thinking rationally, "Niel's mother didn't get to raise him, did she? If it wasn't for you, he wouldn't know her, would he?"

193

"No." Whitt turns away from me, hiding the tears in his eyes. "I love her, you know? Like really, *really* love her. But I don't know how much of that is guilt over what my grandfather did to her because of me."

"If you're to blame, then Niel is– then she is." Reaching out with my fingertips, I grip Whitt's chin. Overcome with the need to comfort him, I lean forward to press an innocent kiss to his lips. "If I've learned anything recently, only blame the ones who are at fault– your grandfather."

"Thank you." Whitt pulls away with a smile on his face and tears in his eyes. "After we storm Misery Castle and take my birthright back, I'll get the courage up to visit my mother. Deal?"

"Deal. But only if you help me cut the cord with mine."

Driving again, Whitt murmurs, "Deal," while showcasing his dimples. "At the end of the street–"

Whitt fails to mention there is only *one* street. Each side of it is lined with giant stone mansions behind impenetrable gates. It's only ten or so, but they are spaced far apart with the acreage surrounding them.

"At the end of the street, there are three roads leading to three of the founders who started it all, with the original right in the thick of it– my mother's family. The Meyers. But the other three, they liked their privacy. So where it branches to the right, a mile up the drive, is Shadow Haven Estates. To the left, three miles up the drive, is Whittenhower Estates– Misery Castle. Dead center, a large Victorian home hides another drive. Ten miles out, on the very edge of the community, is a lake where another house used to stand."

"Jesus fuck!" I shout, eyes bugging out of my skull as we pass a gargantuan four-story home that looks suspiciously like an enlarged dollhouse with a turret. "That's Dexter's house!"

"You're a good guesser." Whitt laughs as I gawk in awe. "Leave it to Dex to be the only original one of the bunch, even if it's a bit of an eyesore. If you ever want to visit anyone, just remember to the right of Dexter is Ezra, and to the left is me, and behind his house is where Marc takes naughty boys and girls to give lectures."

"Thanks for the warning– Marc's threatened me with a trip up there. Only where I come from, when the main boss takes you to the woods, don't expect to leave the woods."

"I'm glad you're leaving that life behind." Whitt turns to the left, driving through yet another gate but he doesn't have to stop because it required remote-access. We enter a tree-lined paved drive that seems to go on for miles.

"Tonight is a night-in-the-life-of-Dalton-Anthony-Fontaine-Marconi, remember?" I tease Whitt. "You'll be dining with Dominion's underworld boss."

"Seriously?" Whitt's eyes widen impossibly. "Fucking sweet! I'll be walking on the edge tonight." He gives my hand another squeeze, informing me he's good with anything I throw his way. "Well, we'll finish up a day-in-the-life… I'm sure Daniel ran off to Diane, and most likely Olivia, the instant we left Wintercrest, so we'll have Misery Castle to ourselves."

"Oh," bursts out of me with excitement. "What are we doing?"

"Mind out of the gutter, babe," Whitt teases, and as much as I hate that endearment, it makes my heart beat triple-time. "It's boring Daniel Whittenhower II for you since it's still daylight. We're playing tennis against Whitney, Prissy, Niel, and Ella. Most likely Ava and Spyder will be there, too."

"I suck at sports," I grumble, feeling like an awkward heroine from a young adult novel. Misery Castle is the perfect setting. "But I'll cheer."

"You do that, babe." Whitt busts out laughing, blue eyes glinting with mischievousness. "You do that."

Chapter Nineteen

"Are you sure my car is going to be safe sitting here?" Whitt looks around the busy street, eyes held wide with fright. We're in the lower-income section of Dominion, where the thugs come out at night. Pretty Boy is under the impression he's either going to be solicited for sex or drugs, mugged at knifepoint, or have his Roadster jacked.

All of which could happen. With a two second scoping of the area, I spot three drug dealers, half a dozen whores of both sexes, and every single person on this street is a criminal.

Except for Daniel Whittenhower II.

Holding in a laugh, I can't stop the amused blush from creeping up my cheeks. "You're parked between a Hummer and an Escalade, what do you think?"

"Yeah, but…" Whitt looks around erratically, his palm sweating against mine.

"Hey, Whitt?" I tug free of his hand, and then climb out of his car. "How can you not recognize that giant yellow Hummer?"

"Dude!" Whitt hops out of his car in a rush, scared to be separated from me. "I've never even been to this street. Are you sure it's safe?"

"That Hummer is probably rolling down the single street in your inbred village a dozen times a day. Really? You don't recognize it? Its owner jogs with Toby and Dex, and the dang thing is always a hundred paces behind anyone with the Zeitler or Whittenhower last name once you leave your gates."

"Oh! That's Gunner's wheels?" Whitt looks noticeably relieved, but his eyes keep flicking around. "Are you sure it's safe?"

"How many yellow hummers are there in the area with a Marine emblem on its ass?" I hitch my thumb over my shoulder. "That Escalade belongs to Stanton Green. Your Roadster now has a '*do not touch*' sign on it."

"Wow," Whitt murmurs in awe, staring at Stan's SUV like it holds a rockstar.

"Stan's just a dude, Pretty Boy," I remind him, and then I walk toward the restaurant.

"An Italian Restaurant?" Whitt quickly catches up with me, giving his car a cursory backward glance. "I feel like I just became an extra on the newest version of The Godfather... and Stanton Green isn't just a dude. He's the leader of the underworld."

"You've been kissing on one for the past few days," I remind him. "Okay." I stop with my hand on the door handle. I have to bite the inside of my cheek to stop myself from laughing. "See that building right there," I gesture across the street. "Alex lived there his whole life until he moved to the Brownstone."

Neck arching backward like mine had been when I took in Misery Castle, Whitt absorbs the reality of a fifteen-story walk-up with a drug dealer hanging out on the corner. "Really?" Whitt's eyes go wide and his voice pitches high, looking like a little kid on Christmas morning.

"Yeah," I nod my head while humming the word. "Bianca grew up in the building at my back, which is still the main point of operation for Stanton. Above this restaurant is where I lived when I arrived in Dominion, until my mother demanded I spy on everyone at Restraint." I grab his hand, tugging a little to get the awestruck look from his eyes. "You're safer standing here than you are on your single street in Crestview. I promise."

"I'm ready." Whitt's vibrating with excitement, and the fear is charging it higher. "I'll even try to be nice to Bianca."

"Sure you will," I mutter underneath my breath, knowing Bianca and Whitt are going to be at each other's throats all night. I wrench the door open, but a large hand on my chest stops me in my tracks.

I look up and up, smiling friendly as my eyes make the trek. Whitt's hand in mine is quivering in fear of the three hundred pound, six and a half foot tall Mexican man guarding the door.

"Hey, Julio!" I chirp, hoping my tone will calm Whitt's nerves.

"I'm glad to see you without that fucking disgusting disguise, Dalton." Julio shivers as if revolted.

"Same here– it's going to meet its fiery death later on tonight." I turn to the side. "Whitt, this is Julian Ramirez, Stanton Green's enforcer. Julio, this is Daniel Whittenhower."

"What's an enforcer?" Whitt whispers in my ear from behind me at the same time he thrusts his hand out for a shake. Ever polite. "Nice to meet you, Julio. Do you have to pat us down for weapons?"

"As much fun as that might be…" Julio grins at us while he checks out Whitt– the suave motherfucker. "My boyfriend might get his tighty whities in a wad over it, Pretty Boy."

"How'd you know my nickname?" Whitt tries to wiggle by me to get inside the restaurant, but I sidestep him.

"Just now celebrating your gaydom?" Julio snorts. "Pretty Boy isn't a nickname– it's what you are. Cory and I'll have to take you guys out to induct you into the club."

"Take us out?" Whitt's voice quivers. "Induct us into the club? Is that like being jumped into a gang?"

"Oh, my God!" A small red-haired man with a smattering of freckles across his button nose approaches us from behind Julio. "Stop taunting the Pretty Boy rich kid, Julian." He reaches around Julio's wide body to shake Whitt's hand. "I'm Cory. Julian's partner of too many years… and he's just jerking your chain."

"Whitt?" Julio steps to the side to allow us entrance. "I meant we'd take you to a gay club."

"Oh!" Whitt's cheeks and forehead bloom crimson. "That would be fun."

We enter a classic Italian restaurant, with its dark lighting, burgundy décor scented with garlic and tomatoes, and padded booths. It's after closing time, and Stanton has the big, round booth in the back set for our family-style dinner.

Julio locks the front door while Cory changes the music to anything but Sinatra, knowing it reminds me too much of Tony. Holding Whitt's hand like a little kid instead of a potential boyfriend, I lead him to the rear booth, with Julio wandering off to locate the rest of our party.

As quiet as a ghost, Levi's the first to sneak in from the back. Not too tall, or too short, hair a shadow on his scalp, my big brother is about as unassuming as the average Joe, but…

"Hey, bub!" I receive a big grin and a shoulder pat. "Looking good, real good."

"Why is Wil here?" Whitt has to work on his whispering skills, because Levi's lips quirk up at the corners.

"Whitt, this is Leviticus Wilson." I gesture between us. "My brother."

"Holy shit!" Whitt takes a step back as if struck. "Our new head of security is your brother? Is that why he showed up when you were attacked?"

"Hey, now–" Caleb struts in from the kitchen carrying a tray a lasagna, with his flip-flops making popping sounds on the linoleum tiles. "*I'm* your new head of security– this motherfucker has a day job."

"Gunner?" Whitt's eyes cut to mine, betrayal written in their depths.

"Caleb Green– Stanton Green's baby brother and Bianca's doting uncle."

"And yes," Caleb says as he sets the tray down. "That is why we showed up to Restraint when we did. But once we were there, Stanton didn't want you guys getting harmed in any way, so we stayed to keep you and the kiddies safe."

"That was sweet of you." Whitt blushes again, eyes drinking down my brother, no doubt looking for similarities. "This is so awkward."

"About as awkward as Dalton with a tennis racket." Caleb's howls of laughter echo around the restaurant. "I was shadowing the Whittenhower Prince this afternoon, so I got a good view of the shenanigans on the tennis court."

"NO!" I cover my face with my palms. "I told you I suck at sports."

Levi holds his phone up in front of my face, wiggling it. "We got pictures, too."

"Can I see?" Whitt sounds like an eager puppy.

"No," comes from several sources– the loudest is the feminine protest coming from the closed kitchen door. Then Bianca walks in carrying a bowl of tossed salad in one hand and a breadbasket in the other. "Good evening, soon-to-be-ex-husband and homewrecker."

"Oh, this will not end well," Levi mutters while wearing a sadistic grin. "I just love a pissed off female– reminds me of my wife's constant disposition."

Caleb hurries over to take the food from his niece's hands– no doubt fearing it will be used as a projectile weapon.

I bite the bullet. I let go of Whitt's hand long enough to go to Bianca. Pulling her into my arms, I kiss her cheek. "Bianca, behave.

Please," I beg. "You know the divorce papers were printed up months ago."

"I'm allowed to be bitter." Bianca pouts, squeezing me tightly. "It's only been since this morning. What kind of girl gets over it in a few hours, Dalton? Gay or not, that's an asshole attitude if I've ever heard one."

Rolling my eyes at a suddenly possessive Whitt while whispering to Bianca, "Your troupe will be doing shows in Europe all summer long– you'll live through my rejection, I'm positive."

"Of course I will." Bianca pulls from my embrace. "But you really need to be a bit more empathetic and look at it from my perspective. All gay men think women are the villains. While I'm happy you're happy, I'm allowed to feel like shit because you kicked me to the curb like trash."

"Point taken." I hold Bianca at arm's length, really trying to understand instead of just flippantly brushing her off while calling her manipulative like my mother. "I've been unfair."

"You have," she accuses, voice warping with hurt instead of anger. "I *am* happy for you. But it's no different than someone saying, '*I'm happy to be away from you– to be divorced from you so I can go play with my new boyfriend without feeling guilty,*' and that's just plain rotten."

"Shit," I hiss, never thinking of it like that. "I know I was being selfish, but I really do believe you deserve someone who can love you back. Truly."

"I know," Bianca stresses. "But the delivery sucked donkey balls big time, Dalton. I feel like a laughingstock. Like everyone is pointing at me and snickering behind my back. '*Bianca was Dalton's beard, but look how happy he is now that he's shaved the bitch away.*' Awesome!" Bianca shouts. "I'm fucking happy for you, Dalton. But don't make me out to be the bitch because my feelings are genuinely hurt and I want to cry– that's not manipulation. I'm not pulling an Olivia. It's just how I feel, and pretending everything is hunky-dory will not change it."

Bianca pulls away from me, and I let her go. She stomps angrily over to the booth to slide in to take a seat. While we were arguing, Julio, Cory, Levi, Gunner, and Whitt had sat down to the table.

Standing in the middle of the restaurant, I feel a bit lost. Shrieking with surprise, my head is drawn back sharply by fingers knotting in my hair. A big, wet smacker is placed on my forehead, then Stanton ambles away, laughing to himself.

Stanton Green, lord of Dominion's underworld, is a big teddy bear. With his tan skin, dark curly hair, and brown eyes, Stan is a younger, hotter version of Vince Vaughn... and Whitt blushes like Stanton is the movie star while he introduces himself.

Shrugging, I walk across the restaurant and take a seat at the end of the booth next to Whitt, across from us are Stanton and Bianca, with the rest smushed in the rounded end.

"I'm glad you could join us, Daniel," Stanton can be just as polite as Whitt. "Most of all, I'm glad to see Dalton's beautiful face instead of the makeup and contact lenses."

"Whitt and I are having a ceremonial burning later on– you're more than welcome to join us." Blushing, I try to make myself even smaller than I am, hating being the object of everyone's undivided attention.

"Next time we eat together, we should do so at my home." Stanton passes the tossed salad around the table, signaling everyone can eat. He doesn't stand on ceremony like many crime bosses do. "We would have tonight, but Levi said you're not allowed to know about his personal life until Olivia is no longer in yours."

"I'm working on it," I mutter sheepishly while digging out a square of lasagna. I raise my eyes to meet Bianca's. "This looks amazing, Binks."

Blushing, Bianca looks like I just paid her the best compliment possible. "Thanks– you know I'm addicted to the Food Network."

Stanton keeps talking as if we weren't interrupting him– in any other family, we'd be punished. But we're a real family. "I don't like to live alone, so I invited Levi and his family to live with me. Caleb and Bianca live next to us, with Julio and Cory across the hall. Levi's wife's Aunt Amelia lives next to us as well. So there was too much risk to allow you into The Green Building if you're still allowing Olivia to influence you."

"I don't care if you stay in contact with our mother." Levi leans forward so I can see him around Caleb. "I just need to be sure you won't do anything she asks. I just found out my wife is pregnant, and I didn't think I could have kids in the first place, so I'm being extra cautious."

"Congratulations!" Whitt and I shout at the same time– we bump our shoulders together because we thought it was funny. "I love having nieces and nephews. Spoiling them, that is."

"This baby is important," Levi says cryptically while looking at Whitt, then Bianca, then back to me. "Now I just have to get my wife to relax."

"That's impossible." Bianca snorts, but Caleb laughs outright.

"You'll have to tie her ass to a goddamn chair." Stanton's words are surly but said with affection. "The pregnancy hormones are making her attitude worse, if you can imagine it."

"Baked goods." Bianca giggles into her napkin. "I just pass her baked goods and walk around her."

"Let's pray for another boy," Caleb ribs his buddy. "Between your wife's attitude and your mother's, if you have a girl, she'll be an atomic bomb ready to blow."

Sharing a rare grin with us, Levi looks proud as hell. "Let's hope the baby gets my temperament."

"Oh, that's so much better," Stanton teases. "I'll have to put a bell on the kid, fearful I'll step on it since you're as quiet as a ghost."

"My wife's son turned out spectacular, even with who his dad is."

Whitt's lips make their way to my ear, learning his lesson earlier. He barely breathes the words to me. "Do you feel like we're the brunt of some cosmic joke right now?"

"Hell, yeah," I mutter back, not caring who hears my side of the conversation.

"Like we should know Levi's wife and just get these hints they're tossing out. But since we don't know what's going on, they're secretly making fun of us at the same time."

"Exactly," I snarl, eyeing each and every one at the table. "But then again, I can't be trusted. Maybe after I can be, they'll let me know."

Lips fluttering against the shell of my ear, a shiver dances up my spine. "I have the sneaking suspicion the jokes on me, too. Green is a Dominion founding father– there's an empty house in inbred valley with Stanton's name on it."

Whitt pulls away from me, our eyes connecting, and it's like an odd partnership is formed. We silently communicate how all of their secrets will be solved. But not because Olivia Fontaine wants to know. Simply because I feel like Daniel and I are connected many times over, and we deserve to know the truth.

"–Backdraft today," Cory is rattling off a story that finally registers when Whitt and I finish our silent communication. "Scary as fuck."

"I missed it," Levi mutters despondently. "I was on bus duty. Three difficulty breathings, a head-on MVA, and the scene of a stabbing. I would have rather run into a burning building than watched a wife mourn the loss of her husband– massive heart attack on their kitchen floor."

"I'd rather be a mobster than a hero." Stanton bows his head slightly, saying a quick prayer for those who were lost today.

"Caleb's the hero," Julio teases, earning a slap upside the head from Caleb. "Cory says it's just another day at the office, and he can't let it get to him."

"It's true," Cory jumps in. "I keep my own log beside the chief's log, tallying the calls. You don't want to know how many dead I've attended to over the years. If I dwelled on it, I couldn't handle it."

"So you're a firemen?" Whitt's mind is spinning, weaving puzzle pieces together I won't even think of by next week.

"Cory's our chief," Levi says without hesitation. "I started out as a paramedic, but I trained to be a firefighter as well. This way I can help wherever I'm needed."

Stanton meets my eyes, smiling like I should be paying close attention. "Never in my wildest imaginings did I believe I'd have a Marine brother, two firefighters, and Daniel fucking Whittenhower II sitting around my table. But *faith* has odd plans for us, and who are we to disagree with her."

"To Faith!" Everyone but Whitt and me lift their wine glass.

Chapter Twenty

"This wasn't what I had in mind when you said ceremonial fire," Whitt doesn't appreciate my sense of humor. We're standing in the back lot behind Restraint, which thankfully has two empty buildings flanking it. Otherwise, I wouldn't be doing this here because I'd piss off the natives.

"Is this how homeless people keep warm?" Whitt asks, looking sheepish as all hell as he adds more cardboard to the burning barrel. "I've never even seen one of these before."

"Cardboard?" I deadpan while handing him another smashed liquor box. "Your world is very small, Pretty Boy. This–" I wiggle the box. "Is called cardboard. It's made of paper, which began its life as a seed, then a seedling, then a sapling, then a tree. Then some hot, burly lumberjack cut its life short and sent it to a paper processing plant. It's all very technical, but happening all over the great state of New York, with our plentiful forests."

Mouth hanging wide open, Whitt just gawks at me.

"Um… I'm giving you fair warning. Once I get to know someone, my sense of humor can come off as more than sarcastic."

"Asshole, you mean. You can come off as an asshole." Whitt grabs the box from my fingertips. "I can see how you wore your disguise so well."

"I'm an acquired taste," I admit, blushing like a sonofabitch but thankful it's dark outside.

"Cardboard?" Whitt eyes me, the firelight making him look sinister. "I meant I've never seen a metal fire pit thing before, other than on TV when the homeless are keeping warm around them."

"And Detective Hotshit is questioning them about a murder, and rewarding them with a bottle wrapped in a paper bag… You watch a lot of crime dramas, don't you?" Of course he does– where else would Whitt have picked up the gang lingo he was tossing around with Julio, making an ass out of himself. Julio was enamored with Whitt by the end of dinner, thinking him adorable instead of a moron.

Whitt actually asked Julio if Stanton jumped him into the gang, like a gang and a mafia family were mutually exclusive. Then he had the balls to ask if anyone besides me had killed before. Needless to say, everyone laughed their asses off.

"Explain to me why we're burning your disguise here?" Whitt shifts closer, placing his hands over the barrel to warm himself. He rubs his palms together, smiling at me like he just learned a new trick.

Teaching Pretty Boy about the real world is going to be a trip.

"Bright stuff hot. Bright stuff burn skin from bone." I enunciate like a caveman, earning a swift kick to the ass. Releasing a delicious sound, Whitt laughs harder than I do, learning how I operate. "What did you envision when I said a ceremonial burning?"

"Out in a field somewhere– maybe some chanting." Whitt, God love him. "Instead, we're in a dirty parking lot borrowing a homeless person's furnace, after stealing cardboard from the recycling bin. There's probably ten very cold people huddled in a ball nearby, planning to jump us right now."

Reaching forward faster than I thought imaginable, I grab the back of Whitt's neck and kiss the ever-loving fuck out of him, all the while laughing harder than I have ever before in my entire life. "This isn't a virgin sacrifice," I breathe directly into Whitt's mouth, and then nip the tip of his tongue with my front teeth. "It's May– sixty-two degrees. No one is cold but you."

"Yeah, well… you were out of your element at Misery Castle today– don't forget that." Whitt taunts me a split-second before his tongue dives into my mouth to steal a taste. Groaning, we try to pull each other closer, finding out that fire is indeed HOT.

"Ouch!" I hiss, rubbing at my hip. "Ceremonial burning first– making out next."

"Deal." Whitt bends down to grab some more cardboard, finding feeding the fire utterly fascinating. "It consumes it so quickly– beautiful," he purrs, on the verge of gaining a new kink.

Arson.

"Did Niel's mother ever teach you that playing with fire meant you'd piss the bed?" I crouch down to sort through the crate of stuff I carried down from my efficiency apartment. A new thought hits me out of nowhere– if I don't have to spy for my mother any longer,

I can move anywhere I please. I miss the apartment Stanton had originally set up for me.

"Um... no?" Whitt answers with an upward inflection, making it sound like a question. "Who taught you that saying?"

"Devlin caught me burning myself," I admit for the first time. "I would hold a lighter against my forearm, with the flame licking toward the crook of my elbow, and I'd see how long I could take it... long time it turns out. Devlin had to take me to the hospital for burn treatment."

"Jesus, Dalton." The concern in Whitt's voice ensures I'll never do something so stupid again.

"So the next time Tony tried to have Bruno burn the fag out of me, I asked Bruno if he wet the bed." I laugh at the memory when most would probably cry. "Tony was so floored, he just stared at me for like ten minutes. Then he hugged me, saying I was definitely his kid."

"So–" Whitt seems hesitant to ask in the face of something so uncomfortable. But to me, it's just my memories. "Did Bruno wet the bed?"

"He must have!" I stand upright from my crouch with a pair of trousers in my hands. "Because he turned bright red, looked so mortified that he wanted to cry, then he ran out of the office." My voice softens, sounding fond when it shouldn't. "Long story short, that was how I stopped the cigar burns, and Bruno kicked his smoking habit."

"Win-win?" Whitt looks at me, clearly unsure how he should respond when I bring up this shit.

I toss Dalton Thompson's brown trousers into the fire, which gains Whitt's undivided attention as the flames lick at the offering. "You don't have to say you're sorry, or try to feel pity for me, or say anything at all. If a memory hits me out of nowhere, I'll share it. But the odd thing is that it's actually a comfort to say it out loud, like Tony is with me. Before, the memories never came unless I was in pain. So exorcising my demons the normal way is a relief."

"I'll bet," Whitt murmurs, eyes never leaving the fire. "Saner and safer– consensual."

"You just ripped off the BDSM motto." I roll my eyes while grabbing a handful of brown clothing. I pass Whitt half of the bundle, knowing he'll get a kick out of feeding the fire.

207

Hesitant, Whitt dips a sleeve into the fire, waiting for it to catch. Flames lick up toward his hand, then he freaks out, dropping the entire shirt into the barrel. Stepping back, Whitt's face is twisted up like the fire disobeyed him by trying to maim his flawless skin.

Laughing, I toss in three shirts and a pair of trousers. "We received vastly different educations. We're complete opposites."

"I think we complement each other well, actually." Whitt takes the initiative by grabbing the rest of the articles of clothing from the crate. Still skittish, he lunges forward, drops the clothing into the fire, and then leaps backward like it's going to jump out and touch him.

"Always be careful not to add too much, or you'll smother it. Pretend fire is a human being– it needs oxygen to breathe." Using the length of wood I stole from next to the dumpster, I stir the fire back to life. "I was the kid who liked what you'd probably call the help. When no one was looking, I'd run off down the street where they'd be around a burning barrel, drinking and swapping stories."

"Well, Kris used to be the help…" Whitt offers as explanation. To anyone else's ears, it would sound like he was saying it was okay to screw your help. But what I hear is how he befriended her– trusts her.

Wig in hand, "This is why I picked the back lot at Restraint for the ceremonial burning. I was an asshole to the people inside this building– I don't like who I became. Because it did affect me in more ways than one. Also, the asshole didn't deserve a field in the middle of nowhere with chanting and dancing around the fire like we came straight out of the Salem Witch Trials."

"Damn… how much time do you and Jamie spend together?" Whitt steps forward, wrapping an arm around my shoulders. "You should visit when Cort comes over– the three of you could do a book club."

"When I was growing up, books couldn't judge, they couldn't make demands, and they never harmed me." I drop the wig into the fire. Fully filling my lungs with smoky air, I take a deep breath for the first time since my mother handed me the wig. "I was mourning my father and the taint on my soul. Olivia– I refuse to call her master now –she came to Dominion with the disguise, handed it to me, and told me to watch Marcus and report back to her. Less than two months later, she demanded I move into Restraint, so I could watch Marc through all of you. I haven't had a life since– I've only lived a life of my own creation for six weeks out of my twenty-four years."

"Olivia didn't like Stanton's positive influence over you, that's what she was up to." Whitt steps behind me, placing his hands around my hips. Pulling slightly, he forces me to lean against his chest. Pleasant warmth blooms in my body, and it's not from the fire.

"I was too blind to see it for what it was," I murmur, eyes riveted to the sight of the flames consuming the strands of brown hair– crackling and popping, it curls before it burns into nothingness. "I just thought my mother cared about me, worried over a hit being taken out on my life. Now I don't know if I'm capable of recognizing when someone is conditioning me to react to their stimuli."

"Not everyone is like Olivia and Daniel, but I'd suggest you stay away from Ezra's mother. Diane Holden would probably have the ability to twist your head." Whitt props his chin on my shoulder, eyes gazing at the fire.

"At what point do we turn into them? They started out as us, being controlled and manipulated by their elders– feeling just as lost and out of control. When I was small, I saw that wild look in Olivia's eyes."

"It's why Grant died." Voice thick with unshed tears, Whitt struggles to continue speaking. "He didn't want to turn into Daniel… and for that, I don't blame him."

"You talk about him as if he's two different people," I murmur so quietly it's barely a whisper.

"Grant *is* dead," Whitt stresses. "Just as Dalton Thompson is no more. Gone. The reason we created Generation Next was because of Grant. We're not going to fall into this trap. The kids will not have someone choose who they should love, what job they perform, or warp their sense of self. Their children will not be created to please their patriarch. No more picking a strong woman because they felt their son too weak. That is how we won't become our parents."

Whitt steps away from me, leaving my back suddenly cold with the loss of his body. He crouches down to grab everything else out of the crate. "You asked how you'll know if someone is manipulating you into reacting–" Whitt dumps everything into the fire. "This is how. The fact that you're burning who Olivia Fontaine created is why you are a member of Generation Next."

Overcome with emotion, I watch as boxes of brown contact lenses and Dalton Thompson's official paperwork and driver's license burn into nothingness. Nearly four years of my life goes up in smoke, and when the flames die out, I feel rejuvenated.

Alive.

No more Dalton Thompson, or Dalton Anthony Fontaine Marconi, as they were both shaped by another's hand, formed in the image of my mother and father and the very men I cleansed from the earth.

The core of what makes Dalton *me* is resurrected.

Chapter Twenty-One

After the fire dies out, we leave the burning barrel in the middle of the parking lot to be moved once it has cooled down. I place the crate near the dumpsters, knowing one of the remodeling crew will scavenge it. Since Restraint has been closed down, the main club is being transformed, as well as the upper floors. We were just given forty-eight hours' notice that the dungeon will be closed while it undergoes renovation.

Tonight I want it to be about Whitt and me and no one else. So we sneak in the side door situated at the rear of the dungeon, and then slip into the hallway. Being snoopy, Whitt keeps looking over his shoulder at our membership. Tonight and tomorrow night will be the last opportunity to play in the dungeon for a long while. The members are going wild.

I catch sight of Sebastian making a new friend with Tobias, sitting side-by-side on the spanking bench, chatting with each other while watching the scene unfolding before them with great amusement. Dexter and Monica are holding court on the sofa, laughing and giving pointers to Aaron and Roarke as they double-team Kayla and Heidi. Stark-naked, Alex is chasing after an equally naked Kristal, with his hard-on flopping all over the place and a riding crop in his hand.

"It's like Lord of the Flies in there," I mutter underneath my breath as I slip up the hidden staircase to my apartment. I pause, noticing Whitt is no longer with me.

Frozen into place, Whitt stares with great longing in the direction of the dungeon. He's pitching the biggest tent I've ever seen. "I'm so horny," he whispers in my direction. "It's like I can't help myself. I don't want anyone in there– I mean, being playful *is* fun. But I want to get off so badly that I don't care how or with who, and that frightens me."

"Whitt?" I call, hating the fear tingeing his voice.

211

"Will I be able to be faithful?" Whitt looks over his shoulder at me, blue eyes darkened with lust and terror. "My mother was passed around like a cheap whore. Grant was married while making kids with another, all the while still in love with my mother. Do you think it's written on my DNA?"

"Truth?" I step out of the stairwell and walk back down the hallway, coming even with the meeting room. "Neither one of us has been in a gay relationship before. Right now, we're just learning to be friends."

"I think that's going rather well, your horrific tennis skills aside," Whitt teases me, and it causes me to grin because it's the truth.

"We're learning about each other. So let's not make it more than it is, and I'm not saying that to be a dick. We can be friends, we most certainly will be lovers, but we can't have a relationship until we get to know whether we even like each other or not."

"So wise." Whitt smiles at me, dimples indenting. "I've always wanted to ask him if he felt like he was cheating on Gwen with the others, and did he love Niel and Ella's mother. Maybe the difference is being in love with someone."

"It's about commitment, Pretty Boy." I tug his arm, leading him back down the hallway. "Commitment *and* respect, and that doesn't equate monogamy. I signed the divorce papers because I felt guilty for having you in my bed. Bianca deserved the respect, because everyone before you didn't matter– you're going to matter to me someday."

"Oomph," is torn from my chest from the force of my back hitting the wall. Whitt sucks the air from my lungs, mouth creating a seal over mine. Groaning, grinding the proof that he's a horny fucker against my belly, Whitt suddenly grows multiple hands.

Sneaky hand slipping into the back of my jeans, my ass is clutched tightly. With every squeeze, fingernails bite in, leaving crescent-shaped marks. My hair, my cheek, even my throat, is caressed as Whitt feasts at my mouth. That same hand moves with lightning-speed, yanking up my shirts while unzipping my pants.

Right in the middle of the hallway, in perfect view of the dungeon, Whitt begins stripping me. As hot as it is, I'm not ready to be on display just yet, not the first time anyway.

Pulling away, hand gripping the waistband of my jeans so I won't trip, I run up the stairs to my apartment, with Whitt growling behind me. "Chasing you is making me hornier, Dalton." His fingertips just miss yanking my hair. "You should know better than that! Jesus Christ Almighty, look at that goddamn ass of yours jiggle when you run..."

The intense longing in Whitt's voice is only eclipsed by his lust, and it makes me feel desired in a good way, instead of the lecherous way my mother's clients made me feel. Bubbles of laughter spilling from my throat, the sound carefree, I dart away from Whitt's demanding hands as I charge up the stairs. I make it all the way to my apartment door before I'm tackled against the surface.

"Got you," Whitt pants breathlessly into my ear. "Hmm... we need keys. Now." Octopus hands and a demanding tongue search me in places no key has ever been hidden– behind my ears, the roof of my mouth, and the column of my throat. Teeth bite my nipples through the fabric of my shirts while two fingertips press forward, searching between my ass cheeks.

"Eh!" I squeak out when Whitt tries to penetrate me. "Front pocket! Front pocket!"

"You sure?" Whitt purrs against my lips. "Hmm... what do we have in here?" Palm cupping my bulge, Whitt squeezes a few times until my knees go weak. By the time he unzips my fly, I'm about to faint. Rubbing the back of his hand against my cock with only my boxers between us, I grit my teeth against the need to drop to the floor, get on my hands and knees, and beg to be taken by Pretty Boy.

"It's no wonder you were so adamant about being searched by Julio," I mutter wryly, trying to distract myself from the way Whitt keeps running a fingertip around the wet spot I'm forming in my boxers.

"I had this insane need to watch that big fucker touch you– Julio's a foot and a half taller than you and nearly three times your size. As wrong as it may be, I was getting off on the visual."

"Keys?" I remind him, because rimming my asshole with a fingertip is so far off base from grabbing the keys out of my front pocket. "Fuck!" My head hitches backward into the door. "That feels way too good."

"Are these keys?" Whitt has my pants to my ankles, with my boxers pulled to my hips– my hard-on is keeping them from falling off. Reaching in, Whitt cups my nutsack, rolling the balls around in his palm. "I'm going to be sucking these later."

213

"Jesus." My legs give out, and only Whitt's hand tugging on my balls keeps me upright. "Get the goddamn keys!"

"You're no fun," Whitt pouts, nipping my neck with his front teeth. Then my jeans are tugged free of my ankles, no longer hobbling me. Fishing around in my pockets, Whitt finally produces my keyring. His bright blue eyes glint in the light of the stairwell and his mouth quirks up into a grin showcasing those dimples.

I want to tongue those devastating dimples... after I rub my cockhead against the divots.

With the twist of the doorknob, I'm propelled into my apartment, only wearing a pair of boxers, my shirts, and a pair of sneakers. I must look ridiculous.

The click of the deadbolt being engaged is deafening in the silence of the room. Leaning against the door, Whitt stares at me from the eyes of a starving predator. I realize if I don't slow this down, some much needed closure on my part will be lost. Unhinged, Whitt's about ten seconds from pounding into my asshole.

"Get on my bed, Pretty Boy," I order, knowing Whitt will only obey me because he wants what I have. "I've never gotten naked for someone before, and I want to do it right."

Eager, Whitt is across the room and hopping onto my bed in an instant. He lies on his back, pants tented beyond comprehension, patiently waiting for whatever comes next.

"I hope you enjoy the show," I whisper in his direction, and a flirty smile curls my lips when he visibly shudders.

Standing in the middle of the room in my tiny apartment, my world shifts on its axis. "Now that I'm finally me, I'm going to find a place that's more my style. A space that's sexy– this is depressing because it reminds me too much of Asshole Thompson."

"It looks pretty sexy to me," Whitt practically growls as he shifts on the bed. "Anywhere you are is unbelievably sexy– I've had a damn crush on you for years. Queen kept trying to convince me it was mutual, but I didn't believe her. She screwed you as a *screw you* to me, and it worked."

Huffing out a laugh, "That explains so much." Hair tickling at my jawline, I shake my head back and forth. "I couldn't understand the woman's cryptic bullshit, but *that* I do understand."

I do the opposite of what most people would do during a striptease. I've seen countless women strip and give a show– Olivia's girls have a rare talent for slow seduction, while Tony's girls were just straight-up whores paid to be naked. I decide on a different approach. After all, I'm a man stripping for a man.

I catch Whitt's crystal, blue gaze with my own, with the pounding of my heart filling my ears, but the loudest sound in the space is Whitt's breathing. He roughly huffs in puffs of air. Rasping, his chest goes up and down rapidly with anticipation.

I'm not a muscular man. Most people would find me different than the norm thought of as attractive. My otherness is what makes me unique. It's what turns them on. I have a slight frame and I'm below average height, but I'm completely androgynous. Women see the man. Straight men see the pale skin, ruby-kissed lips, big green eyes, and silky black hair and think woman. Depending on the type of gay man, they get to pick what they see– a man with a healthy cock, or a feminine-shaped man who they can control. I'm perfect to seduce any gender or orientation.

After spending a few days with him, I still don't know what Whitt finds attractive in a man, but I can be anything but burly.

Striptease etiquette suggests how I should remove my shirt first, and then slowly lower my boxers. But I don't. After kicking off my sneakers, I drop my boxers to the floor in less than a second.

No foreplay or pretense.

Showcased in the bright light glowing from overhead, I show Whitt the obscene length that many men and women– gay or straight – have requested to see, have signed their lives away to touch, and have paid thousands of dollars to suck.

I stand before Whitt in just a long-sleeved shirt with my cock slowly filling with blood from the attention of his gaze. Once I'm fully engorged, the weight is too heavy for my cock to point toward my belly or even stand straight out in front of me. At eleven inches long and thick enough that my cock doesn't look skinny, it hangs low, hiding the nutsack beneath.

Eyes glued to my erection, Whitt roughly gasps in air to fill his lungs as his fingers tangle in the covers on my bed. His reaction has me ready in the blink of an eye– harder than ever before, enough so that my cock is almost sticking straight out.

"Do you have any idea how many people I've been on display for?" I move forward a few feet, cock bobbing in front of me. "But they've never had the look on their face that you have now, nor did they see me painfully throbbing for them." Even as I speak the words, my cock throbs violently. The pulse is visible as it flexes and beats.

"I've been sucked by countless people, until their faces blended together. They were forced upon me, or I simply obeyed orders. One time I had a mouth on me that I wanted and even that wasn't by consent– his or mine. You have no idea what it means to me to know you want me as much as I want you. The look on your face right now makes it all worth it."

Pained, Whitt looks like he's gazing on the divine. All the others looked at my cock and their eyes would widen in lust, greed, and sometimes fear.

I saved my chest for last, because I worry about the marks. I know Whitt felt them last night, but seeing them in the light may change his thoughts on me. I'm also covered in tattoos, and I thought he would appreciate my artwork more than the foot of flesh protruding from between my hips. That's why I saved my canvas for last.

Slowly, I remove my shirt to reveal the ruination of my flesh and the art that is covering most of it. As I pull the shirt over my head, my hair falls around my face and swings until it comes to a rest at my chin.

Standing on display, I feel wanted– desired. Not only in a good way, but the right way.

Whitt sits on the edge of my bed, eyes gone greedy with the need to devour me. He's physically holding himself back, fingers twisted in the covers and the tension in his thighs looks downright painful. He's even clenching his jaw and biting his bottom lip.

"You can touch if you'd like– that is if you don't mind the burn marks." I don't have time to get the words out before Whitt's fingertips make contact with my skin.

Better than I envisioned, I have to close my eyes at the pleasurable contact. Touch tentative, Whitt's fingertip is warm and smooth, sinking directly to my soul. Such an innocent touch has my toes curling, my scalp tingling, and my need blooming.

"This one is exceptional. A true artist took a lot of care on this tattoo." My lips curve into a wide smile at the husky quality in Whitt's voice. I want to shout in relief, because when he looks at me, he doesn't see what everyone else does.

Whitt immediately went for the tattoo that's in honor of my baby sister. He didn't touch my cock and leer while he spoke nasty words– he didn't bend me over the edge of the bed and fuck me without a thought to my pleasure. He didn't use sex as a weapon to harm me or control me with the threat of it.

Smile arching wider, a thought pops into my head. Whitt is a polite gentleman, yet he's always talking dirty to whomever he's with in the dungeon. The real Whitt stands here before me— soft, calm, and looking at me in awe.

"The same artist did all of my tattoos. Derek rented a shop, but the owner lost the building in a card game to Tony. Derek was a good guy and an exceptional artist. I gave him the deed because he deserved to know his business was secure. After that, he wouldn't let me pay him for the work. Instead, he put his heart into the ink, and that's what I needed. Each tattoo symbolizes something for me."

Whitt's fingertips skim my skin as he makes a satisfied noise in the back of his throat–almost a purr. I smile when I realize he's humming a sound similar to a tattoo gun. He does the same thing when he inks the *M* on our new masters.

He circles me a few times, until he finally stops at my back. Eyes burning into my flesh, I know what tattoo he's examining. Air displacing, he moves to trace all the intricate lines with a single fingertip.

"That one is my lineage," I speak of the perfectly round tattoo covering my right shoulder. All of my ink is black with gray shading– no color. When Whitt's fingertips locate the one on my left shoulder, I explain. "That's in memoriam of my father."

I flinch when Whitt finds two tattoos connecting each other. They're for Pierre and Jon. "What does *venger* stand for?" He asks of the tattoo of a knife scrolled with Pierre and Venger.

"It means avenge. With Pierre's death, I avenged my father's death and my mother and sister's lives." Whispering softly, "My life– Levi's life. Anyone that evil bastard touched without consent."

"It's beautifully rendered– extremely realistic. I feel like I could reach out and grasp the dagger handle from your skin... *De sang froid?*" Whitt enunciates slowly, trying to sound out the words. His pronunciation is wrong, and I can't help the smile that curves my lips. I repeat it in French, and he says, "It sounds better when you say it."

"It means *in cold blood*," I explain about Jon's dagger. Whitt huffs in a breath in understanding, then goes back to studying my flesh.

"Why choose a panther in the center of your back?" Whitt's fingers trace the outline of the large creature. The cat is above my heart on my back. Spyder is on my chest because she holds my heart.

"It doesn't look familiar to you?" Chuckles bubble up my throat. "Look closer."

"Oh, wow! I'm dense– Devlin."

Devlin is a large black predator with the only color on my body. The cat's eyes are shaded in pale white-blue. He watches my back just as the man does.

"Where is Olivia's?"

I raise my arm to show Whitt the demon tattooed on my side. "Because Olivia Fontaine is a thorn in my side," I explain before he can ask.

Hand skimming along the tattoo, Whitt presses his chest against my back. My eyes close at the intense warmth while he slides both of his arms around my waist until he's holding me loosely. Burying his face against the nape of my neck, I smile when he rubs the tip of his nose back and forth, moving my hair out of the way. He places a soft kiss on my neck, and I don't bother stifling my groan.

"I will ink every inch of your body– you will be my living masterpiece." Voice aching, Whitt whimpers into my ear. "You have no idea how badly I want that."

Leaning into his touch, my hands skim across his arms until I can twine my fingers with his. "I'll let you. It would be an honor to wear your art on my flesh." My serious tone warps into something playful, so unlike me. "It's your turn to show me yours, Pretty Boy."

"It won't be as titillating as when you did it. I hope I please you. I've um– I've never been with a guy before like this. It's weird. I'm never shy, and I've never worried that I couldn't attract someone, yet I am now." Whitt squeezes me closer, body shaking against mine. "I'm worried you won't like what you see."

"It's okay," I murmur in a soothing voice, understanding exactly how he feels. "You can take as long as you need. But if you don't want me to see, then I don't want to look. My entire life has been about pressure, and I never want to pressure you."

I hug Whitt's arms to me and feel content. Even if he doesn't want me to see him, this is enough for me. It's the most intimate I've ever been with someone. Now I know that there is a difference between intimacy and sex. All the sex I've had either felt horrible, clinical, or nice. Standing here with Whitt feels like every nerve in my body is alive and firing lightning bolts.

"I want you to see– I just don't have the ability to be seductive about it. I'd held out for a long time to be with one woman in particular. She didn't want to do it, but she took my virginity. I loved her, she was safe, and she knew me inside and out. That's why I asked you in the park if you'd ever been with a girl and had it just about the two of you. I haven't. I could look at them and get hard, but it was because I knew the pleasure I would get out of it. I just want to know if something is wrong with me, because I've never felt whole, and I fear I'll always be wandering around, looking for someone who makes me feel that way."

"I answered your question truthfully at the time, because I thought it had been about me and Bianca. But it felt different last night with our hands on each other– better. Just one of your fingertips felt better than Bianca's entire body felt against mine."

"I felt it last night, too," Whitt whispers near my ear. "And I'm terrified to do this right now, only to have it feel like… nothing."

"I know what you mean, and I think a lot of people look their whole lives to find that feeling of completeness. We'll just have to wait and see, because I honestly don't know the answer for either one of us."

"Undress me." Whitt's voice is soft and pleading, just this side of begging. The hungry ache in it just about drops me to my knees. "I would prefer your hands on me when you see me for the first time."

I rotate in the cage of Whitt's arms– he loosens his hold on me so I can maneuver. Heart beating uncontrollably, I'm eager with anticipation, yet filled with trepidation over doing this for the first time. This moment matters to me. It can't replace my stolen innocence, but it's a virginity of sorts. It's the first time the attraction is mutual and has no price tag attached.

Whitt always dresses like a young man playing a businessman. Only he isn't playing. I start on the top button of his dress shirt, working my way down toward his belt buckle. I've never seen him in a tie. I smile at the thought of using it to pull him down to my mouth, then removing it to use as a binding or blindfold.

"If you could dress any way you wanted, what would you wear?" I smile as I slowly unbutton his shirt. Whitt said he couldn't undress for me seductively, but I can undress him that way.

"Will it sound pitiful if I said I didn't know?" Whitt's words flutter the hair at the top of my head– I get off on the fact that he's taller than me, stronger than me. Able to pin me to the bed and fuck me senseless. "This is all I've ever known. When Dexter had us dress differently, Niel and I had no clue, so we went with the absurd."

"What do you know about yourself that isn't a Whittenhower trait?" I peel the shirt off Whitt's shoulders and resist stripping him fast like a kid on Christmas morning trying to get to the surprise underneath all the wrapping paper. Fucking sexy– he has a tight white undershirt on, causing precum to drool onto my thigh.

"The only thing I can say is that I don't like the life I live. I know I love tattooing– creating something that lasts an eternity. I love art, and I've drawn constantly since I could hold a pencil. I have book after book filled with illustrations."

"That's a start." I pluck at the last button. "I'm about to begin another chapter of my life– I need a job, a place to live, and instead of being terrified, I'm enlivened. But I have no fucking clue where to go from here."

"Same here," Whitt breathes against my forehead. "But I can't wait to find out."

"Me too." With a yank, I pull Whitt's belt from his trousers. "We'll just have to try everything until we find our something."

I quickly thread the belt through its buckle and wrap it around one of Whitt's wrists. Eyes glinting mischievously, I tug him to the bed. Crawling up onto the mattress, I kneel before him, putting us nearly at face-level.

"There, this is so much better." Leaning forward, I nip Whitt's lip with my teeth. It takes everything in me not to kiss him senseless, and in the process I almost forget I'm supposed to be stripping him.

Mouth parted, lips reddened from my bite, Whitt gazes at me in stunned silence. I will never forget the look on his beautiful face– the way his big blue eyes glow like bottomless pools of crystalline water, or his slightly parted lips as he drags air deep into his lungs.

"Whoever started the nickname Pretty Boy was a moron." Whitt grunts in reply. "You're absolutely beautiful, and I'm glad that at least for tonight you're mine."

With force, I yank the undershirt over his head to reveal the perfect expanse of his chest– no burn marks, tattoos, not even a hair. It's flawless, golden skin corded with lean muscles, leading down to a deep V.

Kissing him softly on his chest, I lick a path from one nipple to the next. Whitt groans for me when I take his nipple with my teeth, pressing in slightly to test his pain threshold. My hands smooth around his back, touching everywhere I can reach as I worship at his chest.

Whitt stands before me frozen, panting, and moaning, as if he's afraid that if he moves I'll stop. I'd love to tell Whitt he'd have to pry me from his gorgeous body, but that would require that I disconnect from his nipple long enough to speak.

I've never explored a lover. Even with Bianca is was simply biological. With the whores, it was about overcoming my own sexuality long enough to get hard and stay hard. When I obeyed my master, I'd float away in my mind, replaying the book I was currently reading as a distraction from the hand or mouth pulling at my cock. It got to the point that I hated the flesh, making jerking off a chore. All sex I've had was either clinical, a duty, or rape.

Pushing the memories and emotions to the back of my mind, I lock them away until I can deal with them. This is my first act of independence. I want Daniel Whittenhower II, and I'm going to enjoy it without being bombarded with a past I had no control over.

Feeling defiant and alive, I nibble Whitt's abs while my fingers make quick work of removing his pants. Hmm… last night it was boxers. I raise a brow at his underwear choice, and he giggles.

"Did you just giggle?" I tease, and he does it again. The sound is tinged with naughty intent– devious yet embarrassed. "Did someone wear these for me?" I ask of the tiny silk underwear that barely conceals his hard-on.

"Yeah, I didn't want to play with anyone else." Eyes flicking up, I want to look at the blush I hear riding his tone. "Once I got a taste for you, I needed more and more. I think I may have a territorial problem when it comes to you."

"Whether I think it or not, my mind locates you everywhere I go," I admit, my cheeks flushing a deeper red than his are. "Just like in the park, I knew you were there because I could feel it."

Our height difference working in my favor, I bend slightly at the waist to suck at his bulge through the soft fabric of his briefs. Whitt's shocked cry catches me by surprise when he's normally so quiet.

"I like the silk– it feels amazing against my tongue." I demonstrate it by licking him until the silk is saturated, following his length until I get to the ridge where his cockhead begins. He's tight, hard, dick bent to the left to extend to his hip. Tongue dipping beneath the fabric, I get my first real taste of Whitt– my first taste of any man. Rimming his opening, a wash of precum flows over my tongue. Swallowing, it's salty and bitter. Pushing me toward the brink, my cock jerks, nearly touching my stomach I'm so hard.

Whitt cries out above me, fingers tangling in my hair. For the first time in my life, I don't flinch when my hair is yanked. I tell myself it's Whitt and luxuriate in the sensation of his nails biting into my scalp. I know that the mild pain he inflicts is because I'm giving him intense pleasure.

Pulling his underwear down with my teeth, I'm rewarded by his cock popping out to greet me. Whitt is perfect– long, thick, not too veiny, and uncircumcised with a rosy tip peeking out at me.

"Catholic?" I nip the extra skin with my teeth– not hard, just enough for him to cry out again. I'm already addicted to the sound.

"Yeah," Whitt mutters bashfully. His fingers seek more of my hair, tips twisting in the strands. "None of the Whittenhowers are circumcised. Most Catholics do it, but I think it was a way for great, great whatever grandfather to feel superior to the Zeitlers."

"Thank God, I was already circumcised– Devlin helped me convert to Judaism when I was seven. Imagine that."

"Oh, fuck!" Whitt shudders. "Ouch!"

To demonstrate my point, the tip of my tongue slips underneath Whitt's foreskin, then I suck him in until the head hits the roof of my mouth. I suck him experimentally until I can take no more. Licking and nibbling, exacting different pressures, sucking in a few different ways, I use the resulting sounds to determine what Whitt loves and what he only likes.

"This is the first time I've done this, so don't judge me yet." Whitt gazes down at me in surprise, eyes filled with lust and wonder. "I wasn't allowed to give back no matter how badly I wanted to. Clients were fascinated by my cock, not with their own. But I'm glad I waited to do this with you."

Sucking Whitt's cock into my mouth as far as I can, the tip hits the back of my throat. Quieting the unsexy choking sound, I do this several times until I can take all of him into my mouth without gagging. I do this to prove I'm gay, because I glorify in the sensation of Whitt filling my throat, with his precum a viscous wash coating the inside of my mouth, and luxuriate in the sounds he sings as I suck him deep.

"Ah– ah– ya better stop." Protesting, Whitt's moans turn to panic. Tugging at my hair, I allow him to drag his cock out of my mouth. When he pops free, I kiss the tip of him and swirl my tongue around his slit.

"What's the matter?" I roll my eyes up to look through the lace of my lashes. I know what I must look like to him– my ruby-red lips swollen and damp, with my hair a wild mess around my face. I hold his gaze and pant, not bothering to wipe the saliva dripping from my chin.

"My God, Dalton." Whitt flashes me crazy eyes. "I'm going to come just looking at your face. Fuck, I tried to seduce you earlier, and it was child's play compared to you."

"Pray you never see Sebastian like this. He was born in the brothel to a whore. The women took to training him, and he loved every single second of it. I'm a novice in comparison to him."

"Do you promise Sebastian wasn't ever your lover?" Whitt looks down at me with a crazed expression etched across his beautiful face.

"I promise. Sebby's handsome and seductive, but he's my friend first." Back starting to hurt, I crouch down to sit on my heels. "The only guy I have eyes for is you– the only gays I've come into contact with are over thirty and partnered up."

"I'll pretend that doesn't sound like you're playing with me because I'm convenient," Whitt teases me. "Because I know how I feel about you is mutual." Strong hands cup underneath my armpits, lifting me to my feet, and then toss me onto the bed.

I laugh up to the man who has a good fifty pounds on me and several inches in height. Whitt looks thrilled to be able to physically move me, and the feeling is most definitely mutual.

"You make me territorial as fuck." Whitt actually growls from deep within his throat, an animalistic sound that has my cock pulsing in need. "I don't even feel like myself when the thoughts pop into my mind."

I moan loud enough that it echoes around the room when Whitt lies down on top of me. Warmth radiates through every inch of my body. Heavy and hard, the weight is as comforting as it is arousing. Balls smushed against his hip, I open my legs to cradle him between my thighs. I bite back a groan when I feel his cock pressed tight against my sack, with his precum dribbling to moisten my cock.

"Good God, that feels amazing." Moving fast, Whitt groans a split-second before he kisses me. I glorify in the way his mouth moves with mine, instinctively knowing what the other wants and needs.

I've never seen Whitt do an extensive tattoo. Even though, I don't doubt his ability to ink a masterpiece. But I experience how Pretty Boy is a master with his lips and tongue. I meld into the kiss, wrapping my arms and legs around him. Utterly shameless, we rock in time with our mouths, grinding my cock against his abs, while he thrusts like he's trying to figure out how to make an opening in my body. The sounds resonating around the room are a mix of my moans and his cries.

Back bending, Whitt slides down my body while he's still devouring at my mouth. His fingers skim down the backs of my thighs and lift. I gasp when I realize what he's up to— no need to make an opening if you can access one that's ready and available.

Completely pliant, I fall to the mattress, eyes rolling back into my skull just from the thought of what's to come. My fingers clench into the meaty flesh of Whitt's shoulders, silently begging for it. Even my toes curl.

Resting on his knees, Whitt fists his cock, rubbing it between my cheeks to slide back and forth slowly across my pucker. Becoming wet, I can feel his infamous lube smooth the way. I lie back, gasping for air, with my body on fire with need.

"I want it from you— please." Voice dripping with desperation, I shamelessly beg. My fingers tangle in his blond hair, while I push up against him, showing him what I want in case he missed the obvious.

"I don't want to hurt you." Whitt groans in frustration, and I can hear in his voice the control he's exhibiting.

"It's not my first time— or even my hundredth. But it'll be the first time I've wanted it." Rolling my hips, Whitt's cock slides over my asshole. I thrust up a bit, trying to impale myself on him. "It won't hurt me. Trust me on that."

I dig my fingers into Whitt's scalp and use it as leverage to pull myself up to take his mouth in a searing kiss. With brutal ferocity, I bite his bottom lip.

"Give it to me." I may be small, but I'm strong. From deep in my throat, I growl, "Don't make me fucking beg like an animal, because I will if I have to."

"But it won't feel good for you, will it?" Body vibrating, Whitt's gulping air in at a rapid rate, almost hyperventilating. His pupils are blown, eyes glazed over. I can see his need to give me what I want, but he's terrified of hurting me. "That can't possibly feel good– we can just rub together."

Snarling, I bare my teeth. "Stop being such a fucking gentleman and fuck me! We both know you want to." My accent becomes so thick that I'm not sure I'm even begging in English anymore. "I'll show you next time how it feels incredible. What you've heard is just propaganda bullshit that straight men tell themselves so they'll never want it. Because, believe me, once you've had a taste, you'll want more. Please… please… please. I'll beg."

Cock throbbing against my hole, his precum is sliding down the crack of my ass. He wants it just as bad as I do, if not more. Whitt stares at my face for a minute, trying to figure out if I'm telling the truth.

We both know it's going to happen, but Whitt's hesitation is making sure there's enough lube to pave the way, so it doesn't get uncomfortable for me. I've never seen anything like it, in all my years of witnessing men at KINK. Whitt's dick drips continuously like a leaky faucet– it's so fucking hot.

"Um– when I'm done you can, ya know–" Whitt blushes bright red and it's so adorable that I laugh. "I can jerk you off or suck you, or something. It's not fair if it's one-sided."

"Trust me, Pretty Boy. I won't need to." I pull his face back down to mine with rough movements, then I kiss him so sweetly that it makes my heart melt. My body's on fire with need, but I take the time to show Whitt that it can be passionate and slow.

Hooking his arms behind my knees, lifting my rear, Whitt presses me into the mattress until his mouth has access to mine again. The kiss builds from sweet with a fluttering of lips, to scorching hot where we're eating at each other's mouths with lips and teeth.

"Are you sure?" Whitt's eyes are crazed, yet he still asks for permission like a gentleman.

"Daniel, when we're in this position, but in reverse, I guarantee you'll understand why that question isn't necessary."

Without hesitation, Whitt takes me at my word with the strongest thrust I've ever experienced in my entire life. Headboard hitting the wall with force, "Mon Dieu!" I cry loudly when he breaches me, hard cock bypassing restrictive muscles until he's seated to the hilt.

Freezing, Whitt's eyes snap to mine to see if I'm all right.

Head hitching backward into the pillows, my laugh is carefree. "Sorry, I guess you need a translator." Whitt's lips curve up at the corners and his dimples appear. "Mon Dieu means my God." Whitt's chest moves against mine, a rumble of silent laughter. "Please don't stop."

I lift up to reach for his mouth, and Whitt smiles down at me. "You like my kisses?" He leans down slowly to press his mouth to mine, then he lifts away. "I should punish you for scaring me half to death when you screamed bloody murder in French." He kisses me again, and then starts to move slowly, and I know all is forgiven.

"Mon Dieu," Whitt whispers into my ear, following it up with an ironic chuckle. "I think I've been doing this wrong all these years."

"What?" I ask in confusion, but Whitt doesn't answer me straight away.

Rolling his hips, Whitt slowly works his way in and out of my body until I'm left gasping with every thrust. Sweat beads between us, our chests damp with perspiration, creating a delicious friction as our nipples rub together. The feel of his cock sliding inside of me is another form of resurrection– I wanted it, so I begged for it, and he gave it to me because he wanted me just as badly. It's not an experience I've ever had before, and I celebrate it for what it truly is.

A gift to finally own who I am.

"Yes, I've definitely been doing it wrong." Whitt's grunt has my cock going ramrod straight. "This feels right– with you." Shuddering against me, he loses some of the control he's been using.

I'm incapable of breaking our eye-contact, even when we kiss. With vivid blue eyes, Whitt completely captivates me, because he's not fucking me like I assumed he would. Whitt is making love to me, even if this is just a budding friendship.

Whitt's right– I've been doing it wrong, too. I'll never admit this out loud, but a few times with clients it felt rather nice. But it never felt like this, and it sure as hell didn't feel anything like this with Bianca.

Whitt drops all of his weight on me, pressing our bodies tightly together. With every thrust, his movements draw his abs across my cock. It gives a whole new meaning to washboard abs. Angling his cock perfectly, Whitt thrusts against my prostate.

My mind blanks out, body quivering uncontrollably. Stroke after stroke, Whitt does me right. Not too soft, not too hard, the force of his thrusts is perfect. Because in this position, if he were banging into me, the base of his cock would torture my balls. Pretty boy instinctively knows what he is doing.

"You're a savant." A raspy moan wheezes out my throat. "Just like that. Don't stop... I'm close..."

Whitt's mouth is at my ear, breathing in sporadic bursts and groaning uncontrollably. Clutching him closer, my fingertips slide along slick muscles, until I have to dig my blunt nails into his ass to get the leverage I need. Pressure builds in my sack, but it's so much more powerful because he's deep inside of me. My body tenses, and I release a long moan. My hands grip into his ass harder, my short nails denting his skin.

"Mon Dieu!" My spine bows and I arch my neck. I start to gasp for breath as the moans pour from my throat. Whitt releases a long stream of swear words against my ear that shock me.

"Daniel," I moan as he rolls faster inside of me, moving so fiercely the headboard is slamming into the wall. My body tenses and I scream my release. My toes curl painfully, my fingers bite into his skin. My back arches so far off the bed that I'm almost bent in half. Then the flood starts– fiery stream after stream of seed shoots from my cock to flood our chests. It's never-ending in its pleasurable torture. As long as he strokes inside of me, I continue to come.

"Dalton, yes!" Whitt shouts his release, body tremoring against mine, sliding easily in our combined sweat and my cooling cum. The sensation of our bodies gliding so effortlessly almost has me climaxing again.

Whitt's arms slide out from beneath my knees, and my legs slide down to wrap around his waist. He drags his hands up my chest, along my throat, and behind my neck. He cups the nape of my neck in his splayed fingertips. He stares down at me, need still lingering in his eyes. With abrupt determination, he grips my neck and thrusts forcefully inside of me. I grunt from the pain and moan from the pleasure.

"I'm sorry, Dalton, but the moment you let me inside of you, you became mine– and I'm never letting you go."

The look of pure rapture on Whitt's face and the devotion in his voice takes my breath away. I try to respond, but my breath keeps hitching. He smiles at my expression of shock, then he leans forward to takes my lips in a sweet kiss– my lover.

Chapter Twenty-Two

"Seriously?" I toss a cookie at Whitt's face. Fast reflexes have him catching it out of the air, then it's popped into his mouth. "It's after one a.m."

Crunching loudly, Whitt swallows a few times before he can answer me. "It's late– and we only have one more night for however long it will be until the dungeon reopens. Only the diehards will still be down there."

Head cocked to the side, I try to get a read on Pretty Boy. "You really want to fuck me in public?"

Fair face turning crimson, Whitt blushes so quickly it looks like a magic trick. "God, yes…" if his voice got any more filled with lust, I'd think he was coming in his pants.

"We just got off," I remind him. Dangling my fingers into my glass of milk, I dunk my Oreo. "How are you still horny?"

Chomping on a cookie, Whitt follows it up by draining his entire glass of milk. "If I've said it once, I've said it a thousand times. I'm horny. My dick never flags. I can come, and then come again as long as I'm stimulated." Leaning forward, he breathes his cookie breath into my face. "I'm. Horny. All the fucking time."

Whitt grabs my wrist, wrenching my fingers from my cup. Hot mouth opening wide, he steals my cookie, then he sucks the milk off my dripping fingers. "You made it soggy," he pouts.

Jaw hitting the tabletop, I just stare at Whitt in awe.

"You begged me, remember? I warned you once I started, I wouldn't be able to stop." Whitt drains my glass of milk, then slams it on the table. "I want you to walk into the dungeon as yourself, then let me fuck you in front of everyone. They won't even realize it."

"Ugh! And explain how you plan on doing that, Pretty Boy." I close the package of Oreos, hating when they go stale.

"Just trust me." Whitt grabs my arm, towing me toward the door, and I'm thankful I redressed in a pair of pajama bottoms and a t-shirt. He's so pushy, I bet he'd drag me downstairs naked if he could get away with it.

"I'm not sure I should." My voice warbles as Whitt forces me to jog down the stairs. "What if my brother is monitoring the dungeon?"

"My cum is in your ass, Dalton." Whitt flips around to stare at me. "That's about as much trust as someone can have in a person. Don't you think?"

Speechless, I can't argue with that. "Well, lube won't be an issue," I mutter wryly when we hit the hallway. Nervous, I negotiate with Whitt. "No foreplay. No intimacy. This is straight-up fucking until we get off, as quickly as possible. Then I want to get the hell out of the dungeon because I'll be embarrassed."

Walking with a hitch in his step because his pants are too tight with a hard-on, "Deal!" Whitt wrenches me down the hallway, more than eager. "I never use the word giddy– but that's what I officially am. Giddy!"

"You're such a dumbass." I roll my eyes, but something else draws my attention. "Fuck!" I snarl, feeling the telltale wiggle in my pajama pants. My free hand presses against my front, knowing exactly how nasty an eleven inch cock looks wiggling back and forth while I walk– and by nasty, I mean attention-gathering.

I'm hard. Seriously fucking hard.

"See?" Whitt turns to smile deviously at me. "The dungeon is practically empty, and Levi is at home with his pregnant wife who we probably know but he won't tell us."

"Levi was always a very private person," I mutter, pretending it doesn't hurt. "Thank God for small blessings." Only the chatting diehards are still in the dungeon– no sex to be had, just hanging out. Too bad that means all eyes will be on us. Surprisingly, no one bats an eyelash as I walk down here as myself, wearing my pajamas. "Um… how about we postpone?"

Whitt waggles his fingertips at our resident sex-addict. "Goddamnit!" I punch him in the back. "What the fuck?"

"The plan," Whitt reminds me. "Trust me."

Locking my knees, digging my bare heels into the tile, I make sure we go no further than the mouth of the hallway. In the seating area, Ezra and Dexter are chatting together, with Queen and Fate sharing a laptop with a scattering of fabric samples at their feet. Alex has a tape measure in his hand.

"They're working, Daniel," I try to get his attention.

Looking at me pointblank, "Then they need a bit of a break, don't they?" He tugs me over to the wall, not leading me any farther into the dungeon. "I'm celebrating, Dalton. I'm– I'm finally happy with who I am."

In the face of Whitt's voice cracking, I relax. "Okay. But Kristal?"

As if I called her, "Dalton, may I relieve you?" Kristal's leering at my crotch. I will say it's making an impressive showing– the damn thing hasn't softened since I got off. These stupid pajama pants make it look downright obscene.

My eyes seek Whitt, as usual. An intense look of starvation is etched across his face, and my mind goes from disagreeing with my body to being in total agreement. He winks at me, reading the hunger that's mirroring his.

I start to tell Kristal no when Whitt intervenes.

"I'll hold Dalton down while you suck him off." I growl, furious at my lover. "Make me proud, Kristal. I know you're a fabulous cocksucker." You can hear the mischief in Whitt's voice and his blue eyes are twinkling from suppressed laughter.

Whitt's pants show a different emotion. He's so hard I can see all of his cock pressing a perfect outline in his trousers, even the outline of his head. I groan in need and Kristal takes it as permission. She drops to her knees in front of everyone. I start to protest, but Whitt beats me to it.

"Let's go over to the wall where it's more comfortable for everyone." Whitt leads me over to the wall, just a few feet from everyone. They will all have a perfect view of my cock, which I think Whitt is trying to show off. I can practically hear his mind saying, "*It's all mine!*" But at this point, I don't care. I'm so horny that I'm willing to let Kristal suck me as long as Whitt is touching me at the same time.

Whitt leans against the wall and opens his arms to me. I look a question at him in confusion. "Lean your back against my chest. This way no one can see anything but Kristal sucking you off– sleight of hand."

"This better be your plan," I grumble underneath my breath, not liking this at all but it doesn't dampen my arousal. "You know I don't like receiving blowjobs."

"Oh, you'll like this one," Whitt assures me, voice almost taunting yet filled with challenge.

I do as Whitt asked, leaning against his chest, and his arms immediately envelop me. To the spectators, it looks like he's restraining me, but in reality he's just holding me. Quivering, my nerves get the best of me and I start to freak out when Kristal kneels at my feet.

"Shh... It's okay. It'll feel good. Trust me, Dalton, you need a good experience to overwrite the bad." Whitt whispers softly in my ear, his teeth grazing my lobe as he talks. I shiver, and he tightens his arms around me.

Whitt's hand makes a circuit from my chest to my waist, fingertips dipping beneath the waistband of my pajama bottoms. With unhurried movements, Whitt pulls my pants down too far for comfort. For a blowjob, I only need my cock out, but Whitt has other plans. So my bare ass is pressing against his thighs.

Eyes flicking up in terror, I gaze at the crowd, expecting an unnatural level of lust, which would disgust me. But they look at my dick in surprise, as if they can't fathom such a small guy could be packing an eleven inch cock. It's a comfort to see they are only curious.

Like a train wreck, they can't look away.

"Put your hands on Dalton's hips, and don't let go," Whitt orders Kristal. "If you do, I'll punish you. Suck him off with only your mouth. Don't touch his balls, either– he doesn't like it." Whitt laughs about that last part, knowing exactly how much I love just that.

Kristal's small hands cover my hipbones, and I have to remind myself who this woman is. I understand why Whitt's doing this to me. I can't live the rest of my life with nightmares about mouths on my dick when it's one of the most pleasurable experiences on the planet.

I'm a man– we love our dicks sucked.

Kristal is not some woman I was forced to touch. She's Kristal Harris– Whitt's lifelong friend. Alex's girlfriend. She's a very nice person who loves sex more than Whitt does, which is hard to imagine. She's touching me because she thinks I'm hot, and because she enjoys Whitt's attention, not for any malicious reasons.

Kristal is a small spitfire with an incredibly hot mouth, which offers amazing suction and friction. My mind plays out why it's okay for Kristal to touch me as she lowers her mouth to the head of my dick. I'm beyond shocked how it bobs out for her touch. Never have I wanted a mouth on me. Right now, I would let anyone line up and suck me off just as long as that meant Whitt didn't stop touching me.

I want to get off again.

My head falls back against Whitt's chest and my eyes close as the crown passes Kristal's hot, wet lips. I groan, and it's a sound of pure misery. "That feels really good."

Whitt's hand moves behind me, fumbling between our bodies. I try to move when I figure out what he's up to, but his arm tightens around my chest, holding me immobile.

"Shh… no one will see. Kris won't even be able to tell." Whitt murmurs, lips pressed close to my ear. "That's why I'm only letting her touch you with her mouth. It won't matter if she knows anyway– Kris knows that I'm gay." He whispers so softly I barely hear him as his lips press to my ear. "They all do."

"There's not a snowball's chance in Hell they won't notice," I issue my protest, but it comes out breathy and needy.

"If they figure out I'm fucking you, they won't judge." Whitt has a point. Over the years, I've seen them in all sorts of compromising positions. But on the night we popped our gay cherry, Whitt tosses us directly into the fire.

"I want to make you feel so fucking good," Whitt purrs into my ear, arm tightening around my chest. "Kristal is very good at what she's doing, but not as good as this will feel."

I gasp in shock as the head of his cock slips past my cheeks. Whitt's saturated and it drips down the crack of my ass. Kristal looked up at me when I gasped, her hazel eyes bugging out at the prospect that she pleasured me so well. She begins to do it again, hoping she's getting me off for the first time ever.

Rough and raspy, I gasp again, but not because of Kristal.

Whitt tries to work his way into me, but I'm tight, even if I was stretched from our last session. I'm plenty moist, but the position is a difficult one to be in. As Whitt fights his way in, I push out with my muscles, helping him gain entrance. He turns his face to the side and moans into the back of my neck, so no one can see his face twisted with pleasure.

My hands rise on their own accord, fingers wrapping around the back of Whitt's neck. I push my hips out, making a better angle, and end up burying my cock deep into Kristal's throat.

I moan so loud it startles me.

Whitt's fingers grip my hips over Kristal's, not allowing her to move her hands even an inch. He thrusts inside of me slowly, drawing whimpers of pleasure from my lips. He moans quietly into the back of my neck, unable to be quiet as his dick slides in and out of my ass.

"I'm stealing your phrase– Mon Dieu." Whitt's chuckles warp into a groan. "My God, this is seriously the hottest thing I've ever experienced. I'm fucking you, and no one is the wiser." Panting against my ear, he sounds distressed. "There's no way in hell I'm going to last long."

Hard dick sliding in and out of my ass, suction so fierce it's almost painful pulling at my cock, I lose myself in the sensation of Whitt behind me and Kristal in front of me. I envision taking someone while I'm taken, but I want it to be a man.

In the middle of two men. One inside me, with me inside another.

Shuddering, I momentarily feel guilty for using Kristal and not caring about her needs, but she looks lost in her work. She worships at my cock, slurping and sucking with saliva dripping off her chin. Pupils blown, her eyes are glazed, and I recognize that the submissive at my feet loves the force of two masters giving her direction. She loves to please, and right now she is doing an excellent job.

I look to the seating area, curious to see if anyone realizes Whitt's fucking me right now– even I have to admit that's fucking hot. Just the thought has my balls tightening, and it's truly happening to me right now.

Queen and Fate are studiously paying attention to the laptop they're sharing, no doubt not wanting to watch Kris yet again suck someone off. Dexter looks mildly shocked, eyebrow hitching so high it's hidden by his hair. Alex is silently laughing at Ezra, who's wearing the hungriest expression I've ever seen. It makes my heart ache for him. I don't want him, but I know the longing when you don't get what you so desperately need.

"They know." I try to speak to Whitt, but it ends up a rolling moan. With sluggish movement, he looks to the seating area.

Fingertips biting into my hips, his cock grows inside me, proving Whitt loves to be watched.

"Ezra was the first person I came out to when I realized what it meant to be gay." Not bothering to hide it, Whitt thrusts into me so sharply my gasp ricochets around the dungeon. "The poor gay bastard is in love with a man and a woman, but the man won't give his ass up."

"Since they know what we're doing–" My train of thought wanders, head lolling on my shoulders. "God, that feels good. Harder, Ezra needs to see what he's missing out on."

Harder– Whitt thrusts harder into me than he did earlier, when the headboard was slamming into the wall. Crying out sharply, I lose myself to the pleasure of it and allow my worries to float away on a cloud of pure bliss.

Kristal begins moaning, and the vibrations radiate up my cock and into my body. Whitt is groaning too loud for it not to be noticeable. Fiery hot, he starts to come in my ass, and it's my undoing. I scream as jets of cum shoot down Kristal's throat. She's a pro– her fingers dig into my skin and her mouth is pressed tight to my pelvis. Deep-throating all eleven inches of my cock. Shuddering, I didn't think anything could feel so amazing.

Whitt's trying not to move and groan, but he's failing. My spine bows and takes him with me. He fuses to my back, biting the nape of my neck to silence his own scream.

Whitt falls back against the wall and takes me with him. Kristal is left kneeling without a cock in her mouth. She looks satisfied and pleased, and I can tell she found her own release from pleasing us both. I want to hide my cock in my pants, but I can't since Whitt's still inside me. I have no clue how he plans on fixing this without it being too obvious.

Giving us privacy, as if they understand we were showing off our newfound freedom, they all look away– except for Ezra, who seems to be utterly riveted. Without shame, Whitt pulls free of my body, tucks himself in, and then zips back up.

Cock unbelievably half-hard, I bend down to pull my pants back up, cum dripping in a steady stream from my asshole. I flush bright red when I realize what I just did in front of witnesses, and I got off on it.

"I'm not done with you, yet," is whispered into my ear– Whitt is insatiable, and I've yet to deflate. Gasping in shock over how he affects me, I run down the hallway. Yet again forgetting the predatorial drive of a dominant male.

I make it as far as the stairwell before an arm hooks my waist from behind. Flinging me against his chest, Whitt is growling yet giggling the oddest sound I've ever heard.

"This is fun!" Whitt chirps in my ear. "I like chasing you– it's like we get to play, but it's more fun as adults." One hand is locked around my waist and the other is fumbling with the waistband of my pajama bottoms. "I caught you, now I get to claim my prize!"

"Jesus Christ," I mutter in awe. "That wasn't enough for you?"

"No– never," Whitt vows. "It will never be enough." His voice is raw with emotion and his eyes glow in the dim stairwell. "Just thinking of what we did is getting me hotter and hotter and hotter and hotter. Look!" He clutches the ever-present, impressive bulge in his pants.

Wiggling free, I make it two more steps before Whitt is tackling me against the wall. Mouth hot, he devours me from the inside out. Tongue reaching my tonsils, Whitt consumes me.

Stunned, before I can react, Whitt yanks my pajama bottoms off me and tosses them up the stairwell.

"Good throw," I tease impressed. "You made it all the way to the landing."

"I'm glad you didn't wear shoes to the dungeon. It would take too long to remove them." Growling an animalistic sound, he rips my shirt from my back, leaving me completely naked.

"Holy fuck, you're..." I'm at a loss, but I'm enjoying this unhinged side of Whitt. "Wow."

I make Daniel Whittenhower II lose his shit. I do. Me. Holy Fuck.

Ever the horny gentleman, Whitt places my t-shirt on a stair tread and lowers me to sit on it. Without asking, he falls to his knees between my thighs and sucks my semisoft cock into his mouth.

A sharp hiss passes my lips, surprised because I just came five minutes ago and I'm already hardening in his mouth. Vibrating pleasantly, Whitt groans when I reach full capacity, managing to get me even harder for him.

I smile down at Whitt as his blue eyes gaze up at me through the lace of his lashes– a classic cocksucking maneuver if I've ever seen one. It's wild to sit on a step, completely buck-ass naked, and have my dream guy suck me off. And expertly, I might add, for his first time.

"This is your first time, right?" The more I act like myself, the stronger my accent becomes. Whitt groans on me again and it vibrates to my soul. He nods his head yes and sucks me harder.

I laugh from the sheer joy of it. I make Whitt insane– such a gentleman, all prim and proper with his dress shirt and trousers on. The juxtaposition of his demeanor and the wild look in his eyes has me coming into his mouth in a second.

"Mon Dieu, Daniel!" I cry out, my hips thrusting up as I shoot down his throat. He takes me to the root and groans in satisfaction as I take my pleasure from him. Long seconds later, I fall backward against the stairs, gasping for breath.

"No rest for you, Dalton." Whitt flashes me a terrifyingly devious smile. His dimples are even sexier when they take on a sinister edge.

Grabbing my hips, he flips me over to rest on my knees. The sound of metal on metal grinding as his zipper is torn open in a rush has me chuckling against my forearm. Laughter drying up, the wonderful warmth of his cockhead swirling on my well-used asshole has me shuddering in bliss.

"You make me fucking insane. You get that, right?" Whitt pushes in an inch, just his head, only to take it back out again. No doubt watching, he repeats this over and over again. "I've never wanted anything as badly as I do you. I never go soft. I walk around with a constant hard-on."

Resting on my knees with my ass in the air, I gasp against my forearm. "Feeling. Fucking. Mutual. Daniel."

Movement smooth, "Dalton," Whitt calls out as he enters me completely. Without giving me a chance to react, he grabs my hips and begins pounding violently inside of me. All I can do is grunt while gripping the stair tread above me, as I hold on for dear life.

Unbelievable, as soon as Whitt repeatedly batters my prostate, I bloom to full-size. Panting roughly, I bite my lower lip to stay my cries. He takes me brutally, but not out of anger– out of need. It's like once we unleashed who we truly are, we can't stop celebrating the fact.

It feels so damn good that my cock is tight to my belly and eagerly dripping to come again.

A startled gasp surprises me. Jerking, I look over my shoulder at the entrance to the stairwell. Ezra's huge gray eyes are wide with lust, and even from here I can see his chest is rising and falling rapidly.

"I-I-I'm sorry to interrupt," Ezra stutters. "I was going to work in the rooms we're renovating."

Yet Ezra doesn't move to leave– he just continues to stare like he can't look away.

Whitt thrusts into me a few more times, each one slower and longer than the last. "Ez, can you make sure no one else comes up here?" Whitt says over his shoulder. "I'd like to keep a naked Dalton to myself a little bit longer– seeing his cock is one thing–"

Whitt turns to the side, offering Ezra an unlimited view of my body. Skinny with my hipbones protruding, burned and tattooed, ass jiggling with every slow thrust with my dick slapping at my belly and my asshole gaping around Whitt's cock.

Poor Ezra.

Whitt begins to thrust again, never looking away from Ezra while he does it. "You can watch. We don't mind." I'd protest the 'we' but my dick gets harder at the thought. "I'd offer to have you join, but–"

"I can't," Ezra mutters quickly, scared he'll answer differently. "It'd be cheating." He sounds like he is trying to convince himself.

"You can watch– that wouldn't be cheating. You can take care of that, too." Whitt says pointedly at the straining bulge in Ezra's pants. "We'll even pretend you aren't here." Turning away, we pretend to play pretend.

"Why?" Ezra's smooth voice is unusually shaky.

"The three of us in this stairwell know more about longing that anyone else." Whitt stops thrusting, turning back to look at Ezra. "I know you love your wife, but you're married to two people for a reason. It takes both of them to meet your needs, and one of them isn't at the moment. One of them is with Marcus, sucking his cock instead of yours– never giving up his ass or taking yours. So take any pleasure you can from watching us, and then go home to your wife– go home and fuck her while you tell her about what you saw."

Whitt turns around and picks up a brutal rhythm. I can't look over my shoulder anymore because I have to hold on so that we don't slip down the stairs. I white-knuckle the tread with my fingertips and grip my toes on a lower step. I can feel Ezra's gaze on us, and then I hear the telltale sound of a zipper lowering.

Whitt and I don't look back, offering Ezra the privacy he needs. I hurt for his pain and the agony of rejection.

I fall into the connection I feel with Whitt. He keeps whispering my name and nipping at the back of my neck, taking me harder than I've ever been taken. Even when it was force, they weren't allowed to hurt me. But this doesn't hurt– it is the best feeling in the world. Possession. It's the feeling of being consumed by someone you could quite possibly fall in love with, and it heightens a biological experience to that of transcendence.

The very quiet groan that Ezra emits when he finds release rockets me off the edge. I come screaming, the sound echoing off the walls of the stairwell. I pour all over the step and my chest, and I laugh when I hit myself in the chin. The rumble of Whitt's laugher joining in vibrates my back.

"It's my turn– I think I've made you come enough tonight." Whitt groans louder than he has before. Heat floods my insides, and I shudder from the warmth and silkiness of it. Suddenly emotional, Whitt wraps his arms around my chest and holds me tightly for a few moments as our breathing slows.

I look back at the entryway to the stairwell, and Ezra is gone. The light glares off the pool he left on the bottom step, and I release a shocked chuckle– Ezra enjoyed our show. I see the tip of his shoe peeking in the doorway. He didn't leave his post. He just gave us some privacy. But in reality, I think he was too embarrassed to face us after the fact.

Chapter Twenty-Three

Last night and this morning were incredible. Whitt doesn't treat me like I'm something to use and abuse. He acts like he's proud to be around me. We actually went out for breakfast, like a real date, but then he had to go to work all day. After being around him constantly for the past forty-eight hours, it's odd to be alone.

Freedom.

I've celebrated my newfound freedom by making some life changes. First I visited Stanton, asking if he had any apartments available, but he shut me down. Levi had ratted me out about my self-harm, and I was told I wasn't allowed to live alone yet. With my relationship so new with Whitt, I didn't want to fuck it up by asking him. Stanton gave me a suggestion, which was the obvious choice.

My next stop was the Brownstone, where Jamie and I played another round of dirty word Scrabble. I waited him out, knowing he knew why I was visiting. Finally, after four hours of brain-bleeding boredom, Jamie offered me an invitation to move into the Brownstone.

So, here I am, packing up everything to my name into less than a dozen boxes. Restraint is closed, with a small gathering in the dungeon tonight to say goodbye to the old and welcome in the new. So much change is sad, but it's also liberating.

The last thing I do is empty my safe into a fireproof, lockable box. After the dust settled, Bruno sent me our shared items from Tony's desk. Most people wouldn't find an illegal notary stamp sentimental. I also have the original Marconi pictures our family had collected over the last century, with Bruno making copies for himself. The last thing to go into the box is the rubbing I made from Tony's gravestone– I had to commit a selfless act to ensure my father had a proper burial.

I'm not startled by the noise behind me, expecting my new roommate to help me load the boxes into his car. Turning around with a welcoming smile on my face, I realize I made a fatal mistake.

Olivia Fontaine is most certainly not Alex.

"What do you want?" Turning around, I go about my business. With shaking fingertips, I gather deeds and contracts to be placed into another smaller firebox.

"So the rumors are true." My mother's accusing tone is amplified by the sharp clack of her stilettos on the tile flooring. "Do you have a death wish? Hmm?"

"No, Mother." If I ignore her, will she go away?

"Your stupidity is showing." Olivia comes into view, wearing a blood-red dress and a black cape, looking exactly like a vampire. "You're a marked man, yet your need to flaunt your ass around young Daniel has made you irresponsible."

"There are no hits on my life, Mother," I mutter in a monotone voice.

"And yet–" she flings her cape dramatically to sit in a chair at my table. "You were attacked a few weeks ago, nearly killed if I remember correctly."

"Yes, I was." I turn to her, resting my hip on the edge of my bed. "Rescued by the brother I didn't know I had."

Not even a wince. "Ah, yes. I asked if Leviticus was filling your empty head, and you lied to me. Imagine that."

"I'm not going to split hairs with you, Olivia," I practically snarl. "You can evade me, you can try to change the subject, you can blame me, but that doesn't change the fact that I've had a brother my entire life and you kept it a secret."

"Apples. Oranges. I suggest you be a good boy and put your disguise back on and do as you're told." Olivia's voice flexes with manipulation and her destructive need to control.

I snap.

"What in the world are you doing?" Olivia questions me while I tear off my clothes in a frenzy. T-shirt, jeans, underwear, even my sneakers.

"Go to hell, Mother!" Stark-naked, I charge from my apartment, down the stairs, through the hallway, all the way to the dungeon packed with all of our members saying their goodbyes.

Without hesitation, I lunge onto the dais, hearing my mother's stilettos clacking on the slate tiles like the tick of the kitchen timer from my worst nightmares.

"My name is Dalton Anthony Fontaine Marconi," I announce to more than fifty people crowding the dungeon. Whitt rushes up, but with a heavy palm to the chest, he's stopped by Devlin.

"I was created in the unholy union between a brothel madam and an organized crime boss. My mother is Olivia Fontaine." I look to my mother who's staring at me like she's seeing me for the first time, and she despises what she sees.

"I will never call you Master again Mother. I will never bow or kneel before anyone ever again. I am the master of my own destiny." I turn away from the tears glinting in her eyes– tears of fury– tears of betrayal.

"First, I was sent here to keep an eye on one of my mother's victims– Marcus Zeitler, who also happens to be the father of my baby sister. Then my mother gave me another job– to spy on everyone at Restraint. Later, I was drafted to find your mole. I apologize for my asinine behavior. Please blame my mother for making me into an asshole. I'm not *that* Dalton anymore.

"Naked and exposed, I stand before you and finally do the show-and-tell Marcus demanded weeks ago. I share with you my deepest and darkest. Without secrets, my mother has no power over me.

"I was sexually, mentally, emotionally, and physically abused as a child, and that continued until the day I arrived in Dominion when I was only twenty. I was used as a whore. I am a murderer. I was a crime boss, but I gave that up to my brother. I'm going through a divorce. Not only am I a dominant, but also a switch. The FBI forced me to rat out my competition, or they wouldn't allow my father a proper burial. I have a contract on my life, but not one from the mafia.

"I'm gay. If I ever see another vagina in my lifetime, it will be too soon. Sorry ladies, you all smell nice and are soft with pretty voices and beautiful faces, but there can only be one of us in my bed and that has to be me.

"This is who I am. After a lifetime of abuse, I will never be manipulated, extorted, blackmailed, coerced, or controlled again, for any reason at any time." I look through the crowd, searching for Levi. "This is me finally cutting the cord."

"Don't you fucking dare!" Seething, Olivia's on the dais in a heartbeat. "You're a worthless excuse of a human being!"

243

Rage. Unadulterated rage. Red. All I see is red as I turn to my mother and scream into her face. "You. Put. A. Goddamn. Hit. On. My. Life." A collective gasp ricochets around the dungeon. "You tried to kill your own son. What kind of monster does that?"

Leaning into me, Olivia's hand slaps my back. "Venger! What kind of son kills their mother's father and tattoos it on their body like it was a great honor?"

"What kind of mother allows her father to rape her sons? Repeatedly. Over the course of their lives. Witnessing it herself. After he raped her."

"Pierre was my father!" Olivia bellows, tears finally streaking down her face. "I have no idea where he is." Fingers looking like talons, hands fisted at her heart, Olivia screams so shrilly my ears burn. "Where is he? Where is my father? What did you do to him?"

"That's all you give a shit about?" Sneering, I'm utterly disgusted. "You're screaming about avenging your father, when it was an act of vengeance that got him killed in the first place. He shouldn't have killed Tony!"

"You shouldn't have killed Jon!" Olivia volleys back. "You should have allowed him to take from Sebastian, and ignored it."

"That's it– I'm done." I try to walk away from her. "You're too nuts to even get through to."

"I treated you no differently than my father treated me," Olivia says in defense of her piss-poor actions.

"Your father was a sociopath who got off on having his partner rape me while he watched, while he made *you* watch. What the fuck is wrong with you that you'd compare your childrearing skills to his?"

"At least your parents didn't rape you!" she screams back.

"Full-circle. You blame me for killing him one moment, then you want my sympathy because he was a shitty father. Which are you today, Mother? The victim? The martyr? Or the victimizer?"

"My father is dead, and this is how you talk to me?" Olivia looks around the dungeon, honestly believing they should be on her side.

"I killed the bastard for you, so don't pull that victim bullshit with me. I'm deaf to it from now on. He treated you badly and you didn't like it, so why would you allow it to happen to your own children?"

"I kept Spyder from it," she says as if that takes away the abuses I endured for her.

"I hate you," I hiss.

"I know," she mutters flatly with a shrug. "I feel nothing for you, so we're even."

"What's that supposed to mean?"

"I'm my father's daughter. Fontaines are more attached to things than people. People can hurt you because you have no control over their emotions. But you own things, and if you take care of them, you can have them forever. People try to grow up and become independent. The moment you were married, I knew I'd lost you. You were no longer a thing. You've been very helpful to me, and I feel bad that I've lost that help, but I don't love you." Olivia's face scrunches up in confusion. "Or at least I don't think I do. I feel bad right now, but I don't know why."

My knees give out and Devlin catches me, settling me on the edge of the dais. Whitt hops up next to me, taking my hand to comfort me.

My mother is completely unhinged. My love and adoration for her blinded me. She and Pierre are one in the same. She never batted an eyelash as she watched my punishments. The shame I'd seen flash across her face was shame that she felt nothing when she knew she should.

Head bowed, I stare at our tangled fingers, concentrating on how secure Whitt makes me feel. "I don't want to see you ever again," I whisper to my mother, knowing her bat-like hearing will pick it up.

"I live here now, Dalton. You've made my life extremely complicated. I've never seen anyone get a divorce, or sign their property over so fast. Your death does me little good now."

"What? I thought the hit was a way to control me, to make me think I couldn't shed the Dalton Thompson persona and just be me." Heart beating a rapid tattoo against my chest, it's hard to breathe. "You truly meant to kill me?"

"You're such a fool, just like your father." Olivia paces on the dais, her heels clicking on the surface. Tick. Tick. Tick. "I'd asked Pierre to arrange my marriage to Anthony. I made you on purpose because I needed you as my tool. It was simply a waiting game as I fostered you to be exactly who I needed you to be. You became willful, so I needed another child to keep you in line. An old friend sent Marcus my way, and Spyder was conceived as a backup plan. It was foolproof, except you weren't as foolish as I'd thought."

Glaring, Olivia paces on the dais, grumbling a steady stream of swear words in French.

"I had Pierre set up your marriage with the Greens. It made you an even more valuable asset. You played into my hands perfectly. After twenty-one years of marriage, I'd forgotten that Anthony was foolish in all things except for money. You were to kill Pierre after he killed your father. That was flawless. You even took out your competition, creating the largest organized crime syndicate that had money flowing in like water. The only problem was that my father's body was never recovered."

Olivia paces nervously, like a caged animal, and growls underneath her breath.

"It takes three fucking years– three years for a missing person to be declared deceased. Finally I had Pierre's death certificate, and I went to collect my inheritance, but there wasn't one."

Snorting, I shake my head back and forth, continually snorting. "That's why you're pissed? Not your undying love and devotion to Pierre Fontaine, but that you had no idea where I put his body." I turn to my mother with an evil smile on my face. "Devlin held Pierre down while I cut his dick off, and then I sliced his throat. If you want to know where your father is, don't look at me."

"Devlin?" Olivia breathes, real betrayal tingeing her voice. Instead of focusing on that very real betrayal, she spins her web of lies. "While I was playing Anthony, he was playing me. It seems you were the sole heir to my father's holdings. Meaning you own KINK. So I devised a plan to remove you. But Bruno and Stanton are very good at protecting you from the countless hits I placed on your life. I wanted my club back, and if you died, I would gain the Fontaine, Marconi, and Green holdings. I would have been set. As I said before, I want property, not people."

"You wanted me to die, and you just admitted it like you're ordering a coffee." Head in my hands, I can't even fathom how I'm supposed to feel right now. "I'm your son. You carried me for nine months in your womb."

"I've never said I loved you and meant it, have I? What I love is KINK. It's my legacy."

"Then why are you here?"

"Why do you think? That bastard child of your father's kicked me out. The minute the death certificate was legal, Bruno was on me and he took everything that was rightfully yours. I have no money, no club, and no need to be in Vegas. I came to Dominion to get my property back, but you divorced Bianca in a heartbeat. I was okay with that because I didn't need her father's holdings. Then I find out that you gave your brother everything. You gave that bastard Marconi spawn my club!" she screams in fury.

"I don't want to hear any more of this. Just leave me alone." I want to cry, scream, and fight. But all I feel is defeated– numb. After the life I've lived, I shouldn't be surprised. The members of Restraint are my family now. My mother, my master, she wanted me to die so she could keep her precious club. She orchestrated the deaths of my father and hers to keep her club.

I lean over the side of the dais and dry heave, with Whitt holding me up to keep me from falling to the floor. The violence that erupts from my throat as my stomach contracts has me whimpering in pain. I sob and quiver while the retching takes over my body. It lasts for several long minutes, with Whitt trying to calm me.

A random person hands me a water bottle and a washcloth from one of the private rooms. I take it with a thanks, and then drain it dry, wiping my mouth afterward.

"Are you finished with your theatrics?" My mother's heels press into my hip, she's standing so close. "May I continue?"

"Why not? I'm sure it can't be any worse than admitting you ordered hits on your   own son," I mutter sarcastically. "Why did you have me do that stuff at Restraint?"

"For an old friend. Loyalty is important," she says, and I snort at the atrocity of her word choices.

"That tells me nothing, Mother."

"I considered killing Marcus so that Spyder would inherit his fortune. But that wouldn't work. No one knew she was his except for him. Plus, I'd have to kill all the Zeitlers. It was just too much wet work, and I never do the wet work."

"Wet work? Jesus Christ," Whitt whispers in awe. "I couldn't get the actual mobsters to talk that shit, but a demented cunt will."

Either ignoring Whitt, or not hearing him, Olivia continues to prattle off her lists of crimes against humanity. "I've become quite fond of my daughter. I wouldn't want to take her life for monetary gain. Besides, Marc's wife should inherit the bastard's money."

"You're a fucking lunatic," I mutter in mystification. "You need to be at Wintercrest with Adelaide Whittenhower."

"Prove it," Olivia challenges from above me. "You're my son, and you can try to commit me, but you'd have to prove it," she taunts.

Hand arching to include the entire dungeon, "Proof? There ya go. Lots of witnesses."

Olivia paces a few laps around the dais while collecting her thoughts, and I suspiciously wonder if she knows it reminds me of the nightmare kitchen timer. I contemplate matricide for the billionth time, but I'm better than her. I will imagine it, but I won't actively try to kill her, even if I'd enjoy every second.

"My plan at Restraint was perfect," Olivia praises herself. "It was my friend's idea, really. The hits weren't working, so I tried a new idea. You were to create havoc and make them hate you, so that when I needed your life to end, it would look like an accident or assault. It would benefit my friend, because how could Restraint stay open after a murder occurred in its dungeon, especially with all those pesky riots? It's such a shame that Dexter Hayes is so moral. Pity," she says in heavily accented French.

"Who's the leak, Mother?" I demand.

"Ah... yes, the ironic beauty of the mole. Poor Adelaide Whittenhower, rotting away in Wintercrest. She was the perfect patsy for the books. She didn't write a word of it. A Whittenhower wrote a few passages." Olivia releases a maniacal laugh that reverberates around the room, causing everyone to shudder.

"Ms. Whittenhower's girlfriend needed a clear divide between Adelaide and her enemies. Adelaide was always in the middle, much like yourself. Her name as the author solidified her pariah status. Sheer brilliance," Olivia praises herself.

"The mole, Mother?" I remind her again.

"Ah... yes, the ironic beauty of the mole," she sings, tone warping into gloating. "Having you investigate the mole was the most impressive part of it all."

"Why is that?" I ask, wanting to get this over with so I can throw up, get drunk, or beg for punishment. Because once she says the words, I'll want to kill myself. The majority of the people in this crowded dungeon already know the answer to this question. They've known for days– maybe even weeks. I'm going to be sick...

"It was you, son." Olivia announces loudly for all to hear. "You're the mole."

With the sweep of her cape, Olivia bows, and then she leans over to kiss my cheek. Stunned, we all watch as Olivia Fontaine stalks out of the dungeon.

Fifty shocked gazes gawk up at me from the dungeon floor. They allow Olivia Fontaine to leave because they're so stunned by what they've just heard.

I bow my head in shame, pretending I'm not silently weeping. Going into protector-mode, Whitt removes his shirt, and then tugs it over my head to hide my nakedness. As soon as I'm covered, he pulls me into his arms and rocks me like a baby.

"Roarke, escort Ms. Fontaine from the building," Marc issues the order. "Take her to Edge and remove her possessions. Inform her she has one hour to vacate the premises, is not allowed anywhere that I own, and how I will have her arrested for trespass if she ignores my request."

Despondent, I start to sob as realization dawns. My mother tried to kill me over and over again. My mother is a sociopath. I'm the mole that I was trying to protect us from. I leaked the information that ruined us. I had a hand in Restraint being shut down. I'd unwittingly fucked us all.

This is what Dexter and Levi wouldn't tell me– why they demanded I cut the cord. They already knew, and still they trusted me. They were waiting for me to see my mother for the twisted person that she is. They wanted me to join their quest of my own volition. I've never respected them more so than I do right now. On the flip side, I've never felt so ashamed and in pain as I do right now.

"I was the leak." Guttural sobs are wrenched from my chest. I cling to Whitt, needing an anchor. "I'm so sorry." This hurts so much.

"You didn't know, son." Marcus tries to comfort me, but his concern only makes me feel worse.

"I need to be punished," I whimper.

"No, son, you don't." Marcus lays a heavy, reassuring hand on my shoulder. "We all understand."

"I'm suffocating– I can't breathe." Gasping, I plead, "Release it. Please."

"Devlin, escort Sebastian to Edge, because he shouldn't see Dalton like this. Make sure Olivia is gone from the building, please." Marcus takes charge of the disaster Olivia Fontaine left behind.

"Katya, go with Devlin and fetch my daughter– it's time to bring Spyder home to Shadow Haven. Then go get Niel and Ella, so all of the kids can be a comfort as she acclimates and deals with the bitter news about her mother."

"What about Whitney and Prissy?" is all I can make out as Kat whispers to Marcus. "Do you really want them left alone at Misery Castle while all of this is going down? Didn't you say Daniel was involved?"

"Take them to your house," Whitt mutters gravely. "I'll pick my kids up when Dalton is feeling better."

Marc's eyes scan the room, searching. "Regina, Fate, and Kris, go help Katya. Please." Then he turns to look for someone else. "Ezra, if you've ever trusted me, you will do exactly as I say," Marcus warns.

"What? You know damn well that I trust you in all things," Ezra replies in confusion.

"Get your mother out of our house before my daughter and Ella show up– she can't see either one of them. Trust me on this. Drive her to the jet and physically place her on it. Tell them to fly her to the Hastings, and make sure it goes to California."

"Why?"

"Don't ask," Marc clips out.

"I'll try my best," Ezra says as he turns to leave.

"Don't try– do it!" Marcus bellows, losing control, and we all flinch.

"You know how my mother is. Saying I will do my best is the best you can hope for. What's going on?"

"Your mother's best friend was just escorted from this building, after admitting countless crimes against us all. You better hope Diane is still at Shadow Haven when you arrive. Having the two of them plotting our demise will make what they've already put us through look like a fucking walk in the park... then you add Daniel to the mix."

Ezra bolts from the dungeon at a dead run. His facial expression was the same as the one I wear. I guess it's the night to find out that your mother is a sociopath hell-bent on your destruction.

"Cort and Alex will take your belongings to the Brownstone, Dalton. Finally. Welcome home, son. I'd have you come to Shadow Haven, but I know you'd be more comfortable with Jamie and Alex."

Marcus squeezes my shoulder a few times, and then leans down to kiss my forehead. He whispers into my ear, "While the guys are moving your belongings, Dexter will ease you of your agonizing suffering and guilt."

Chapter Twenty-Four

Standing below me while I sit on the edge of the dais, "You don't have to do this, Dalton," Dexter says for the tenth time.

"Yes, I do," I utter as strongly as I can.

"No– don't!" Whitt pleads, pulling me closer to his chest. "Don't do it."

Clutching at my throat, my fingers turn to talons. "I can't breathe... it's a heavy blanket of darkness suffocating me."

"Dalton?" Levi walks right up to me, getting into my face. "This is the last time. The only time. I don't give a flying fuck if you're a masochist. As soon as you heal, you're going to therapy and you're hitting the pavement. But you will never allow anyone to hit you again!"

Teeth chattering, I force the words out. "I promise– I mean it. Therapy. Gunner's survivor fitness group. But I need to make this sacrifice tonight."

"Fine!" Levi bites out. "But I'm not watching– I can't." My brother turns his back to me, head bowed. "I'd harm Dexter with the first lash of his whip."

"Hey?" I rest my palm in the center of his back, muscles so tense I fear he's hurting. "Go home to your wife, and I'll call you as soon as it's over. It doesn't take long, so I bet you won't even get home first."

"The Green Building is four blocks from here," Levi mutters, showcasing where my sarcastic attitude and warped sense of humor comes from, because he's actually teasing me– not that anyone would ever know.

"It won't take longer than five minutes." Dexter doesn't get the joke. "Can we at least do this in private?" With unease, he gazes around the dungeon. "Do you really want your boyfriend to witness this?" Dexter steps from side-to-side, scratching at his curls.

"Ah, shit! I'm sorry, Dexter. I know you don't like being on exhibit, but my punishment is for all of them."

"I understand," he mutters in defeat.

Walking toward the exit, "Call me," flows from Levi as my hand falls away from his back.

Dexter has tried to talk me out of it for the past hour. I wouldn't do it until all the members were back. Ezra returned with Katya after the girls were settled. They left them in Niel's capable hands, with Kayla watching the twins. I was informed that my sister was nearly hysterical and that she'd finally passed out from sobbing. We were also told that Diane wasn't at Shadow Haven and my mother gave Roarke the slip. No doubt the women are together somewhere. Whitt's grandfather was sitting in his study, looking as innocent as a child, which means he's harboring the women somewhere, according to the public consensus on Daniel Whittenhower I.

Swinging up beside me, Dexter crawls to his feet. "Master Dalton would like to formally apologize before he receives his punishment," Dexter says from atop the dais.

With Whitt reluctantly releasing me, I pull myself onto the stage and take a few breaths to center myself.

"I want to apologize for unwittingly leaking information that was used in the *Mistress & Master of Restraint* books. The consequences of my actions have caused Restraint's doors to close and created the media frenzy. I apologize for all of the problems that my actions have caused you and your families, and the effects it had on your jobs and lives. My mother was my master. She was the Master of the BDSM Lifestyle Authority and she used that position to make me think I was helping rather than hurting you all. I want to apologize individually to each and every one of you for my heinous behavior. However, I will not use my master's commands and demands as an excuse. Please take my punishment as atonement."

The St. Andrew's cross is directly in the center of the dais by my request. I wanted to be in full view as I took my punishment. I strip Whitt's shirt off until I'm completely bare to the skin. I walk up to the cross and get into position. I haven't been whipped since my father did it when I was a boy as he tried to whip the gay out of me.

I take a deep breath, and then nod to Dexter to signal that I'm ready.

Dexter straps my hands and feet to the cross with leather cuffs. The entire time he runs his hands over my body, massaging my muscles. The touch isn't sexual. He does it out of respect to calm me and to make sure I don't cramp. My body falls lax under his expert touch.

I don't panic because I know what to expect. Fear is for the unknown, or the things we cannot bear to endure. This type of pain I've endured my entire life, using it to bleed the agony, shame, and guilt from my soul. My body feels so full of agony that I can barely stand to breathe. The ache– the pressure is unbearable.

This isn't just about my guilt and shame over being the leak– the mole. It's about the ignorance I feel for allowing myself to be blindly led. It's about the loss of my father. I believe Tony was an honorable man who allowed my grandfather and mother to twist him into an unrecognizable monster. This punishment is for my mother who was tainted from birth. Olivia Fontaine's nature was not as it is now– it was nurtured, fostered by the very men I murdered to save us all. I do this to expel the very same monster I've allowed them to turn me into. The guilt and shame over my past transgressions try to release through the sobs that keep building, but it's not enough. It'll never be enough.

I need the punishment to relieve the pressure from knowing my mother didn't love me, was incapable of loving me. That she didn't think I was good enough to love, to be safe and happy– to live. Olivia thought of me as an object, not a human being. But I know I'm good enough, that I deserve to live. It's a right that is afforded to us with our birth, and no one has the right to take it away. I grieve because my mother is that broken, that she feels nothing inside but bitterness and an evil wrongness. I'm ashamed to call the woman my mother because she saw a club as her reason to live. She thought our lives were mere game pieces to bargain for the club.

I use this punishment to let go... to let go of the past and move on to an unknown future.

I use Dexter's gift to heal.

"Word of advice: do not go into a memory. Stay in the here-and-now. Become one with the pain, and your mind will convert it for your release. Release your pain from that deep well inside of your mind. Know when this is over, the emotions that placed the pain inside of you are gone. You will have atoned for your sins...

"Anything else you're bombarded with is just baggage someone else has pushed onto you instead of having dealt with it themselves. They are the cowards, not you. It takes an immense amount of courage to do what you're doing right now, Dalton. Own it– respect yourself," he whispers rapidly into my ear.

"Heal!" Dexter screams over the crack of the whip.

"Ahhh…" I moan as the leather strikes the flesh of my left shoulder. With no buildup, no practice or warning strikes, Dexter whips me.

The pain is so intense that it eclipses everything inside of my mind. My mind tries to protect itself by delving into a memory, but I hold out even as the next strike connects with my thigh. I scream through the pain. I will myself to stay in the here-and-now because I can't heal if I live in the past.

Each hit is more intense than the last, but I make less noise each time. I feel pride well up, knowing I'm powering through and overcoming the agony. My mind no longer tries to dredge up the past and fling me into things better left in my subconscious. Instead, I experience the sensation of the leather slicing across my flesh. The hot sting that radiates from the welt sears the ache away.

I let go… I finally let go.

My body arches in my restraints. A guttural moan spills past my parted lips. My seed flows down my thigh in a scorching torrent. My mind blanks into the perfect clarity of a cleansing release. I feel nothing but a disconnecting bliss. Mind and body break apart and reform as one being.

I heal.

Chapter Twenty-Five

There's a disadvantage to living with a therapist. When Alex tries to get me to talk, I go next door and spend time with the mute. Sure, it's creepy as fuck to stare at the man who is an older version of my boyfriend, but at least he's enjoyable to look at... and quiet.

The Brownstone is two separate living spaces connected inside by a common foyer and staircase. On the right is the training side. The entire bottom floor is room after room with different themes. I spent a great deal of my training in the impact room at the hands of Alex. The second floor of the right-hand side of Brownstone is Jamie's domain– no one is allowed up there but him.

On the left side of the Brownstone is Alex's apartment, with a shared kitchen at the back of the house. It's nice and quiet with a homey atmosphere. There is plenty of downtime because Jamie requires it. But otherwise, it's a revolving door for Marcus and Dexter. If Jamie's had enough, he'll just get up mid-conversation and go upstairs to his lair. It could be an hour later, or two minutes, but you'll never hear him return. So it's best you keep your secrets and gossip to yourself, because the walls have ears, even if the inhabitants are mute.

I've been here for a total of ten days, and I understand Jamie's propensity to just get up and leave the room. At first I thought it rude, but then I met the real Alex. His constant hovering, mothering, and the *'how are ya?'* and *'you wanna talk about it?'* are driving me batshit.

It's bad enough I was dragged kicking and screaming to The Edge Building last week, where I was tossed on a sofa and cerebrally fucked by Ezra. For the foreseeable future, Dr. Zeitler will delve into my psyche for three sessions a week.

So when I come home, Alex's constant hovering drives me next door. Which is exactly why I'm on the right-hand side of the Brownstone, sitting on an antique sofa, eating pizza and playing dirty word Scrabble with Jamie.

It sounds fun and easy until you realize that you have to be creative to come up with words to play. You'd think that being a BDSM Master would give me an advantage over the straight, submissive man. Nope, he's a mute author of BDSM literature, living in a BDSM training ground. Jamie's life is words– I'm losing miserably.

R U O K Jamie spells out the sentence with Scrabble tiles on the board, and I jump from my seat and yell, "You've got to be fucking kidding me?"

Smirking while choking on his ghastly laugh, Jamie rotates his tray around. **J K**.

Jamie can't laugh or talk thanks to an assault he survived– I've asked everyone for details, but they're tight-lipped. By the way Marcus looks at Jamie, I can tell he barely lived through it. Sometimes, Marc gets misty-eyed and hugs Jamie for no apparent reason, and Marcus isn't a cuddly guy, either.

Q U E E R. I play on a triple word score, flashing a proud grin.

If I played that, you would've gotten offended. Jamie writes on our conversation tablet. I know a bit of sign language, but the notepad is faster.

"Yeah, right, wheezy," I tease. "You used fag and cocksucker last round."

Jamie's gnarled upper lip sneers at me. He's a beautiful guy if you don't look at his mouth. White-blond hair, bright blue eyes, and dimples are a gorgeous combination. I'm assuming Jamie's a hermit because if he stepped foot out this door, you might as well hang a Whittenhower sign on his ass.

"I want to ask you a question," I mutter hesitantly as I select four more tiles from the bag. "Did you love the mothers of your children? Also, do you think cheating is a Whittenhower trait?"

Releasing a creepy moan, Jamie gains my attention. One of the hazards of being mute, if no one looks at you, you can't communicate.

Really? He scrawls on the tablet. *Little Daniel needs to get his ass in here and talk to me himself!!!! Damn it!*

"Says the man who hides when the doorbell rings." Looking down at my tray, I arrange the tiles to spell out **Q U E E F**.

Knuckles rap on the coffee table, knocking my tiles over. *I loved their mothers very much. They are different people, so my feelings were different for them, but no less intense. & no, cheating is not a Whittenhower trait. I did NOT cheat. EVER! & neither did*

Wilhelm, or Jackson and Daniel. You know as well as I do, negotiated sex is not cheating.

"Hmm… so there's more skeletons in the Whittenhower closets yet to fall out, is what I get from that last sentence, being as Whitt is the first Whittenhower to enter the lifestyle."

Jamie narrows his eyes at me– he and I have an odd relationship. He's a brat, through and through. But so am I. So we fight and get along in equal measure. Whitt's been pissed off at him for fifteen years, so that tends to taint Jamie's and my interactions.

Tile after tile is placed on the Scrabble board, spelling out **A S S H O L E.**

"Hey!" I grab the bag off the table, hiding it from Jamie. "Cheater. I'm passing these bitches out from now on. You're probably a horrible banker in Monopoly, too."

My sincerest apologies–

"How can the written word sound like a *fuck you* when you write it?" I pass out seven replacement tiles now that Asshole is on the board.

My sincerest apologies. I've been testy with today's celebration. I'm scared, Dalton.

"Shit!" I reach over to grab his hand, forgetting how Jamie might be able to dish it out, but he can never take it. "Are you storming Misery Castle with us?" He nods his head, looking faintly ill.

I won't be coming home with you afterward. I'll be staying there to keep an eye on everyone. All of my children will be under one roof, and I have my suspicions that our missing antagonists are hiding in my ancestral home.

"Jesus, you're coming out? For real?" I lean forward, clutching both his hands. "That's not healthy for you, Jamie. You can't go back there."

I'm doing it for my children– I have my reasons, but they belong to me.

And just like that, the asshole cuts me off. I'm just lucky Jamie didn't ghost away upstairs to pout, stew, brood, or whatever the hell he does up there besides write and sleep.

I lay **Q U E E F** out on the board, ignoring the fact that Jamie is sniffling. He's like an injured baby animal, and I have no idea how

259

to handle it. I'm just about to call for Alex when he calls to us instead.

"Whittenhower alert!" Alex yells from his side of the house.

Like a mouse, Jamie freezes, and then thaws. He quickly signs *later*, and then runs to the back of the house. I hear his footsteps pound on the back steps, and then his bedroom door slam shut. He does this for every visitor. I'm used to it after training here for over a year.

"In here," I call to Whitt.

"Interesting," he drawls when he sees the Scrabble board. "I see Jamie was with you," he says as he picks up the tablet and reads what Jamie had written throughout the course of the game.

"Hmm…" Whitt frowns at the words on the page, and scrubs a hand over his face. "That is not a good idea. But I'm not going to convince him otherwise. Jamie does whatever the fuck he wants."

"He's not too bad to be around. Chatty Cathy over there was driving me nuts. Jamie's muteness is a godsend."

"Just tell Alex to knock his shit off. It's what Kristal does when he goes on his addict tangents. He won't mind."

Rising from my seat, I finally greet Whitt properly. "Happy Birthday, Pretty Boy." Wrapping my arms around his waist, I draw his front tightly against mine. Grinding on him a bit, I show him how happy I am to see him.

"Thank you." Whitt gives me a quick smooch that quickly evolves into ten minutes of ravenous kissing. Pulling away, "We have to behave– I have a hair-trigger around you."

Sighing, I step from his embrace. "Are you ready for this?"

Vivid blue eyes glowing with excitement, with his devastating dimples making a showing, "Yeah, I am. It's been twenty-four years in the making."

"Holy fuck," my voice quivers. "Even I'm scared, and I know I'm coming right back here when it's all said and done."

After another quick kiss, Whitt pulls away. "Dad!" he bellows– and a shadow moves in the corner of the room. Jamie detaches himself from the wall, just like a ghost. "Creepy." Whitt shakes his head to clear it. "Ready to storm the Castle?"

Epilogue

Marcus whittled down Restraint's membership to fifty, and put a cap on it. All fifty members plus our security force stand proudly in the street outside of Restraint. We're blocking traffic, and we could give a shit less. It's a day of celebration. Our club has a huge *Grand Reopening* banner wrapped around the building.

We all had a hand in remodeling Restraint, inside and out. Kristal was in charge of designing the main club with Queen and Fate's help. The upper floors are office spaces and our new private rooms. A security hub was designed by Aaron, Roarke, Gunner, and Levi– even in my head I can't call him Wil. The hallway where our old private rooms were is now lined with theme rooms for the members to get their kink on. Each master created a theme room to their liking. Dexter and I shared a space since his sadism complimented my masochism, but Levi won't allow me to participate. Whitt, with his obsession with restraints, created a room that's a hybrid between a hardware store and a stable. Katya's room looks like a vampire lair. Every person who peeked into Ezra's room busted a nut– Dr. Zeitler is in the house.

Marcus and Devlin renovated the dungeon, and none of us has seen it yet.

We all ignore the albatross that glows neon pink next to us. Restraint used to be flanked by two unoccupied commercial buildings, now there's only one. To our right is a new club with its own grand opening sign, but it says **French Kissed Kink** instead.

My mother is haunting us from next door, with her new strip club offering illegal specialties in the back. The excess members we chopped from our ranks flooded next door. We all sneer as we see the bright lights in our peripheral vision. Olivia Fontaine thinks she's won– she can think again.

I snap open the newest edition of Generation Next, and gloat. I can feel my mother's stare directly on me as she stands in the third-story window of her new club. I tip the pamphlet in her direction, and then reread it for the fiftieth time.

Generation Next
Your BDSM Lifestyle Authority Insider

When you fall from on high, you fall hard and fast.

Master Olivia Fontaine is a traitor. She has been banished from the very community that she helped create. Her world-famous KINK is no longer in her possession. She helped incite riots at Restraint in hopes that it would close. During these riots, she paid five men to kill her son, Dalton Anthony Fontaine Marconi. These actions led to the media storm that surrounded Restraint's membership. She was the leak of information on all of the masters in her organization, which led to the two installments of the Mistress & Master of Restraint series. Tonight is the grand opening of her new club, French Kissed Kink. FKK, which ironically is directly next door to Restraint.

If you have any loyalty or ethics, you will avoid this club at all costs. How can your identities remain safe when she is the one who will publicize them? One day, you may be driving your children to daycare and hear on the radio that you get off on cock-and-ball torture. This is what happened to the Masters of Restraint. Don't be so arrogant to think it won't happen to you. Beware: *Generation Next* will out any members of the Lifestyle who dare to enter French Kissed Kink. If Olivia Fontaine doesn't out you, we will. You've been warned.

RESTRAINT GRAND REOPENING

Our beloved Restraint has been closed for months. While Olivia Fontaine would love to take credit for this, she is mistaken. Restraint has been closed for a revamp. When you arrive tonight, you will find a brand new club, a redesigned dungeon, and a dozen theme rooms to feed all of your needs. The upstairs now houses the masters' *private rooms and VIP membership rooms that are available by reservation-only.*

Come out and congratulate the Masters of Restraint
*Marcus*Devlin*Dexter*Ezra*Cortez*Syn*Whitt*Queen*Dalton* Alex*Katya*Aaron*Niel*

~Happy 24th Birthday, Pretty Boy~

News Alert

Diane Holden is missing. She is a tall, lithe, fifty-year-old female. White-blonde hair, gray eyes, 110 lbs. She is the beloved wife of Marcus Zeitler, mother of Ezra Zeitler and family. If anyone knows her whereabouts, please contact the Masters of Restraint. Our thoughts and prayers go out to the missing matriarch.

We deviate from our usual parting message

~Good luck storming the Castle~

Checkmate

Please visit www.generationnext.com for subscription details.

May dominance and submission feed your needs. Happy controlling and kneeling, boys and girls.

Jarring me from my reread, "Whitt, are you ready?" Marcus asks excitedly. The tension in the air is palpable, or it could be Whitt's anticipation reverberating through my hand from where our fingers are intertwined.

"I'm so ready!" Whitt hops up and down as he speaks. "I can't fucking believe it's the day. Marc, we've waited for fourteen years," Whitt's voice shakes with unshed tears.

"Are you ready, Regina?" Marc asks the woman who's nearly jogging in place.

"I'm beyond ready," Queen growls. "Let's do this!"

"Ready?" Marcus asks the crowd.

Eighty-two people scream at the top of their lungs *R E A D Y!*

"Well," Marc drawls. "It's time to storm Misery Castle!"

Jaded

Mistress & Master of Restraint #5

The long-standing Mistress & Master of Restraint series is dark and mysterious, with a warped sense of morality. Erotic romance fans, would you prefer something just as twisted, but not as dark? Try the Blended Series, beginning with Good Girl. For a mix of both styles, try the Rusty Knob series.

To purchase any of Erica Chilson's titles, please visit her website (ericachilson.com) for details.

-Acknowledgements -

A lot of work goes into writing a novel, and it isn't just by the writer herself. **My parents:** for their unconditional support. **My readers**: thank you for reading my twisted words and spreading my books to the masses. For without you, no one would have ever heard of my stories. My readers are my lifeblood. A shout out to the members of the **M&M of Restraint Group on Facebook**: thanks for the endless entertainment and inspiration. Thank you to my street team: **Erica Chilson's Deviants!** You guys ROCK! **Wicked Reads**: (in all its incarnations) **Angela G.**, thank you for taking over and making Wicked Reads better than I could have done by myself. & thank you for helping promote my work and the work of other authors. Angela? Have I told you lately how much I appreciate you? A huge thank you to the **Wicked Writer's Betas** for keeping me grounded and encouraging me to keep trudging along when I get frustrated. Your thoughts and observations are invaluable. ((Hugs)) Beta readers: **Kris | Suz | Darcy | Sandy | Di | Angela | Diane | Jacki | Linsey | Alexis | Alicia | Billie Jo | Shelby | Tassie | Liz | April | Caroline | Judith | Jodi Lynn | Jodi | Lakecia |** Someday, I'd love to meet you all in real life– it would be the experience of a lifetime.

About the Author

Erica Chilson does not write in the 3rd person, wanting her readers to *be* her characters. Therefore, writing a bio about herself, is uncomfortable in the extreme.

Born, raised, and here to stay, the Wicked Writer is a stump-jumper, a ridge-runner. Hailing from North Central Pennsylvania, directly on the New York State border; she loves the changes in seasons, the humid air, all the mountainous forest, and the gloomy atmosphere.

Introverted, but not socially awkward, Erica prides herself on thinking first and filtering her speech. There are days she doesn't speak at all. If it wasn't for the fact that she lives with her parents, giving her a sense of reality, she would be a hermit, where the delivery man finds her months after expiration.

Reading was an escape, a way to leave a not-so pleasant reality behind. Reading lent Erica the courage she gathered from the characters between the pages to long for a different life. Writing was an instrument of change, evolving Erica into the woman she is today– a better, more mature, more at peace thinker.

Erica has a wicked mind, one she pours out into her creations. Her filter doesn't allow all of it to erupt, much to her relief. Sarcastic, with a very dark, perverse sense of humor, Erica puts a bit of herself into every character she writes.

I love hearing from readers. If you would like more information on release dates, works in progress, teaser chapters, and random bits of madness, please visit my Facebook Fan Page: https://www.facebook.com/thewickedwriter my website: ericachilson.com or please contact me via email: wickedwriter.ericachilson@gmail.com

DEVIANTS ONLY, if you'd like to join Erica Chilson's closed Facebook group, M&M of Restraint: https://www.facebook.com/groups/MistressandMaster/

www.ingramcontent.com/pod-product-compliance
Lightning Source LLC
Chambersburg PA
CBHW070849250626
47159CB00003B/996